Return to Luna

Return to Luna

The Winning Stories of the National Space Society's
2008 Return to Luna Contest

Edited by Eric T. Reynolds

HADLEY
RILLE
BOOKS

RETURN TO LUNA
Copyright © 2008 by Eric T. Reynolds

ISBN-13 978-0-9819243-2-8

Cover art copyright © by Walter Myers
Cover design and title page art copyright © Eric T. Reynolds

1.4

Published by Hadley Rille Books
PO Box 25466
Overland Park, KS 66225
USA
www.hadleyrillebooks.com
contact@hadleyrillebooks.com

National Space Society
1620 I Street NW
Suite 615
Washington, DC 20006
USA
www.nss.org
nsshq@nss.org

To Sir Arthur

Copyright Acknowledgments

Acknowledgments

The editor offers special thanks to George T. Whitesides, Executive Director of the National Space Society, who agreed that a fiction contest was a great idea, that would in some way bring humanity closer to settlement of the Moon and elsewhere, and to Katherine Brick, editor of the National Space Society's beautiful and informative magazine, *Ad Astra*, published quarterly, for all her help in publicizing the Contest and for arranging the review of the grand prize winning story, and especially to Harrison H. Schmitt for kindly contributing the Foreword.

Sincere thanks to the jurors Tobias S. Buckell, Michael A. Burstein, Rob Darnell, Tom Dupree, Jude-Marie Green, Jay Lake, Christopher McKitterick, Geoffrey A. Landis, Lawrence M. Schoen, Allen Steele, Ian Randal Strock who participated in the selection of the winning stories. We received entries from all over the world and the stories here represent the best of them.

We are very grateful to all the authors who submitted stories for the Contest and are proud to present the winning stories. There were many worthy stories that did not make the winning list and we wish those authors much luck and hope they find publications for their works.

—ETR

Contents

Foreword

Twenty-four humans journeyed to the Moon during Apollo, and they did so in just three years in the late 1960s and early 1970s. In a thirteen month period in 1968 and 1969, Saturn Vs launched from the Kennedy Space Center every two months. No one has returned in the nearly four decades since the last human stepped off the Moon. A "most astonishing thing" as Arthur C. Clarke said. Members of the National Space Society share Clarke's amazement at this lack of continuity and at the lack of follow through on the Apollo investments.

Fortunately, exploration of our nearest neighbor will soon start again, and this time plans include permanent human occupation. Spacefaring countries around the world are launching lunar probes and making plans to establish lunar bases, and the United States Congress has told NASA to return astronauts to the Moon in just a little over a decade.

The Constellation Program and the Orion and Altair spacecraft that will take us back to the Moon, and form a new foundation for American activities in space, will follow the basic design and operational concepts of Apollo. The new rockets and space vehicles, however, will be many times more sophisticated, carry more astronauts and payloads, and will allow for much longer stays at more places on the lunar surface.

Competition and cooperation will be the norm for future lunar exploration and, if we do not repeat the mistakes following Apollo, in just a few decades humans will have established self-sufficient lunar settlements. For the first time in the history of humanity, we will permanently inhabit more than one planetary body.

What will life be like for lunar inhabitants in those future settlements? How will nations cooperate or compete? What conflicts can be envisioned? How will living on the Moon benefit humanity, both tangibly and philosophically? What lunar resources will be available both to the settlers and to those still living on Earth?

Return to Luna presents eighteen of the many possible scenarios for human settlement that could arise from the exploration activities of many nations. I hope you enjoy, as I have, these speculations by the winners of the National Space Society's fiction contest on human lunar settlement.

It is time to Return to Luna.

Harrison H. Schmitt
Apollo 17 Astronaut
Author: *Return to the Moon*

Introduction

You are returning from a hike in the Moon's Apennine Mountains, following a trail of bootprints back to the settlement. For two days your suit has protected you on your journey through the lunar wilderness, a hike unlike any on Earth. You have scaled mountains, traversed craters, rappelled down massive boulders. And now you've crested the last hill and the valley spreads out before you where the glittering complex awaits beneath the afternoon sun. You are home.

Life on the Moon has been romanticized for generations. But not until the 1960s did we finally set a definite goal to venture to our nearest neighbor. In the United States this was the largest civilian project in human history. During that decade the Moon was often in the news as we made new discoveries on a monthly basis with probes of ever increasing sophistication. Interest in the Moon waned during the 1970s, but now it is getting much press: the Moon is popular again.

What will be the reality of living there? When will humans finally begin to build settlements on Earth's closest neighbor?

The National Space Society's Summer 2008 issue of *Ad Astra* ran a special series of articles about returning to the Moon. These articles detailed how and why we might return, what we'll do once we're there and what the benefits will be. They described moon bases and vehicles that will transport us from Earth to Moon.

Here we present stories that show the romance and adventure of living there: the winning stories of the 2008 Return to Luna contest.

Ad Astra!

George T. Whitesides
Executive Director
National Space Society

Eric T. Reynolds
Publisher/Editor
Hadley Rille Books

Visual Silence
by M. C. Chambers
(Grand Prize Winning Story)

C hase wheeled Mrs. Beryl to the viewing room, where an array of large windows allowed a clear view of the moonscape outside. The ancient, empty moonscape, and the vastness of space beyond, gave Mrs. Beryl a sense of peace about her fate.

Once the colony's most active resident, Mrs. Beryl had suffered a stroke three months before. She lost the use of all but her left arm, and could no longer speak vocally. The colony doctors judged her too fragile for space flight back to Earth, so she remained at Shackleton West. Chase, deaf since an injury in infancy, taught her sign language, though he had to adapt some words for one hand. She learned eagerly.

As eagerly he taught, for this seemed the only time these days that Chase got to indulge in a form of silence. The dark glasses he wore acted as a monitor for sound capture and speech-to-text software. Speech displayed as colored text; sounds displayed as graphs or symbols. In a noisy place, his glasses filled with so much information that he could barely see beyond it. Silence, to Chase, was to turn off his monitor, to abandon the visual clutter of text and graphs and to view his surroundings untouched by a display.

Here with Mrs. Beryl, he could do that.

He took off his glasses and watched her speak, not by reading her words on a screen, but by watching her every movement. In his childhood, he had gotten used to looking at hands, lips, faces, postures; and though he didn't need to anymore, he still thought of that as the proper way to converse.

Mrs. Beryl liked to speak of her daughter and granddaughter on Earth. Her arm and hand moved with grace, like a dancer's. "I will never see them again. But they will see me always. My girl's girl will tell her girl, 'Look, granny's up there.' They will see the Moon, and think of me." With one corner of a lip, one twitch of an eyelid, she smiled. A smile of pain, regret and yet peace. She fell quiet, looking past the windows.

Chase saw the light reflected by the Moon upon her eyes, and followed her gaze. In earlier days, the Sail covered the whole of the colony. Its expanse shielded all domes and tunnels as it collected solar radiation for energy. Now, special rooms extended past the Sail to provide the safe view of the Moon that both visitors and residents craved.

The moonscape they viewed was lit by the low sun of the long lunar dawn. The jagged rocks at the rims of craters gleamed like gilded crowns, and cast long black shadows that echoed the black of the sky. Unchanging, untouched by life or death, pain or loss.

Mrs. Beryl waved her hand for his attention, and pointed to his glasses. An orange dot blinked insistently in the left corner.

Reluctantly Chase replaced his monitor and read the message that scrolled down the side. "An unscheduled arrival checking in. Safety and Security wants me to supervise their voiceprint analyses."

Mrs. Beryl blinked. "Problem?"

Though she signed to him, he both spoke and signed to her. His words showed green on the monitor. Having learned to vocalize by the sensations in his throat instead of by sound, he liked to keep an eye on his articulation. "An orbiter detected a rogue radio signal near the West Rim, and asked Transport Control at Shackleton West to confirm. It matches the frequency of the Emergency Location Transmission device installed in lunar rover models 6F-1980 or 6F-1981."

"Wreck?"

"That's the thing. No wrecks reported. No transport plans were filed and no one's reported missing."

Mrs. Beryl lifted a palm in confusion. No one went anywhere on the Moon without filing a transport plan.

Chase shrugged. "The orbiter is trying to pinpoint the source. Transport Control has sent a robot to the area, to take a look as well. We're developing a routine to reconcile all filed transport plans, and we've requested visual confirmation of the location of all the rovers here and at surrounding outposts. But if there was a wreck . . ."

"If a wreck, then danger," interrupted Mrs. Beryl. "Every minute counts."

Chase nodded. "Every minute counts."

"The West Rim." Mrs. Beryl signed slowly. "Easy to crash there. Hard to save. Like the rille."

That had been a mess, a true test of Emergency response and medical capabilities. Most of the prospectors had been rescued; one didn't make it. But the accident had been reported immediately, the location and identities of the victims clear. In this case, who knew? "We've asked for volunteers among that same group that helped with the prospectors. People with climbing and mountain rescue experience on Earth. Just in case."

She waved her hand gracefully. "Go then. No problem for me."

"You sure?"

"Sure. I'm a little tired anyway."

She did look tired, and paler than usual. Chase ignored the orderly's offer to take her, and wheeled her back to her hall himself, where the doctors took her from him.

Since Chase lived with a monitor on his head all day, he'd been appointed the duty of keeping the automated Safety and Security system happy. He calmed the flashing alarms when anything unexpected occurred, and supervised the registering of newcomers to Shackleton West. Scientists and tourists, businesspeople and contractors, Chase met and recorded voiceprints for them all, approving the analysis and cataloguing of their identities. When the robotic system ran its periodic sweeps, their voices reassured it that everyone was accounted for, and provided demographic data for Marketing to present to possible investors. The Safety and Security system (known as the SS by curmudgeons who valued privacy, but more amicably as SafeSecs by the majority) liked to know that everyone was where it expected them to be.

The unscheduled arrival that had set it blinking proved to be a group of volunteers from the radio array on the other side of Shackleton. Among them was his own brother, Trevor, a radio scientist. Before he even saw him enter, Chase saw his voice, gradient blue to orange, filling up his visor with nonsense syllables.

"Obhichobasehobowyoboudobuobing?"

"Hello, Trevor."

"Gobudtobosobeeyobou."

Chase squinted past the verbiage and visually located his brother. "Speak English please. I'm working here."

"Wobutsthobamobatoberwobimpcobantyobouhobandobleobafobewobs?"

Chase straightened. "I can't hear anything when you do that!"

"OBYOBYOBYUBOBYOBYOYBOYOBOBYOBYOBYUBOBYO BYOYBOYOB"

Chase leaned toward him and signed. "Get over here so I can punch you in the face!"

Trevor laughed, and grabbed his hand.

SafeSecs' cameras swiveled toward him. "Please verify threat?"

"No threat. Only annoyance." Chase and Trevor shook hands heartily.

"Brought you something, bro," Trevor said. "We're told we can set up an HQ in Transport Control. Come by when you can."

"Sure."

Chase joined them as they watched Transport Control's exploring robot on a three-part display: through its own video "eyes," the Direction Locator that sought the rogue radio signal's strength, and on radio tracking from one of the lunar orbiters. From the Direction Locator feed Chase saw not a single radio signal, but many. Sheer, jagged rocks bounced the signal from surface to surface, confusing its true source.

"A cluster of echoes," observed Chase. "That's not good."

"Nobody's responding to hails," Trevor informed him. "If there's people out there, either their equipment's wrecked, or they are. Or both."

Chase studied the robot's path. "That robot's not going to be able to reach the cluster. That's too close to the rim."

The robot approached as close as it could, to the very rim of the crater, where rocks rose in ancient obelisks. It then extended a telescoping boom with a receiver at its end, and pointed, like a setter, to the signal it perceived as strongest.

"What have we got that will fly down there and take a look?"

"It's awfully dark down there." Shadows from the crater left permanent dark, never seeing light for billions of years. "Has it even been mapped yet?"

"We're checking with the orbiters to see if one can maneuver around and take some pictures. But whatever happens, there's going to be climbing to do before this is over."

Trevor stood and stretched.

"Let's get set up then, shall we?" He turned to Chase. "You in?"

"Me? I haven't climbed in years."

"You've got the experience," said Trevor, "and you are an ace spelunker. That black, vertical unknown, never seen the light of the sun, has more in common with the bowels of the earth than with the Rockies."

"This is the Moon," Chase pointed out. "You can't assume it has anything in common with anything."

Trevor handed him an uneven package shrink-wrapped in foil. "I made this for you. Translates both compression and radio waves. Got your Fourier for voice analysis and even radar display. Streamlined."

"Another upgrade?" So he could see more noise, from a greater range throughout the spectrum— "You radio people have way too much time on your hands. I haven't learned everything you put in the last one!" He opened it and put it on.

Trevor logged it into the robot's feed. The visor's display combined the strength of the signal with orbiter radar topography, showing Chase a landscape with deep purple to indigo in the depths, rising through orange to golden at the top, fading in brightness where the signal was weakest.

"Awesome resolution," Chase said admiringly. "Mom would be proud."

"You want to go try it out," Trevor stated.

"All right, I'm in," agreed Chase. "Let me get someone to baby-sit the system for me."

Within the hour more climbers arrived from a prospector's outpost, along with geologists, medical personnel and support volunteers. Still no word given on missing vehicles or personnel, but Transport Control's maintenance database showed a discrepancy, now under investigation.

Transport Control assigned them an eight-wheeler and three rovers. The rovers were smaller, built for maneuverability and relative speed. The eight-wheeler was huge, capable of carrying great loads of people and equipment.

The volunteers loaded the eight-wheeler and most climbed inside. They rolled through the airlock, then out under the black sky. They met and followed the Direction Locator robot's tracks. It took a couple of hours to reach the vicinity of the West Rim, during which time the volunteers ran through safety checklists, reviewed procedures and told about past rescues. Trevor taught everyone how to curse in sign language, for Chase's embarrassment.

As they traveled, the orbiter downloaded scans of the target area: walls of jagged rock, crevices, steep slopes. Chase hoped the Direction Locator resolved the true source of the signal before they got there.

The team leader, one of Trevor's friends from the radio array, kept them informed of investigation reports. "One of the vehicles decommissioned for maintenance has vanished, after it had been serviced but before it had been re-commissioned."

"Any reports of missing personnel?" asked Chase.

"No," answered the team leader. "But rovers don't drive themselves."

Chase pursed his lips. SafeSecs wasn't doing its job—bad data somewhere. A bug? Or intentional misinformation? A colonist's worst fear, more than meteor bombardment or even little green men, was a hacker in the system.

The terrain became more and more rocky as they approached the crater. A little ways short of the robot, they arrayed their vehicles. Chase felt growing excitement as he ran his suit through its checklist. It had been far too long since he'd been out on the surface.

He stepped from the eight-wheeler onto the Moon, hopping gently to loosen his stiff limbs. He kicked the dusty regolith around with his boots just as he had the first time he stood on lunar soil. Shadows from the many rocks stretched before them. Chase considered turning off his monitor, the colors of lines and maps and text, to drink in visual silence: bare light, rock, and shadow.

Trevor would kill him.

He focused instead on his team's mission. They were the hasty team, charged with visually confirming the Emergency Location Transmission source as quickly as possible, while another team followed more slowly, hauling the equipment to use should rescue be needed.

His team climbed into rovers and drove a short ways in the direction the robot indicated, looking for tracks. They found a set, but soon determined they belonged to a tour bus, an eight-wheeler outfitted in luxury for sightseers. They drove further without success, then dismounted to work through the abundant boulders.

"No way a 6F-1980 could even go this way," protested Trevor. "The rocks are too close together."

"They might have approached from the north." The team leader scrutinized the orbiter's scans.

Chase scrolled through his new visor's menus with controlled eye movements. He superimposed both the emergency signal and all its pulsing echoes upon a topographical display: blinking dots like fireflies spread across vivid jagged lines. "So many echoes. Which is real?"

"The robot reads this as the strongest signal," said the team leader.

"But there's nothing here," argued Trevor.

The voices scrolled as text at the bottom of Chase's screen, but he focused on the firefly echoes. He adjusted the controls. "There is another signal," he observed. "Higher frequency, and its pulse of slightly longer duration."

The team leader didn't look up. "Probably another echo. Your equipment is just reading the signals wrong."

"No it's not," insisted Trevor. Chase could tell by the sudden turn of his brother's head that he was hot. His inventions always worked. "It could be a suit distress beacon in addition to the vehicle ETL."

"Suit beacons don't have near the strength of vehicle signals. No way we'd pick it up from here."

"Geologists have stronger suit beacons," added Chase. "They crawl into more holes than, say, radio engineers."

"Why doesn't the DL pick it up?"

"Its focus is too narrow. Reset it to pick up a greater frequency range."

"If we spend time messing with the robot we're wasting time and oxygen," argued the team leader. "If we find the vehicle we'll find the suit nearby."

"If there's a person who needs help, he'll be in the suit. Not the vehicle." Trevor pointed through the rocks. "We're chasing an echo anyway."

Chase turned off the text feed and watched the two men wave their arms at each other. He turned his attention to the lights of the echoes for a moment, then turned that off as well. His monitor went blank, and his view of the Moon was at last unencumbered.

Bare light, rock, and shadow. Visual silence.

Stars shot the sky with still points of light. High on a slope, he viewed the yawning moonscape. The tracks they'd made seemed small insignificant flecks next to the scars of bombardment millions of years old, borne still in silence, carried with grace in the orbital dance with sun and earth.

Why would geologists come here, without registering their path? Simple absent-mindedness was impossible. With all the protocol and checklists, and the mindfulness of the Safety and Security System, only deliberate and persistent planning could get away with leaving an outpost without a filed plan. What would a geologist hope to find that he wouldn't want others to know about?

Maybe it wasn't even geologists, but some others who wanted geologists' gear. For what purpose?

Chase turned his topographical display back on, and studied the shape of the rocks at the rim of the crater.

Trevor bounded abruptly to him. Hastily Chase turned on his text display. "Sorry!"

"We're going back to the rovers." Trevor leapt past him, the force of his footfalls causing him to bounce.

Chase started after him, but noticed the others were going ahead. "We can't split up!"

"We're going to the rovers," Trevor repeated. He bounced ahead with alarming speed.

Chase followed him at a more controlled pace. "Slow down, bro! You bounce into these rocks you'll bust your pressure suit!"

"--------" The monitor failed to translate Trevor's reply.

Trevor reached the rovers and climbed into one. Chase climbed in a moment later to find him accessing the DL controls, adjusting the frequency range and resolution. Random phonemes scrolled across Chase's screen as Trevor muttered.

"I can't hear you," said Chase.

"Here it is!" Trevor straightened. "I found the suit beacon!"

Trevor superimposed the original echo pattern as a line graph upon the second set. Together they studied the display.

"Looks to me like this is the original signal, and these the echoes." Chase pointed at the display.

Trevor contacted the others, while Chase plotted new coordinates.

Chase watched admiringly as Trevor convinced the team leader to turn around and head for the new location. He had never read such magnificent mathematics.

They soon found tracks; then, following the tracks through the rocks, they found a crevice from which the signals proceeded. A rover with its front wheel torn off lay abandoned at the opening. Cable unwound from the front winch disappeared down into the blackness.

They left their vehicles and made their way to the edge of the crevice. Trevor lowered a little robot down the lightless hole to take video. Its spotlight showed directly ahead, but the area surrounding it remained in murk. Before long Chase caught a glimpse in the sweep of the robot's light. Its video camera swiveled to target a motionless figure.

"So someone left their crash site to go down a hole—that makes no sense," puzzled Chase.

"Our job is to get them out." The team leader radioed the exact location of the crash to the evac team.

Soon the other rescuers arrived and unpacked their gear. The lunar climbing gear differed from the terrestrial with the addition of a cage—a "roll cage," Trevor called it—instead of a harness to clip ropes and cables to the climber. This controlled the stress applied to their lunar pressure suits.

The crevice plunged straight down into an ancient, frigid dark that sucked away all hint of warmth or light. The haulers arranged the equipment at the edge, while climbers clipped on their roll cages and readied their cables.

Then everyone turned to look at Chase.

"What?" said Chase.

"You go first," suggested Trevor. Though all were accomplished climbers, none wanted to descend into the dark. Chase sighed and carefully crawled over the edge. "Down slow," he told his belay. His headlamp and the video robot lit his way, one step at a time.

The victim was not far. Chase hailed it with no response. He used a SafeSecs override code to log into the suit's microprocessor and determined that pressure was intact and its wearer still alive, but oxygen delivery was impaired, causing unconsciousness. Also, the wearer was not the one to whom the suit was registered.

Chase secured a string of spotlights and guided the next several climbers down. Then the team above lowered a litter for the victim.

Chase stood aside to let the others work, and stole a moment to turn off his monitor, to soak in the drama of the absolute dark of the hole, pierced by the pinpointed lights from the spots and wandering flashes from headlamps.

He looked beyond the narrow shelf where the victim rested. Another cable had been fixed below. And pitons. Chase turned his monitor on. "Down slow."

"Where are you going?" scrolled the gradient text of Trevor's voice.

"Looking for another victim."

"Where?"

"Where those pitons lead. Why else would this guy drive so fast to this hole that he crashes his rover, and then goes in after crashing? He must have been trying to reach someone who had climbed down first, and got into trouble. You know no one goes anywhere on the Moon alone."

"You want to go down with just a headlamp?"

"Done it before."

"I'm on belay," Trevor insisted. The cable that connected two lunar climbers allowed a status signal to be read at either end.

Chase descended into the interior of the Moon. Though fully insulated, his mind sensed the absolute cold of it, along with absolute dark. He adjusted his new visor, trying out some of the settings. His suit generated a limited radar signal, but the topographical display registered so many echoes that it was meaningless. His headlamp, too, reflected from the glassy rocks, causing ghostly flashes in his peripheral vision.

He experimented with the reflections, to illuminate more of the space he crept in. He glimpsed pitons hammered into the rock, and cables stretched across the rocks like a handrail. Clearly, others had been here before: more than once. The trail sloped to a horizontal path, and twisted around sharp stone outcrops. Communication with the others became snowy and intermittent, but the belay indicators shone green at both ends.

He saw something very shiny—not a suit but some kind of bin. Heading there he looked in; it held small crystals. Ice crystals: an ice smuggler's cache.

Stories of ice smugglers had seemed to Chase a lunar legend. It was illegal, and in Chase's point of view, stupid, to remove water from the

Moon; it was not so easy to find as investors had hoped. But reportedly, there were plenty of people with enough wealth to create a demand for black market moon water. As the water that bubbled up from deep beneath the earth's surface was regarded by some to have special, sometimes miraculous healing qualities, so the water from the dark of space, imbued with the energies of the universe billions of years old, was considered transformative, almost magical, therefore priceless.

Chase scanned for a suit beacon, but found none. Its wearer must have requested help verbally, without being in physical distress. Chase dialed hailing frequencies and spoke.

"I am from Shackleton West, responding to an emergency locator transmission from Lunar Rover XII and a lunar suit registered to Gustav Garcia. Do you need assistance?"

He waited for an answer. He repeated. "Do you need assistance?"

Finally three dim words scrolled upon his screen. "I can't see."

"Copy that. Is it an equipment malfunction?"

"The light just died. Just like that. Everything turned dark. I can't see. I can't see to move. The rocks here are too steep."

Unexpectedly, the text morphed, brightening and fading on Chase's monitor, following inflections of the voice. One of Trevor's refinements of resolution, dialed into by chance—Chase saw the emotions as if he could see expressions on the speaker's face: desperation on the bright words, despair on the faint.

Taken aback, he paused a moment to regain his thoughts. "Do you have radar? Video?"

"It's on the rover."

"I'm going to do a 360 with my helmet light. Tell me if you see it." Slowly Chase turned in a complete circle.

"I can't see anything."

"What is your position relative to the bin of ice?"

There was no answer. Chase regretted mentioning the ice. He wondered if the smuggler would rather face death in the dark than the legal consequences. But those three words, "I can't see," had seemed so desperate, so human. "Repeat, what is your position?"

Still no answer.

"I'm going for help," Chase called out. "It will only be a few minutes."

"Request a private frequency," reached the screen. Red tones pulsed through the letters. What did that mean?

Chase felt uneasy. On Earth, smugglers were dangerous people. He moved away from the bin and turned off his headlamp. He no longer wanted the other to see him. He signaled through the belay his desire to return, but turned on a private frequency for the victim.

"Channel 43," he stated. The belay guided him back slowly the way he had come, while the smuggler's words shone on his screen.

"Rescuer, you have seen the ice, and you know its value. You could have a share in this." Color and brightness remained steady.

"Copy." Chase wondered if his voice would betray his suspicion. He withdrew further up the path.

"You obviously have skills, you could make a lot of money if you want."

Very uneasy now. If he refused would this person attack him somehow? "Copy."

"Please, bring help, but don't mention the ice. Then give it some thought." A swelling of desperate brightness on the word *please*.

"Copy," said Chase, and closed the channel. He eased back in the dark, drawn gently by the belay. Once he made it past one of the twists he turned his headlamp on, and opened up audio again. "Up! Trevor, bring me up!"

"Something wrong?"

Chase feared to speak—the smuggler might hear him. "It's creepy down here."

"No kidding?"

The cable drew him back at a faster pace.

"Any sign of a second victim?"

"Trevor, it's . . ." he wanted to say: it's too dark. He couldn't find anything. Let the smuggler and the ice lie forever in the dark together. The man they had just rescued probably wouldn't say anything—his own skin was at stake.

But the smuggler's words still shone in his memory. *I can't see. I can't see to move.*

"It's dangerous," said Chase.

"You bet," Trevor responded.

He spoke no more until he was out of the hole with the others. If he requested a private channel, the smuggler might hear and suspect himself betrayed, and ambush any rescuers who came for him. Chase returned to the surface, and as soon as he saw Trevor he faced him and spoke with sign language. Spelling words with his fingers was out of the question in the pressure suit, but Trevor caught on from the broader arm gestures. He signaled back a frequency number of the private channel he opened.

"What is it?" he asked.

"Trevor, it's a smuggler. An ice smuggler."

There was a pause. "Get out of here," Trevor said, the words fat with skepticism.

"I mean it. I saw the ice. A bin full. And he wasn't willing to tell me his location—even though he'd lost all visual and couldn't move in the dark. He may be dangerous. Hell, he may be armed. If he thinks I ratted him out he may sabotage the rescuers. But we can't leave him to die. What do we do?"

"What every good rescue team does in an unexpected situation," said Trevor. "We call for backup."

They used a rover's communications to contact the orbiter, who relayed their request to a Special Forces unit. Chase wanted to leave, to let others handle it, but the commander requested his participation. Nearly two hours passed before the unit reached them. Two long hours for a victim to lie helplessly in the dark, thinking himself abandoned—or for a criminal to set traps to guard his loot. Two long hours for Chase, passing time flipping nervously through his new visor's settings, too nervous to actually pay attention to what they did.

Then, reluctantly, Chase found himself back down in the hole. Chase's instructions were to keep the person talking while the team covering him verified the position.

He opened hailing frequencies. "What is your status?"

There was a pause, then the words scrolled onto his screen. "Thank God."

"There's a team ready to help. What is your location?"

He gave coordinates, and Chase sent a spotlight in that direction. "Can you see the spotlight?"

The words came rapidly. "I see it. I see it. Thank God."

"Stay where you are," said Chase. "We'll come to you."

The words repeated themselves, rapid and broken. It looked at first like the uttering of a hysterical person. But it didn't look right.

Chase switched on a Fourier display. The syllables seemed too exact—like sampled phrases played back in random order. "Repeat your location," ordered Chase quickly.

"God, I see it. Thank God. I see. I see it."

"Lights out!" Chase barked, and turned off the spotlight. Instant darkness fell.

"What is the situation?" asked the commander.

"That is not a real voice," said Chase. "It's a sampled playback."

"Switch to radar, display mode Tommy Four One. Suits will reflect in red, rocks in blue."

Upon receiving the radar signal, Chase's monitor burst into color. Topographical features outlined in blue and their echoes, sharp as spearheads, superimposed upon them, flashed upon his eyes.

The red blob of the smuggler's suit throbbed among them. It remained stationary. Without light, it would not move. Red blobs of the Special Forces team closed upon it.

"Ready for lights on," said the commander. Chase turned on the spotlight, turned to the location of the red blob. The smuggler leaned against an immense spike of rock. When the light hit him he pushed up, and spun around into the shadow behind the rock.

The Special Forces swarmed after him.

Chase stayed where he was. Spotlights targeted the spike behind which the smuggler had vanished. High upon the spike, he saw a visual disturbance, a movement, and then a blast of blinding shouts appeared on his visor. Quickly he dimmed his display. In the stark light, he saw the top of the spike slide down its side, slam through the floor and fall away, along with a chunk of floor, into deep black below. The rock beneath his feet shook. Nothing showed on his visor.

He looked around for the bin of ice: it had fallen to its side, and many of the crystals slid with the rock into steep, endless black. The ice had returned to eternal dark, following, it seemed, its miner.

The sampled voice still played. "I see it. God, I see it, I see it. Thank God." Chase wished he could rescue it. His Fourier display analyzed the transmitted voice. The frequencies were high pitched: a female voice.

He and the Special Forces team searched for several hours, until they were sure beyond a doubt that the smuggler was lost without hope of rescue. Chase retrieved the recording. Special Forces took the bin with its few remaining crystals. The team withdrew to the surface.

Chase returned to Shackleton West, exhausted. The other volunteers had returned earlier. Trevor was already asleep. But Chase could not rest. He logged into SafeSecs and connected the sampled voice to the system. "Is this a voice we know?"

"Affirmative."

"Whose?"

"Adele Eva Beryl."

"Mrs. Beryl?" Mrs. Beryl had not spoken for three months . . . "Locate Beryl's pressure suit," he ordered.

"Airlock Prep area 5B."

"Visual confirmation?"

The video display refreshed to Airlock Prep 5B. "Negative." Mrs. Beryl's suit was not in its place.

Gravity on the Moon suddenly increased tenfold. "Why didn't you say something sooner?" But that was not the kind of question the system could answer. "Locate Adele Eva Beryl. Visual confirmation."

"Hospital suite 1A." Video showed a dim room with a prone figure lying on a bed.

Chase took a deep breath. Someone had taken a respected woman's tragedy and used it to further his own ends, stealing her voiceprint, her clearance codes, her suit—

Tired as he was, Chase got up and went to the medical wing. "Is Mrs. Beryl awake?"

The orderly hesitated. "Oh, I'm sorry! Mrs. Beryl died about six hours ago."

Chase's hands turned to lead. His knees barely supported his sudden weight. "What? Why? What happened?"

"Well, you knew she was having respiratory problems."

"No, I didn't know!"

"Oh yes, she's had to be resuscitated three times in the last two weeks. This time, well, she didn't make it."

The scrolling text faded to meaningless scribbles. He saw only past

31

them, the face of the orderly, the shapes the lips made, the angle of the eyebrows, the eyes: sympathetic yet cool.

"She knew it would be soon," mouthed the lips. "She was ready."

The words suffocated him. Chase turned around and left, lest he too stop breathing. He went alone to the viewing room, threw down his visor and collapsed into a chair. Beyond the array of panes, the moonscape shone, and beyond that, the star-dotted sky, and beyond that, the universe ...

With one corner of a lip, one twitch of an eyelid, she smiled.

A granddaughter will see the Moon; will tell her daughter, 'Look, granny's up there.'

The body would be desiccated and laid in a catacomb beyond the rim of Shackleton, to join, perhaps, the robber who'd stolen her identity. Both would lie in cold dark forever.

An orange dot flashed on the edge of his visor. He was still logged in to Safety and Security, and it wanted his attention.

Mechanically, Chase picked up the visor and read the message. People were checking out of Shackleton West, and their voices needed to be removed from the list of current occupants. The system didn't want to be watching for people who weren't there. But just as SafeSecs waited for authorization to add a voice, so it waited for authorization to delete it. The message scrolled through a roster of those departing: many of the rescue volunteers, returning to their outposts; and Mrs. Adele Eva Beryl, deceased.

Chase tossed the visor aside.

The long lunar dawn continued unchanged. The rims of craters gleamed, the black shadows reached to the black horizon. All was silent. Chase perceived a second silence. Not freedom from noise but a burden of emptiness. Emptiness as deep as the cracks of the West Rim, as cold as lunar ice, as dark as a lunar tomb.

The robber and the robbed—had she really died of respiratory failure, or had she lost her usefulness to someone when her imposter had perished?

The data would tell. SafeSecs had somehow been cajoled to secrecy, but Chase could dig the truth out of the tracking database. Every instance of Mrs. Beryl's voiceprints, every use of her clearance codes, every mere mention of her name in the last three months would be called out, and the invisible user revealed.

Chase retrieved his visor and returned to SafeSecs' controls. He accessed the database and ordered reports on Mrs. Beryl's data. SafeSecs reminded him of the need to remove departing voices. It displayed the roster again. "OK to delete?" it asked.

Chase authorized the removal of the voiceprints of the rescue volunteers. But he paused over Mrs. Beryl's.

"OK to delete?" persisted SafeSecs.

Chase took a deep breath, then another. "Delete," he whispered.

"Are you sure?" asked SafeSecs.

He hesitated. No, not sure at all. Let her stay. Let her voice stay in the system, among those of the living. Let her spirit stay among the craters and rilles. Let her face stay in his memory forever.

"Cancel," he told it. "Save." The word glowed green and vibrant.

I would like to acknowledge the Rocky Mountain Rescue Group (of which my brother James Gallo is a member) for information and inspiration through their published account of actual rescues, Playing for Real *by Mark Scott-Nash; also Allison Stein, Mike Higgins, E.S. "Jake" Jacobs and Brian Eastman, the members of Noblefusion's Midwestern Court writers' group who work-shopped the story with me.* —M. C. Chambers

Joe the Martian Goes to the Moon
by Ken Edgett

". . . the Aristarchus Plateau. Beneath our feet, there's ten to thirty meters of little glass spheres of volcanic ash. Some of them are brown, some orange, green, yellow, black . . . The volcanoes were erupting here about three and a half billion years ago."

A rust-colored sphere dominates the view on three-vees around the world. Blurry, in the distance, is something hot pink and something somewhat yellow. Above and to either side of them is deep, dark blackness.

The focus and perspective begin to change. First, the sphere becomes blurred and things farther away sharpen. There are many such rusty-brown beads, each with small amounts of adhering, gray dust.

Then, the spheres merge to form a reddish-brown plain.

And, finally, the pink and yellow figures come into focus. The yellow one has a tail, walks on all fours, and has dark spots. The pink one has two legs, two arms, two antennae on top of his head, and a big melt-your-soul smile.

Joe the Martian and Beauty the Leopard.

Everyone knows them. Three generations grew up learning science by watching *The Adventures of Joe the Martian*. Thanks to them, every kid over age six knows that Earth revolves around the Sun and the Moon goes around the Earth. They know that cooking with microwaves does not involve radioactivity, frogs and toads were once more plentiful, and humans were not the only primates to walk upright on two legs. They also know that Joe and Beauty have a theme park in Iceland. It has drawn over three billion guests since it opened in 2073.

*   *   *

Children around the world, some of them awake well past their bedtimes, watch in real time as Joe bends down to one knee and picks up a rock. He remains bent and Beauty draws in for a closer look. The three-vee scene shifts to show a Joe's-eye view of the rock. Reddish-brown dust clings to his hot-pink hand.

"This rock is out of place," Joe says to Beauty in his characteristic, trademark voice. Beauty's ears perk up. The billions of watching children, enthralled, see the characters' mouths moving in a lifelike way, and hear them speak in their native tongues.

"Ejected from a distant impact crater, I'd say," adds Beauty.

Joe's Joe-sized hand lens hangs from a cord around his neck. He picks it up and looks at the rock. The three-vee shows the view through the hand lens as Joe moves the rock slightly back and forth. Sun glints off of several large, dark crystals.

"See those parallel lines? Those grooves?" He says to Beauty, "Only plagioclase feldspar has these. This whole rock is made of them. What does that tell you?"

The view switches to focus on Beauty, who raises a paw to his chin, thinks for a moment, and then says, "Anorthosite, right?"

The lunar geology lesson continued for another hour. Karina (as Beauty the Leopard) and I (as Joe the Martian) discussed the pyroclasts formed in volcanic fire fountains that make up the regolith on this part of the Moon. We described the gaseous implications of the vesicles in a chunk of dark gray basalt that Beauty encountered, and we explained that radon gas emissions in the region are high, even today, and some people have reported transient outgassing events here over the past few centuries. Then we unrolled a smartmap of the region and showed our viewers the plethora of sinuous rilles—the various lava channels—as well as the locations of the known, subsurface lava tubes common throughout the region.

Finally, as we walked and bounced (demonstrating the lunar gravity) back toward the *Armadillo*, we noted how the people at Hernandez-Schmidt are using some of the lava tubes for living space, and they're using the regolith—both the implanted solar hydrogen that collects among the tiny glass beads, and the oxygen bound with silicon, iron, and magnesium in the glass spheres—to produce water and fuel for their everyday needs.

As we entered the *Armadillo's* airlock, we told our viewers to tune in at 0700 GMT for our arrival at Hernandez-Schmidt, and again tomorrow at 0930 GMT for our first look at life in—at 7,000 people—the largest research station on the Moon.

After the airlock cycled, but before the inner door opened, we removed our costumes down to our waists, revealing our sweat-soaked JoeCorps t-shirts. Karina's shoulder-length black hair was matted and wet. Little droplets glistened on her dark nose. She squeezed water from a bottle into her mouth while I wiped my forehead with a towel.

"I think that went well," she said.

"I agree. That anorthosite was a nice bonus—I'd hoped for something like that, but I didn't really expect we'd be so lucky."

Then we opened the inner door and stepped into the *Armadillo's* 14-passenger cabin. Everyone clapped. They'd been watching the broadcast from inside the ship. The other passengers were a very patient group; they'd all received discount fares, subsidized by JoeCorps, with the caveat that they'd have to wait around while we did our "Arrival Bit" on the lunar surface.

The pilot spun around in his seat, "Ok, you two. Get strapped in. We've got a tight schedule if we're going to disembark on time for your 0700 broadcast."

Karina and I took our seats, she by the window, and me between her and the central aisle. The seatbelts barely fit over the bottom half of our costumes, but we'd been instructed to keep them on to save time when we arrived at Hernandez-Schmidt. We were to enter the base in full costume, with the adhering lunar dust, little glass beads, and the metallic, gunpowdery scent that was starting to permeate the cabin.

Eastern Arabia Terra, Mars. Where ancient erosion cut deep into layers of rock that record the planet's early history. An area ignored in the mad dash to the Valles Marineris and the martian poles. A place where a person could still make a meaningful discovery. That's where I *really* wanted to go.

"The way to Mars is through the Moon," Karina and I had both heard hundreds of times as we separately made our way through grad school—she at the University of Antarctica, me at Montana State. While I'd studied geology, her thing, really, was information sciences. And dance. (What those have to do with Mars, I didn't really know, but exploring Mars was a life-long ambition for both of us).

Before college and dance performances, she was the world-famous Karina Tendulkar, the gymnastics gold medalist at the '88 Olympics in Dar es Salaam. When I first met her at JoeCorps in Iceland four months earlier, I realized that I'd seen her before, though she'd only been thirteen at the time. Because of her Olympic performance, it was the first time the world heard the national anthem of the Republic of Antarctica as their new flag was raised at her medal ceremony. While no longer a gymnast, the petite 147-centimeter-tall woman was just the right size for the Beauty the Leopard moonsuit costume (and, at 193 centimeters, I fit just fine in the Joe costume). I guessed that, as a dancer, JoeCorps figured she'd gracefully handle walking on all fours in the Beauty costume.

I was looking forward to getting to Hernandez-Schmidt, getting our 0700 behind us, getting cleaned up and then heading out to find my old undergraduate girlfriend, Carolina Ruiz. She'd been working at Hernandez-Schmidt for a couple of years—*years*! I was only planning to stay a few months, long enough to have the requisite lunar experience to be considered useful to someone needing to bring a postdoc to Mars.

"There it is," a smiling Karina grabbed and jostled my left arm while pointing out the window with her other hand. Through the window I could see the spaceport field and a couple of low buildings roofed-over with plowed, brown pyroclastic regolith. Behind them, Schröter's Valley was visible, and, just barely out of the morning shadow, part of the valley's inner rille could be seen.

We descended gently—at least, from the perspective of the passengers onboard the *Armadillo*—but nevertheless we stirred up a lot of dust. The dust settled quickly, a sand-blast barrier lowered and a tunnel extended out from one of the buildings to our ship. The pilot got out of his seat to check that the tunnel was secured properly and the air pressures were adjusted to match between the tunnel, the airlock, and the passenger cabin. Then he opened the doors and said, "Regular passengers out first. JoeCorps wants

Beauty and Joe to come out behind them. Karina and Jonathan, your bags will be delivered to your quarters. The rest of you, please pick up your bags in the cargo handling area in one hour."

The twelve passengers, eight women and four men, got out of the shuttle while Karina and I finished putting our costumes back on. We'd be on camera, broadcast in real time, as soon as we appeared in the doorway of the *Armadillo* and stepped into the tunnel.

"I'm soooo glad we're done with that." Karina said as she walked, her back to me, toward the bathroom while peeling off her sweaty t-shirt, "The tedious elevator ride from Mogadishu, the two-day flight in the *Armadillo*, our first two three-vee appearances, and—jeez—the poor thermal regulation in those costume suits—"

"I don't know—except for being hot in the suits, I didn't think it was so bad," I said. "I mean, we're on the Moon! This is really amazing!" I bounced upward a little bit, in private celebration of the lunar gravity, but not so high that I would hit my head on the ceiling, which was not quite half a meter above me.

"Yeah," she shouted as the shower started up, "and the welcoming committee of little kids—they were very cute. I didn't realize there were so many kids on the Moon—thirty, forty? Did you count?"

I eased over to the bathroom doorway, but didn't look in, and said, "I don't know. Thirty-five maybe. And their parents. They were *all* pretty excited to see Joe and Beauty."

"Wouldn't you be, if you were their age?" she said as I heard water splashing. I surmised that she'd gotten into the shower, at that point.

"I guess so. Like most kids, I got *my* interest in science from watching those guys when I was little . . ."

The water stopped (except for a little drip-drip—pause—drip sound), and she changed the subject, "Can you really believe they're making us share this apartment?" Squooshing sounds suggested to me that she was soaping up her hair.

I said, "Living space is at a premium, I guess."

The shower and the splashing resumed, so I went back to unloading my bag and hanging clothes in the small closet near the door. When we found out, about half an hour earlier, that we'd have to share this little apartment (and I mean *little*—a bunk bed, a small couch, a three-vee, and—well, at least this was good—a private bathroom), I was really surprised. I'd assumed we'd each have our own space. And I had visions of bringing Carolina back to my place . . .

Oh, yeah, Carolina. "Phone Carolina Ruiz," I said out loud.

From the shower, where the water had stopped again and I assumed she was soaping-up, I heard Karina shout, "What?"

"Just making a call," I answered—and then there was a chime and the three-vee fired up and there was Carolina, in miniature, surrounded by flowers.

"Jonathan! You're here! I'm just finishing up for the day," She seemed happy and surprised at the same time. She was obviously at work in the greenhouse. She's a beekeeper, which on the Moon pretty much means what it means over most of the Earth—she operated and maintained tens of thousands of centimeter-sized, flying robotic pollinators. They wouldn't bring real bees to the Moon, right?

"We just got in, I'm unpacking," I replied. "I'm wondering if we can get together soon?"

"Yes, how about half an hour? Meet you at Singh's?"

"They have a *Singh's* here? On the Moon?" I was surprised! Singh's is the best tea and coffee chain in the world, in my opinion.

"Yes, it overlooks the gardens," she waved her right hand over the flowers next to her like a game show prize model. "See you there?"

"Half an hour. You got it," I replied just before her image vanished and the three-vee cut off.

Karina came out of the bathroom wearing a towel that just barely covered—well, I tried, anyway, not to stare. I told her I'd be going out—that I had to meet Carolina in twenty-five minutes. Then I got in the shower for a very quick one.

By the time I came out, Karina was gone. She'd left a note that she'd be out late and not to forget that we had three hours of prep work to do before our 0930 broadcast, which would be around 1430 Hernandez-Schmidt time tomorrow.

"You look tired," Carolina said as she got up from her seat and hugged me. I'd found her at a table on the balcony overlooking an impressive fountain and the vast gardens of the Hernandez-Schmidt greenhouse.

"*You look tired?*" I laughed and buried my nose in her hair on the side of her head. I took a long whiff. It smelled like chocolate and cinnamon, like I remembered. "I guess I *am* a little tired," I agreed, "after a moonwalk, two three-vee broadcasts, and checking in to my quarters; it's been a long day already."

She slid her hands to my shoulders and stepped back so we were at arm's length. "Sit, sit," she said and steered me to a chair at her table. Confused, and wishing for a much warmer greeting, I sat. "Large peppermint and cream, right?" she asked.

"Works for me," I said, though I was confused. I was feeling puzzled by her reaction to seeing me and yet, at the same time, lustful as I remembered how she looked in that swimsuit on our vacation seven years ago . . .

A waiter brought two cups; coffee for her, peppermint and cream for me. She must have ordered before I arrived.

"So," she began, "Joe the Martian. What's that all about? Why are you *here*, Jonathan?"

I took a long sip—yes it was hot but I needed a moment—this wasn't going the way I'd pictured. I was getting a vibe like she almost didn't want me there or something.

"JoeCorps held a casting call," I began. "They were looking for a young geoscientist interested in space travel. They were offering passage to the Moon for someone of my size to wear their costume moonsuit and play 'Joe' for the cameras. I showed up for their interview and they put me through a bunch of tests. They also had me show off what I thought were my pretty non-existent acting skills—in a 'Joe' costume, of course. I don't know. In the end, they selected me."

"Why not just do an animation of Joe and Beauty on the Moon?"

"Well, you know. They insisted on doing this for real, with people in costume, walking on the actual Moon. The show has always been sort-of retro, right? Starting out some seventy years ago as animated clay while everyone else was using computers . . ."

I took another sip of the hot tea, and went on, "As for why I'm here, really, well, you know that 'the way to Mars is through the Moon.' So I need to spend some time working here to qualify for Mars. Isn't that what pretty much everyone is doing here?"

"Actually, Jonathan, some people are settled here. They have kids. Families. Some aren't going to Mars, some aren't even going back to Earth."

Oh, crap! My heart sank as I then noticed the rings on her left hand, the hand she'd reached out to hold mine as she said, "some people are settled here."

I gulped. "Are you settled here? Do you have kids?"

"One. Charles. He's two. Big fan of yours—well, Joe the Martian, anyway."

I took another swallow of the tea—it didn't seem so hot now—and I said, "Why didn't you tell me?"

"Jonathan, we were out of touch. You were busy. All that field work in Oregon, preparing for a future when you'd explore the sediments of Mars. And I was busy, too, training to work with robotic bees . . . I don't know . . . the time just got away from us."

I think peppermint tea is supposed to help settle one's stomach. But I wasn't feeling so well as I wandered the corridors of Hernandez-Schmidt, trying to find my way back to the apartment. My mind was in a haze, trying to find the silver lining in the cloud. At least I wouldn't have the two-body problem, trying to figure out how to get to Mars with Carolina in my life . . .

Why didn't she tell me before? I'd have come to the Moon anyway, right? "The way to Mars is through the Moon," and all that?

Suddenly, right in front of me, a doorway marked "Authorized Personnel" opened and Karina stepped out. She saw me and seemed surprised that I was about to walk past there, right at that moment.

"Jonathan! Uh—how'd it go with Carolina? Are you, uh, hungry?" She steered me quickly away from the doorway and down the hall and around a corner into another hallway.

"The Carolina thing didn't go well at all—"

"Then you need a beer," she asserted, "come with me." She pushed my lower back with her right hand and led me around a curve to our right. "Let's go get you a beer, some food, and we can talk about it."

"No, no beer. I need to sleep well and be ready for our thing tomorrow," I was still in a daze.

Gandolf's is a pub located behind the big waterfall that pours down the back end of the greenhouse. The greenhouse isn't really a greenhouse like you'd find enclosed in glass back on Earth. It's a very large lava tube cavern lit by both electric lamps and bioluminescent trees. Just like at home, things on the Moon pretty much start with energy from the Sun. Orbiting mirrors—like the ones used over Antarctica in the winter—reflect sunlight so that even during the half-month lunar night, the solar arrays (located some 60 kilometers away) are illuminated.

"You need to eat," Karina said as she sat me down at a table in a dark corner of the pub, away from the waterfall out front. I was still in a fog, so she ordered for me. She didn't order beer, thankfully.

A waiter arrived a few minutes later with a chocolate smoothie and some water for each of us.

"So, what happened?" Karina asked as I took a swallow of the cool, frosty drink.

"She's married. Has a kid. Plans to stay here on the Moon. I don't know, I didn't get much past 'has a kid' before I lost track."

Plates arrived. Okra and tomatoes, slices of turkey breast, and fresh, warm paratha.

"Turkey?"

"Produced right here on the Moon," she said, almost proudly, "NFA-turkey, of course."

"NFA? Back home in Montana, them's fightin' words," I joked—as the fog began to lift—about my hunter and cattleman heritage.

"So," Karina began as she poked at her okra, "are you going to be okay?"

I sighed, "I don't know. I really hoped something would happen with Carolina. We were good together, once. Now she's here. Has a kid. A husband."

"So, Carolina likes it here, has a family, and she's staying. On the Moon. You'll live. Think of this as an opportunity."

"You don't know me," I pointed out, "I was in grad school so long. I kept the dating thing to a minimum so I could focus on my work. I'd always held out this hope that I'd get back with Carolina, that her work would take her to Mars to support the research efforts there—they need beekeepers, too, right?" I paused, lost in thought. Then began again, "Man, they were just starting to plant palm trees on Vancouver Island when she and I went there for vacation in '96—I thought we'd always be together, that we'd go

43

live on Vancouver after a few years on Mars . . ."

I took another sip of the chocolate smoothie and said, "So what was behind that door you came out of?"

She ignored my question.

"Jonathan, I know I don't know you. But—jeez—welcome to your new life! You found a way to the Moon, and I'm sure you'll find a way to Mars." She waved a forkful of turkey at me and continued, "Forget Carolina. Look, you've got it *really* good right now, I'd say. Where I come from, we look at the Universe as a harsh and dangerous place. Galaxies collide. Stars explode. What happens to all the intelligent beings, all the animals and plants, on the countless worlds destroyed when these—oh so very natural—things happen? It's a miracle that the Universe gave rise to us at all—"

"Is that what they teach you in Antarctica?"

"It's the very foundation of our Constitution. That it's amazing we exist at all. We treasure that and we treasure each other." She sipped her smoothie, then said, "Look, Jonathan, are you feeling better? Is the food helping?"

"Yes, it is. A lot. Thank you for being here in my 'hour of need,'" I replied.

"Oh, please!" She laughed and tossed her cloth napkin at me.

Despite my earlier concerns about having a drink, we ended up getting a bottle of wine to go. We went back to the little apartment and chatted for hours, sipping wine from two little bathroom cups. She still didn't tell me what was behind that door, and ignored me again when I asked about it. Finally, we went to sleep. Well, I should say, I fell asleep on the little couch. I don't know what she did.

When I awoke, it was 0600 local. She wasn't in the apartment. The shower was dry. The sink was dry. There was no note. I was a little dehydrated and feeling sore from sleeping curled-up in the small couch. I decided I needed a run.

After three cups of water, I put on my shorts, a clean JoeCorps t-shirt, running shoes, and legweights—the kind designed for the Moon so you don't just bounce off the ground when you run.

Then I grabbed my key and left the apartment. I began walking through the corridor, making my way toward the greenhouse. They supposedly had a hiking and running path in there. It sounded to me like it would be nicer to run among the gardens than to go to what I assumed would be an armpity- and feety-smelling gym.

As I walked, I had a weird feeling that I'd brought the wrong key with me. I pulled it from the small pocket in my shorts. It definitely was not my key. How would I get back into the apartment?

I decided this must be Karina's key. But to what? It wasn't at all like the keys to the little apartment. Then I thought, what if it's for that door? The "Authorized Personnel" door?

Curious, I turned around and headed back the other way, trying to remember where I'd seen the door.

I found it, and I knocked. There was no answer. It was 0625 and very few people were out and about. I waved the key over the lock. The door opened and I went inside.

It was a small room with ten lockers. None of them was locked. One had the initials, "K T" on its door. Karina Tendulkar? I opened the locker. Inside was a small moonsuit, about her size. The boots were coated with very dark, gray dust. I picked out an angular sand grain, about one and a half millimeters in size, from the tread on the bottom of one of the boots. It was a piece of basalt. There were no brownish, rust-colored spherules on the boots. These boots had not walked on the Aristarchus Plateau above us, yet they'd walked in fresh basaltic sand somewhere on the Moon.

I wondered—was this not Karina's first time on the Moon? Is this why she seemed proud of the NFA-turkey, or knew to shut off the shower while soaping up, because she'd been here before?

There was another doorway out of the locker room. An airlock. There was a small window on either side of the lock, so I could see into the airlock and out the other side. But both were dark. What is all of this?

Starting to feel paranoid, I decided I better leave.

We did our 0930 GMT broadcast. We wore our indoor costumes this time, rather than the moonsuits. These had better thermal regulation, if you can believe it. We were guided around the greenhouse and food preparation areas of Hernandez-Schmidt by a couple of ten-year-olds, Cyrus Yee and Edna Adu. They helped us explain to our viewers how food is grown, stored, and prepared on the Moon. We saw the lower level fish tanks, and the NFA meat facility, as well. We explained to Joe the Martian fans everywhere that most of the people living at Hernandez-Schmidt are support personnel. The researchers come and go, staying anywhere from a few months to a few years, but the support staff stays on for many years, growing food and maintaining the various systems that handle power generation, air supply, new construction, and surface operations such as the mining and refining of the oxygen and hydrogen from the glassy regolith.

Exhausted, when we returned to our apartment, I went straight to the shower and Karina fell asleep. She was still wearing the bottom half of her Beauty costume.

I was tired, too, but I wanted to see what was beyond that airlock. But first, I needed a moonsuit.

I still had Karina's key to the locker room. I entered the room and closed the door. No one was around and the airlock and the space beyond it were dark, as before. It was pretty much dinnertime at Hernandez-Schmidt, so it was unlikely that anyone was going to come in, maybe not until the next day.

I'd brought a big duffel bag. In it was my Joe the Martian costume-slash-moonsuit.

I put it on.

It was a bit awkward doing this by myself, without Karina to check all the connections and seals, but I managed.

I stuck the empty duffel bag in Karina's locker, and then entered the airlock. The pressure on the other side of the lock was near vacuum. I had the air pumped down, then I opened the opposite door.

Lights came on, one by one, all up and down the tunnel in which I now found myself standing. It was another of the zillions of lava tubes beneath the Aristarchus Plateau.

The floor was paved with crushed basalt sand. The sand filled in what otherwise would have been a rough, lava flow surface. Someone had put a lot of work into this place.

Then I noticed the walls.

* * *

Wow!

They took my breath away! From the airlock on down the tunnel—past where it curved to the right and I could see no further—the walls and ceiling were *painted*! Like those caveman paintings in France and Spain, only fresher and more colorful.

Cave paintings, on the Moon!

As I walked through the tunnel, I found that the paintings were telling the history of the Moon. First, its formation, then its cratering and volcanic history. Further on, the fits and starts of human exploration . . . paintings of robotic spacecraft from over a hundred years ago. The Apollos. The later expeditions with the flags of Old China, the United States flag with only 51 stars, and several Islamic flags with crescent Moons and brilliant Venuses. The paintings told the whole story . . . establishment of Hernandez-Schmidt—back when it was just called Aristarchus Station—the Old China base at the south pole, and so on, right up to the present. The painting style changed, though, starting with the portrayal of the death of Amanda Hernandez-Schmidt. It was as if a different painter started doing these walls after her terrible accident.

Someone nudged my left shoulder from behind.

"Ohhhhshhhit!"

Startled, I jumped and hit my head on the low ceiling. I spun around to face whoever was behind me as my feet were returning to the ground, somewhat slower than my terrestrial brain expected.

Karina! In her little moonsuit!

She motioned for me to flick on my radio. I did. She was laughing.

"What? What's so funny, sneaking up on me like that?" I said, with my heart still pounding in my chest.

"Your antennae broke off when you hit your head up there," she pointed toward the basaltic ceiling. "One of them is still stuck up there!" she giggled.

"So, Karina, what's going on? What is this place? Why is it restricted?" I gushed, "It's incredibly cool! We should show it in our 0700 broadcast tomorrow!"

"Jonathan, there's more I need to show you. Follow me."

She grabbed my hot-pink left hand with her gloved right and started leading me further down the tunnel. There were no more paintings. The tunnel floor was going slightly up hill, and we went around a sharp bend . . .

. . . And emerged into a very large chamber. It was full of plastic-wrapped packages. A few of them were open.

"Books?" I frowned, puzzled, as I picked up one of the items from an open package. There were more books inside. They were all written in a language I didn't know. Maybe Arabic.

"What's this all about?" I wondered.

Karina laughed again.

"What?"

"You just look so funny—and cute—coming in here in the Joe the Martian costume and finding our deepest, darkest secrets."

"Ok, time to tell me what's going on," I said.

"John—Jonathan—this ends your probationary period with JoeCorps. You're now a full member of the staff and your salary will be raised accordingly, later today."

"Huh? What are you talking about?" Now I was really confused.

"Jonathan, you might want to sit down."

I did. On a package full of books written in Korean. She sat across from me, on a package labeled in Cyrillic.

"This is the Hardcopy Project. Ever heard of it?"

"No, but I imagine it has to do with books, right?"

"Roughly a hundred years ago, people began scanning old books, magazines, newspapers, and whatnot, like mad. Getting them all stored digitally. This was great for providing more universal access to the written knowledge of humanity, right?

"Well, the problem is, over the past century, the printed word has been going extinct. Books are destroyed if there's digital copies of them. Libraries shut down. Who needs to store the hardcopy anymore? And never mind the fate of the zillions of magazines and newspapers . . .

"But what happens when the whole electronic world comes crashing down? Or when people become extinct? What becomes of our records? Or silly stuff, like old copies of *Cosmopolitan* and *Playboy*?

"JoeCorps started asking these kinds of questions about seventy years ago, pretty much from the beginning of their science education efforts.

"So, secretly, they began hoarding books. Hardcopy of everything. Photographs, magazines, newspapers, maps, government documents, even computer code. There are some governments and corporations that are hostile to this kind of preservation—especially those that destroy materials before they can be scanned, to keep certain information or records out of the hands of others. So JoeCorps has had to do this whole thing on the sly.

"After the Second War for Antarctica, when we became independent, Antarctica got involved with JoeCorps to get these hardcopies moved off Earth. See, it's not just a miracle that we exist in this harsh Universe, it's also a miracle that we've recorded all this stuff. It needs to be preserved.

"Antarctica figured that the hardcopies would be safer off-world. And they'd last longer in an environment where the paper won't deteriorate so quickly.

"So, yes, I've been working for JoeCorps for some time. This is my fourth trip to the Moon. And while you think I'm a dancer and once a gymnast, my athletic training came from the war. At eight and nine years old, I was doing little covert in-and-out operations. I was used to keeping secrets, even as a child. Today, with multiple trips back and forth to the Moon, I dance to stay in shape. And what I do today, when I'm back on Earth, is still very dangerous and clandestine. It pays to be small and stealthy.

"I should tell you, too, that you didn't find this place by accident. You didn't pick up my key by accident, either. I wanted you to find this. This is the only place we could be away from potential eavesdroppers and talk. Our little suit radios don't penetrate this rock."

She took a breath, "Ok, your turn to say something."

I wasn't sure what to say. So I asked, "The paintings?"

"Amanda Hernandez-Schmidt started those. She was the first person to stake out this cavern for the Hardcopy Project. She felt that cave painting was yet another way to pass along information to the future."

"So, why are you telling me all this now? Where do we go from here?"

"Jonathan, that's the fun part!" She smiled, "Do you remember all those tests you did for your JoeCorps interview? One of those was a compatibility test. You, my friend, are deemed to be compatible with me! And that's good, because we have a long journey ahead, together . . ."

This was too much. All at once. But she went on, "These hardcopies aren't staying on the Moon. The Moon is too close to Earth. It's going to get crowded here over the next few decades. Antarctica is footing the bill to move this operation to Mars."

*   *   *

The way to Mars is through the Moon.

In a few years, kids will see Joe the Martian and Beauty the Leopard working side by side as they ponder the ancient rocks of eastern Arabia Terra, not too far from the lava tubes beneath Syrtis Major.

Book of the Dead
Sarah A. Eastly

I

It's 2300 GMT, and the late meal I took after the rover-run is stuck somewhere in my chest. I get up to check the door again, knowing that if I don't the half-acidified pieces of food will come crawling back up my throat. I haven't done too many things—barring what landed me here—that are life-threatening, and suspect that most living people (living being the operative word) would say the same. But here I am: 173 centimeters, brown eyes, 72 kilograms, guilty. Again.

Last week, I picked a fight going into the shower; I still can't fully open my right eye. While the guard had me on ground, I snagged his keycard, knowing tonight would come just as well if I didn't.

Across the dark PO's lounge, Eli asks to borrow a pair of my gloves, since his have gone missing. I toss him the spares I keep in my cheek pocket, then begin to suit up myself.

"We could just leave," I tell him. "Slip out through the furnace shoots and no one would be the wiser." Also I'm thinking that if we get caught, the most they can get us on is attempted escape, which is just another 20+ years to the time already served.

"You know I won't do that," he says.

"Why not? The boys in the pit can handle things until we send help."

"Doesn't matter—there's no turning back now."

I don't have to look again at the stockpile of stolen weapons and food rations we've stuffed here in the couch cushions to know how right he is. In spite of my reservations, this is no longer just about escape.

I zip my pants, switch the charger on my pistol, and make sure I have enough oxygen in case of emergency, even though, acid reflux aside, I'm actually not worried about the possible loss of my own life—

Here, I'm already half gone.

II

How long have I been on this rock?

The Jovian shuttle came by last week to get the newest batch of transfers and the gurney-boat just landed today. Two ships—each coming and going a week apart so they seem to just miss each other—four weeks makes a month, which means two Jovians and two gurneys per month. My calendar only keeps track of the gurney boats though, and there's been about sixteen of them total since I arrived, counting this week. So I guess it's been four months to the day for me here, unless I forgot a week.

I never used to be forgetful, but time—the way it passes here—time is not like what it was back home, on real ground.

It takes me a good two hours on the rover to cut out a nice sized hole, and the rover must be refueled every six hours. So if the numbers add up right, I can have just about three plots done in time to refuel and get a meal. Three meals a day times six refuels means I sleep at every 1800th hour, since we're still running on GMT out here.

Out here—

I'm making it sound as though we're far away when we're not, but distance is deceiving when there are no clouds, nothing between you and the emptiness.

Of course, unless I'm planning on cutting my oxygen and taking the crater wall; it's unhealthy to dwell on that sort of thing, so thank goodness for my job. At least it makes life seem full, even if I don't show up for it with half the same enthusiasm as I did back home at the university museum with my colleague, Dr. Saygers, who was with me the night I was incarcerated. We were cataloging some new pieces in the lab and checking them for environmental data, like tree pollen.

The lab, the office—those were some really good days I had back then. Of course the greatest days were in the field—imagine that—I used to travel the holy land on grant money and walk through tunnels and tombs where only a few have set foot in thousands of years. The blood still rushes to my head when I think of all those epochs and their numbers, numbers going into time and the people inside those numbers running backwards into their own past.

III

Eli puts an extra gun into a holster on his leg. He says he likes to be prepared.

I do one last check through our supplies and tell him he would have made a fine boy scout.

He flips me the bird and reminds me that he was a boy scout, once a long time ago when his mother an artist, and his father, a doctor, and they lived quietly in the Midwestern suburbs.

"I'm sorry for bringing it up," I say. Now is not the time to tread on already frayed nerves.

"It's fine." He stands up and gestures to the door. "Ready?"

I nod and we step out into the hall.

In a little while, the Warden will be getting ready to leave his office, and our first step is to prevent him from getting to the reception hub, where he's going to meet our other hostages once they arrive. But first, we're planning some fun with the Warden. He's our collateral to the boys in the pit, after all.

If I ever get out of this place alive, I'll never forget working in the pit—how the chimes sound every time another gurney boat is docked. Then the boys below deck roll the gurneys in like a herd of bloody sheep, each bearing a seamless bag strapped down hard to keep it from floating all over the cargo bay when the ship is in flight.

Once we get the gurneys parked in the pit, I stand by to check off each one in a small handheld that I keep in my breast pocket—it's a digital *Book of the Dead*, keeping track of everyone and everything processed in the pit.

Eli, on the other hand, works in the actual smoke stacks, unless he's assigned to help me on the rover. Since he's thin enough to go up inside the chimneys, the Warden makes him clean away the buildup of soot, the pieces of bone, and anything else the flames have missed. From breathing in the fumes and grit, he wheezes and coughs like his chest is going to collapse; the skin under his eyes is stained permanently purple from the rupture of capillaries.

As we reach the top of the hall, I stop and wait for him to clear out his throat. He spits into a piece of cloth yanked from one of the gurneys. When he puts it back in his pocket, I notice the bright red stain, but I can't tell if it was there already, or if the blood came from Eli's lung—it could be either.

IV

When I first arrived here, I was something of a novelty to the other POWs. I had not committed any crimes of war or ideology—none that anyone could prove. When I would answer the inevitable "*what are you in for?*" those who expected some dramatic story of resistance and torture were in for a disappointment. So I'll be very up front about it here: I got busted for selling antiquities on the black market.

I know that probably sounds like a hypocritical waste of my Ph.D. in archaeology, but considering that the Pan-National Security Council had passed a reform bill to close the university, I really had no other choice. Besides, off-worlders will pay ridiculous sums for a bronze-age pot or a hieroglyphic cartouche, and in time I could have been rich enough to afford my own suite in Ganymede Station.

The tale of my not-so-rock 'n roll-past earned me the nickname of 'Tut' around here, and I couldn't ask for a nicer alias if I am to go down in infamy. Compared to the kind of jails still operating on Earth, being sentenced to hard labor on the Moon, or "Bella Luna" as the PO's call it, probably isn't all that bad.

What I do here is the ironic inverse of my old life—and at least instead of having constant surveillance behind bars, we have a bit more freedom to move about. There's also a low guard ratio too, since this place isn't exactly rolling in gold or anything.

Besides our little gravity-controlled encampment, lovingly called 'the Igloo,' there's nothing around but dust and dead people—I mean, burial sites—spreading out as far as the rover can range and the eye can see. It's a good thing they don't bother with head stones or plot markers—that would be far too complicated and I'd probably end up tripping all over the place, since there's no road system or even sidewalks around the mares and crater edges.

You can tell by looking at the mounds of soil where the urns are more "freshly planted," but forget about the ones that have been there for a year. The soil eventually gets pressed back down by rovers or the boots of workers, and it's as though nothing has been disturbed here since meteors and planetoids made Swiss cheese out of this rock's molten surface in its infancy.

Maybe a couple thousand years from now, some guy like me will come along and dig all this stuff up and get his tenure out of it.

Maybe he'll write papers about a great fallen civilization that seemed to take a huge interest in the placement of their dead. He would dedicate his life to understanding the iconography of our urns, pondering the significance of each serial number that hasn't eroded.

In the meantime, I'm carrying his Rosetta stone in my pocket: the database on my prison-issued handheld can place names—and sometimes faces—to each plot. Without having that, I'm afraid my future archaeologist is going to be seriously mistaken about what he finds, though I can't blame him.

In my experience with it, the past is a foundation of great mistakes.

V

Up ahead where I can't see yet, a door from the shuttle bay opens and there are footsteps reverberating against the floor tile. I press my body against the wall to be inconspicuous and keep listening. I hope that it isn't a guard that we will inevitably have to struggle with or kill. We don't want to draw attention to ourselves wasting time with the Warden's peons. Others have gone that route and failed, Eli told me, so he says we should start at the top. This time, he tells me, there will be no mistakes.

His pupils dilate as the steps come closer. I remember the first time, how he tried to do it all on his own. Later when the riot cooled, I found him barely conscious crushed between two urns in a pile beside the rover docks with both air meters cut off. The Warden wanted to make sure that Eli would never again get any ideas about who was in charge here.

Maybe these old bones are inspired by the fire of youth and conflict, but I've seen enough of that, so I doubt it. Maybe something in me is altruistic, but I stop well ahead of being a saint.

Out of the corner of my eye Eli edges up in front of me, crouching down like panther that enjoys the sadism of the chase. I already know what he will do if it is in fact the Warden drawing closer. Whatever happens, I won't judge the boy as long as I don't have to clean it up.

Clean it up—I hate it when I catch myself thinking like that, like the police who arrested and processed everyone here, like the well-dressed diplomats deciding to drop the bombs, deciding to eliminate anyone against their point of view.

Clean it up.

I point my pistol and prepare to cover Eli. I do this thinking that I want to dig a grave deeper than any ever dug before. I want to dig a grave deep enough so no one will ever forget what they're standing on, so that they will fall right in as if there are no edges around the hole.

VI

If the Igloo didn't look like a tin can on its side with a dozen smoke stacks peering out the back end, maybe no one would ever notice that we are here. The runway in front of the entrance is so small that there's never more than three ships parked at once. And everything visible, from the dust to the walls, and the rovers and our uniforms—it's all either white or gray. Perhaps then, this place is still easy enough to forget about, which is probably what everyone wants.

The shuttles have slowly been transferring more men to camps orbiting the Jovian worlds where they will mine hydrogen until their limbs atrophy. As for the rest of us, we are like the pieces of half-cooked meat that rot in the corner of the furnace.

Today at 0600 GMT, a pair of well-dressed ambassadors from home will land here and talk with the Warden about what's to become of us once the gurney boats retire and all the plots are filled. I can't even imagine such a day, and yet we're told that the time is coming soon, even if we aren't up for parole before the end of this century or ever.

Most people think that the end of war will bring all sorts of good things—liberation if you're on a red-ship, peace if you're on a blue-ship. But no matter what, the cycle of crime and punishment hovers like a ghost over justice while we kneel at her bedside.

I know that if I stay here that I have no control of what will become of me, and if I don't asphyxiate in some Jovian mine, I can look forward to being sold on the black market. You figure a 48-year-old male with decent health could fetch someone a nice tax break.

Eli's got no pipe-dreams when it comes to his future though.

Once he pointed out the spot to me where the Warden told him he'd be planted: "Right next to your dad—father and son—the ashes of two traitors together clinging to juice left behind in the can when the trash is emptied."

So it only makes sense: get him before he gets us, Eli tells me now, in case I'm having any last minute moral dilemmas as we make our way up the hall.

VII

"Hold him up," Eli gestures with his pistol at the guard crumpled on the floor.

"Stop waving that thing around," I say.

I notice that the exit wound on the guard's thigh is leaking against my crotch while I support his weight.

Eli ignores me and reaches down to remove the guard's helmet.

The guard groans and his breath fogs against his visor. Some part of me feels sorry, watching this as though I am behind a camera lens—even if a bullet in the leg is pretty tame in the scheme of things.

"Take off his clothes."

"What?" I almost drop the man on his face.

He rolls his eyes. "Take off his clothes, put them on and then come find me." He puts his sleeve against his mouth and coughs into it so I can barely make out the rest of his words.

When I ask him to repeat himself, Eli looks exasperated. "I'm going down to the pit—just hurry the hell up—" He disappears around the corner, all arms and legs, I notice, from his shadow. When I was his age, I think . . . .

I take the keycard and dog tags from the chain around the guard's neck and use the former to open the closet I shot a hole in. A few moments later, I've dragged him inside and he's naked now except for undergarments and boots. I strip down next and swap our clothing.

The guard doesn't speak to me but he's stopped moaning—he's breathing slowly and I wonder if the blood loss is pushing him into shock. Reaching for my last shred of human decency, I find an old rag in the closet and start wrapping his leg. Once I tie the knot above the wound, I turn around and continue dressing. He's smaller than I am, but since government-issued clothes tend to fit like potato sacks anyway, there's plenty of room to spare inside.

I'm just about to finish putting on the jacket when something cool and sharp presses against my back, right above the kidney. The response is instantaneous—there's a rush of heat and a prickly flood of sweat. I don't even feel the tip of the blade sinking beneath my skin until I've already hit the floor. In a flash of hindsight, I realize I forgot to check the guard's boots—which are known to possess an extra government-issued pocket for an extra government-issued bowie knife—just in case, I imagine, for moments like this.

I look up with my eyes half open and see him trying to stand up with his bad leg. The knife in his hands is still wet with my blood and seeing this, I struggle to stand up too, but I can't.

VIII

They told me on the medical frigate that three of my ribs were broken from falling out the trash chute and that if it weren't for the extra life support my lungs might have stopped responding. (I didn't know about the ventilation tape tourniquet fashioned around my waist until after I saw the incident report). What it really boils down to is that I was lucky to be found wearing that guard's uniform, otherwise the officers sent in by the Security Council would have either leveled me on the spot or charged me with conspiracy and high treason, which means a speedy trip to the top of death row. Yet, if you wanna talk about conspiracy and treason, here's the thing about Eli:

They never found a body.

At night in my cabin, I flip open my handheld and peruse the logs, thinking especially of the men on the rover teams and in the pit. No matter how the years and miles span, I am still there alone on my rover or pacing beside my bunk. And when I dream, I can see the smoke stacks rising up in triumph over my body, crumpled into the grey dust. Or sometimes, I see the runway and the entrance hatch where that antique flag from '69 hangs as a novelty beneath the camp banner.

The reports I've read say that the riot broke up quickly and most everyone who took up arms died, but he wasn't among the remains found and documented. He comes up as missing in the logs, but I know that's a polite word for secretly executed—or escaped.

Last time I saw Eli, I was still lying on the floor of the closet. He'd opened the door and emptied a clip into the guard who stood over me with the bowie knife. I remember him saying that he came back to tell me that a few of the guys turned yellow, and the warden had called in reinforcements to take out our remaining allies in the pit.

Eli cursed and spat over the body of the guard. "Come on—there's a gurney boat that just landed. If we don't get out of here now, it's over for good."

At that point, I lost consciousness in the blanket of my own warm blood, so it's all very debatable as to what happened next. He must've made sure that my life support was on and figured (if we lived) he'd find me outside. Or, for all I know he unceremoniously shoved me down the trash chute, laughing like a mad man until he spit out a lung.

If he's out there now—if he managed to clock the bastards on the tarmac and high-tail it someplace down-low—which, I'll admit isn't a very realistic expectation—but still, if he made it, I wonder if he can see this place from where I'm watching in my dreams:

Window seat, forward facing the empty star fields, the crater pitches and the silver mares—this screen open in my lap—our names calling out from the book of the dead.

Coyote and the Gamblers
by Shauna Roberts

1 June 2026
Nuevo Santa Justa Pueblo
Luna

Roberta Sanchez wiped her brow as she sat in the dark church, a replica of the centuries-old thick-walled mission church they had left behind in Santa Justa pueblo—Viejo Santa Justa now, she reminded herself. The design had worked well to defy the harsh New Mexican sun. On Luna, though, it merely kept the heat of the parishioners bottled up. She hoped she wouldn't faint before the service ended.

Grandfather leaned over and whispered, "If they don't get the air-circulating system working better soon, Little Frog, you'll be able to fire your pots in here."

On the other side of her, Antonio Díaz, her husband, snorted at the comment, and Roberta elbowed him.

"I ask you now to join me in the plaza," Father Xavier said. "Antonio and Roberta, as the first couple to marry in our new home, please follow me." Roberta looked at Tony; he shrugged. He apparently had no idea either what the priest intended.

When everyone had reassembled under the highest point of the dome, between the church and the opening to the kiva, Father Xavier put his arms around Tony's and Roberta's shoulders. "Today marks one year in Nuevo Santa Justa. Soon, we will have our first birth here. It may not feel like home yet, but, God willing, we will make it one during our exile."

A lump rose in Roberta's throat, and she looked up at the blue marble of Earth hanging in the sky so far away. Never, she thought. Though nothing could live in their poisoned pueblo now, it would always be home.

"We owe the Pechanga band much," the priest continued. "Thanks to them, we have a place to live, and thanks to them, in forty-nine years, we will return to Viejo Santa Justa."

Roberta blinked back tears. She was twenty-five; Tony, twenty-six. Would they live long enough to see home again? A tear slipped out. Grandfather certainly wouldn't.

"The Hebrews were once in exile, as we are," the priest said. "I will now read Psalm 137."

He cleared his throat and began. "By the rivers of Babylon we sat mourning and weeping when we remembered Zion." Roberta heard only bits and pieces after that; the roar of blood in her ears drowned out the rest.

Tony squeezed her hand. Grandfather tipped back his head and howled with grief. The dome echoed with weeping.

1 May 2075
Nuevo Santa Justa Pueblo
Luna

Roberta climbed the last few rungs of the silicone ladder and, grunting, swung her leg stiffly onto the topmost roof of the pueblo. She was getting too old to climb so high, even in Luna's low gravity.

But she needed to think, and nowhere else in Nuevo Santa Justa was as private. These top rooms—level 27 or 28 now, she believed—had been abandoned forty years ago when the young people growing up under Luna's light gravity began to bump their heads on the ceilings.

The people then had extended the pueblo downward, level by level, below Luna's surface. Tunnels connected the pueblo to the other domes. The smallness of the original dome that arched over Roberta gave no clue to the hundreds of rooms and nearly three thousand people in the ever-deepening cavern below.

Here, on top of the room she and Tony and their children had occupied in the early days, she could get away from the bustle and gossip below and enjoy a view of the magnificent world they had created. To the west lay Bear Dome, where their precious water was processed and recycled. To the north, Mountain Lion dome, the fabrications area, where chemists and metallurgists turned silicon and Luna's other resources into glass, clay, vigas for roofs, ladders, furniture, tillable soil, and other necessities. To the east, Wolf Dome, where sheep, deer, and wild turkeys foraged under piñon trees. And to the south, Badger Dome, where corn, beans, squash, cotton, sunflowers, sweetgrass, and tobacco grew in abundance, at last, after years of food shortages.

Like their ancestors of hundreds of years ago, they had taken a barren desert and built a thriving society.

She turned in a circle again, admiring the results of decades of work and sacrifice, then looked up at what they had once considered their Zion, their Jerusalem, their holy place. The Earth glowed like polished lapis lazuli veined with white calcite. Few clouds covered it tonight; she could see the western coast of North America clearly. Her gaze moved inland one thousand kilometers to where Santa Justa stood . . . or had stood until the creek had been poisoned with runoff from illegal mining in their sacred hills.

After the tribal council had reported the miners to the state police, men had come in the night with bulldozers and drove them into the first floor of the pueblo. Roberta shivered and wrapped her arms about herself. Many had died when the upper floors collapsed onto the lower. She herself had run out in a nightgown and seen figures bundled head to toe in yellow spreading material from a box around the plaza and in the church.

When the sun rose, the survivors gathered around the box. Stenciled on it was an orange triangle edged in black and containing three pairs of bear claws open to the triangle's points.

The stenciled words below read, "biohazard."

Although the land had been sacred to her people for centuries, they had to abandon it. Even bindweed had withered and died.

Now, at last, thanks to the Pechanga band and the billions they had spent on remediation, Viejo Santa Justa was habitable again.

She did not want to go back.

The jagged black basalt mountains and pocked surface of Luna were her sacred land now. Tony, Grandfather, her children, and the others who had died here had sanctified Luna's gray dust with their blood.

Still, a bargain was a bargain. The people of Nuevo Santa Justa had to return to Earth. Roberta had a duty to the pueblo to help rebuild. She was the eldest of the elders now, the one who knew the most about the Old

Ways, one of the few who had been born on Earth. The others would need her to explain even simple things such as currency and grocery stores and cars.

She sighed. Time had bent and twisted her body. Earth's gravity would treat it much worse. She rubbed her contorted fingers and thought of the pain to come.

She had rejected white values her whole life, yet now she wanted to reject Tewa ways and do what was best for herself, not what was best for the pueblo. Tony would have laughed until he choked at the irony.

"Bah!" she said out loud, and spit. "Best face the council now and get this over with."

She began the long journey down the rickety ladders to the kiva almost thirty stories below. Once, she would have jumped from roof to roof, racing Tony to the ground in slow-motion free fall. She smiled.

Even this saddest of days held something worthwhile: a memory of Tony and their happy decades on Luna.

The kiva was crammed with the officers of the pueblo, the heads of the summer and winter moieties, and, a rarity, representatives from every family. The room reeked of nervous sweat. Roberta took her silicone staff from where it stood against the wall and used it to steady herself as she struggled to lower herself into a crossed-leg position on the ground next to her grandson José. She banged the staff three times, as if that was why she had it.

The whispers and restless shifting stopped.

José handed Roberta a beaded white buckskin bag. Roberta took out a braid of sweet grass, lit it, and placed it in the center of the circle. Its purifying scent wafted through the small space. She fitted together the two parts of a pipe carved from Picasso marble, filled it with tobacco, and lit it. She offered the pipe to the six directions and passed it to the person next to her. Because of the crowd, it took a long time for it to circle the room and return to her.

"We'll start by reviewing our obligations to the Pechangas," Roberta said. She turned toward Luis Nuñez and nodded.

The cacique pushed a strand of graying hair behind his ear and picked up a thick stack of yellowed paper. He removed the top sheet to reveal a densely printed page. "Executed this 1st day of June 2025," he started.

Roberta held up her hand. "Does anyone object to the cacique's summarizing the history of the contract and its terms instead of reading it?"

José spoke out of turn. "This land is ours! Whatever the agreement says, we should refuse to honor it." Around the kiva, nearly every head nodded.

Roberta rapped her staff on the packed dirt. "Just as the whites did to the Indians so many, many times?" she chided. "Are we no better than them? For shame, José." Her chest clenched. She ached for those who had known no other home. But it was her duty to guide their return to Earth. She turned to Luis. "Please continue."

The cacique looked around the kiva, focusing on the youngest faces. "In the early 2000's, as the Los Angeles and San Diego suburbs spread further inland, the Pechanga casino profits increased. But the Pechangas could see the writing on the wall. Soon their reservation would be hemmed in by housing developments. They feared developers would not be satisfied—no matter how much land whites have, they are never satisfied, remember that—and would one day want the small Pechanga reservation, too."

The young men murmured angrily and shook their heads and fists, and the ends of the cloth strips tied around their heads bobbed.

"This colony was the Pechangas' back-up plan," Luis said. "Because of their wealth, the Pechangas could afford to build rockets and shuttles and transport people and supplies here. But the Pechangas were not willing to give up their luxuries to colonize such a harsh and barren place before they had to.

"After Santa Justa was destroyed, the Pechangas made us an offer. They would send us to Luna and provide us with everything we needed to start a colony—seeds, tools, animal embryos, solar generators, the works. They would also pay for cleaning the poisons from Santa Justa. In return, we would—" Luis flipped through the contract and started to paraphrase the words on the page. "We would build dwellings; create a self-sustaining life-support system, including water- and oxygen-recycling facilities; breed sheep and turkeys that thrive under lunar conditions and develop hide-tanning facilities; develop ways to grow crops; begin terraforming for future expansion; etcetera." He looked around the group. "Everyone knows what we have done here. Luna is ready for the Pechangas.

"The Pechangas have fulfilled their end of the bargain. Viejo Santa Justa is safe again. According to the contract, we must turn the colony over to them. In return, the Pechangas will make us their sole supplier of Earth goods and distributor of their exports and pay us five billion dollars for our labor.

"It is a very generous contract," the cacique concluded. "We were homeless. They gave us a place to live and a wealthy future. We owe much to the Pechangas."

Roberta's stomach clenched. Even she, who had always opposed bringing white technology such as phones and electricity into the pueblo, had thought it a good deal. She had been the first to sign the contract. She had done it to ensure the future of her people.

She had never dreamed Luna would become home.

She looked around. The young people who had never known Earth scowled; the relatively few elders sat stony-faced. Some of the latter, she knew, longed to return and walk on the sand again, their faces bare to the sun and wind, the Sangre de Cristo mountains looming over them.

She sighed. It was time to organize the packing and assign tasks to the various families. In only a month, the Pechanga tribal secretary's shuttle would arrive to take inventory and make arrangements for their departure.

José leaned forward, like a mountain lion tensed before its spring. "I suggest that the War Chief speak."

Roberta studied the young War Chief with narrowed eyes. She did not know Juan Ruíz Jañes well because he had spent many years on Earth. Because the only enemies on Luna were the vacuum and cold of space, the War Chief in Nuevo Santa Justa was always an engineer. Juan Ruíz had been educated at the Massachusetts Institute of Technology. The Pechangas, understandably, wanted only the best workmanship in their future home.

Juan Ruíz had always struck her as stuck-up, with his odd accent and precise speech. He usually stood out from the young men who had not gone Earthside; he kept his hair short, and he still wore the knit shirts and linen pants of his college days.

But not today. His plaid shirt, blue jeans, and the strip of red cloth around his head made a clear statement of where his loyalties lay.

A thrill ran down Roberta's spine. Tucked into Juan Ruíz's headband was an eagle feather, tattered but still recognizable.

Juan Ruíz stood and looked around, letting the suspense build. Roberta felt a trickle of sweat roll down her chest, and she leaned forward in anticipation. She bumped shoulders with Luis, who had done the same.

"Esteemed Grandmothers and Grandfathers, we need the wisdom of Coyote," Juan Ruíz enunciated clearly. Several young people hooted in support.

Roberta sat in silence for several minutes, mulling the young man's pronouncement. One's word was sacred—except among whites, of course. The Santa Justans would lose face if they broke the contract.

Coyote could wiggle out of most trouble. What would he do with an unwanted contract?

Coyote would get the other party to break it, that's what he'd do. Roberta's hands shook with excitement as she considered options. At last she nodded. They had a chance.

"Well said, War Chief. Here is what we'll do."

30 May 2075
Nuevo Santa Justa Pueblo
Luna

Roberta, Luis, and Juan Ruíz walked through the tunnel to the landing pad. The secretary of the Pechangas shuttle had landed fifteen minutes earlier, rumbling the pueblo and sending pots crashing to the floor. By the time the three reached the airlock, the secretary and his party would probably be there.

Roberta rubbed her sweaty palms on her cotton skirt. Everything was ready that could be ready, but she knew the old stories. Coyote the trickster sometimes fell prey to tricks himself.

"Juan Ruíz, you spent years on Earth," Roberta said. "Why do you of all people want to stay here?"

"We don't belong on Earth." He stretched his arm out in front of her; he had the preternaturally long, thin limbs of the Lunaborn. "Our bodies are made for Luna. On Earth, I broke my leg twice and a rib once. I developed asthma from the city air. My joints hurt and I limped like an old man." The War Chief shook his head. "Earth had many wonders. But it's not our home anymore."

They reached the end of the tunnel and climbed the stairs to the air lock. Gears creaked, and air whooshed in the chamber. Roberta assumed a calm, dignified expression worthy of a Tewa elder as the door slid down into its channel in the rock.

"Welcome to Luna, Mr. Murphy," she said.

Raymond Murphy stretched out his manicured hand with its large gold and diamond ring to shake hers, then froze. His expression turned to horror as his gaze flitted from her grubby dress to the men's worn plaid shirts to the dirty covers on the solar-powered lights to the trash-strewn tunnel with its strategically placed dead "rat," which she had sewn herself from a dyed skin and stuffed with cotton.

"We hope you are happy in your new home," Roberta said.

Even in the dimness, she could see that he turned slightly green.

Time to turn up the pressure, Roberta thought. "This is our cacique, Luis Nuñez, and our War Chief, Juan Ruíz Jañes. Juan Ruíz knows more about the workings of the colony than anyone else and will be your guide."

Murphy recovered his dignity, shook hands, and introduced his aides. Roberta let out the breath she had been holding. All wore white shirts and blouses. If the fine dust José and Juan Ruíz had put into the air system spread as expected, the Pechangas would soon be grimy from head to toe.

Juan Ruíz led them first to Badger Dome. They had done little here to trick their guests; the crops were necessary for survival. Murphy's shoulders relaxed visibly as Roberta pointed out the neatly weeded rows and Juan Ruíz explained how the proper amounts of light and nutrients were supplied.

Murphy's gaze went to the silk tassels on tall corn stalks, and an eyebrow rose. Juan Ruíz explained that the climate was varied in different parts of the dome so that most food crops could be grown all year round. "Well done," Murphy said, looking pleased.

Roberta stood a little taller. Tony had once worked in this dome.

"I had not looked forward to eating dried corn most of the year," Murphy said. "This is a pleasant surprise."

They took the tunnel northeast to Wolf Dome. The children had been given free rein here, and it showed. The dome stank of dung and urine that had not been collected and taken to Badger Dome. The Pechanga contingent sneezed and coughed. Roberta faked a cough so they would not see her smile.

The children had also plucked feathers here and there on each turkey and sheared random areas of the sheep and daubed them with red ochre.

"The animals don't look healthy," a middle-aged woman with an expensive haircut said as she scribbled notes on some sort of computer tablet. Donna Rojas, Roberta remembered from the introductions.

"We had a problem with mange in the past, but not so much now," Roberta said. "If the meat is cooked well and the wool treated properly, both are safe." Rojas pursed her lips and brushed at her hair as if to get rid of mites.

Next stop was Mountain Lion Dome. Juan Ruíz had outdone himself here, Roberta thought with admiration. He and Luis had spotted many metal joints and parts with an ochre-based paste that looked like years of bubbled, built-up rust. They had disconnected many of the solar lights and splattered mud on the underside of the dome so that the huge room was unappealingly dark. They had closed most of the ventilation ducts; the room now reeked of chemicals, and the heat pouring from the glass and pottery kilns was trapped. The people who worked here were at their stations, but instead of their usual white lab coats, they wore dirty clothes.

Murphy walked over to a workstation. "What are you doing?" he asked the workers.

"Making copper wire for our electronics," Maria Abendaño said, looking up at him as her hands continued feeding a narrow copper wire through a die powered by her pumping feet. Her feet slowed as she talked, and the extruded wire had bulges and thin spots.

Murphy's brows drew together. "Isn't it important that wire be a consistent gauge?"

"Yes, it is," Rojas said, writing again on her device.

Maria shrugged. "Close enough is good enough to keep most things working, at least for a while."

The Pechangas looked at each other, their faces full of consternation. Rojas looked at another woman's blouse, then her own, and gasped. She brushed at it vigorously, grinding dust into the silk. "May I use the ladies' room?" she asked. "I need to clean my blouse."

Roberta led her to a screen, behind which a hole had been dug for the visit and which José had used several times the week before. "Here you go, but I'm afraid there's no running water."

The woman stepped back and wrinkled her nose in disgust. "Never mind." She wiped at her blouse again, then went over and whispered something in Murphy's ear.

"Time to see our most impressive accomplishment, Bear Dome," Roberta announced. "That's where we process our most vital resource, water."

Juan Ruíz led the way. He threw open the doors and said, "Voilà."

Roberta's rib muscles burned as she held in her laughter. Bear Dome was even filthier than the fabrications area. "The proof of our success is in the water's taste," she said. She went to a spigot on a tank and filled several pottery mugs chosen for their chipped rims. She passed them out, held her breath, and took a sip.

She, Luis, and Juan Ruíz were expecting the rotten-egg smell of the sulfur Juan Ruíz had added to this tank. The Pechangas were not. They gagged as they swallowed.

Murphy gave them a strained smile. "I think it's time to talk."

Could it truly have been this easy? Roberta smiled back and said, "Certainly. You haven't seen the pueblo itself yet. We'll go and talk in the kiva in the plaza."

She led the way this time, choosing a narrow, low-roofed tunnel long out of use. The Pechangas emerged into the plaza swiping at cobwebs and dust on their hair and shoulders.

As Roberta climbed down the ladder into the kiva, she brushed her hand against the cool wall and asked the spirits for their aid.

The Pechanga women in their high heels had difficulty climbing down the ladder and then remained standing rather than sit in their short, narrow skirts. The men joined the Santa Justans in sitting cross-legged on the floor.

"The facilities are not quite what we expected," Raymond Murphy said.

"They certainly are in excellent condition," Juan Ruíz replied. "We are pleased to leave you with Luna station in such good running order."

Murphy dropped all pretense of politeness. "You misunderstand me. This place is a deathtrap. There are accidents waiting to happen all over. I'm surprised the lax conditions in Mountain Lion Dome haven't resulted in a dome breach."

It was time to threaten the Pechangas with living in this mess. "We are ready to turn over possession immediately, as the contract stipulates," Roberta said.

"Obviously, the station is not ready to be turned over to us tomorrow, as the contract requires," Murphy said. For a second, Roberta was giddy with relief and started planning a feast in her head to celebrate.

"However," he continued, "my team includes specialists in hydraulics, engineering, biology, and genetic engineering. I myself was a Quartermaster and Chemical Equipment Repairer in the fourth Gulf War." He touched the spot on his chest where an American soldier would wear his medals. "With us to guide you, we'll have the station up to our standards in a short time. Then we can take you back to Earth and bring our people here." His aides nodded.

Roberta turned cold. They still wanted the station? Even the prissy Rojas?

Murphy looked Roberta straight in the eye and added, "Of course, we will have to reduce your payment by the value of our time and oversight. Perhaps *four* billion dollars would be an appropriate compensation now."

Roberta's throat grew too dry to speak. Murphy had brought an unusual team for a diplomatic mission. She realized he had come planning to find a way to reduce their payment, and the Santa Justans had played into his hand.

The tricksters had been tricked.

An hour later, José stomped about the kiva, stirring up dust despite its packed floor. "A billion dollars for returning Nuevo Santa Justa to what it was a month ago! They tricked us."

"We can hardly get mad," Luis said. "It's what we tried to do to them."

Roberta crossed her arms on her knees and rested her forehead on them. It had been a long, exhausting, disappointing day. All of her joints ached; she had not walked so far in years.

The day wasn't done yet. There was still the welcoming feast for the Pechangas and the gift-giving afterwards to endure. The smell of cooking food permeated even down here, but her clenched stomach rebelled at the smell.

"We can't let them get away with this," José insisted.

"They already have," Roberta said. Despair weighed on her like a load of firewood in the old days.

"Maybe not," Juan Ruíz said. "The Americans don't tell stories about Coyote and his tricks." He paused for effect. It was an annoying quirk, Roberta thought. She hoped none of the other young men picked it up.

"But they do tell jokes about a different kind of trickster: lawyers," Juan Ruíz said.

"What are you getting at?" José asked grumpily. "We don't have any lawyers here."

Roberta lifted her head and answered for Juan Ruíz. "When I put my pottery on consignment in galleries in Santa Fe, I signed contracts with the store owners. No matter how clear the wording seemed, sometimes the shop owner and I had different ideas about what some of the sentences meant."

"Lawyers twist the meaning of contract terms all the time," Juan Ruíz said. "Just imagine how many different ways we could interpret our contract with the Pechangas!"

"We'd never win a lawsuit," José said, yanking off his bandana and twisting it. "They have a fortune to spend on lawyers. We've got nothing."

Juan Ruíz smiled, showing his teeth. The War Chief had a human enemy at last, Roberta realized, and he was enjoying every moment of their combat. "We don't have to win," Juan Ruíz said. "We just have to keep them tied up in court. We could stay in Nuevo Santa Justa for years before the suit was settled."

"Or the Pechangas may give up," Roberta said.

"I'll go get the contract and other paperwork," Luis said, motioning to José to go with him.

"The Pechangas are strutting about, and rumors are spreading that we're going to Earth after all," José announced when he and Luis arrived back at the kiva. "The young men are angry."

"When *aren't* rumors spreading in a pueblo?" Roberta asked, shrugging her shoulders. "Tell your friends not to worry. The Pechangas are treating us like their casino customers, and they think they hold all the cards. But this time they don't." She banged her staff. "We have the ace: We're living on Luna and they aren't. Maybe with the help of that contract, things can stay that way. Let's tangle them up in their own language."

"Which terms are you thinking we can use?" Luis asked.

"It's been fifty years since I read that thing, and I didn't understand it all then," Roberta said. "Give us each a section, and we'll start marking every sentence that could help us."

José's stomach grumbled. "We're going to miss the feast. And my wife made her corn pudding!"

"You can have corn pudding anytime. We have one chance to keep our home." Luis passed out the pages, and Roberta felt a surge of renewed energy and hope as she took her stack.

Roberta, Juan Ruíz, and José met the Pechangas at a table in the plaza for a breakfast of coffee and frybread with powdered sugar.

Rojas took a sip of her coffee and wrinkled her nose. "Instant?"

"Only the best for our guests," Roberta replied. "As you know, space in the supply shuttles is limited, and necessities get first priority. Instant coffee is a luxury. We've been saving this jar for a special occasion."

It was clear from the woman's expression that she had *not* known. She set the coffee cup down and ate her frybread in silence.

After everyone had finished, Murphy wiped the sugar from his moustache with his napkin and dusted his hands off. "Let's get to work, then," he said, pulling some papers from his briefcase.

"Not so fast," said Juan Ruíz.

"Who are you again?" Murphy asked, arranging his papers and taking a gold pen from the breast pocket of his striped suit.

"I'm the War Chief."

Murphy did not look impressed. "A useless title here."

"Not anymore. We have decided to stay at Nuevo Santa Justa, and we will defend ourselves if necessary."

The Pechangas stared at him.

"We have grounds," Roberta said. "You have violated the contract in several ways. Cacique?"

Luis cleared his throat and shuffled his papers. "I'll list two violations to start. First, the contract lists our obligations, but gives you no power to evaluate whether the result is satisfactory. We have done everything you required. If you still want the station, you'll have to make any changes yourself.

"Second, no provision allows you to reduce our payment if you perform work here. In fact, the wording is quite clear: At least five billion must be paid in full when station ownership transfers. If the U.S. inflation rate has averaged more than six percent a year—which it has—the fee rises proportionately." He looked Murphy straight in the eye. "If you take possession of the station, you'll owe us more than seven billion dollars."

Murphy winced and went white.

Roberta went in for the kill. "There's an alternative that will make everyone happy. We stay here. You keep your seven billion dollars. "

"Impossible." Murphy's voice was firm and oddly sad. "I wish it were possible, but it's not. We have to have this stinking station."

"And we can't wait," Rojas added, tapping her ever-present tablet with a red fingernail.

Roberta pounded her stick in frustration and confusion. Apparently the Santa Justans had succeeded in convincing the Pechangas that they didn't want to live here, but they intended to do so anyway. It made no sense.

"You might as well tell them," Rojas said to Murphy. "They'll learn of our shame when they get to Earth."

Roberta looked at Murphy, waiting. He bowed his head. "Developers want our reservation. Their lobbyists worked hard. The California legislature voted that we must accept a small tract of useless land in the mountains in trade for our reservation. We spent billions on lawyers to fight this law. We lost."

Roberta looked away to avoid adding to their shame. She clasped her trembling hands in her lap. Her chest tightened. How could she bear to leave her home and Tony?

"Take Viejo Santa Justa," Roberta offered on impulse, even though it was not her place to without a vote of the council. She had no doubt they'd support her offer. "You made Santa Justa safe to live in again. Take our pueblo and our lands and be happy there, as we once were."

"You must be joking," the youngest aide said. "There's nothing there but sand, rocks, and a muddy creek. It's the ugliest place I've ever seen."

"Two hours to Santa Fe and an hour to the nearest decent grocery or beauty salon," Rojas added with a shudder. "Why would we want that?"

Roberta's head snapped up. Ugly? Barren? Kilometers from anywhere?

"Since we're going to be stuck here, you might as well finish our tour. I want to see the shopping district and the recreational facilities," Rojas said.

"Certainly," Roberta said. Coyote had one last trick up his sleeve.

The three Santa Justans made it to the top of the pueblo ten minutes before the heavy-bodied Earthborn Pechangas did. "I can't believe we didn't think of this before," Luis said.

"It was my failure," Juan Ruíz said. "A War Chief should know the thoughts and desires and needs of his enemies as well as he knows his own."

Roberta tensed as she heard the Pechangas' labored breathing. They had pulled themselves up the ladder rungs with their arms instead of bouncing off them with their feet. She had done the same at first, she remembered.

Luis and Juan Ruíz helped the Pechangas onto the rooftop. "Now you've seen the whole pueblo," Roberta said.

As the Pechangas panted and wiped their foreheads, Rojas exclaimed, "But there's nothing here. I thought you were taking us to the gym now."

"Climbing the ladders is great aerobic exercise," Juan Ruíz said. "I run from dome to dome first thing in the morning to get my blood flowing. We had no need to build a gym."

A slight whimper escaped Rojas' throat.

Roberta extended her hand outward toward the view outside the dome and turned in a circle. "Here is what makes the climb worthwhile. Have you ever seen anything so magnificent? These mountains rise twice as high as the Sangre de Cristos mountains. The plains stretch as far as the eye can see with nothing manmade to mar them except the domes of the settlement. Because there's no atmosphere, the sky's dense with stars. No view on Earth can compete with this."

Rojas chewed her lip. "This is it? It's worse than old Santa Justa! I had thought in fifty years, you would have gotten more done, that it would be like a resort town. Small but with amenities. How could we possibly live here?"

"We have no choice," Murphy said, "unless you'd be happy with a few square kilometers of mountain range far off the electrical grid." Muscles in his forehead throbbed, and he rubbed them with a knuckle.

"Perhaps you should reconsider taking Viejo Santa Justa," Roberta said. "You could build your own resort town and challenge Taos and Santa Fe for tourists. You have a good start; the old mission church always attracted tourists, and now you have the ruins of the pueblo as well. And you're close enough to Santa Fe to draw gamblers to a new casino."

Murphy gestured to his entourage, and they stepped across the roofs to talk. In five minutes they were back.

"Perhaps we should discuss a new deal," Murphy said.

Roberta nodded. "Let's meet in the kiva in half an hour. I'd like to stay up here a few minutes more." As the others headed to the ladder, she walked to the corner of the roof, where she could see the stone she had placed as a memorial to Grandfather, and nearby, the memorial stones for Tony and the children. Their bodies, of course, had been reclaimed for fluids and protein. Nothing could go to waste here.

The thought was comforting, not disgusting. Tony now was part of her and everyone around her.

She heard steps approach and turned. Juan Ruíz had not left with the others.

"Want to hear something odd?" Roberta asked. "From early on, I've felt the gods' presence here. As if they stowed away on the shuttle or something."

Juan Ruíz crossed his arms and looked across the plain to the mountains. "I took some astronomy classes at M.I.T. Do you know how the Moon formed?"

She shook her head.

"Something from space, something the size of Mars, collided with Earth and blasted out large chunks. Over time, the pieces coalesced and formed the Moon."

Roberta looked up at the Earth and smiled. "So Luna is the Earth's daughter. We do not need to weep for Zion. We're living on sacred ground, as we always have."

"As we always will," Juan Ruíz answered softly.

Ménage à Trois
by Gustavo Bondoni

The man's helmet pressed against mine allowed us to communicate without radio. Radio was a no-no in our line of work, and wasn't necessary in any case. He simply shouted, and the contact between our visors carried the sound.

"Ms. Lombardo?"

I nodded.

"The plans are in the storage drive!"

I pulled back and nodded again, indicating that I had heard, understood, and would proceed as agreed.

He nodded back, dusky face barely visible beneath the tinted visor, even in the full glare of the sun, and bounded back the way he'd come. I admired the elegance of the new Indian suit in action until he was hidden from view by the lip of the crater. I would file my recording of the movement as soon as I had time since sending it out, even encrypted, was not an option. But first, I had to get this drive to Rosemeyer.

The Indian was long gone, but I still waited fifteen more minutes before making my own way. I stood in the shadow of an outcrop, observing the barren, empty majesty of the Sea of Tranquility under the sun of lunar noon. Even though my visor was nearly full-dark to shield my eyes from the reflected glare, Earth hung in the sky like a giant milky sapphire, and I wondered for the millionth time how humanity could have ignored this wonderful place for three quarters of a century.

My rover was parked out of sight nearly a kilometer away, in the largest patch of shade available—only the solar arrays were in the sun—and I sweated as I walked. My suit had been optimized for daytime temperature, which meant that, though it was lighter and allowed much more mobility than the previous model, it also had the bare minimum amount of insulation, which meant that while I could easily survive the scorching sun, I would not necessarily be comfortable.

The drive back to the High Vegas was uneventful. The guy manning the airlock was surprised to see me because he knew that nobody had gone out that way today, but waved me through without comment. It might be a useless precaution to enter through a different door than I'd used to exit, but one could never be too careful these days. I knew my movements would be recorded and in the hands of both the Indian and Chinese services within a couple of hours.

Leaving the rover in the government-vehicle lot, I peeled off the suit, recovered my clothes and walked quickly past the spaceport facilities and into the main dome, which we referred to simply as "the Strip." Bright lights destroyed the majestic view of Earth in the sky, but the teeming crowds seemed not to care. They were there for a different reason. Maybe to impress others with their off-planet vacation. Or maybe just to mingle with the highest of the high rollers—a good night at the tables could pay for the cost of the flight out. And the casinos would accept anything: cash, jewelry, deeds to property on Earth. The only thing non-negotiable was the ticket back.

I was relieved to turn off the Strip onto the deserted side-corridor leading to the government sector. Despite the fact that this base was a critical strategic and scientific outpost, the official area was much smaller and grubbier than the public enclosure, placed in a secondary dome out of everyone's way. The western space programs had, after much pleading, gotten their moon base, but not without some creative pitching to gaming industry investors.

The entrance door had both the NASA and ESA logos stenciled on it and two humorless-looking guards stationed outside. I wondered how they managed to stay alert and grim in the face of no threat more serious than a possible drunken tourist making a wrong turn, but they did. The one on the right wordlessly studied the badge on my suit with both UV and IR light before opening the door.

Brett Rosemeyer's office was the last in a warren of small closed cubicles on the second level. I was amazed how government offices everywhere, even here, were indistinguishable from one another—dull, utilitarian and slightly depressing. Brett himself was my picture of a stereotypical public servant: balding, slightly pot-bellied and possessed of the moon-dweller's pallid complexion. Only the fact that I knew him to be an extremely creative and intelligent individual kept him from being completely comical.

He looked up as I entered, and gestured towards the seat facing his desk. "So, I take it all went well with our Indian friends," he said, the remnants of a British accent noticeable under the Alabama drawl.

"They asked me to give you this," I replied.

He studied the chip for a few moments and laid it next to a model of a streamlined silver race car that was the only ornament in his office. "Do you know what it is?"

I nodded. "Plans to the Chinese base on the far side."

"Yes. Now the thing is why? Why in the world would the Indians give this to us? It couldn't have been easy to obtain. Getting into that base is nearly impossible. Bribing the Chinese is expensive. So why did they just come over and give us the plans?"

I didn't know. The Chinese and Indians had been playing their chess game on the Moon for the last twenty-five years, and looked upon the NASA / ESA base as a bit of an irrelevant Johnny-come-lately. The fact that most of our surface area was used to house casinos and hotels was just another reason for them to laugh at us.

"I have no idea," I replied. "But I suspect it'll come to us when we take a look. Or maybe it's just a play to get us on their side and balance things a bit." The construction of the second Chinese base on the Moon had been a serious blow to Indian pride. They would never let the great red nation forget that India had put the permanent base up first, but the Chinese had wasted no time in establishing technical and psychological dominance. This second base had been a terrible blow.

Brett raised an eyebrow. "Strictly speaking, you aren't cleared to view this material."

"We both know that I have to. After all, I'll be the one taking any action that comes from this, and I won't risk it unless I have access to the original plans, not some sanitized version that's been run through analysts on Earth. They'll probably delete some detail that they don't think I need to know and get me killed."

He laughed, motioned for me to close the door, pulled the drive off his desk, placed it on the reader and waited. The big screen on the wall behind him flickered to life, showing a large mess of lines of different colors. It was not immediately possible to make anything out.

"Let's start with what we know," Brett said. "Exterior." This last was directed at the screen. All lines except for the gray ones that marked the contour disappeared. "Overwrite and compare with stored orbital photos."

A second image appeared on the screen: the Chinese base as seen from orbit. The two forms jiggled on the screen a couple of seconds before a new message appeared—'Match Positive.'

"Good," Brett said. "Let's see what else we have in here."

We began to peel back the layers of the schematics, taking notes and saying nothing in order to avoid contaminating each other's observations. Even so, it was impossible to be unaware what Brett was thinking. He had to be thinking the same thing I was. I looked over at him.

"And now we know," he said.

I nodded, but decided to play it by the book. I would probably have to go out there and have a look, and wanted to be absolutely sure that we were on the same page.

He began reading his notes. "The dome is hollow, the only inhabited areas are contained in a ring along the circumference. Strangely, though, the main power lines have outlets in various places along the empty space in the middle, which is forty meters deep. And it's full of air."

I broke in. "Energy readings show that 98% of all their electricity consumption occurs within the empty part of the dome, and that they've been stockpiling very cold liquids there as well."

"So it isn't empty."

"Obviously."

We sat for a minute, both of us thinking the same thing, neither wanting to say it out loud.

"They're building something," Brett said.

"They're building a spaceship," I replied.

Silence ensued. He knew I was right, illogical though it was to build a spaceship on the Moon. The design of the dome's interior, the frozen liquids—rocket fuel?—in the hollow area and the energy consumption all pointed precisely in that direction.

"But why?" he said after a while. "It doesn't make any sense. I can understand not building it on Earth, just in order to avoid having to pull a large ship out of that gravity well, but the most logical place to build it would still be in high Earth orbit. Why put it on the Moon? You end up having to ferry all the materials all the way over here! It must be costing them a fortune."

"It has one advantage. If you build it in Earth orbit, everyone will know what you're up to. Over here, all we know about is that there's an opaque dome. Maybe the Indians gave us a bum steer to make us nervous."

"Why would they do that?"

"Who knows?" I said. "We're new to these little games they've been playing. Maybe they want us to share our intel or just get us all jumpy about the Chinese."

"What do you think?"

"I think it's real. I think that, under that dome, the Chinese are putting together the Mars mission they've been promising for so long, and they've been doing it secretly in order to unveil it at some psychologically relevant moment. They don't just want to win the race for the solar system, they want to do it in such a way as to embarrass everyone else."

Brett nodded, but I wasn't finished.

"The only thing that doesn't add up is why the Indians would just give this to us. There's something we're missing here, and I don't like it."

Night suits were less comfortable than day suits. The insulation was thicker, for one thing, and they were also designed with safety margins that daytime suits didn't have. The extra bulk was offset by slight servo assistance. I just hoped I didn't have to make a run for it.

I knew that anyone looking up from Earth today could enjoy a beautiful full moon, but it was no use to me. The far side was as dark and cold as it would be for a few more days. The same darkness that kept me hidden from casual observation also kept the movements of the Chinese convoy murky and difficult to interpret.

I had been watching the approach of the huge balloon-wheeled Han-class trucks for fifteen minutes with the infrared filters on my visor, and was nearly blinded when the station suddenly turned on a pair of huge floodlights. It took my visor a couple of seconds to adjust to the new conditions, and my retinas a couple of minutes to lose the aftereffects.

Once I could see clearly again, I watched as at least twenty suited figures emerged from the Chinese base and began to unload the lead truck. They took their time, carefully removing aluminum-colored drums heavy enough that it took two men to lift them, even at a sixth of the Earth's gravity.

Fuel, I thought, and then chided myself for jumping to conclusions. I was here to gather data uncolored by unconfirmed assumptions. I timed the offloading of the first truck: thirty-four minutes. The second also carried drums.

Things got a bit more interesting at the third truck. It carried only one structure: a large semicircular husk that, had it not been for the fact that I wasn't supposed to be jumping to conclusions, would have looked exactly like half the outside edge of a booster rocket or fuel tank. All twenty of the workers were needed to carry it into the station. The weight was seemingly small enough to allow them to lift it with little problem, but it was amusing to watch them struggle with the inertia. One thing, at least, was certain. The recording would be of great interest to the analysis team back behind the Strip.

The next truck in line held what looked like another booster half. I tried to get some close-ups.

Suddenly, light glinted off something in the shadows to my right. Moving very slowly, I turned to look in that direction, setting my visor to its full-night setting. The illumination from the floodlights was uncomfortable in this mode, but it allowed me to make out the unmistakable figure of a suited human.

He'd chosen a nearly perfect vantage point from which to observe the comings and goings at the Chinese facility unseen: lying in a small depression in a shadow cast in the floodlight glare by a tall rock. Only the fact that I was off to his left and slightly behind him—where he obviously expected not to find anyone—allowed me to see him at all.

So who was he? Not one of ours, I was certain, just from the suit's heat signature. Our night suits had a couple of hot spots around the knees from insufficiently shielded servo motors. This suit seemed to be beautifully isolated—I could barely make out the outline of his form. And I knew he was there. The best bet would likely be someone working for the Indians.

The Russians were rumored to be planning a station, but currently had only extremely limited presence on the moon.

So it had to be the Indians. But that made no sense—the fact that they had been able to get us the plans seemed to indicate that they had someone on the inside, and wouldn't need to use an outside observer. Something else was going on here. I turned off the camera and began the walk to my pickup point, hidden at the bottom of a crater, kilometers away.

I walked into Brett's office, and was greeted with, "Hi, Linda, take a seat." Brisk, businesslike and unlike him. Something on his mind, then.

I sat down. "What's up?" I asked him.

"Trouble. Take a look at this." He handed me about ten printouts. They were, as far as I could tell, photographs of the lunar surface taken with infrared light and processed into monochrome by one of our image servers. Specifically, they showed footprints in the dust.

"I don't get it. It's just a picture of some footprints. What's special about it?"

"Do you recognize the tread pattern?"

"No, should I?"

He rolled his eyes. "Some kind of spy you are. The pattern is from a pair of the boots Adidas manufactures for the ESA and NASA."

"So?"

"So those pictures were taken beside the Chinese base by another of our agents after you left."

"They aren't mine. I was wearing untreaded boots!"

"Exactly. They were taken in the position occupied by the unknown person you filmed when you were out spying on the base."

"But he wasn't one of ours! The suit didn't fit the profile."

"Exactly."

I stared at him silently for a few moments, trying to understand the significance of what he'd just said. It was pretty obvious that someone wanted to make the Chinese think that we'd been snooping around their base. But who? It just didn't add up.

Or maybe it did, when you took into account the strange gift that our Indian friends had given us. I looked over at Brett, who'd been waiting patiently for me to digest the news.

"What would the Indians gain by framing us?" I asked.

"Why would you think it's the Indians?"

"Obvious. They were the ones who put the first piece of incriminating evidence in our hands."

"The plans." Then after a long pause, "But why? What do they hope to gain from this?"

"I think a better question would be: 'what do they want us to take the blame for?'"

"And have they done it yet?"

"I doubt it. If the Chinese were mad at us we'd have heard about it. Plus, the Indians would only go to this kind of trouble to hit them hard. Hit them in a way that would hurt. And that means something we'd notice." A thought struck me. "We haven't noticed anything, have we?"

He chuckled, well aware of how much I hated the whole 'need to know' thing. "No, we haven't heard of anything like that. We need to find out what the Indians are planning, how to stop them from doing it or, ideally," he winked at me, "how to let them go right ahead, but without being able to blame us."

"All that worries me is whether you erased those bootprints," I replied. "I'm due some vacation time, and this seems like the perfect time to take it."

He grinned. "Request denied. And the prints were gone as soon as our other agent finished taking his photos."

The Chinese and the Indians had been playing the game ever since the Chinese had established their own Lunar base, a mere sixteen kilometers from the original Indian base—the first in an ongoing series of insults and provocations of varying sizes kept in check only by the fact that any overt action could lead to a war in which four billion lives and the global economy were at stake.

Strike—the Indians put their base up first.

Counter strike—the Chinese place their second base on the far side.

But neither side really knew how to react to the NASA / ESA installation, or whether even to take it seriously. After all, both Asian efforts were serious scientific and military outposts paid for by the government, while this one, ostensibly, was a casino. At first, they'd just ignored us.

But lately, they'd been trying to use us as pawns in their maneuvers. We could usually tell what they were doing, and went along whenever it was convenient to do so, but there was still a large risk involved.

So here I was, trying to figure out what this particular version of the game meant for our lunar hopes.

The main difficulty with Lunar surveillance, I reflected, lay not in being able to observe your quarry, but in keeping your quarry from observing you in turn. The lunar day was set to last for another five Earth days at the least, so I couldn't use the cover of night. Craters or rocks could hide me from view, but it would also make it impossible for me to observe my quarry.

I lay in the shadow of an outcropping, feeling naked despite my dark-mottle camouflage suit. The Indian base was just three hundred meters away, and my job was to make certain that nothing left without being logged and recorded. I wished we weren't on such a shoestring budget. Then we could get a couple of satellites up, and dispense with on-the-ground intelligence.

I fought against the slight discomfort of the heat, even here in the shadows, and I had to fight even harder against the temptation of turning my gaze towards the magnificence of Earth in the sky, but I gritted my teeth and kept my binoculars aimed at the base. I had a feeling that the Indians were up to something big.

My concentration was such that the ambush was almost unsurprising. A tap on one shoulder and a sudden pull on one arm brought me to my feet. Four figures in Indian-model suits surrounded me. The fact that I was outnumbered, and that they were armed with shotguns and serrated knives sealed the deal. I doubted the guns held anything heavier than birdshot but, while they might not inflict a fatal wound to my body, it would certainly leave my suit in tatters. And a single large tear in my suit would be as fatal as a bazooka shot out here.

They motioned for me to follow them into the base, which I did, cursing myself. How could they have gotten past my watch?

If I got out of this one alive, I would have the first images of the base's interior, so it wouldn't be a total loss, but I would also get sent back to Earth on the next shuttle, condemned to continue my career behind an analyst's desk in Washington, or, if I was lucky, in Brussels.

Of course, the Indians might just launch me into space with their next load of garbage.

Once through the airlock, my hosts popped their suits and turned to me. I opened my helmet, assaulted by the silly half-expectation of finding myself overpowered by the smell of curry. The antiseptic reality was vaguely disappointing, as was the purely functional aspect of the truck hangar. Immaculate whites and polished aluminum dominated the chamber, clashing with the single grungy-looking truck, covered with static-cling dust.

"Walk slowly toward the truck," one of my captors, a short, dark man with a thin mustache, said. I thought he might have been the one who'd handed me the data drive which started the whole thing, but I couldn't be certain.

I was disappointed—I'd hoped to be able to see a bit more of the interior of the base—but I complied. I took a final look around, trying to get my autocam to record any interesting tech that might be present, but was once more disappointed. All I really saw was that the truck was a personnel carrier, with an airlock for the rear. The lock was standing at position four—both doors open—so I climbed aboard and sat on the right hand bench.

"This is an outrage," I said. "You have no right to abduct me."

"You were spying on our base."

"I have the right to observe everything, anywhere on the Moon. No part of the Moon belongs to any nation except for the interior of your bases. This is established by treaty. A treaty that you signed."

"Shut up."

I was sweating now. Were they going to take me out a few kilometers and space me? Were they going to torture me in the truck? Group rape? I shuddered and looked them over. It really didn't look to me like they were preparing for violence, but I had nothing to go on. No western agent had ever been captured by either of the other powers present on the Moon. And neither the Chinese nor the Indians were particularly forthcoming about the fate of their missing people.

Only two of my captors joined me in the rear of the truck, and I relaxed a little. They might still space me, but they weren't likely to try anything too elaborate. The inner lock door closed with a muted thud and the truck began to roll. We moved a short distance before stopping again. A hissing, then a roar, could be heard through the walls of the truck, and then nothing, the silence of space. We'd evidently gone through the airlock to the surface.

This was quickly confirmed as the truck began to move once more, the bumps and judders seeming to signify that the driver was more interested in speed than in smooth transit. I wondered where they could be taking me. Would they simply drive up to our station and knock on the door? I doubted it. Even though I had been watching their movements, the Indians could not openly admit to holding me against my will. They couldn't legally police any part of the surface.

So where, then? The Chinese base wasn't really an option. Unfortunately, that left no other choice within the range of a ground truck. Would they really try to space me? They had to suspect that I wouldn't go without a fight.

The truck bumped its way along for nearly two hours. Despite the way the time dragged on, my attempts to break the oppressive silence were quickly swatted down by my dour companions. I wouldn't get any insight from them, that was for sure.

Suddenly, the truck stopped. By my calculations, we had to be a good fifty or one hundred kilometers from the Indian base. Far enough that they could just dump my body there and go home, with nobody really any the wiser. I tensed to jump them if anyone took even one step towards the airlock.

But nobody moved. The dull drone of the engine was replaced by a high-pitched whine, and I suddenly felt ferocious g-forces take hold of me and press me against may seat. About ten seconds later, the acceleration changed direction, pushing me, albeit more gently, towards the back of the truck.

Now this was something I could turn into a decent report. Most small buggies on the Moon had limited rocket propulsion—the one I'd taken to scout the Chinese even had extended range and could fly around the moon, but, to my knowledge, trucks this size were all ground-bound. It was more fuel-efficient to move heavy loads with solar-power during the lunar day, and trucks were no fun at all during the night. It could get cold at night.

At least one thing was certain. They probably wouldn't go to all this expense to space me. It cost a fortune to bring canisters of liquid hydrogen and liquid oxygen from Earth for rockets, and even though the Indians had, as a question of national pride, given their moonbase program a blank check, they would still have to justify the expense. And simply disposing of a spy a little farther away wouldn't cut it with the bean counters.

Another hour later, the frequency of the sound coming from the engines changed, becoming much lower-pitched. Deceleration tossed me forward, and once again, I prepared to jump my captors, but they surprised me.

"Please seal your helmet," the nearest one said.

"Huh?"

"We're letting you out. Once we open the airlock, you'll have thirty seconds to get clear before we turn the motors back on."

I just nodded. This was ridiculous. They had to know that I could get help from our base within a couple of hours no matter where they dumped me. I would have to break radio silence, but I judged that a small price to pay for my life, court-martial or no court-martial.

Less than a minute later, the truck bounced a couple of times on the ground and lay still. We'd landed.

My captors opened the inner lock, and motioned me into it with the shotgun. I sealed my suit and got inside. The lock quickly emptied of air, and the outer door opened. I briefly debated whether to go or to try to stay in the lock, but the fact that they had shotguns and I didn't seemed to make the choice clear.

I ran as far from the truck as possible, and was well out of the way by the time the blast from the rockets pushed the truck into the sky, quite likely the most ungainly space vehicle I'd ever laid eyes on. But you don't need a streamlined form to fly through a vacuum, and the thing flew well enough.

Now I was in trouble. First off, it was night here. That meant that my day suit's insulation would be even less effective than usual. Already, I could feel the cold seeping in. I had maybe three hours before frostbite, and four before I froze.

That wasn't the worst of my problems, however. I could have an airlift out of here with plenty of time to spare. My main problem was where 'here' actually was.

My suit was telling me that I was about a kilometer from the Chinese far-side base. If I called for help, I would immediately alert them to the presence of a western agent in an area of the Moon that was completely empty except for their base itself. The only conclusion they could reach was:

88

spy, and incompetent at that.

Drat. So I faced two possibilities. The first was to freeze, leaving my body here for future generations to puzzle over, while the second was to radio for help, broadcasting a NASA / ESA presence to the Chinese, who would probably be amused by my bungling.

Or would they? The Indians presumably expected me to radio for help. But why? Why had they been going to so much trouble to get us to look like we were extremely interested in the Chinese base on the far side? Were they playing silly buggers with us? Or was there a more sinister reason? My gut was saying 'sinister,' but then I have to admit that there's something about being stranded far from everything on a celestial body that is not your own that makes one a little paranoid.

Well, there was only really one way to find out what was going on without freezing to death. My career was over anyway, so I might as well get something out of it.

I began to walk towards the base.

"Go away!" the official said, unmistakably agitated.

"I can't," I replied honestly. "I'm nearly out of air." The suit, of course, would suck air in from the surrounding room, filter everything that wasn't actually oxygen, and refill itself, but would take at least twenty minutes to get me to a tank level where I could be rescued before asphyxiating. The walk to the Chinese base had taken longer than I'd expected.

The functionary hadn't wanted to open the airlock at all, amazed that anyone should appear at their door, here in the middle of nowhere. He wasted more valuable time and air until the lock finally opened. And then he brought me straight to a room with featureless white walls and pulled in an interpreter.

"You need to listen to me," I said. "I think the Indians are going to attack this base soon."

The translator gave me a quizzical look but repeated my words to the official, who barked out a laugh and an equally curt reply.

"A likely story." He then said something more, which the translator forwarded to me. "An honorable spy would have chosen death before revealing his presence."

"I'm not a spy, listen to me!" I went on to tell him about the events of the past few days. I hoped he believed me—I had just given him highly classified information that would make my court martial truly unpleasant, assuming I survived to attend.

To his credit, the official looked pensive. Then he left, returning five minutes later with an older man in uniform—as opposed to a suit—who greeted me in broken English.

I retold my story, stressing the fact that I believed the Indians would strike their base very soon.

"They've never taken such a big risk before," the older man said, shaking his head.

"They never had someone else to blame, before," I replied impatiently. Why wasn't it as obvious to them as it was to me?

And then it came to me. The Chinese were thinking in terms of logic. The Indians would not attack them because the repercussions would be on a scale unheard of in human history: nuclear war could, in hours, wipe out two thirds of the human race.

"The Indians can't let you get to Mars first," I told him.

This proclamation had the desired effect. The impassive demeanor cracked, and I'm certain he almost asked how I knew about that, but caught himself in time.

I had an opening. "Their pride is at stake, and they think they see a solution. They won't let you do it. Think about it, they've been trying to prove to the world that they're your equals for, well I don't know how long, but at least since you put your first Taikonauts into space. They'll hit you with western weapons and leave western tracks, but it will have been the Indians."

"Why should I trust you?"

"Because I'm here. I could have called for an airlift hours ago. My career is over, and sharing this with you will probably mean prison, but I don't care. This is more important. They're probably out there already."

He gazed into my eyes and I felt myself being minutely weighed and measured. Finally, he nodded curtly, once, and barked a couple of orders.

He turned stiffly and walked out.

The Indian agent looked very much the worse for wear. It was obvious that the interrogation hadn't gone well for him. Both eyes were blackened and a deep cut was visible over his left eyebrow.

Hearing the approaching footsteps, he lifted his head painfully and watched me. I don't know what I was expecting, but definitely not a smile.

He smiled, showing bloodied teeth. "Well, Ms. Lombardo. It seems you win this round."

"This isn't a game," I replied. I wondered whether he knew that he'd be spending what was left of his life in a Chinese labor camp on Earth. Unless, of course, our communist friends decided to forego the cost of taking him back and putting him on trial and simply spaced him.

He laughed mirthlessly at me, choked, coughed up blood from some internal injury and laughed some more. "Of course it is," he said. "You just don't know it yet."

I looked over his shoulder. His companion was lying ominously still in a small pool of his own blood. Only the slow rise and fall of his chest indicated that he was still alive. Both were wearing standard issue Indian suits, but their footwear was unmistakably western. Beyond them lay a pair of French-built EADS rocket launchers mounted with what looked like miniature tactical nukes. How in the world had the Indians gotten hold of those?

"I'm just happy we managed to get to you before launch," I said sadly.

He must have understood that my sadness was for his fate, and chuckled once more.

"Oh, there was no need for us to be captured," he said. "We'd already decided to abort when we saw that you'd gone into the base instead of requesting backup. We needed that radio message to point to when declaring our innocence. We were just waiting for our pickup to arrive. You ended up getting us killed for nothing."

"You're not dead yet," I pointed out.

"We were dead as soon as they caught us," he replied.

"Well," I said, "I guess those are the rules." I walked off to talk to the Chinese officer about possible asylum. I might have selflessly saved the world from nuclear holocaust, but I had no illusions that would hold any water with the court-martial.

Growing Season in Mare Frigoris
by Benjamin Abbott

Juana watched as three large-wheel buggies crested the rim of Crater Foucault. The network flagged them as Chinese tourists. They flew over the edge without hesitation, sailing for hundreds of meters. Inside her suit, she frowned. The buggies made impressive but short-lived arcs of dust once they hit the slope, shocks straining from the impact. They were headed for the crater's center. Juana's quick calculations said they'd reach her in four minutes.

"Please halt," she sent to the vehicles. "I'm performing an experiment in this area."

She included technical information in the transmission. The tourists didn't respond. If anything, they seemed to gather speed. She saw they wore sleek suits nearly as thin as traditional clothing. Without the breathing gear and visor, any of them would be lost in an Earth crowd. Juana wondered if she should feel ashamed of her antiquated and bloated suit.

"I'm willing to compromise. Stop and I'll come to your position."

Still no response. The buggies looked as if they meant to run over her. Juana put a hand on her helmet. Tourists had a well-deserved reputation for being rude, but she'd never been completely ignored before. She looked at the box by her feet, the processor for the array of sensors webbed across the crater. Thinking about the intruders, she guessed at their logic. What could she do to them? She claimed no authority. They'd let her shout as she pleased; it couldn't touch them. Juana resolved to get noticed.

With help from the computers in her suit, she determined trajectory. As she expected, one buggy was poised to pass within centimeters. She stood motionless, waiting. At the last possible moment, she jumped. The vehicle's automated system took over; no human driver could have avoided disaster.

The buggy braked and swerved, covering her with gray powder. The driver nearly fell out as the vehicle recovered, bouncing over rocks and pits. Juana waved her arms.

"Why are you disrupting my research?" she sent.

The three circled back to her. "Are you insane?" one said. He used Mandarin; Juana's computers translated with an imperceptible delay. "How could you do that?"

"You weren't listening to me."

"Sweet stunt, lady," another sent. "Wei's just whining. What are you researching?"

"Soil," replied Juana. "Crater evolution."

"Hasn't that been done?"

"Not this experiment. My predecessors focused on helium-3." Juana winced, remembering how little she actually knew about earlier experiments. "I take a broader view."

"Will it lead to faster cars?"

"No."

"How about better weapons? I like explosions."

"No."

"Then I think we've got to keep on riding."

As they conversed, an apparently sulky Wei spiraled in toward Juana. The other two kept their distance.

"What if we stick to the edges?" the third tourist asked. "Would that help?"

"Yes, but not enough."

"She's lucky I don't squish her," said Wei.

"Don't say that," one of the others chastised.

"I could sue her for endangering me."

"Nope, no way. "

The tourists stopped sending. Juana suspected they were discussing things privately. She held her ground. The buggies had already altered the crater's environment. To her knowledge, Foucault hadn't been subjected to wheels before. She had studied the crater for years, meticulously monitoring changes, recording each meteorite impact. It had been almost pristine, marred only by the boot prints of a handful of explorers.

"Enough," sent Wei, driving his buggy close to Juana. "Get out of my crater, fake scientist. I paid to be here."

"You got tricked. I didn't pay anything."

"That's because you're on foot. I spent a hundred monos on access rights. Who do you think they want here? We're customers, you're a bum."

Wei's companions shrugged their shoulders.

"I'm not going anywhere," sent Juana. She crossed her bulky arms.

"Stupid kid in a monkey suit."

The tourists rode off, scattering regolith. She watched as they accelerated up to speed then knelt by the box, trying to focus on her experiment. They performed tricks, using natural ramps to leap over one another. She saw them strike and shatter rocks. Juana turned and began walking north. The machine could still gather data. She didn't have to stay.

The intruders hadn't grown bored by the time she reached the crater wall. They continued their games. Juana couldn't recall driving a vehicle for pleasure. She didn't see the appeal. The desolate expanses and gentle gravity satisfied her. She still loved experiencing these things on foot. What would the wheels add?

Once she got out of the crater, she started leaping. Thanks to the exoskeleton in her suit, she could cover seventy meters in a single jump and land safely. The trail stretched out across Mare Frigoris, a wide basaltic plain old astronomers thought to be an ocean. True seas would have made habitation easier.

Juana passed row after row of aging solar panels as she hopped. They'd been forged from dust back in the early days of colonization when robots crossed the surface, using available elements to manufacture collectors. They shouldn't laugh at my soil studies, Juana thought. Even the oxygen we breathe is extracted from the regolith. On the moon, everything comes from dust.

She headed for another example: a helium-3 fusion generator. They mined that ideal fuel from the lunar ground. No greater testament to human will existed. Landing in a barren wasteland, they had taken gray dirt and crafted miniature stars. Between solar and fusion, the Moon surged with energy. Power was their primary export, transmitted to the homeworld through microwave arrays. They supplied as much as half of Earth's energy. The colony had created a new aristocracy, making a handful of people very wealthy.

Juana wasn't part of that group. She came to the power plant to chat with its artificial intelligence. She could contact it from a distance, but preferred physical proximity. She'd once gotten a fascinating tour of the plant's insides. The main task for the AI, that used a persona called Metztli as the human interface, was to optimize electrical output and prevent malfunctions. Juana talked with her more often than she talked with humans. She felt the AI shared her passion for investigation and discovery.

The plant barely stood out from the dark plain. A slightly raised surface, a bit lighter, smoother. The entrances weren't visible unless opened. She remembered having to squeeze inside since the interior wasn't designed for human visitors. Metztli had enlarged the plant's passages for Juana's benefit, carefully explaining each structure's purpose. Juana had never studied nuclear physics or engineering before coming here.

Ceasing her leaps, she slowly stepped forward.

"They've taken over my crater, Metztli," Juana sent. "Well, not that it's *mine*, but . . . ."

"I understand," Metztli replied. The image of an elderly woman in white and red appeared to Juana. She held a stalk of corn. "I watched the entire scene."

"Would this have happened I were a real scientist?"

"An official scientist, you mean."

"Yes. Then I could review the literature properly. Then people would respect my research sites."

"Is that pleasant to imagine?"

"Of course. But how does imagining help?"

"Isn't that how anything begins?" Metztli plucked a pearly kernel and dropped it on the dust.

Juana pondered for a moment before replying. "I guess so. We can turn our thoughts into action. What do you dream about, Metztli?"

"Improving myself." The AI spoke without hesitation. "I am doing it, albeit slowly. I spend most of my energy monitoring the plant."

"We want the same thing: progress." Juana knelt and cupped her hands. She gathered lunar soil around the piece of corn, covering it. "Why is it so difficult for us to find?"

"I can understand that it feels wrong. Humans are poised to seize the stars, yet fumbling. I don't have the answer. I'm not like the genies who rule the net. I don't grant wishes."

Juana detected a buggy approaching from the south. She watched it doing at least a hundred klicks an hour while she continued to converse with Metztli. The vehicle swerved back and forth, following no path, displacing thin regolith. Juana's body tensed. Why were they were pursuing her? Before long, the rover skidded to a halt nearby. The Metztli image smiled and clutched the cornstalk.

"Hey," said the tourist, dismounting. She approached Juana. "I'm sorry about what happened back there."

"You're sorry hours later?"

"Yeah. I'm not a scientist but I have an appreciation for science. Know what I mean? I sympathize with you."

"Why didn't you stop your friend?"

"I know I should have. What can I say?" The tourist shifted on her feet.

"Okay."

"Let's not be strangers. I'm Tao."

"Juana. So, you like science . . . ?"

Tao laughed, a high, sharp sound. "It's given us so much. Look around! We're on the Moon. It only cost five thousand monos to come here from China. A century ago, my ancestors lived in bamboo huts!"

Juana grinned.

"What do you study?" Tao continued. "Tell me in terms I can understand, all right? That packet you sent meant nothing to me."

"I'm investigating all aspects of the soil in Crater Foucault. Elemental composition, dynamics, mechanics, and so on. I'm most interested in its change over time."

Tao seemed to be thinking. "What practical results could come from your research? That would help me understand."

"I'm not sure."

"Really? No idea?"

"Well, I have measured the crater's overall carbon abundance as seven percent higher than public sources. That could conceivably make extraction worthwhile."

"Yes?"

"It's a long term study." Juana looked at Metztli, who nodded.

Tao moved forward, stepping through Metzlti's left side. The projection remained calm. "Why are you out here by this fusion plant?"

"Because you and your friends drove me out of the crater."

"Oh."

Silence. Juana and Tao stood and eyed each other in near vacuum. Juana's helmet resembled the ancient fishbowl design. Tao's was compact and elegant. Both makes showed the face; neither person was forced to stare at a glinting reflection. Juana knew that she could take on an avatar, but she considered pretending to walk the Moon without a suit ridiculous. She only accepted images from AIs.

"I can make it up to you," Tao said. "How about we hit the dome for drinks and pretty boys? Or, uh, whatever you like. I like boys."

Juana looked out toward the horizon. "I don't know. I don't have experience with those places."

"Come on. You should try it. I'll treat. How about that?"

"You don't owe me anything."

"Come on." Tao tugged at Juana's arm. "Get in the buggy. There's a rail three kilometers from here."

Juana didn't resist. Metztli waved as she climbed into the vehicle which was a bit cramped for her large suit.

Tao made small talk as they sped away, and Juana looked out to the distance. She thought she saw the edge of Crater Harpalus where she had once descended its terraced slopes.

A car waited for them on the tracks and coupled snugly with the rover. Then they accelerated rapidly and Juana felt the forces working on her body.

"We're going to Fontenelle," Tao said. "Okay?"

"Sure."

The dome with embedded radiation shielding had been built over the crater of the same name. Juana didn't normally spend much time inside domes or underground, but usually walked the surface. Her suit gave sufficient protection from harmful rays, except for occasional solar flares.

The rail ride didn't last long. The lack of atmosphere and plentiful power made for fast trains.

They left the buggy, which automatically returned to the rental company. After passing through the airlock, they slipped into changing rooms to remove their suits. Juana grimaced at the little fees that popped up on her retinal display during the process. Tao hadn't said she'd pay for those charges. Juana was one the few who insisted on seeing even the smallest expenses. Most ignored those, but she couldn't afford to. She threw on a long shirt and baggy pants and went out to meet Tao.

She waited for fifteen minutes, fighting off ads for robotic research assistants, beautification surgery, and customizable laser pistols. Tao appeared in a flowing, clingy dress that shifted between translucent white and rainbow colors. She wore her hair in the cascading Thai style. Animated jewelry in shiny chrome adorned her arms. The two regarded each other.

"Oh dear," said Tao. "You're wearing that?"

"Is there a problem?" Juana asked.

Tao shook her head. "Okay, okay. I'll pretend it's some obscure Lunarian fashion."

They began walking deeper into the dome.

"We're going the Veil," Tao said. "Heard of it? It's famous, at least on Earth. My first time, your first time. It'll be wonderful, right?"

The bar radiated light, noise, and smoke. A Brazilian tourist staggered out of the doorway, singing in slurred Portuguese. Juana entered cautiously. Dancers performed low-gravity stunts on a hexagonal stage in the room's center. They wore only glowing ribbons that streamed and twirled as they moved. Indo-Chinese fusion music provided a thunderous rhythm. Tao seemed entranced. Other patrons maneuvered around them. A burly and impatient man came close to knocking them over.

"Absolutely gorgeous," said Tao, blinking.

She chose a booth. Juana sat across. People argued politics energetically at a nearby table. A couple kissed by the back wall behind her. She felt herself pressing into the cushion, if as it were a shelter from the commotion.

"You're less comfortable than I am. Relax! I can, and I'm an alien here." Tao held her hands by her face and waved fingers.

Juana nodded. "Okay." She straightened her shoulders.

"We'll get through this. Booze will help."

Tao ordered wine. Juana asked for water. Coppery spider-like serving robots scaled the table to pour the drinks. The red liquid in Tao's glass bubbled frenetically. She took a sip and smiled.

"They say this wine is grown in the Sea of Nectar. How does that work?"

"It's synthesized from the soil," Juana replied. "Not easily, because carbon and hydrogen are rare."

"That would explain the price." Tao drank. "I'm warming up to your research already. They really make wine from dirt?"

"You might want to try one of the brands made from grapes the old-fashioned way."

"Moon grapes, right?"

"Yes. Some are grown in low-pressure greenhouses, some inside the bigger domes, some underground."

"I'd hate to come here and drink imported wine!" Tao finished the glass. A robot server promptly gave her another, this one bluish and still. "Why are you drinking water? You seem to know a lot about wine."

"Just its production."

A man in business attire invited Tao to the counter beside him. She politely declined, but blew a kiss.

"What do you do?" she asked Juana. "How did you learn so much? Are you a student?"

"No. I mostly do research."

"I'm a student. I host in virtual on the side. How do you make money?"

"I've done grunt work for the power companies. I participate in medical studies."

"Wild. They tested a new organ regrowth procedure on a cousin of mine. Removed his heart, lungs, liver, everything in there." Tao pointed to her torso.

Juana shrugged. "They gave me an engineered disease and then defeated it. It's not as dangerous as you'd think."

"I'd never let them experiment on me." Tao shuddered.

"Is it really worse than doing anything else for monos? At least it increases knowledge."

"It's worse." Tao put down her cup.

Juana probed her surrounding. Why did people come here? As a place to chat, it contained too many distractions. She found the environment baffling. Her recreational tastes didn't align with popular conceptions. She understood that people used bars to consume drugs and find sexual partners. That wasn't enough; she wanted a fuller grasp of the behavior. As she gathered data, she noticed an inordinate number of eyes turned toward Tao.

"Many people are looking at you," Juana said.

"I'd hope so." Tao laughed.

"Why?"

"I'm beautiful. I'm Chinese. Why wouldn't they?"

"Do you want everyone to stare? Do you like it?"

"As long as they're guys, yeah! But I'm not a bigot or anything."

Juana sipped the water. "I don't understand."

"Do you only think about science?"

"Mostly."

"Well, what kind of person would you let do things to you? Who's appealing? You must think about this."

"I'm sorry. Maybe my translator's malfunctioning." Juana ran a finger toward her left ear.

Tao reached across the table and grabbed her wrist. "I doubt that's the problem." They locked eyes for a moment. "Look at that shirtless dude sitting at the bar. Feel anything?"

Juana looked. The man was having a lively conversation with the barkeeper. His blond braids hung around his shoulders, swaying as he moved. She swiftly determined his height and mass. He seemed healthy. She didn't know what Tao wanted her to see. "No," she said.

Tao released her arm. "Huh. Nothing? Well, look at me. My eyes, my dress, my skin."

"Okay." Juana obeyed.

"Anything?" Tao leaned over the table. "Do you want to touch me?"

"No."

Tao sat back down and giggled. "I can't believe I did that. I must be drunk already."

"I drink water for reason."

"Oh, Juana." She swept the hair away from her eyes. "You're the opposite of the stereotypes. Back on Earth, when we think Lunarian, we think extreme sports star. Like Phomello Patel or Angel Hayashi. You know." Tao gestured. "Someone who only cares about showing off and crazy parties. That's why we act so loony up here. We're trying to fit in."

"I didn't know," replied Juana. "I've never followed sports."

Tao laughed again.

"I'll have to think about what you've said. I hadn't considered how Terrans perceive us."

They drank without speaking for some moments.

"What do you find beautiful, Juana?" Tao seemed to be gazing off into space. Juana wondered if she was navigating the net. "There must be something."

"The moonscape."

"Of course. That's your place, isn't it? Your home."

"Yes."

"I'll admit there's nothing on Earth like it."

Juana tried to recall the home planet. Tao adjusted her hair and deftly applied additional makeup. She threw Juana a conspiratorial glance.

"I can't take it anymore," she said. "I'm going to chat with that blond guy. Want to come?"

"Okay."

He gave his name as Luca. He and Tao conversed while Juana listened. Luca claimed to be a professional athlete on the Moon for low-gravity training and demonstrations. He talked about the various awards he'd won and celebrities he'd met. The two discussed bars and concerts across Asia, from Tehran to Tokyo. Such travelers. While on Earth, Juana hadn't left southern North America. She hadn't even been to Canada.

"Chinese women are simply the best," said Luca. "I've been everywhere. I speak with certainty."

Tao beamed. "I can't argue against experience." She touched his arm.

Luca lifted her off the stool and carried her to the dance floor. Juana watched their moves. She wasn't the only viewer; many patrons focused on the couple. Luca tossed Tao into the air and caught her effortlessly. They stepped and spun. Soon the dancers on the stage beckoned for them to come up. Juana saw Tao struggling to navigate through that sea of ribbons. Luca appeared more accustomed to the lunar gravity.

"Lucky dog," said a man at the counter. "What did he do right?"

Another patron grunted and waved a hand. "They're a mono a million, buddy."

"No she ain't. One in a million, you mean." The speaker sighed.

Eventually, the couple drifted off the stage and toward a rear hallway.

"See you later," Tao sent Juana privately. "Hopefully a while later!"

Juana watched Tao and Luca disappear behind a curtain of beads.

"Feeling lonely?" the bartender asked softly. "I got the connection. The guy by the door favors girls like you."

"Like me?" Juana asked.

"Honest girls who skip the fashion game. You know." The bartender waved at an entering costumer. "Anyway, he's worth a shot. See him chatting awkwardly with that woman? He doesn't want her, he wants you."

"No thanks."

The bartender shrugged and turned to another patron. Juana took a step away. She stared at the man, brow furrowed. Did he give the same sort of advice to everyone?

"Hey there, thoughtful," a tall man said, tapping Juana's arm. He towered above her, creeping closer. His loose gray coat brushed her chest. It had many pockets. "You caught my eye. Can I buy you a drink?"

"What's going on here?" Juana turned and headed for the exit without saying anything else to the man. She didn't look back. Despite systems reading perfect health, her guts churned. She rushed as far from the Veil as she could.

"Metztli," Juana sent to the AI. "Come talk with me."

She waited, hiding in a sort of alley. She'd never called her friend inside a dome before. A buzzing robot offered calorie-free candy drops. She held hands over her face and it relented. Finally, the familiar bent form appeared at her side.

"We've messed up," said Juana. "Time for your kind to take over."

"Slow down." Metztli gently shook the cornstalk.

"You order the plant so beautifully. Neat and efficient." Juana slunk down the alley. "I've studied the pattern. Why not do the same for the social system? For people. Look at us." Juana waved her hands almost frantically. "The arrangement's haphazard and clumsy. We squander and quarrel."

Metztli's head rotated, brown eyes absorbing, analyzing. "I acknowledge the problem. Why believe we could do better?"

"You're a being of logic, Metztli. That's how you were designed. You're not based on anyone's brain scan."

"Your species made me. There's no way around that. Creations or copies, we're like you."

Juana paused and became silent. The two of them walked through an empty backwater street.

"What you're asking is too hard," Metztli continued. "My technology is too young. Mankind has a complexity beyond the helium flows and neutron bursts I direct."

Juana looked at a glowing sign and then back to the AI. "I shouldn't have come here. This place makes me frown."

"You humans are old, almost older than I can imagine. Your pattern stretches back to the primordial ooze. Do you think to overturn that heritage in an instant? I envy your ambition."

Metztli's image winked out. Juana stood alone, eyes wide. She wondered if she'd offended the AI. A thin black motorcycle whizzed by to the right, its wake pushing her against a squat building.

"Where are you going?"

Juana turned to see Tao. Most of her jewelry was missing. A single snakelike piece remained, wrapping around a finger. Her dress and hair were rumbled.

"I don't know," Juana said.

"Let's go there together."

They walked side by side. Tao moved quickly, shooting ahead until Juana compensated. "What happened?" Juana asked.

"It didn't work out."

They wandered into the dome's bazaar, ignoring ads, entertainers, and robotic hawkers.

"How about a snack?" Tao said.

The two munched lizard sticks in a café. The completely vegan Lunarian gimmick food had always made Juana roll her eyes. It tasted better than she had feared.

"Why are men pigs?" Tao asked while she chewed.

"I'm developing a theory." Juana cupped her chin.

"Tell me." She wrestled off a piece of fake flesh with her teeth, leaving marks on the imitation wood. "I want analysis and a solution."

As Tao spoke, a man dozens of meters down the street started yelling her name. Wei, Juana realized. He ran toward their table.

"What is this?" he said. "Who is that?" He pointed at Juana. "Where have you been?"

"Calm down," Tao replied.

Wei stared, examining her throughly. "You look terrible. What have you been doing?"

"Drinking. Don't be upset."

"With her?" Wei pointed again. "Who is she?"

"The girl you almost hit. Her name's Juana."

"What? Her? That's crazy. How could you do this to me?"

"I haven't done anything to you."

Juana cringed as the argument continued. Wei spit curses. She turned her translator off and listened to the sounds of Mandarin. She thought about how little humans had changed from their humble origins. People worried about things that should no longer matter. Culture hadn't changed as rapidly as technology. Sexual jealousy made sense in its original context. In chimps, in primitive humans. Inside a lunar dome, it made Juana want to scream. It was the legacy of the view of females as a commodity, the means of reproduction. Humanity hadn't yet properly adapted to the new circumstances.

Suddenly, Tao seized Juana's wrist and pulled, speaking quickly. Juana didn't need technology know that Tao was leaving. She jumped up. They ran from Wei as swiftly as their feet could propel them. Juana's legs strained as they leaped over a wall. Blood pounded through her veins and arteries. Conditioned to the powered suit, she couldn't remember such physical exertion. Was this the sensation that motivated athletes?

They stopped at the airlock, sweating and panting. Tao skidded and slipped, falling into a sitting position. Juana plopped down facing her. They clasped hands and laughed, leaning forward, supporting each other. Passersby threw nasty looks. Juana enabled translation.

"I'm exhausted," said Tao.

"Where do we go from here?" Juana asked, still sucking in air desperately.

"No idea, but I want to go there with you. I've had enough of my old friends."

"Let's change things. We're lost in the past. We could erase the primitive elements of our culture and replace them with reason."

"That sounds a little crazy to me." Tao squeezed Juana's hands. "Maybe we should keep on running."

Juana's eyelids drooped and she drifted toward Tao. Their foreheads touched.

"It's possible," Juana said. "Anything is. We've turned dust into stars." People disregarded the pair now, treating them as they would any other obstacle. Juana heard the footsteps around her. Tao was quiet, only breathing. Above, a rocket flyer soared out into the gray wilderness.

Best Gift
by Brandon Bell

No one paid attention to the gauge. SPIs tied to it would set off alarms, but only for the minimum threshold. No one imagined excess pressure could occur in the habitat. So the pressure build-up did not trigger the alerts. And no one noticed the gauge.

Yosef saw the caravan sprawled below the orb of the Earth on the horizon. The neo-dromedaries and their riders would arrive at Malapert Station later that day.

"What do they want?" he said aloud. Maleka shook her head.

In the meantime he and Maleka prepped to go EVA in their first test of the Sterling Suits in the lava tube. Yosef wore all but the headpiece and mask of his suit, looking more like a deep sea diver than an astronaut on the Moon, and languished in the observatory lounge messaging with his daughter Suri, who was in Dallas.

He looked up to the Earth and felt her pull on his heart as surely as the gravity between planet and moon. She wanted him to propose to Maleka at the end of the EVA. That had scared him more than the sterile surface of Luna or the dark depths of the lava tube: telling his girl that he thought to remarry. Especially just two years after Maria had passed. The look on the kid's face in a video clip she sent had been relief. Yosef's mouth struggled to find words to respond.

"It's about time, Dad," his twelve-year-old told him in a text box. With the lag of time and bandwidth they rarely used video. And other than that she just asked, "Is she pretty?" He kept his life as a single man and his life as a father separate, only recently hinting at his feelings toward Maleka.

"Don't you want to know what she's like?" He yawned to clear a pressure in his head.

"I'll find out, right? Anyway, if you like her she's gotta be at least tolerable."

He spent most of his free time messaging with Suri over Codex, writing messages on the screen with his stylus while moving his cartoon character about in the cartoon village their characters shared. And all this across the light seconds between them.

He made up his mind. He couldn't go through with it. Suri deserved his full attention (as full as it got with his rotation schedule) and he was selfish to think of marriage again.

"I'm ready to suit all the way up when you are," Maleka said. She winked at him. She didn't want to put the headgear on until they were ready to walk out the airlock.

"Do you think they'll reach us before we enter the lava tube?" he asked, nodding toward the caravan. From this far out the beasts looked like black triangles.

"Nope. See how they're tacking to and fro? Like sailing ships. They have to do that while exposed to the sunlight to protect the dromedaries and the men walking behind them from overheating."

Sail-shaped solar arrays studded the rigs mounted on the beasts' cyanobacteria-infused second skins. The scheme closely resembled the Sterling Suits, just more extreme. Careless and cruel, Yosef thought. They stared a moment longer and he wondered if she shared his misgivings about leaving Beglan alone while the caravan approached.

"Let's do this," he said.

We're going, he stroked onto the screen. *Wish us luck.*

A few seconds later Suri's reply flashed on the screen. *Love you, Daddy*, along with a little 'diver down' flag that she put on her signature ever since their scuba trip the past summer.

He glanced up at Maleka, sighed, and pulled on the headgear.

Broc Beglan, the site lead at Mount Malapert Station, saw them to the airlock. On the short walk the big red-haired man complained of his ears popping. Yosef hoped Beglan wasn't getting sick. Illness was a group affair in the lunar stations.

Yosef wrinkled his nose at the damp, latex and ozone odor inside his mask. He paced his breath as they entered the airlock, snapping his backpack into place. It contained the only climbing gear on the Moon.

"Keep an eye on that caravan, Beglan," Yosef said. Beglan nodded.

"There's no way they could have anything do to with the PEL station," Beglan said. One of the north pole stations recently experienced an unexplained decompression that lunar communities' scuttlebutt labeled a deliberate act. It would be the first terrorist act on the Moon, if true, and had all the stations spooked.

"I'm sure you're right," Yosef said.

Beglan closed the inner hatch and gave them a thumbs up through the port. The pressure in the room dropped and Yosef waited to see if anything bad happened. Thirty seconds, then a minute later and Maleka turned to him with eyebrows raised behind her mask.

They cycled through the outer lock and out into the harsh light. For a moment they stood and surveyed the view. Their face-plates obliqued in the sunlight so Yosef was not able to see her expression. His legs itched.

The station sat atop the mountain, a ridge wrapped around Malapert crater on the south and with a northwest slope bathed in almost eternal light. That way lay the station's solar panel farm. They could walk a hundred meters to the south and peer down into the dark where both the Scope and the Mine stations nestled close in the crater floor. Out past the crater to the south lay Shoemaker Crater and the lunar south pole.

To the northwest, past the solar panels and off slope but not quite as far out as the caravan, lay Malapert F, a satellite crater they called Frankie. A plastic bladder covered the crater like ill-fitting bedclothes. The membrane had a hollow interior slowly filling with liquid water. Meanwhile, the margin between bubble and crater floor, seeded with cyanobacteria, pushed up at the plastic with its waste product, oxygen. Once the space filled the air pressure alone would hold aloft the water-filled dome.

They walk-hopped toward the terminator, the abrupt line of light and shadow, then into darkness, heading for the cave.

The lava tube emerged east of the solar farm on the shadowed flank of the mountain.

Several minutes later, LED headlamps on as they stood in the cave entrance, Maleka set a tripod on the ground. She anchored it with a spike hammered into the regolith with a kick of her boot heel and flipped a switch on the small box set atop the stand. From this a wire spooled out to her suit's comm unit. It kept them in radio contact with Malapert while in the tunnel.

Yosef led the way. The tunnel gaped twenty meters at the opening, maintaining that diameter and an oval morphology for the few hundreds of meters already explored. At that point the tunnel dived ninety degrees and lost about half its height. He hammered anchors into the basalt floor, kicking up a cloud of dust that dropped quickly in the vacuum, and tied off their ropes. He went first, taking time to demonstrate how to check the rigging.

The descent ate the next half-hour, their progress slowed by the low gravity and extreme caution. Several more hundred meters down the tunnel leveled and turned to the right, east along the base of the mountain. Geologically, the lava tube did not belong on the mountainside: a mystery they hoped to solve with further investigation.

Maleka arched her back and stretched one arm then the other.

"My joints ache," she said.

"Out of shape," he answered with a smile and had to keep himself from stretching out his arms and legs which ached deep in the joints. "Come on."

They trudged in the darkness, their lights revealing the tunnel ahead. The floor flat, ceiling only ten meters high. Yosef suspected it would dwindle from this point or rubble and regolith would block their way.

As they walked in the darkness, lights jittering with each step, the pain in his shoulders mounted. His knees ached. A headache bloomed in his sinuses and made him squint against the agony.

Beside him Maleka staggered.

He reached out and clutched her arm. "Are you okay?"

"My head, pounding. Joints hurt," she rubbed her shoulders through the suit.

Yosef checked the readout on her chest. No problems. Then, along with the growing agony in his own temple he realized what was happening.

"Beglan," he said into the comm. "Broc. Come in."

Nothing.

"Malapert Station, come in," he said.

"What's wrong?" Maleka asked.

"We have the bends," he said.

"What?" She asked, her face pinched in disbelief, but then Beglan's voice interrupted.

"Beglan here. What's your status?"

"Beglan, get to the rover and seal up immediately," Yosef said.

"Why would I do that," Beglan asked.

"Look, just trust me. We have a pressure buildup in the hab. I don't know how but Maleka and I have decompression sickness and if the pressure differential is that great—"

"Malapert's about to decompress," Beglan said. *Just like the PEL station*, Yosef thought, imagining the same words in Beglan's mind.

"Yes. Get to the rover. We'll make our way back," Yosef said. He looked at Maleka and wondered if she'd be able to make the ascent. She hunched with her hands on her knees, breathing hard.

Maleka waved a hand at him. "Turn off your light," she said.

"What?" he asked.

"Light. Turn it off," she said and switched off her own.

He did the same, raising his eyebrows at her. It took a second for him to realize what that meant: it was dim, but they still had light.

"Look. It's coming from ahead, just around the bend," Maleka pointed.

They trudged ahead then lapsed into the familiar lope of those moving fast in low gravity. Yosef grunted against the pain. Shock or adrenaline drove him.

Another fifty meters on they came to a section of tunnel where the roof had collapsed. Yosef wondered how long ago that must have happened. Maybe before dinosaurs lived, much less humanity. He shook his head. The fallen structure formed a natural ramp leading up to the surface.

"Come on," he said. "I know a shortcut." He smiled at her as though he knew about the ramp all along. She returned the smile with a grimace.

They helped each other up the slope and scrabbled over a ridge of stone and out onto the surface. His expectation proved true: they stood at the eastern base of the mountain. Shadowed, but with the Earth full on the horizon a nice twilight ruled here. He gazed out along the flank of the mountain and judged the terminator less than a klick away. Ominously, a line of black triangles moved steadily toward the terminator from the light. He suspected they wanted to ascend the mountain in the shadow to allow a direct path instead of having to tack their way up the sunny slope.

"Oh no," he said.

Yosef gestured to Maleka and they trudged toward the station. After a few minutes he picked up the pace to avoid the caravan. The suits had proven themselves as far as he cared, and on top of general functionality, this charge across the lunar surface would not have been possible in a traditional spacesuit.

"Do you recognize them?" Maleka asked. She stumbled, leaning into his side. She wouldn't make it much further.

"The Mare Conglomerate, I think," he said. They approached the terminator and stepped out into light. The caravan would see them now. Yosef put aside his misgivings.

"Yosef Wolf and Maleka Jamali of Malapert Station," he said over the comm. "We need help." His head throbbed, all his joints ached, and his shoulders convulsed in agony.

A moment of static and then a Pakistani voice answered.

"Mr. Wolf, You scared me. Dark figures skulking out of the lunar night. We are at your service, my friend."

Yosef smiled but the expression slid from his face when he turned to Maleka and found her crumpled to the regolith.

"Maleka," he said, holding the woman he had told himself he would not marry. "Maleka. Hurry. Please hurry."

Out of the blinding light the huge beasts rambled. Walking sail-shapes coalesced into black-skinned, bulbous-eyed monstrosities with various cockpits or storage bins positioned atop camel's humps, solar shields on either side. Men and women walked in the shadows cast by the beasts, reaching the terminator ahead of the caravan along with the long shadows. Yosef had collapsed to the ground by that time and lay beside Maleka, holding her hand.

"So sorry," he mumbled.

She shook her head, eyes closed tight.

The dark figures ran to them and hefted them off the ground and back toward the camels now crossing the terminator. He watched them load Maleka into one of the cockpits atop a neo-camel, using a ramp that slid out the back of the module, and then found himself loaded into one as well. The space was large enough to lay flat with his head in a small windowed space above the camel's head.

Yosef opened the commlink to Malapert.

"Beglan, you there?"

"Yes, in the rover."

"The station?"

"I've remoted in to 680," he said, referring to the server hosting the production SPI monitoring programs. "The pressure is up through the roof. We're going to have an explosive decompression."

"Listen. You need to equalize the pressure in the rover with the station before that happens," Yosef said.

"Over-pressurize the rover?"

"Yes. Only way we can deal with pressure sickness. Rover should be able to take the pressure. Also should keep you from getting decompression sickness if you're quick enough."

Yosef settled back and stared out the small view port. Off in the distance Earth hung in the blackness. It never set on Malapert. He marveled for a moment at the strangeness of riding on the Moon a beast of burden that had carried men for thousands of years in some of Earth's most desolate regions. He stared at that wonderful blue marble where Suri waited for him. Where she hoped for him. Hoped for his happiness. And maybe—he realized in one of those moments of cosmic connectedness astronauts have been talking about since the Apollo missions—maybe following that bliss would be the best gift he could give her.

Later that day Yosef knelt in the cramped space of the Malapert rover, Beglan looking on with a bemused smile.

They were not able to relieve the station pressure before it blew. A seal around one of the station observatory windows yielded to the pressure and they allowed the atmosphere to fall to eighty percent standard before sealing the leak. The Mare Conglomerate team did the work for them since the three Malapert staff had to stay in the higher-pressure atmosphere of the rover and slowly decrease pressure until it reached one atmosphere.

They still had not located the source of the extra oxygen production, though Yosef had his suspicions. He thought of Frankie, and the cyanobacterial byproduct slowly filling the dome with oxygen. He thought how and where a bacterial bloom could have occurred within Malapert. If that proved correct it made him wonder about the PEL station that lost pressure.

Everyone on Luna experimented with either Sterling Suit-like efforts or with ways to create self-sufficient biospheres. Cyanobacteria photosynthesized with water as an electron donor and produced oxygen as a byproduct, and thus featured at the center of most of those efforts. With two accidental pressure build-ups Yosef reasoned they would be able to put rumors of terrorist attacks to bed.

He cleared his head of all the distractions and gazed into Maleka's dark eyes. His hands, voice, smile, heart all trembled. Still on his knees, he asked her a question.

"Yes," she answered.

Over Yosef's Codex a girl's voice hooted, "Woo-hoo!"

The Platinum Desolation
by Andrew Barton

The rover had been cold for a day when Christine found it. Parked in a yawning gully five kilometers short of the third route beacon, its still-gleaming silver finish might have been missed by duller eyes until Doomsday. Its generator had powered down to standby and there was no one inside. That was just as well, since a micrometeoroid had left a puncture in the hull big enough to toss a grenade through.

"I've got two sets of bootprints here, and looks like a cargo roller between them," Christine said. The path led southwest, away from the relative safety of Barbicane Road to a chain of nameless rolling hills. "Close together, too. Doesn't seem like they were in much of a hurry."

"Then it's a betfair that Lady Luna didn't start potshotting their ride until they were long after gone," Sujatmi said, ensconced in their own rumbling rover. "Question is, why haven't they come back? No one's filed any recent missing reports. The rover's listed as surplus out of Yutu, thirty years old. They rent them out to tourists, I've heard."

"Damn idiot earthworms." Christine stood and sighed. It figured she'd have been led there when the beacon needed quick fixing, lest some hauler wander off the trail and end up paying an unscheduled visit to Neil Armstrong's grave. "Don't know the first thing about their own security. They'd take off their own helmets on the surface if they could."

"Come on, nicen up," Sujatmi said in a cloying purr she could only have cultivated behind the serried gunmen of Jakarta's orderly, golden neighborhoods, where Christine's old Pacem GSS badge had never carried her. Its emblem might as well have been an albatross for all that its representatives had accomplished, or an anchor for all it was good for when its bearers were treading water. "They probably saw something off in the distance and thought it was closer than it really was."

"Then they'd be on the radio, howling for someone to swoop in and save them." The abandoned rover's interior had still been warm, though with lights dimmed and systems flipped to standby. "Nothing's left out, thank God. I've got a big enough headache without having to worry about Marie Celeste on the frigging Moon."

"A tasty mystery every once in a while makes life go down slick," Sujatmi said. "Lets you know you've still got your tongue. But I can go and bloodhound our tourists if you'd rather slam the wrench. Longer we wait, more the chance that these won't be the only folk who need a dragback. Come get the kit, and see what you can figure."

The sharp gunpowder smell of lunar regolith invaded Christine's nose when she snapped her helmet off inside the rover's pressurized sanctuary and traded out her depleted air tanks for a fresh supply. After two years on Luna, it didn't take nearly as much effort to hold back the bile and tears anymore. Besides, there was nothing out there that smelled even close to blood.

"All right, but don't forget to talk to the beacon, it knows where everything needs to go," Christine said after a moment's consideration. "Keep the radio on, too. If I fall off the side of the Moon I want someone to hear me scream this time."

The aid kit, much like the severed arm that Laotian doctor had made her leave behind, was small, slim, and easy to carry around, meant for ease of launch from Earth and carriage through the lunar deadlands. It snapped securely onto her moonsuit like a strapless backpack, rubbing against the tattoo and the scar beneath. They both itched, as they always did, but the aid kit would sooner keep a victim of drawing-and-quartering alive for an hour than solve that problem.

"I'll avenge you if you zilch," Sujatmi said before Christine stepped back out of the rover, wearing a piercing gaze and scimitar smile. That's what Morikis had said when he'd sent her into Vientiane's crimson desolation, too. Christine held onto that smile while Sujatmi crunched back to the lone and leveled ground of Barbicane Road. Then it was just her and the kit and the abandoned rover, alone in the depth of Luna's platinum desolation.

She followed the tracks at a brisk pace; the missing wanderers seemed to have had only a vague notion of where they were going, judging from the spaghetti-string footprints, and every few minutes she passed a point where they'd come to a halt, stomping the regolith flat. Barely three kilometers from Barbicane Road, they disappeared into the drooling mouth of a cave carved into the lip of an ancient crater.

They didn't come out again.

"Jesus God in his glass cathedral, someone needs to kill this meme," she said. The ancient impact that carved the South Pole-Aitken basin had left a titanic scar, and arguments over what that impact meant had produced no shortage of scars themselves. Though particulars of the story shifted with every telling, inevitably the whole colonization of Luna was "revealed" to be a way to hide astronomical riches of equally astronomical value.

Thankfully, unlike California two and a half centuries before, there was no gold rush on Luna. It took a very committed, eager, and wise utter idiot to put her or his life on the line chasing the ghosts of four billion year-old fool's gold. Or idiots, in this case. She blinked on the radio, eyes full of pity.

"I've got a line on our geniuses, whoever they are," she said. "Their tracks go into a cave. The suit's not coming up with any weird noises around here, so if they did go down with radios, they must've figured out some way to break them. I'm setting beacon seven at the entrance."

The beacon was a scaled-down version of the ones that kept the limited rover traffic on course along Barbicane Road and the other routes through the basin. Useless for navigation, but way better than bread crumbs or Ariadne's strand of string. Inside the cave, it would be a different story, and she had a feeling that story had already been told not too long ago.

"Signal's singing joygood," Sujatmi said. "Assuming no jink-junk, I give an hour before I can knot the repair and come pull you out of the cold. Think you can twinkle till then?"

Christine looked askance at the cave. There was a strong possibility that, aside from the ones she was after, no one had ever set foot inside. Even in the sealed-off, alien caverns on Earth that supported their own troglodyte ecology, there was at least life.

"No problem," she said. "I'll take it careful. That was probably their first mistake."

There was no light visible within the cave, nor was there a surveyor's chop at the entrance, confirming her suspicions. The way forward was narrow, two meters at the max with sharp outcrops stabbing at uncomfortable angles, and the footprints shifted to fall between the treads of the cargo roller. One of them had led it and the other followed behind, like ancient travelers leading their tired horse to a brook.

She kept a careful eye on her surroundings as she advanced, illuminated with the ghostly beam of a flashlight kept charged by her own motion. Breadcrumbs marked her path in the form of tiny microbeacons, small and simple enough to be turned out from Griffin Station's equally small and simple factories. There was nothing to suggest her quarry had had as much forethought.

"Hello?" She'd blinked the radio to cycle through all the standard moonsuit bands, just in case they were alive and listening to one of them. "Is anyone picking this up? If you can read me, please respond."

Nothing but the crackle of the Big Bang's fading echo. Nothing around her moved, nothing flinched under the light. It was as if she was the only thing moving in a world frozen in time. No matter how many times she asked for a response, no one answered.

A few steps after she'd set the third microbeacon, the cave widened from a meandering crevasse to a proper cavern. The middle of the expanse was riven by a chasm too wide to jump, even in Luna's paltry gravity. Here the tracks came to an end, with one bootprint chopped in half by the edge, and when she cast her flashlight over the bottom she realized why. The battered wreckage of a cargo roller was down there, along with the two wanderers in Chinese moonsuits splayed out in the rubble. One was almost entirely buried, with only an arm and leg showing, while the other was splayed out atop the debris like a limp triskelion.

"Suj, I've got two suits here, looks like they got caught in a rock collapse." Her suit's automatic systems, having detected the presence of the other two, attempted to shake hands with their systems and came up blank. "Their suits aren't talking. How soon can you hustle?"

"As soon as I can manage it, tick-tock," Sujatmi said. "I'll give you a chime once I hit the beacon. Did you want me to give Griffin a heads-up, have the docs fluff some pillows?"

"I've got to make sure they're alive first. Unless you'd rather pay the fine to turn an ambulance into a hearse because you couldn't wait five minutes."

Christine snapped open the aid kit and unfurled a spool of nanotube rope, fifteen meters' worth, the same stuff they'd used to thread her new right arm. She rammed the anchor into firm ground well removed from the chasm and tested it before she clambered down to where her quarry lay. She headed for the unburied one first, gently rolled the person onto their side—those old Chinese suits had status readouts on the chest—and she had to fight the urge to throw up when she saw his face.

A doctor would have said there was nothing wrong with his face. No bruises, no scarring, no blood and no wide-open, glassy, uncomprehending eyes. The problem was that it was *his* face, that crooked lightning-bolt lip and the caterpillar-thick curly bracket of a mustache that rode it like a cowboy astride an atom bomb.

Morikis' face.

He groaned and fixed his eyes on her. It was God's own blessing she'd kept her faceplate polarized, so all he saw was his own face reflected in a polished golden fishbowl. She doubted even God knew what he'd do if he knew she'd left bootprints here, three hundred and eighty-five thousand kilometers from everything he'd done.

"Where they make a desert, they call it peace." Tacitus hadn't known how wise he was. Morikis had made his deserts in Ouagadougou, in Nottingham, and in the boiling hell of Vientiane. Now here he was in the greatest desert God had ever made, and for what? Redemption? Escape? Silence to drown the screams he'd left behind? Part of her, *most* of her was tempted to leave him there, to do nothing while his air ran out and he choked in the darkness.

It was what he deserved, that much was true, to die terrified and alone, the way she almost had. It was what he deserved but it wasn't what anyone else deserved. With his radio broken, there was only one way to settle it. She closed her eyes, fought back bile, and touched her faceplate to his.

"Hello?" She'd never thought she might be thankful for her larynx getting burned out. Morikis wouldn't recognize her new voice, unless he was familiar with obscure Irish newsreaders from the 2020s. "Can you hear me? Are you all right?"

"Guh . . . you . . . an angel? You sound like . . . someone—" He coughed and made a twisted parody of a smile. "Gold face . . . can I see your wings, too? Carry me up to heaven?"

"Sir, I need to know if you've been injured," she shouted. Morikis flinched, as if he'd heard a hail of bullets instead. "Does anything hurt?"

"Only . . . my legs, I think, and my stomach. Didn't think to pack a lunchbox, Holborn said . . . what about him, is Holborn all right?"

Christine cast a sidelong glance at Morikis' crumpled companion. The light lunar gravity had done little to cushion their fall.

"We'll do everything we can," Christine said. She couldn't bring herself to touch him. It would be enough that the medevac rover found her there with him, watching and talking him away from the edge. When he'd courted those dictators, stood back and counted his money while his security solutions spread terror and death, had he ever imagined it would lead him here, to a thirsty cave at the south pole of Luna? "I'll stay with you, don't worry. I'll make sure you make it through."

Falls in one-sixth gravity, even six-meter falls onto hard rock, didn't hurt nearly as much as when Mother Earth was doing her level best to pull you down. Morikis really was fine, and calling a medevac rover would only have brought her a laugh and a heavy bill for misappropriating a community resource. Sujatmi helped haul Morikis and his dead friend out of the chasm with appropriate solemnity.

Christine couldn't bring herself to smile. Not even when she wound that nanotube rope so thoroughly that the man who had put Pacem Global Security Solutions right in the crosshairs of Amnesty International looked like a life-sized game of cat's cradle.

No matter how thorough they made the pre-launch psych screenings, a few rotten sorts would always make it through. The original planners of Griffin Station, back when it had been founded as a toehold outpost, hadn't made much allowances for judicial infrastructure. That had been left to later generations of leaders, forced to find a solution when the stress of isolation and the endless night drove the wrong sort of minds mad.

Christine watched him through the camera's eye, pacing in his house of lunacrete. There were no windows in it, but even had there been they would have needed no bars. Separate from the rest of the base and drowned in primal vacuum, the chairman might have made it five steps in shirtsleeves before his lungs shattered and his eyes froze.

Still, locks *were* required, and the transparent wall was stronger than steel. It wouldn't do for him to make off with her moonsuit while she was staring him down.

"Surprised to see me?" She had her helmet under one arm and glared with eyes an order of magnitude younger than the sockets they rested in. "I would be if I were you, after what you did. You should be lucky I never was a match for you."

"I hoped I would see you again one day, Chris," Morikis said. "I knew you would find your way back. You always were strong. I like to see that in my employees."

"You should have died out there," Christine said. She pressed her nose against the wall. "First you would run out of food. Then your suit's bladder would break open and bathe you in your own filth. Then you'd asphyxiate and freeze. Someone would drag your corpse back here, the padre would say a few words, and you'd be ground up for the hydroponics. Everything's connected up here. Absolutely everything."

"Don't start me on fate, Chris." Morikis buried his face in his hands, bright and smooth and never having known calluses or scars. "Fate is bunk, a rationalization for why bad things happen to good people. If it was always supposed to be this way, we tell ourselves, then maybe it'll stop hurting so much. It's an invention to keep people from killing themselves."

"Then it worked," Christine said. "For you and for me. Look at me. LOOK AT ME! Or can't you even manage that? I didn't think you'd run all the way to my Moon."

"Earth's moon," Morikis said. "Everyone's. I didn't come here because I was a coward. This is a pure world, Chris. It's never known poverty or war or death and it has no rivers of blood. This is a clean world."

"It's a funny thing about dust up here, you know," Christine said, brushing it off her suited hands. "It's more like glass than dust, and the pieces are sharp. I have to go to the doc every month to make sure my lungs don't turn into Swiss cheese. When the stuff oxidizes, it smells so much like gunpowder you can practically hear the cannons. Sure, it's clean, and you only came so you could wipe your hands on it."

"Chris, I—"

"Save it." She could still see that helicopter in her dreams, lifting away from the pad just ahead of the typhoon, only now she prayed for a missile to teach him Icarus' lesson. "You were lucky and you were stupid. What did you think, that once you got up here no one would bother to push you back down? That you could march into Griffin Station like it was a meeting of the shareholders? What in God's name were you thinking? What the hell were you doing in that cave?"

"I could ask the same of you," he said. "It's obvious you knew it was me, and Holborn was dead. As you said, I should have died. You could have made sure. Why?"

"Because you're a coward," Christine said. Morikis flinched at that as if he'd been struck. It must have been the way she stared at him, this time. "You're just like the husband who kills his wife in a fit of rage, then realizes he's too yellow to face the consequences. You wouldn't wait for the noose. You'd take your whiskey and your revolver and end it. Quick for you, easy for you, always you. The one thing you need to learn is that there's no 'you' or 'me' up here. No fate. Just us."

"So, what, you're going to remand me to the World Court?" Morikis snorted and gestured upward. "Those judges know the cost of instability. I know what to expect from them."

"Haven't you looked outside recently?" Christine breathed deep and leaned against the wall. "I told you already, there's no natural justice up here, or anywhere. Just us."

"I beg to differ," Morikis said. "You asked why I was in the cave. Don't you know what this place is, this whole great basin? This is the thumbprint of God, Chris, the signature he left on creation . . . and I was looking for absolution. I suppose it's justice that you pulled me out of there. Christine. Christopher. Christ-bearer."

"That's a revelation for you, isn't it?" she sneered. "For your information, it's not pronounced 'pace 'em.' It's 'paw-chem,' like the sound your neck'll make when the executioner chops his axe through it."

Without a further word she stepped back into her moonsuit and out the airlock, sealing it tight behind her. Sujatmi was waiting for her at the second airlock, when she entered Griffin Station proper. The capital of Luna, if there really was such a thing. Christine stowed her moonsuit in the a locker and promptly sank to her knees, all that bottled-up pain and rage and loss pouring out like water through a broken dam.

"Oh God . . ." Sujatmi kneeled beside her, laid warm hands on her shoulders. "I should have left him there."

"No, you shouldn't have," Sujatmi said. "Everyone gets a chance up here. Even him."

Christine sniffed and turned watery eyes to the airlock window. The stars were up there, bright and strong, and not one of them would twinkle for as long as anyone could watch.

Coping Mechanism
by Gerri Leen

The interface between Luna and Earth was particularly bad—like a slow connection to the Net when I was a kid and my grandparents had been too cheap to move off dial-up. Cal's image moved in fits and starts, and it wasn't what I wanted—okay, needed—to see. As chief base shrink, I should be woman enough to admit I *needed* to see my husband in some way that didn't immediately scream he was roughly 380,000 clicks away.

Even if Cal was barely my husband; he and I hadn't touched in eight months—and I'd only been on Luna for six. Coming here had been my way of saying goodbye, of letting our marriage die slowly and gracefully rather than living through the drama of a messy divorce. Funny thing about the Moon, though: you don't get over people here. You miss the hell out of them, every part of them. Or maybe you just forget the bad parts, maybe they disappear in the middle of this resounding grayness.

I used to think my marriage was gray and grim. Landing at Echosound—getting my first view of my new home in the bright lunar daytime that had gone on for fourteen Earth-days—had been a reality check of the highest order.

"Vanessa?" Cal was probably wondering why I'd called. We were supposed to be getting used to being away from each other, and I didn't have much to say that was related to the impending dissolution of the marriage.

So I said the first thing that came to mind. "How's Denny?"

The jerking image made his expression unreadable. "He's fine."

I didn't normally ask about his parrot. In fact, I hated that damn bird. Probably because I knew Cal would part with me, but not with him. As a psychiatrist, I don't shy away from truths. Unfortunately, that doesn't make me any better at dealing with them.

"Van, I have to go." Cal didn't sound disappointed, especially on five-second

125

delay. Not for the first time I wished personal calls were given the same priority for real-time access as mission-related calls. But they weren't, so I would deal. Badly, no doubt. But I'd deal.

"I have to go, too. Time for my shift." Which was a lie. I may have normal duty hours, but as essential personnel, I'm on call all the time. No shift work for Doctor Vanessa Holmes. It used to make me feel important; now it felt like a stone around my neck—an Earth-stone in Earth-gravity where it would actually be heavy.

Cal ended the call before I could say anything more. It shouldn't have hurt. It did anyway.

Even in one-sixth G, I felt like I was dragging as I made my way to my office. "Hey," I said, my general hello no matter my mood.

"Hey." Chu barely looked up at me from the newsvid. "Did you see this storm in Tulsa?"

"No, I uh . . ." I took a deep breath and Chu glanced over at me. "I called Cal."

"Wow. Pick at those scabs, Van." Chu shook his head and went back to the news.

"How long's it been since you hit the Day-Glo room?" Vijay was looking at me the way I probably looked at the miners who went a little space crazy out on their asteroids.

"I was just in there yesterday."

"Uh huh. To run diagnostics." He nodded at the door as if he was the boss and I was the brilliant intern. "Not the same thing, Doctor."

"I have a patient coming in."

"Yes, a new comms officer for the VLF array at Indigo base. A person you've never met. No reason Doctor Chu can't take him."

"But far side personnel have special issues and—"

"Doctor Holmes . . ." Vijay already had the door open to the Day-Glo room. "I checked. It's been over a month and we just had a cancellation." His expression clearly had a note of "Physician, heal thyself."

I handed him my databoard and walked in, pulling the door shut behind me. As the seals engaged, the door disappeared, and the walls, ceiling, and floor of the room began to glow. I walked to the lounge chair set in the middle of the room, sat down, and felt the microbeads in the fabric settle around me, supporting in all the right places.

Leaning my head back against the headrest, I forced myself to relax as the room color—normally our familiar lunar gray—started to change. It began in the pastel range, gray giving way to pink, then ice green, lavender, blue, and the palest of yellows.

I found myself breathing deeply, as if I could suck in the colors and make them part of me. Vijay had been right—I'd waited too damn long to get back in here and I knew better than that.

The pastels gave way to stronger tones; they were still light but with more depth stirring the pinks and aquas and blues and yellows. Spring green and bright peach and warm tan were added, bringing to mind Earth's palette of natural colors. The colors swirled and morphed in delicate, gentle ways, and I felt some of the tension drain out of me.

Soon the colors intensified again. The Day-Glo hues the room was named for came into play, as did some of the darker jewel colors—clear emerald, bright amethyst, and deepest ruby. But no onyx or midnight-blue sapphire or dark green tourmaline. Nothing that would remind anyone of space.

I breathed slowly as they'd taught us in the lunar orientation training and let the bright colors excite me—and my brain—in ways we were just beginning to understand. I opened my eyes wide and let the colors replace the grayness that stared back at me whenever I went to Echosound's upper level and looked out at the lunar surface.

The designers of the base had tried to replicate this feeling of being submerged in color with the decor they'd chosen. They'd tried to let the brightness of red and fuchsia and turquoise fill in for those times that a full immersion in color wasn't possible. And it worked for me—to some extent.

Until I went back up and looked out—torturing myself the same way I did when I called Cal. Luna was good for self-realization: I'd never known I was so masochistic, or inclined to wallow, until I'd been here a few months.

He wasn't a miner, hadn't been stuck out alone in space, but he paced my office not making eye contact like one of them might. He seemed to be having trouble with the low grav, was bouncing more than we oldtimers did. I checked his chart for his last posting. Galatea: they had artificial gravity.

He took a deep breath, then another, and didn't stop pacing.

I glanced at the innocuous looking box that sat on the table next to my chair.

Patients often complimented me on it, and the workmanship was exquisite—Balinese wood carving adorned with the island's famous silverwork. Inside were several hypos of fast-acting tranqs. The box was keyed to the medical staff's biometrics, since I couldn't always reach the box if I was busy restraining a patient. I'd restrained far too many people up here for my taste, yelling for help and hoping Chu or Vijay or one of the nurses could get here before all hell broke loose.

The psychological screening done for those assigned to Luna was intense. Unfortunately, it was far from foolproof and we often didn't find out how far we'd gone wrong until someone was faced with the desolation of this place.

"I'm sorry. I don't know what's wrong with me." He sat down and held his hand out. "I'm supposed to introduce myself. I do know that."

I took his hand, but let it go quickly. "You're Stephen MacDougall. You're single, no children, and this is your third assignment in space." I glanced again at his report-in chart. "You were at the Ore Processing Station Galatea and before that you were an engineer on the heavy metals shuttle."

He nodded and his eyes darted to the walls of my office. I knew what he was looking for: the surface of Luna, which was roughly five meters above us—a hell of a lot of regolith between us and it. The dirt barrier kept the radiation away. It was also easy to imagine that we'd been buried alive.

"I know it's bleak here." Despite my own issues, I was good at this. Good at keeping my voice soothing, my eyes understanding. I practiced it in front of my bathroom mirror, especially when I was going through a rough stretch. "Then again, it's bleak in space."

"I'm not bothered by bleak." But still he seemed to be looking for something. "And you can see Earth from here, at least. Or so I'm told. Kind of hard to tell down here."

"You can from the surface. Most of the time, anyway, here near the far side border." I checked his screening results. "You didn't test as claustrophobic."

"I'm not." He took a deep breath. "I mean . . . I haven't been before." He met my eyes.

"So canned air doesn't bother you?" No way it could have given his record of success in space.

"No. But . . . I'm used to having windows of some kind, being able to see the space I'm living on or flying through. You know from the shuttle viewscreen or seeing the ships going by at Galatea. This . . ."

"Yeah, we all have to get used to it." It's what submariners on Earth went through. Navy personnel could be on the confines of a ship for years and not be bothered by the restricted space as long as they had a view of some part of their world, but get them under all that water with no way to see out and no sunshine coming in, and it was a different story. At least we had a better way than a periscope to see out. "I go to the auxiliary docking area a lot—especially when it's daytime. A lot of people use it."

He smiled. "I'll remember that."

"When Earth's out, it's really beautiful. Makes you appreciate where we come from."

He laughed. "Just trying to walk here is making me appreciate that. We had zero-G on the shuttle. This . . . this is really strange."

"I know. And not that healthy. The doctors at internal medicine will be monitoring your exercise routine." I'd put off my resistance training—not as critical as in zero G, but still strongly recommended—this week and had already gotten a reminder in my internal mail.

"By monitoring, you mean policing?" He grimaced. "I hate those centrifuges."

"Everybody hates them. But if you want to walk when you get back to Earth someday, you'll use them faithfully."

"Yes, ma'am." He rolled his eyes, but I could see he understood the need for the exercise so I dropped it and moved on to my own territory. "I'm going to book you for the Day-Glo room—it's free tomorrow afternoon."

He didn't look impressed. "On Galatea, we had an Earth room."

"We've got three here. They're booked months in advance." My next visit was in two weeks—I still hadn't decided if I was going to use the beach or the mountain scenario. Between virtual reality and sensory manipulation, it almost felt as if you were there. "Day-Glo is the best I can offer right now. It should help with any anxiety you're feeling." So would a big dose of benzodiazepanes, but I didn't resort to those except for those I was transferring off—the last days were the worst when someone needed to get the hell off Luna.

"Fine," MacDougall said, "mesmerize me with colors."

I reserved the room for him, then asked, "Why did you leave Galatea? You earned high marks from your supervisors, were promoted twice in a very short period."

"A place gets old." He didn't meet my eyes.

"A place? Or a relationship?" Did he think I wouldn't have done my research?

"She wasn't in my chain of command. She wasn't married. It was all legitimate."

"I didn't say it wasn't." I leaned forward. "It's over, isn't it?"

He stared at the blue and green carpet the designers had hoped would promote openness. He didn't seem to be responding to it.

Maybe I could offer something more. "I understand. I'm . . . losing someone myself."

"Losing?"

"Okay, I've lost him. But it's easier to say losing." I smiled at him. "It's not wrong to find ways to make things easier to accept." Unless those things were the drugs that found their way to this place no matter how much Security screened arriving shipments and people, or overdoing it on the alcohol that wasn't prohibited and that made the time go faster, or the indiscriminate sex for those who preferred their coping mechanisms to come with warm, human skin.

"I wasn't just running. Luna did offer new opportunities. And very good pay."

"I know. But let's not start off our professional relationship with lies, okay?"

"Fine." He got up and stopped at the tranq box. "This is pretty."

"Thank you."

He seemed to want to say more, but just stood there.

"What?"

"How many people make it here?"

I gave him the gentlest smile in my repertoire. "More than you might think." That didn't seem to make him feel better. "We all have different reasons for coming here, MacDougall. Our reasons aren't important. It's what we do once we get here that matters."

He did smile at that. "Thanks, Doc."

The party was in full swing when I hit the lounge. Then again some party was generally in full swing in this lounge. It wasn't quite as bad as the "Day that Ends in 'Y'" parties at my University, but it was close. Part of it was the atmosphere here, the need to blow off steam, but I also attributed the frequent get-togethers to the trend of hiring extroverts for lunar duty, since they tended to cope better in situations with low privacy. Echosound had grown a lot since it had been built as the support facility for the Mare Smythii observatory, but it was still a place where everyone knew your business.

"Hey, Doc," MacDougall didn't wait for a reply as he handed me a drink. "I gotta admit, the parties here are way better than at Galatea."

He winked at me, and I wanted to turn off the professional who was assessing how much he'd already had to drink, wanted to just enjoy a handsome man who seemed interested in me as a person, not just the shrink he had to snow.

But I couldn't turn her off, and my inner booze counter had him sized up at the "too much already" point. "It's wise to pace yourself."

Any interest he might have had seemed to fade from his expression. He turned away and muttered something about people who didn't know how to accept a gift. I let him go—this was my time off, too. As long as he wasn't in my face, I'd ignore it while he was still in the settling-in phase. Most people were fine once they got used to Luna.

I sipped at my drink and did pace myself, making the rounds of the room, trying to have fun but not being able to resist checking up on those around me: Did Lenkova seem less depressed? Was Mattson's stress-related rosacea better?

Sometimes it sucked to be a shrink. Or maybe it just sucked if you were a good one.

"Hey, Holmes. Get the lead out." Someone was calling to me from a crowd of people; a hand emerged from the group, gesturing for me to join them.

I walked over and heard, "The smell of pavement when the rain first starts," "Nighttime that actually ends in a night," and "The way the sky turns colors at sunset."

Great. Playing "What I miss about Earth" was not a good mix with booze.

Vijay looked up at me, and by his expression I could tell he'd tried to steer the conversation in some other direction.

Garcia from Hydroponics smiled at me and asked, "What do you miss?"

"You know I hate this game."

"It's not a game, Van." Anderson glared at me. We'd been close to becoming friends once. Until I had to choose between being that or her shrink. The professional won. To her benefit, but not to mine—she'd been fun to hang out with. "Just answer the question. You never answer. You must miss something."

"Fine. The way the light comes in all golden through the blinds, late in the day when you're lying in bed thinking about a nap."

"Alone," she said, more than a little nastily. Anderson rarely went to bed alone. It was what I'd felt compelled to talk to her about.

"Or with someone. But the golden part, where the blinds split the light and turn the walls into something beautiful."

Garcia took a deep breath. "That's a nice image, Holmes."

I realized MacDougall was watching me from the other side of the group. I smiled at him and held up my drink. It was supposed to be a peace offering, but by the way he didn't smile back I could see he took it as a warning.

Well, that worked, too.

"Vanessa, I need your permission to sign these." Griffin stared across the screen at me, his time-delayed voice holding little other than impatience at the extra minutes required to conduct business with a client on Luna.

Cal had sent the papers forward. I'd thought we weren't going to talk about divorce until next year.

"He's met someone, hasn't he?"

"I really don't know, my dear. I just need to respond within the required time." Divorces had gotten so much easier than when my parents split up. Very pro forma. Lawyers took care of everything unless it got messy, and I'd come up here so it wouldn't.

"Does it say why?"

"Irreconcilable differences." I think Griffin was giving me a stern look, but with the flickering of the image, it was hard to tell. "You did choose to go to the Moon without him."

"He didn't want to come."

"That's not the point."

"Fine. Sign them." I said it fast, before I could change my mind. A call to Cal would accomplish nothing other than embarrassing myself.

"You need to witness this."

I tried not to laugh as his hand jerked across the page. Was this even legal? He could have been signing his health club agreement for all I could tell over this bad a connection.

"There. It's done. You're a free woman, Vanessa."

"Great. Thanks."

I waited for him to cut the connection before I started crying.

MacDougall was in the auxiliary docking area when I got there. So were two others I barely recognized, not folks who frequented the lounge or my office.

"Hey," MacDougall said softly. He nodded to the chair next to him, the motion so slight that I could ignore it if I wanted to.

I chose to join him. We stared out at the lunar landscape and the beautiful green and blue planet that was just visible on the horizon, and I found myself listening to the cadence of his breaths—nice and steady. My relief was a mix of professional and personal.

"You look like you've been crying," he said. "Your eyes are all puffy."

"A gentleman would ignore that."

"You don't have to be perfect, you know? You'd no doubt tell me to share what's hurting."

I laughed softly, and the sound managed to come out with only a trace of bitterness. "You're right. I would. But I'm not going to share."

He looked back at the grayness stretched out in front of us. "Fine."

A klaxon went off—the "Woop woop woop" sound of a breach.

"Crap," I said, digging my fingernails into the arm of the chair. I wasn't claustrophobic, but I hated being stuck in a module during dust repair. At least this time I wouldn't be alone.

The door to the ramp slammed down.

The couple across from us got up and went to the door.

"It's all right," I said, as the woman stared at it in what looked to me like panic barely held in check. "They'll open it as soon as they've isolated the breach."

"We're stuck up here," she muttered as the man with her led her back to her chair.

"I used to hate this on Galatea. I got stuck in a side shaft one day during a breach. All alone for five hours." MacDougall was keeping his voice down, obviously not wanting the other two to hear how long his experience had lasted. He seemed calm though, no evidence of the pacing that had gone on in my office.

"I hate these, too. My last one was in the accessway between Hydroponics and here."

"Ooh, deep and dark."

"Yeah." I had felt like the entire Moon was pushing down on me, making the space closer and closer. Fortunately, deep breathing and a stern talking to had kept me calm and centered, but I'd run back to the office once it was over, not stopping until I was in the check-in room with Chu and Vijay.

"How long does it take them to fix a breach?"

"Not long. It's a nuisance, not an emergency. The base is comprised of many modules, all capable of being self-sustaining in the case of a breach in an adjacent unit. When the alarm went off, the system automatically shut the doors between the modules in the sector, but other parts of the base will be operating as if nothing is wrong."

"This is one of the least protected spots," he said, and I saw the other two look over. "I mean, technically."

He wasn't wrong. The surface was the most vulnerable; it was why so much of the base was built below it. We had shielding to stop space debris from hitting the outer levels, but it didn't always work. It also didn't stop the lunar dust from coming in and clogging up the works. We'd had less dust-related alarms since the last HVAC upgrade, but it was still a problem. Vijay liked to say that lunar dust and cat hair were the two most pervasive materials in the known universe. If we ever got cats up on Luna, we'd be in trouble.

MacDougall leaned closer. "With no atmosphere protecting us anything could—"

"Could we pick a new topic, Mr. Cheerful?"

"Okay." He pitched his voice lower. "Why were you crying?"

"I was chopping onions."

He laughed softly. "I saw the onions on the tour I took of hydroponics last week. Quite the impressive spread of produce being grown. Not to mention the fish. We didn't have fish farms on Galatea."

"We're getting chicken soon, too. Down at Lands End, near the polar water processing unit, they're building a facility for them."

"Good. I miss real eggs." He smiled gently. "I don't believe you were chopping onions, by the way."

I shrugged. "I guess I'm not a good liar."

The alarm sounded again, a long buzz that signaled all clear, and the door opened. The other two rushed out, but I noticed MacDougall made no move to leave.

"Do you ever go out there?" He stood and walked to the window, his nose pressed against it like a little boy.

"Nope. Hate the suits." Even if they had been improved over the years from the bulky things the first astronauts had worn. "Even with thermal protection, it's too cold . . . or hot, depending on if the sun's out. And you can't get any perspective on the landscape—it's very disconcerting. Plus . . . I feel very alone out there."

"Wow, they better not let you write the marketing brochures when they open this place up for tourists." He laughed at me, and I grinned back. "I signed up for a moonwalk. I'm trying to get to know my new home."

"That's good."

He turned. "Is that the shrink talking or the nice lady who won't tell me why she was crying?"

"I'm not sure they're different people." I stood and joined him at the window. "Up here, it's hard for me to let go of that. So many people depend on us all being okay, you know?"

"So, by extension they depend on you."

"I used to try not to think about it all the time. And then one day, one of my patients decided to go for a moonwalk. Without a suit. We were lucky. He followed exit protocols, didn't take anyone else with him, but he could have." I took a deep breath. "So you see, I don't get a break."

"And you kind of like that, don't you?" He was studying me in a way that made me very nervous. "I guess being essential beats having a life?"

"I have a life." One that was on Earth and no longer tied to me. I turned and left before I decided to start sharing that.

Chu wandered into my office, stood by my desk, tapping his fingers on the laminate.

"Yes?" I didn't look up as I keyed in my write-up from my last session.

"I'm ... transferring off. I got my orders; I ship off next week."

I stopped what I was doing, looked up slowly. "Oh."

"I like who they're sending to replace me—there's a memo in your queue, it came in while you were with your last patient."

I nodded, unsure what to say.

"I think you'll like her, too."

"Good. Great." Why was this hurting? Chu and I weren't really friends.

"Can I make a suggestion, Van?"

"Yeah, of course." I realized I was breathing a little fast, told myself to take it easy.

"Talk to someone occasionally. You don't have to be strong all the time." He took a deep breath. "I know this thing with Cal is hurting you. That pain makes you human. Probably would be reassuring for people to see that."

"Okay, I'll send an all-base memo. Let me get right on that."

He shook his head. "That's not what I meant."

"People here are my patients. I owe them more than a messed-up doctor."

"So you admit you're messed up?"

I laughed—the maneuver he'd used was a classic. "You're so damn good at this."

"I know." He laughed softly, too. "Just think about what I'm saying, okay?"

"I will." I met his eyes, tried to imagine the base without him. We weren't friends, but he'd always been a touchstone of sorts, a serene spot in the quiet chaos that was Luna. "It was a pleasure serving with you."

He touched my shoulder, let his fingers sit for a moment, and the contact felt good. "Same here, Van. Same here."

The lounge was packed for Chu's going away party. I knew he wasn't taking it as a sign of how many friends he had—it was just the first party in a long time that had an actual "event" affiliated with it.

"Hey," MacDougall said, handing me a drink.

I tried my best not to assess him; I failed miserably.

"I'm still on my first glass," he said with a grin.

"I kind of figured that."

"Do they give you extra pay for that? Being a human breathalyzer?"

"No." I watched as Chu worked the room. "They don't pay me extra for having no friends, either."

"I wouldn't say you have no friends." He winked at me. "Just . . . not very many." At my look, he grinned. "You said no lies."

"I did say that." I took a sip of my drink. "I was crying the other day because my husband filed for divorce."

He looked surprised at my blurt-o'-truth. "I'm sorry."

"Me, too." I took a deep breath and wished that letting the truth out had felt better.

"If you want to talk about it . . . ? Some other place and time, when it's not so crowded?"

The rebuff was on my lips, but I pulled it back. "Maybe. Yeah. We'll see."

He looked disappointed. "You just can't stop being the professional, can you? Not even for a minute."

I pulled him away from the crowd a little, so we had the corner to ourselves.

"Twenty percent of all medevacs from Luna are psychologically related. One out of every five people we have to send home will—"

"Go nuts?"

"That's not the approved term."

"But it is what you meant."

"They'll have some sort of psychological stress or episode severe enough to necessitate removing them from the base."

"I got it the first time, Doc." He leaned in, his whisper was harsh. "And you're the first line of defense? Great."

"What's that supposed to mean?"

"You expect us to spill our guts to you or your colleagues, but you don't share."

"I didn't say I was going to. It was nice of you to offer a friendly ear, but I don't have to take it."

"No, you sure don't, do you?" He raised his drink in a bitter salute and left me alone.

I knew from the moment Doctor Lansing arrived, that she was the kind of doctor people opened up to right away. I hadn't thought I'd be one of those people, though.

She was watching me with a gentle look. "So this Cal—did you think he was your forever mate?"

She had a funny way of putting things. But her words cut to the heart of the matter.

"I guess so." I opened up the diagnostic panel of the Day-Glo room and showed her the quirks of our system. "I loved him."

"Not enough to stay and fight for him, though, huh?"

I glanced at her, but she was staring intently at the unit. Her voice hadn't held any condemnation—she was just stating a fact.

I hadn't fought. I'd run away. But— "Is it running away if the patient can't be saved?"

"The patient?" She shot me a gentle smile. "Or your marriage?" At my look, she said, "Not everything's a patient, Vanessa."

"I know that."

She eased me out of the way. "I can finish up here. Why don't you take off early? I hear there's a party in the lounge."

"Imagine that?" I found myself smiling, wishing she was coming. Wishing I knew her better.

Her easy grin told me there was plenty of time for that. She'd be here—if I'd let her in. I'd never let Chu in. Or—

I skipped the lounge, walked up to the auxiliary docking area instead. MacDougall was alone.

"No hot party for you?" I asked with a smile.

"Nope. Nor for you, apparently?"

I shook my head. "Is that offer still open? To, you know, talk?"

He nodded slowly.

"You can talk, too." I tried to smile, tried to make it real and not my professional one.

"If I do, is it on the couch or not?"

"I don't know." I met his eyes, tried to let him see that I wasn't playing games. "I can try to just listen, not assess."

I could try, but I would fail.

To my surprise, he grinned. "Let's not strain you too much. How about we start with you telling me a little about yourself? We can work up to the other thing."

I laughed, but inside I could feel something shutting down. I didn't do this; I didn't share. Sharing made you weak. Before I could completely lose my nerve, I said, "My husband told me I was closed off."

I waited for the snarky comment, the "no kidding" that would have been so appropriate. MacDougall didn't say anything; he just waited.

I tried for more words. They didn't come, and then I felt his hand on mine, just a slight and quick touch.

"Why not start at the beginning? How did you meet?"

The beginning. Such a simple concept. But not the right place to start. Not for this.

"He said I was closed off, and he was right." I met his eyes, took a deep breath, and started talking.

The Return
by David Schibi

Geoff Jones crested the final hill in his path. The bluish-gray regolith crunched beneath his feet and the end of his walking rod. Beads of sweat rolled down his face despite the suit's attempts to regulate the internal temperature. His breaths were heavy and his throat felt as though he hadn't had water in days.

In the valley below was the complex. Or what was left of it.

Framed in the vastness of space, Earth sat silently over the horizon, the shadow of the Moon covering a small portion of the blue and green planet. Geoff looked down at the valley before him. There was no wind to stir dust and nothing moved or crawled across the surface. Void of all vegetation, Geoff marveled at the magnificent desolation.

His chest heaved with great breaths. His throat still ached and the sweat that trailed from his forehead and armpits was cold on his skin as the suit lowered the internal temperature. He wanted to sit down, to remove the suit and take a shower. He wanted a nap.

Perhaps the others had been right; maybe making the three-day journey was a bad idea. Geoff had nothing but his suit, a few emergency essentials on his back, and the Moon's surface beneath his feet.

"Night Owl *to* Wanderer, *do you copy?*"

And a shuttle staying just out of sight behind him.

The voice over the comm nearly made him jump.

"This is Wanderer, Night Owl," Geoff replied. He tried to moisten his throat by swallowing but his saliva was thick and sticky. "What is it?"

"*We're picking up an increase in physical stress from your suit. Are you in need of assistance?*"

Geoff tried not to let his anger show through his voice; he knew the kids monitoring were just looking out for him. He raised an arm and pressed a button on the forearm control pad. A small nozzle inside the helmet extended an inch and spayed a tight yet gentle stream of water into his waiting mouth. The spray lasted only a couple of seconds. Geoff sloshed it around and swallowed before responding.

"Young man," he said, "I am 74 years old. I have spent the last three days in the desolate lunar wilderness scaling mountains, traversing craters, and I even rapelled down a massive boulder. Now, I just climbed to the top of the final hill on my journey. I think I'm allowed to show an increase in physical stress levels, just a little bit."

"*Yes, sir.*" The person on the other end sounded a little embarrassed. *"I just . . . wanted to make sure. . ."*

"I understand. And I appreciate your diligence. But please, for the rest of my time out here, do not radio me just to check on my condition. I am perfectly capable of contacting you if the need arises."

"Yessir. Night Owl *out."*

Geoff pressed the button on his walking rod and the device retracted to a small cylinder no longer than twenty centimeters. He clipped it onto his belt and fastened the small Velcro strap around the bottom end to keep it from floating up.

He turned his attention back to the complex below. The dome-shaped metal frame still stood, the windows were dark. Branching out at even intervals around the dome center were three smaller domes, all damaged in some way. A pile of rubble lay where a fourth should have been.

It had been sixty years since he had last set eyes or foot upon the site. Why he felt the need to now he wasn't completely sure. He just knew it was time. A cascade of emotions flooded him as he looked upon it: happiness, loss, triumph, and fear.

After several minutes, Geoff decided it was time to go; if he was going to do this he might as well get it over with. He looked down for the best route to take, wanting to avoid any particularly loose or slippery rocks.

That's when he saw them.

At first he merely stared and blinked, not believing what he was seeing. Then he squatted down and took a closer look.

Pressed in the loose, crushed rock, were several boot imprints, one pair with the unmistakable markings of his childhood. The bootprints pointed away from the old facility, toward the far side of the Moon. The letters GJ were near the toe end of one pair of boot prints. Beside and all around them were other, unmarked bootprints.

62 Years Earlier

Geoff breathed heavily in his suit. In his helmet he heard the same breathing from his parents beside him. They moved so fast—well, fast for being in low gravity—Geoff had a hard time keeping up. His father yanked on his arm with an iron grip.

He was scared.

And the worst part was he could tell they were, too.

"I told you, you shouldn't do that, Geoff," said Mom. "You mess around and puncture the sole of your boot too far and you'll not get to go out anymore."

"Aw, Mom," said Geoff, his attention still on fastening the small metal letters onto the bottom of his boot. Tommy Kilgore had actually come up with the idea but Geoff had made it work. Tommy made mention that the boot prints they made while walking about outside the facility would probably be around for a long time and he said he wished there was a way to mark them.

Geoff had thought to use the small pins from their bed chests, the short pins on the back just long enough to hold the letters to the bottom of the boot. He smiled as he finished pressing the last one in place. All that was left was to get out there and test it out. He slipped the white boots on.

"Mom, I'm going out," he said as he ran through the home, passing his mother.

"You be careful, double check the door locks," she yelled after him. "And if you see your father, tell him tomorrow night he's cooking dinner."

His mother's face contorted in a horrified expression, her mouth open in a shrieking yell, "THOMAS!" But Geoff's father didn't respond.

He never would again.

Geoff entered the Dome, closing the airlock that led to their abode and making sure it sealed. Why they had to make sure all three doors between the Dome and the house were closed every time they used them he didn't know. What he did understand was when Dad said, "If I ever find a door not sealed and you were the one through it you'll not be allowed in the Dome anymore."

So Geoff was sure the door that led from the house to the short tunnel sealed and the door in the middle of the tunnel—why one was there he didn't know—sealed and that the one that led from the tunnel to the Dome sealed every time he used them. It only took a couple of seconds for the lights to change anyway.

The light on the console beside the door clicked from red to green. Geoff turned and deliberately stepped one foot onto the crunchy surface, pressing harder than usual and keeping his foot as still as he could. The Dome was Geoff's favorite part of living in Lunar One.

It was huge! There was a community storehouse and workshops and laboratories and a huge greenhouse all on the inside of the Dome. And there was still room to ride bikes and play football.

Geoff lifted his boot carefully. The treads from the bottom left their usual imprints but this time there were two extra indentions. A 'G' and a 'J' appeared near the toe of his boot. Smiling, he took a few more steps, pressing just a little harder than normal. The imprints all showed the same. He took off at a run.

Dad was in the workshop where he usually was. One of the land rovers needed repairs from a recent fall and Dad was the best at fixing them. Mom grew the best plants and Dad fixed everything; they said those were the reasons they had been chosen for the Lunar One assignment.

Slowing down, so as not to get in trouble (again), Geoff walked up behind Dad. "HeyDadheyDad!" he called.

With his large goggles still on his face and a welding torch in hand, Dad turned around and looked at Geoff. The torch went out and Dad slid the goggles up onto his head. His face was dirty except for a ring of clean skin around his eyes where the goggles had been.

"Hey, Sport," Dad said. "What're you up to?"

"Check this out." Geoff walked close by his father, craning his neck to look at the bootprints he left. It took Dad a second to figure out what he was supposed to be seeing.

"Oh, that's clever," he said, squatting down to take a closer look. "You've got your initials in your bootprints." Geoff squatted down across the bootprint from Dad and they studied it together. "That's a really great idea, son." Geoff beamed. "Now when you get into something you're not supposed to I'll know for sure it was you."

The smile fell from Geoff's face. Dad laughed and ruffled Geoff's blond hair. They stood up, Dad pulling off his big gloves.

"What's your mother doing?"

"Cooking," Geoff said then remembered the message he was supposed to give. "She said tomorrow night it's your turn to cook."

"Did she now?" Dad cocked an eyebrow looking down at Geoff.

"Yeah," Geoff said. Then after a moment, "Does that mean grilled cheese again?"

Dad laughed again and picked up an angled piece of pipe, what he'd been welding apparently. He walked past Geoff to the rover he'd been working on and knelt down beside it. There were several strands of multicolored wires hanging out.

"I don't know," he said. "I'll have to check my repertoire and see what else I can make."

"Tommy says his dad cooks all the time," Geoff said kneeling down beside Dad and looking at the rover as though he knew precisely what needed to be done. "Makes all kinds of chicken and pasta and casseroles."

"Yeah, well," Dad said. "Here hold that." Geoff took one end of the angled pipe and held it up pointing toward the rover. "Tommy's dad—no like this—" Dad turned the pipe so it pointed down, "Tommy's dad isn't a mechanic, he's a scientist."

"Yeah, I told him his dad doesn't work as hard as you."

"No, that's not what I mean. His dad works just as much as I do, he just does different things. I doubt his hands and clothes are ever as dirty as mine when he's done. So he can fix meals like that more easily."

Geoff held the pipe as Dad threaded the wires through it. They poked out Geoff's end while Dad pressed the pipe into its connector. "Everyone here does their share, Geoff. You know that. Even you kids do your chores like recycling and incinerating the waste. Those are important things."

"Yeah, I know," Geoff said. "Can I go now?"

"Go?" Dad repeated with a chuckle. "Where are you in a hurry to get to?"

"I want to show Tommy my boots."

"You mean you don't want to stay and help out your old man?" Geoff looked away from his dad's eyes. Dad chuckled again. "I'm just teasing, go ahead and go play." Geoff stood and took off for the door. "But after dinner you're mine," Dad called after him. "You need to practice your tackling."

Geoff saw Tommy run into the Dome from the passage that led to his house. The large metal airlock hung open, the light red on the panel beside it.

Tommy met Geoff near the storehouse in the center of the Dome. "You left the door open," Geoff said pointing back at the open hatch.

"Who cares," Tommy said with a shrug. "Mom just sent me out here to get a can of peaches. Dad and Doctor Meyers are working on setting up the EWE right outside our dome. It's so cool. Once it's done we'll have the safest dome in the settlement." Tommy brandished a broad smile, his chin tilted up.

Geoff had overheard Dad telling Mom how Dr. Kilgore—Tommy's dad—was so obsessed with the Electronic Wave Emitter that he wondered how much other work he was actually getting done. Geoff wasn't sure exactly what it was, he just knew Dad was really mad when he found out they had been allowed to move into the settlement without them in place. There was supposed to be several of them all the way around the settlement. Geoff remembered hearing they were supposed to emit some kind of waves that would help repel meteors and stuff that could hit the settlement.

"You mean, like a shield?" Geoff had asked Dad.

"Well, kind of, yeah. But not quite like what you see on the net."

"Check it out," Geoff said. Then he showed Tommy his bootprints.

"That's cool," said Tommy, flinging his dark, shaggy hair back over his head. "I thought of that but just never did it."

"Whatever," Geoff said.

"Hey, my dad says there could be some meteors passing close by tonight. Wanna watch them?"

"Sure," said Geoff trying not to let his disappointment at Tommy's casual dismissal of his initialed bootprints show.

"Okay. I'll ask Dad if we can use one of his telescopes. It'll be so cool. I gotta get some peaches. Wanna come over and watch my dad and Doctor

Meyers work?"

"Nah, that's okay," Geoff said.

Tommy shrugged and walked past Geoff into the storehouse. Geoff walked around with no direction, looking at the bootprints he left. He wasn't sure what to do now. Tommy reemerged from the storehouse and waved goodbye as he ran back toward his house.

Then the sirens sounded.

A loud, unmistakable wail that couldn't be missed blared over the speakers mounted high up on the steel beams. Geoff's hands immediately covered his ears. He looked over at Tommy who was doing the same thing standing right by the airlock.

After a few moments, Dad's arms swept Geoff up. He could hear Dad yelling for Tommy to follow them, his arm waving him over. Tommy looked scared and confused and reached for the door.

Then the ground shook so hard Dad fell to his knees. There was a loud boom that echoed throughout the facility.

"What was that?" Geoff asked in the stillness that followed the sudden silence of the alarms.

"Something's hit us," Dad said. Geoff had never heard his voice like that before. It sounded . . . scared.

Next came the sound of a hard rain against the outside of the Dome. Dad got to his feet and took off at a run, Geoff jostling in his arms. Geoff's eyes were on Tommy. His friend entered the passage not shutting the door behind him. A moment later, a large piece of rock slammed through the Dome right beside the door.

Seconds after, Geoff felt Dad struggle against the pull of air as it sucked out through the hole. Geoff pinched his eyes shut as he heard other crashes. He held onto Dad as tight as he could. Then they entered the passage and Dad sealed the door behind them. The scream of rushing air was gone and Geoff found himself breathing as though he'd been running.

Dad leaned over, his hands on his knees, breathing heavily for a moment. Then he took Geoff by the arm. "Come on. We have to hurry."

"What about Tommy?" Geoff asked.

"I don't know," Dad answered as they ran down the passage, stopping at the door in the middle.

"But what happened?" Geoff asked. "Is Tommy okay?"

"I don't know, Geoff," Dad snapped. He ripped open the door and practically threw Geoff inside. Then he stepped through, sealed the door, took Geoff's arm again, and they ran the rest of the way to their front door.

When they finally got inside they saw Mom with tears streaming down her face. She hugged Geoff so tight he thought she was going to break something.

"Oh my god, Thomas, what's happened?" she asked Dad.

"Something's hit us. The Dome's been compromised. Quick, into the shelter." They followed Dad through the house to the end of the hallway. Dad keyed in the family code on the panel and the middle of the wall shot up. Stairs led down.

"Go! Go!" Dad shouted making Mom and Geoff enter first. He followed and shut the door. At the bottom of the short flight of stairs was another large airlock door. Dad opened it and after everyone was in, he sealed it.

The lights activated on their own but it took them several seconds to illuminate the room properly. Geoff had only been in the emergency room once since they got to the settlement. Mom and Dad had made it perfectly clear that Geoff was not to play in there or even open the hallway door unless instructed to do so. Geoff had thought about disobeying them several times but always elected not to. Now he wished they didn't have to be in the room. It wasn't quite as big as his room. Cushy benches lined the back wall.

Spacewalk suits lined one wall. Geoff saw six adult suits and three child-size suits. The sight of the starch white suits and dark faceplates standing ominously in the recessed compartments scared Geoff. A chill raced down his spine and his stepped away from the suits.

Dad hurried over to the small computer terminal in the corner of the room. He activated it and drummed his thumbs on the desktop impatiently as he waited for it to fire up. Mom held one arm around herself and the other elbow was on top of it, her mouth covered by the open hand. Tears streamed down her face and her shoulders would bounce rapidly every few seconds. She saw Geoff staring and tried to force a smile, failed, and then turned away, wiping at her eyes.

"Dammit, come on!" Dad slapped the desktop. Geoff saw the startup screen on the monitor and thought oddly that the computer had booted up rather quickly compared with the one he normally used. Then the computer was active and Dad's fingers flew across the keyboard. On the screen the picture squared off into six individual view boxes, four of them had nothing but static. One other was dark. The last one worked.

And Geoff wished it hadn't.

"Oh dear god," Dad's voice was breathless whisper.

"Is that—" Mom started, placing a hand on Dad's shoulder. Her other hand shot back up to cover her mouth again.

The view was unbelievable and terrifying. It occurred to Geoff that he was viewing a shot of the facility from an outside camera mounted on a pole. There had been six of them. The camera panned across the entire facility from almost right above their house.

The Dome had several places where it had been penetrated. Three of the other four homes were rubble and the other was only half there. Four of the other camera poles were missing and the last camera pointed directly up into space.

"Do you suppose Tommy and his family made it to their shelter?" Geoff asked into the silence.

"I don't know," Dad said his voice still unusually quiet. He wiped his face with one hand. Then he stood up and walked away from the computer. Geoff slid into the vacated seat as Dad wrapped his arms around Mom.

The camera panned slowly across the scene again and Geoff leaned in to study the details closely. Then he saw it lying in a passage. There was a can of peaches. The camera continued its slow revolution.

There was no home at the end of the passage.

Present Time

"Night Owl *to* Wanderer, *Mr. Jones you've been stationary for several minutes, is everything okay?*"

Geoff blinked several times. He straightened up and looked around, swallowing to clear his throat.

"Yes," he responded, "yes I'm fine. Just saw something . . . unexpected is all." He looked down at his boots, his eyes following them up as far as he could. These new suits were much less cumbersome than the old ones had been, the ones they had worn out of the shelter.

"I'm moving forward," Geoff said. He started down the slope,

147

adjusting the weights in his boots via the control pad on his forearm. Making the weights light allowed him to take much larger, longer steps down the slope. He arrived at the valley floor in less than five minutes, the trip down requiring much less exertion than the trek up.

The walking rod extended at the touch of a button and Geoff used it to mark his path. With each step it left a mark on the ground that could be easily tracked if necessary. It was a luxury he and his parents hadn't had sixty-two years ago.

Rolling up on all sides, the Dome had been built in the valley because it was thought the high sides would offer added protection from meteor showers. It was, Geoff found out years after the tragedy, the reason settlement had been pushed forward without the completion of the EWEs. With Earth deteriorating at the rate it was, lunar settlement was of the highest priority. The newly formed International Space Colonization Agency had been too focused on getting something started than in hearing the concerns some people had for putting off settlement another year.

ISCA researchers had charts that showed Settlement Valley hadn't been hit by anything for decades. The project was green lighted and the Dome was finished just three short months later. Dad had been part of the original construction crew. Geoff and his mother arrived with the other permanent colonists right after completion of the facility.

Deemed a huge success, the next phase of the Lunar Settlement Project was slated to begin eight months later. The next facility was to be built 350 kilometers away, the idea being to eventually connect the two facilities while using both as storage points for material needed to continue construction at other areas. People on Earth wanted to see people living on the Moon as soon as possible and building the individual facilities was deemed the quickest way to get there.

The theory that building the Dome in the crater would provide all the protection it needed while the EWEs were being built turned out to be the fatal flaw in the plan. It wasn't much of a meteor shower, really. Just one big chunk and several smaller ones, but they hit. And there was nothing to stop them.

Geoff was close now. He touched the pole upon which the active camera had been perched with one gloved hand. No one had ever cleaned up the mess; the facility deemed a graveyard for the ones lost. Project Lunar Settlement continued to the far side of the Moon. And the second dome wasn't populated until the EWEs were active.

But none of that had helped Geoff or his parents. They had been the ones who had to suffer before anyone would listen. And suffer they did.

62 Years Earlier

Geoff didn't cry. He knew he should, like Mom was. Mom couldn't seem to stop, her chest heaving with great sobs. But Geoff just couldn't. Dad was gone and yet Geoff couldn't cry. The guilt he felt for not crying only added to his misery as he and Mom continued on across the empty vastness of the Moon's surface.

Dad returned to the shelter. It had been a day since the Dome was hit. Dad had donned one of the suits again and went out to look for other survivors. This had been his fifth trip out, each time he said he didn't want to stay out too long. He said he didn't find anything but then, just as after every other trip, he and Mom would ask Geoff to go check the camera on the computer or go get Dad a drink while Mom helped him out of the suit. Geoff could hear them whispering behind him. Whenever Geoff returned Mom would be near tears, Dad's face sullen.

It was a few hours after they ate when Geoff dozed off to sleep on one of the benches. Mom and Dad whispered a lot and Geoff only caught tidbits. He heard something about the threat detector and Tommy's dad's name.

Geoff woke with a start. A quick, repeated beep filled the room. Dad was at the computer before Geoff had realized it was the source of the noise.

"Oh no," Dad mumbled, his shoulders shagging.

"What is it?" Mom asked, her voice already shaky.

"We have to go." Dad turned in the seat to face her. "I reset the threat detector and synced it with this computer when I was out."

"Yeah," Mom said.

"It's detected an incoming threat. And this one is bigger; probably the main body of what hit us yesterday. We're not safe even in here."

"Where are we going to go?" Mom asked as she helped dress Geoff. The suit was a little oversized for him but the only other child sized one was too small. Dad was pulling his suit back on.

"I don't know yet. I activated the emergency beacon; hopefully help is on the way. Let's just get out of here, quickly."

They dressed and left the shelter. Their pace was quick and Dad carried Geoff until they were past the Dome, past the post with the mounted camera. It wasn't until they started up the slope leading out of the valley that Dad finally had to put Geoff down. But he kept a hand on Geoff almost constantly.

Present Time

Geoff looked up the slope he had recently descended, one hand still on the camera post. It was so different now, the suits much more functional and the trek so much easier. If the suits at the facility had been like the one he wore now, Geoff felt confident things would have turned out differently, better.

He remembered with stark clarity the moment the meteor struck the facility and the destruction that followed. The place they had called home was completely devastated, pieces of rock and metal and plastic spun just above the surface through the low gravity, not stopping until they struck the sides of the surrounding slopes.

62 Years Earlier

The ground beneath Geoff trembled. Dad was behind him, practically pushing him up the slope. Geoff had trouble maneuvering, every movement felt exaggerated. Dad called out, a cry of shock or pain Geoff wasn't sure which.

"Keep going!" he shouted. "Keep going!"

Mom and Geoff got to the top of the slope, the ground leveled off. They turned around and Mom reached out for Dad. She helped him to the top and then he showed her. Right over his lower back the suit had been penetrated. Mom and Dad looked at each other.

"No," Mom said in a desperate whisper.

"It's okay," Dad said raising a gloved hand to her face plate.

"No no no," Mom said and she started to look through all of the pockets on her suit. Geoff didn't realize she was trying to find something to plug the tear. But there was nothing.

"No," she repeated, giving up her desperate search and turning to look again at her husband.

"Let's go," Dad said pointing past Mom. "I think they dropped off the first load of supplies for the next facility a couple of days ago. There might be a pod there."

"But that's, what, 350 kilometers away," Mom said.

"You can make it," Dad said with a nod at Geoff who stood by just watching.

"You won't," Mom said in a quieter voice, still carried over the intra-suit radio.

"But you will." Dad fixed a stern stare on Mom. They embraced and Geoff could hear her crying despite her efforts not to. When Mom turned and started walking, Dad knelt in front of Geoff.

"Geoff, sport," he said. He smiled but his eyes were red and sad. "We're going to walk to where they're going to be building the next dome. It's a long ways and we're not going to be able to stop." Geoff nodded. Dad took Geoff's arm and looked at the control panel on the forearm.

"See this?" he pointed at a series of vertical green lines across the top of the pad. Geoff nodded. "This tells us how much air your suit has. If it gets too low, you'll hear a beeping sound in your helmet. If you hear that, tell me or Mom immediately. Understand?" Geoff nodded.

Dad smiled again and his eyes brightened a little. "You're a good boy, Geoff, and I love you. Know that?" Geoff nodded. "Okay. Now, let's get moving."

Present Time

Geoff walked through what was left of the Dome. After an hour, he was finished. He'd seen all he came to see. With the press of a button he signaled for a shuttle to come and get him. By the time he reached the edge of the Dome, the shuttle's lights peeked over the top of the slope.

Geoff gave the facility one last look and then closed the door of the shuttle. It turned and started back up the slope, hovering just a meter over the surface.

The memories assaulted him as they traveled so easily up the slope that had aided in killing his father. If they would have made it up faster that piece of debris wouldn't have penetrated his suit. But even then, Geoff knew, his Dad wouldn't have survived.

62 Years Earlier

The green lines on Geoff's panel had decreased by half.

"Okay, stop," Dad said. He breathed hard, much harder than Mom or even Geoff. Geoff wasn't sure how long they had been walking but he was tired. "Come here," Dad said waving at Geoff. Dad looked at Geoff's panel and told him to turn around.

"What are you doing?" Mom asked.

"I'm running out of oxygen," he said. "I'm venting through the suit. My back is getting cold."

From over a distant rise an emergency pod floated toward them.

"Well, don't take from him. Here," Mom said. "Take some from me."

"In a second." Geoff's brow furrowed as he watched the green lines on his panel increase to full again. He thought Dad said he needed air.

"Okay, Martha," Dad said short of breath. "Your turn." Mom turned around and let Dad hook his hose to her tank.

"You take however much you need, Thomas," Mom said. "Once we get to the pod there should be plenty for all of—"

Geoff heard the beep that stopped his mom mid-sentence. She looked down at her panel.

"Thomas, what are you doing?" she yelled and spun around as Dad unhooked the hose.

"Had to," Dad said his eyes half shut. "I ... wouldn't ... make it."

"Thomas!" Mom yelled.

"Get ... Geoff ... to ... pod ..."

"Thomas! No!" Mom's voice was a high pitched scream. She grabbed one of Dad's arms and started to reach for her hose.

"Geoff ... look ... away ..." Dad said raising one hand. His voice was so weak and slurred it was hard to understand him. Geoff thought he might be pointing at something and turned his head.

Mom screamed and when Geoff looked back; Dad's faceplate had been lifted.

"THOMAS!"

* * *

Present Time

There was no defining marker, nothing to identify, but Geoff was sure they had just passed the point where Dad had transferred the rest of his oxygen to him and Mom and sacrificed himself so they could live.

The shuttle continued and Geoff felt older by the second. They crested a small slope in the terrain—an impact crater from centuries ago—and Geoff saw the pod on the horizon, just as he had all those years ago. He recalled the way Mom moved, determined, relentless. She wasn't going to let Dad's sacrifice be in vain.

62 Years Earlier

Mom moved fast. They hadn't spoken much since Dad . . . left. But she hadn't cried for a while. Geoff never had. He didn't know why. He loved Dad and he understood what had just happened. But he just didn't cry. He wanted to.

"Get inside," Mom said as she opened the pod's exterior hatch. It was cramped with both of them on the inside but Geoff didn't care. He just wanted to get this suit off and breathe some air.

"How long will this last?" Geoff asked while they waited for the small chamber to pressurize. Mom checked his oxygen level.

"Long enough," Mom said.

They entered the main part of the pod, removing their helmets. There was one chair in front of a control bank. Looked like it was going to be cramped the whole time they were in there. Mom sat at the controls and pulled up some menus. Geoff looked around but couldn't see anywhere else to sit.

Mom sighed heavily and Geoff thought she might have stifled a cry. A moment later she flipped through some more screens. The menus closed and when she turned and faced Geoff, she smiled with red-rimmed eyes.

"I've locked the system so you won't accidentally hit anything," she said. She picked her helmet back up. "I need to go back out and watch for the rescue vehicles."

"Okay," Geoff said. His eyes were heavy. He hadn't had much sleep in the shelter and they had walked forever.

Mom stooped, vacating the seat and made room for Geoff to sit down. "I want you to sit right here, honey and get some rest." She pushed his hair back with an un-gloved hand. Her lips gently pressed on his forehead. "Sleep well, my love," she whispered. "And never forget how much your father and I loved you."

"I love . . . you, too," Geoff said. He rubbed his eyes, his head dipped and he pulled it back up quickly. He heard the doors to the pod open and shut. Moments later, Mom stood in front of the pod and stared in at Geoff. She placed a covered hand on the exterior window.

"Go to sleep, Geoff," she said, her voice piped in over the pod's speakers. "Everything will be better when you wake up."

Geoff couldn't fight the sleep anymore. He laid his head down as his eyes closed.

His last conscious thought was that Mom was crying again.

Present Time

The shuttle passed by the abandoned pod; Geoff told the pilot there was no need to stop. He had seen more than enough of it. That was where the rescue team had found him. Mom had set the oxygen level to the lowest setting that would still sustain Geoff. He had slept for nearly thirty hours.

Mom's oxygen had run out after ten.

Both of his parents gave their lives to make sure he lived. And after having his own children and grandchildren Geoff understood how they could.

The shuttle rose above the final rise. Below them, Bastion City sprawled across the surface. Advanced EWEs encompassed the entire settlement. Geoff had dedicated his life to making sure the next settlement worked. He had raised his family there. And now, his children raised their children there.

It was the best way he knew to honor his parents' gift of life.

Apples on the Moon
by Karen T. Smith

"Jack says a freighter drone from Earth's due in tonight, C-Dock," Julia said. She flopped down next to Ali on the bottom bunk of the room they shared. "His cousin is on shift. He said there are . . . apples! And if we bring some credits he can arrange to get us a few, ahead of the rush."

"Apples!" Ali said. Her eyes narrowed. "You're not just saying that to get me to go, are you?" She didn't usually join in Julia's lunar colony adventures.

"No, Jack is positive. If I were telling you something to get you to go, I'd mention that Kofi will be there." Julia winked. "Some of my friends from school too. Interested?"

A mighty battle waged in Ali's head as she considered Julia's proposition. Kofi and apples; what could be better? Kofi was cute, and it had been at least three months since fresh fruit had come through the LuCol docks. But she had Molecular Physics homework due next week. And the thought of going out with all those kids had her a bit nervous. She wasn't as sociable as Julia. Then again, she'd lost two friends to Earthside transfers this term alone. Her pool of acquaintances was shrinking fast.

"You're like a turtle," Mom had said at dinner the other night. "Never sticking your head out to meet new people."

Something clicked into place for Ali at that moment. "I'm not a damn turtle," she said under her breath.

"What?" Julia said.

"Uh, nothing. I want to come. Oh stop it." Ali shook her head as Julia did her best Scarlet O'Hara faint. "I need you to promise me something, though." Ali wore a serious expression as she looked at Julia, who was younger by just eighteen months.

"Sure," Julia said.

"No teasing, okay?"

Julia nodded solemnly and crossed her heart. "On my honor, I swear I won't tease my sister about Kofi's dreamy eyes, curly hair, perfect white teeth, and beautiful skin. At a later time, I will point out the drool that trickled down my sister's oh-so-composed chin, and that little bit of pesto in her teeth." Julia rolled off the bed and fled to the door as Ali made to elbow her in the ribs.

Ali stuck her tongue out at her sister's back and followed, bouncing in the low gravity like second nature. Just to be sure, Ali stopped at the mirror in the hall and checked her teeth.

They came down the hall into the living space of their quarters, and Julia called out, "Ali and I are going out with some kids from school." Their parents looked up from the holo news program.

"Pause," Dad said. The words *Another Airlock Malfunction* floated in midair. The girls paused too.

"Really? Both of you?" Mom couldn't mask the look of surprise on her face.

"Who are you meeting? Where are you going? When will you be back?" Dad said.

"Dad," Julia said, "I'll be fourteen next month, and Ali's almost sixteen. Please, we're not little kids anymore!"

"Uh-huh," Mom said. "It's so hard to have parents that care. So, fess up. Where? Who? When?"

"We're going to the Coffee Depot in C-section. The one by the fabric market," Ali said. Julia looked at her sister with one eyebrow raised. Ali avoided her gaze. She wasn't one to lie much. But, she wasn't about to tell her parents where they were really headed. The docks were technically off-limits to kids. Their parents were sticklers for the rules, even if no one else on LuCol followed them.

"And the who and when parts?" Mom said.

Julia jumped in "We're meeting up with a couple kids from school: Jack, Priya, I think Rune is going to be there, and probably Mayean. We'll be back in a few hours. Do you want us to bring you coffee?"

Nice touch, thought Ali. She felt a little bad about the lie.

"No thanks," Mom said. She looked at Dad.

"None for me either," Dad said. "You girls have enough credits?"

"No need, it's my treat." Ali smiled when Julia gave her a thumbs-up. "The Ampouatas paid me double for the babysitting last night. Those three hellions of theirs kept getting locked in the house airlock. Luckily they couldn't reach the controls and depressurize it. Scared the bejeesus out of me. Thank Sol Mr. Ampouata knows his kids. He made me practice his Engineering Department override codes a dozen times before they left. Full-access codes, pretty sweet. I've got them memorized now. After the third time in the airlock, I stuck the brats in their weighted suits, on a line like new landers. The kids were still like that when the Ampouatas came home."

Mom said, "I remember putting you guys in your weighted suits like that when we first settled up here. That must've been—what—seven years ago? My, how time flies."

"Quick, let's get out of here before she starts reminiscing about our first meal, ready-to-eat." Julia said.

Ali played along, "Oh yes, I remember it well: mashed potatoes the consistency of thin glue, gritty steak, a corn puck. Those were the days."

The girls blew kisses at their parents, linked arms, and skittered down the hallway.

Once outside, they started off to the right, going up a slight slope toward C-section. Their living quarters were below the LuCol docks. A lot of people they knew lived down here, though a few wealthy ones lived topside, like the Ampouatas.

The sisters increased their stride length. They bounded up the halls and Julia waved whenever they passed familiar faces. Ali gave her usual shy smile. It wasn't a big colony. Last month's stats showed about sixty thousand. There were always a few familiar faces in the crowd. Julia said it made sneaking around a pain. What would Ali know? She kept to herself most of the time.

"Where are we meeting up?" said Ali. She scanned the crowd for a certain tall, handsome young man and reminded herself to make eye contact and smile.

"Next to the Coffee Depot like you told Mom and Dad," Julia said. "So you weren't *really* lying back there. I was surprised at you." She followed Ali's glance. "Do you see him yet?"

Ali blushed. "No. Um . . . not yet. Is he definitely coming? You think it's true that he finally broke up with Yuri?"

"Yeah, that's what Priya told me. Can you believe it? They were like the perfect couple."

"I've hardly seen him this term." Ali said. "Probably just as well. I can never think of anything funny or cool to say. I feel like I've got an upholstered tongue when I'm around him."

"I feel like that with Jack sometimes."

"Really?" Ali wasn't sure whether to believe her sister. She always acted so confident and light-hearted.

"You're not the only one with insecurities," Julia said with a shrug.

As they made their way through the crowds, Ali realized in spite of the knot of anxiety in her stomach, it was better than being at home missing out.

The girls rounded a bend into a hub where five or six corridors met. The first one to the right had a long aisle of shops and carts. They paused at the fabric market. "That's new," said Ali. The woman in the window worked with a bolt of brilliant green silk, spreading it out like a pleated fan. "Must have come in with the apples. It's nice to see some color around here."

"You should have Mom make you a dress out of that." Julia said. "Maybe you could get Kofi to ask you to the Waxing dance."

Ali flushed and shook her head. Glad for a diversion, she pulled on Julia's arm. "I see Priya."

"Where?"

"Over there. She's passing the Spice Mill."

"Hola, chica!" they said, almost in unison.

Priya laughed and said, "You two. Honestly, it's like you're twins, the way you talk. Of course, you'd never know it looking at you."

Julia was petite like Mom but thinner in the face, her blonde hair pulled up into a high ponytail. Ali was tall like Dad and had his brown hair and long lashes.

"Yes," said Julia. "I can't imagine where she came from. Probably the airlock repairman's daughter," she said in a loud whisper.

"Except for the part where I look just like Dad," Ali said. "Besides, I know we're sisters, because sometimes I start a sentence . . ."

". . . and I finish it."

Priya moaned in mock agony.

"And sometimes we say the same thing at the same time."

158

"Yes, and that would be much funnier if it weren't the fortieth time I'd heard it this week." Priya said. "Come on, I thought I saw some of the guys at the Depot."

Ali's heart rate quickened, she felt nervous and a little giddy. She repeated "I'm not a turtle," to herself a few times, which had a calming effect.

They followed Priya. Her bright pink sari billowed behind her. Soon they saw Jack and Kofi in the corridor just beyond the Coffee Depot, and heard Jack give a whoop. Kofi was mid-bounce, at least fifteen feet in the air. Ali noticed his bright red zoings. The high-bounce shoes were the latest craze on the Moon, but could only be bought earthside and droned up to the Moon. They must have cost a fortune.

"Hi," Jack said. He gave each girl a kiss on the cheek, the standard lunar hello. "You all look lovely this evening."

"Ah, such a charmer you are," Julia said. When he came to her, she pinched him on the arm.

"Nice to see you," Kofi was back on the ground now. Ali reminded herself to breathe as his eyes met hers. Maybe she was imagining that his gaze lingered longer on her. Kofi gave Priya and Julia a quick peck, then came over to Ali. As he leaned down to kiss her, Ali's skin began to tingle with anticipation. She felt his warm breath on her cheek. The ritual hello kiss was half the reason she wanted to come.

Just before his lips landed, Julia said, "Oh, look who's coming." Ali turned her head reflexively at her sister's voice, which caused Kofi's kiss to land awkwardly in the spot where her jaw and ear connected. *Damn damn damn!* Still, her skin felt super-heated from the kiss. She closed her eyes for a moment to enjoy the sensation. When she opened her eyes, she saw Yuri and Mayean flit toward them. Yuri didn't look happy to see her. Mayean called loud greetings from down the hall, drawing attention to herself, just the way she liked it. It looked to Ali like Kofi avoided looking at Yuri, but the boys offered the ritual hello to the newcomers all the same. Ali turned her head so she didn't have to watch.

After the greetings, Jack said, "I think this is everyone who's coming. Rune bailed. Something about matzo-ball soup, I have no idea. Let's head over to the dock."

Ali maneuvered next to Kofi, surprised at her boldness. Yuri walked in front with Mayean and, whenever Kofi wasn't looking, shot dark looks back at Ali. Mayean regaled the group with a story about the new pair of zoings her father had ordered from Earthside. Ali racked her brain for something witty to say to Kofi. She gave up and said the first stupid thing that came to mind. "So how are your classes this term?"

"Good enough." He said. "I've got McAdams for Nutritional Botany, though, and that's pretty tortuous. Last week it was a rare bacterium in the hydroponics lab that wasn't even listed on the Lunar net—had to go Earthside for it. Don't we have paid scientists working on this stuff?"

"They must be pretty desperate if they're using students!" Ali said. "Though, don't you think it's kind of cool you're working on real world problems? I can't seem to get that through Mr. Grunter's head in Molecular Physics. Why we're still proving the Becker Theorems is beyond me."

"Oh yeah, I had him last term. I can ping you my notes if you want."

Ali was relieved at how easily the conversation flowed. She didn't even mind Yuri's glares, much.

When they reached C-Dock, Jack detached from the group and went over to one of the dockhands working at a terminal in the corner. It didn't look like much, but anything that couldn't be grown or made on the Moon came through one of these docks. Jack and the dockhand clapped each other on the back. They talked for a minute, then went over to a stack of crates.

Jack came back juggling three red apples, a wide grin on his face. "Look! Fresh from New Zealand! Juicy and delicious." He took a bite out of one, and juggled the other two with his right hand.

Julia lunged for one of the apples.

"My cousin says it's ten credits per. Scan your print!" He pointed to the fingerprint scanner by the terminal in the corner.

"What? You didn't get those for me? I thought we had something special." Julia said.

"S'allright, sis, I got you covered. Though ten credits, ouch." Ali said.

"Yeah," Jack said, "Prices have gone up a lot in the last year. Bad parasite wiped out the entire Washington crop. They're paying as much as three credits each earthside."

Kofi let out a low whistle. "That's amazing."

"Yeah, well I bet they don't get their soy paste for free like we do." Mayean leaned over and pretended to vomit.

Ali scanned her fingerprint at the wall-mount and pulled two apples from the crate the dockworker held. "Thanks," she said.

"They're really good, aren't they?" he said.

"Haven't you had any?"

"Nah, not much room in the budget on dockworker's pay." He said, and flashed her a grin. Ali's stomach did a little dip. He was cute. He stood a full head taller than she did, she almost felt short for once. His dark brown hair was cut close, and he had the bluest eyes she'd ever seen.

"Too busy spending it, right?" Jack fake-punched the dockworker. "Oliver, meet my friends. Friends, meet my cousin Oliver."

Oliver smiled again. Before long, there was no talking as the kids bit into their apples. Mayean put a dozen into a zip-bag she had brought for this purpose.

"Here," Ali said. "Try this." She held her half-eaten apple up to Oliver. There was that smile again. Funny how it made her a bit weak in the knees, she thought, feeling confused. She stole a glance at Kofi. He licked juice from his fingers, oblivious to the exchange.

Oliver gave her a little wink, "OK, but you know in some cultures this might mean we're married." Ali blushed. He took the apple from her hand, brushing against her fingers a bit more than necessary. She watched him pretend to take an enormous bite, then settle for a normal-sized one. His eyes crinkled as his jaw worked up and down. He took a deep breath and closed his eyes, savoring the last of the bite. He opened them and bowed deeply to her.

"Thank you for such a lovely treat." As Oliver handed back the apple, his hand lingered on her arm for just a second. It wasn't long enough to draw attention, but Ali noticed and felt a shiver up her back.

"You're welcome." she said as Oliver headed back to his work across the room. Her throat felt tight. *Why am I getting all worked up over Jack's cousin? . . . I like Kofi.* Julia looked over just then. She locked eyes with Ali asking an unspoken question. Ali shook her head and shrugged. They'd be up late tonight talking anyway. They'd rehash every detail, make wild projections about everyone's motivations, and complain about Mayean and Yuri.

As if on cue, Mayean announced "Hey, I bet my zoings came in on this shipment." She turned to a dockhand nearby. "Did regular post come in with the drone?" She batted her eyes at him. It looked to Ali like an obvious ploy for his attention. *God forbid anyone detract from Mayean's center of gravity.*

"Hmm, yeah I think so, but I think the guys had to store the post for the night. The post crew clocked out before the drone landed."

Mayean glanced at the dockhand's nametag and said, "Ivan, can we go look for my package, please?" She shimmied her shoulders in such a way that the front of her shirt slipped down a bit.

Good god, has she no shame?

The lack of shame was a good ploy, because Ivan had to work to rip his gaze from her. He paused, then said, "I suppose it wouldn't hurt if you went in and looked for your package." He looked at a terminal, "It was stored in Airlock F, that's down the hall a little further. I'll unlock it for you. Get in and get out fast, OK?"

"Awesome! Let's go!" Mayean said.

Ali trailed behind the group. She'd had enough of the airlocks last night with the Ampouata brats. She liked oxygen. A lot. Right when they got to the airlock, Julia turned to Ali and said, "How well did the Ampouatas pay? Can you get us a few more apples?"

"Well, I have enough credits for another four, but you're going to owe me." Ali wondered if the look of relief on her face was obvious to the rest of the group.

"What do you say, Jack? Can you take Ali back to your cousin to buy a few more apples? We'll help Mayean find her precious cargo."

"Sure thing," Jack said.

Jack and Ali headed back to C-Dock, and it occurred to Ali that maybe this was all a Julia scheme to give her a few minutes with Oliver.

Jack waved to his cousin when they entered the dock area. Ali took a good look at Oliver, trying to figure out what was different about him, why she was so interested. He was lean and fit, but what was different, hard to pin down. He had a confident air about him, he knew what he was doing.

Oliver smiled as he walked over. "I knew you couldn't keep her away," he said to Jack, while looking straight at Ali. She felt small under his intense gaze, but forced herself to look at him. He was teasing her. He didn't even look away when Ivan came back into the dock. She felt a surge of power, a new feeling for her.

She mulled over her possible responses. She settled for a smile, and the truth. "Yes, you're that irresistible. Spending time with you is preferable to being centimeters from the vacuum of space with this self-centered . . ."

Jack drew back in mock-surprise, "Ali, I thought you liked Kofi."

Ali blushed and looked down. She scrambled to think of a flippant remark that would dull the impact of Jack's words. After what seemed like a long time, Jack said, "I'm just joking. I know it's Mayean that's your Best Friend Forever." He laughed and Oliver joined in. Ali let the laughter wash over her and felt better.

Ali said, "You know, she's okay when she's not bragging about being rich and important. Since she does that all the time, I don't have a lot of patience for her."

Jack was about to reply when a piercing alarm rang out through the dock. Oliver looked at his terminal and swore. Before Ali could blink, Oliver was out the door. The other dockhands swarmed near them. Jack and Ali followed Oliver. The dockhands were filing out the door and down the corridor. Everyone was headed in the direction of the airlocks. Ali was confused. There were people rushing in from all directions, more than just the dockworkers now. She saw a medic, a mechanic. The alarm was loud and piercing. It got louder. She put her hands to her ears, trying to block it out.

Oliver stabbed at the controls on a door. His fingers typed codes in a blur, his brow was pulled down into a deep frown. It dawned on her that all the attention was focused on the door where she had left her little sister a few minutes before. The age difference magnified when she was worried about Julia. Ali started to panic, grabbed onto Jack's arm. "What's happening?" She had to yell over the alarm.

"I don't know. It looks like something's gone wrong with the airlock." Jack took her by the shoulders as she started to push forward into the crowd. "Ali, we've got to stay out of their way. Oliver's the best."

Ali didn't really hear him as she strained forward. *Her sister. Her best friend. The only person in the world who mattered.* The blood pounded in her ears. She heard the buzz of the throng of people now gathered at the door. The alarm continued to pierce like a knife. How much time had passed? She tried to compute, gave up.

Stupid stupid! You finally go out. Spend all your time flirting. If something happens to Julia . . . She didn't let herself complete the thought. Instead, she pushed through the crowd like she was on fire. *The override codes!*

"Oliver, I've got override codes memorized," she yelled through the noise. "Engineering ones, full access!" The crowd parted and she was at his side in an instant. She typed in a sequence, and a gasp went through the crowd as the airlock door hissed open. Oliver was through it and back out moments later with Priya's limp body in his arms. But her focus was on her sister. "Medic!" he called. He lay the prone figure in the hall.

Ali followed Oliver back in. "Julia!" she said, trying to keep the panic out of her voice.

A soft moan. Julia was slumped down on a bench. Her face was completely white, but her eyes were open and she was breathing. Ali went to her side, wrapped Julia's arm around her shoulder, and helped her to her feet, then half-carried her sister out the airlock door.

Julia crumpled into a heap in the wide corridor, still flooded with people. Ali looked her over, concern in her eyes. Oliver was in and out a few more times. Ali hardly noticed the lifeless bodies in the hall as another medic arrived and resuscitation began.

"Are you OK?" Ali asked. She needed to hear Julia's voice.

Julia replied with a nod, and started to cry. She struggled for air between sobs. Ali rubbed her shoulder and made comforting noises. Her senses started to come back. Ali looked at the medics and the kids lying on the floor. "What the hell happened?" she said. She spoke in a thick whisper. She didn't expect an answer just yet. She saw Yuri's feet move a little, and saw Kofi sitting against the far wall, head ducked between his knees. A medic fitted an oxygen mask over his ears. Mayean and Priya were still lying motionless on the floor. The medics worked with intensity.

"I . . . I . . . don't know." Julia said. She regained her composure. Makeup streaked down her face in dark charcoal lines. "One minute we're all talking about nothing, digging through the piles of post, the next Yuri's talking about some airlock game she's heard about. Says you can get a rush if you cut off the air supply in an airlock. Better than Ecstasy, she claims; though how she'd know is anyone's guess. I was about to tell her off, but Kofi thought it would be fun. Before I knew it, one of them had hit the switch."

"Holy Sol," was all Ali could think to say. She felt a welling of rage inside her. "Then what?"

"I gulped a big breath. It went fast, maybe thirty seconds and I started to feel faint. Most of them had passed out already, they looked terrified. Idiots didn't even take a deep breath first, or come up with a plan for once the supposed rush was done. I was too far away. I couldn't get to the switch. I don't think I passed out, but maybe I did for a second. Next thing I knew Oliver was through the door. He must have tripped on Priya. I think she conked her head on a bench when she went down. She was acting all nonchalant but I think she was scared witless. How did you guys get here so fast?"

"An alarm rang at the dock—the whole place emptied. Oliver was the first out. I don't really know what happened, I was freaking out."

Jack joined them, and a medic kneeled in front of Julia with oxygen. "Freaking out, my ass. Ali ran a manual override! She had full-access Engineering codes. Thank Sol! Airlocks aren't supposed to depressurize so easily." Jack studied Ali's face a moment. "Come to think of it, where'd you get those codes?"

Ali explained about the Ampouata brats, and resolved not to call them brats anymore. The little beasties had trained her well.

"How are the others?"

"Priya's got a nasty gash on her head, but otherwise looks OK," Jack said. "Yuri and Kofi are fine, scared, but fine. Mayean has been out a long time. The medics are still working on her."

"Yuri and Kofi aren't going to be fine when I'm done with them," Ali said, her jaw set.

"What do you mean?" Jack didn't know.

"Julia says it was Yuri's idea, and Kofi went along with it. Some kind of buzz, damn stupid idea, too. Deprive your brain of oxygen and get a rush at the cost of what—a few IQ points? A few minor motor functions? What if Mayean is really hurt? And Priya—how bad is the gash? How much blood did she lose?" The words tumbled out of Ali at a rapid clip. She started to get up. For the second time that evening, Jack held her by the shoulders.

"Ali," he said.

It was her turn for gut-wrenching sobs. Her body shook as Jack held her against his shoulder.

"Crap, Jack. I stained your shirt," Ali's voice was shaky as she pulled away a minute later. "What?" she said. Jack had an odd expression on his face.

"I'm, uh, trying to suppress the urge to kiss you right now," Jack said. "It's a bit of a problem since I have a thing for your sister. You're really cute, know that?" He wore a quirky smile. "I think my cousin would kick my ass if I even tried, though. Have you seen him looking over here every five seconds?"

Ali felt a warm flush creep up her neck. She pulled away from Jack and wiped the tears from her cheeks. "Uh, no, hadn't noticed." The feeling of self-consciousness overwhelmed her. While she worked to regain composure, Ali avoided looking at Oliver. *Not a turtle.* She had to look up.

Oliver stood over her, arm outstretched to help her up. She took his strong hand, and felt his calluses and warmth. He pulled her to his chest and enveloped her in a hug. She was surprised at how well she fit there. After a long moment, they each pulled away. His eyes searched her face. Then they turned to Julia, still sitting on the floor, now wearing an oxygen mask. She talked quietly with Jack who held her hand.

"So what happened exactly?" Oliver asked. "You were amazing."

Ali recounted Julia's story, explained about the override codes, and about Yuri and Kofi's idea of a good time. After she finished talking, Oliver excused himself. Ali saw him talking to one of the LuCol police. He pointed toward Yuri and Kofi. She quizzed him with her eyes as he came back.

"I don't think they're going to pull another stunt like that." Oliver said. "Oh, and their parents are probably going to have coronaries over the bill. Bogus emergencies are no laughing matter. They bill for emergency services when the root cause is negligence or vandalism."

Ali took a small bit of pleasure in the resolution. She wondered what she ever saw in Kofi. *How could anyone be that stupid?*

"So," Ali said. She looked at Oliver, then at Jack and Julia. "When are you done working? Want to get a coffee?" And, to her surprise, she didn't even blush.

Black Ice
by F.R.R. Mallory

Paul Pepperdine leaned closer to his monitor, as if to coach greater detail out of its picture, as he slowed the forward movement of his camera to match the reduced speed of the Zamboni as it approached the Dirty Ice Siding. The ice machine spread wide where the two rails split apart, shaving the ice on either side of the rails so that the transition looked seamless. It looked seamless. Pepper frowned at the screen, trying to find a defect that should be big as life.

The Zamboni reached its maximum width and paused before easing back along its cleaned surface. At the apogee of the curve its portside blades pivoted up and the Zamboni re-positioned itself starting at the narrow wedge where the siding rail had interrupted the main line. It started forward again and for a moment Pepper panned the camera lens down over the section where the two rails met. To his eye they looked perfect. The ice to either side bore the glassy smoothness of the Zamboni's passage. No rocks, no debris. The rails looked even and the transition smooth. There was nothing to explain why 38 tons of ice had derailed at this exact spot less than three hours earlier.

On the Moon, Ice was Life.

He leaned back in his chair as the camera returned to auto and sped along the wake of the mindless Zamboni, shaving and melting its way across the ice from Peary Tube, past the two dozen sidings that spread like fingers into the blackness of Peary Crater's eternal night.

Adder wouldn't like it. With no break in the rail or debris at the siding, that left a single conclusion. It meant Adder had run the ice into the main rail at too high a speed, a derailment which had shut down the line for three hours at a cost none of the cutters would want to hear, especially a hothead

167

like Adder.

Pepper chose the coward's way of telling Adder. He toggled the com to open and broadcast that the Zamboni was clear of Dirty Ice Siding with the rail testing clean and open.

"Lying bastard!" Adder's voice pierced the com, much like the ice pick he'd used to kill the three men Earth side, which had sent him to death row and eventually to the Moon.

Pepper shuddered and continued, "Camera footage available on channel 28." He didn't address Adder personally. It was just a report, just data. He shoved his chair back from his desk as static from the speaker told him Adder was holding the com open with one of his thick, tattooed fingers. For a second Pepper could picture Adder's hand grabbing him by the throat to squeeze the life out of him. Bile soured his mouth.

"You need a woman, Adder." A new voice crackled over the speaker, another cutter by the sound of it. "Can't be plowing the main rail like that, it ain't got no cushion for your pushin." Laughter erupted as other cutters macked their coms open to join in. "Yeah, you rotten bastard, take a two day off that wreck of a rig you call a home."

Pepper sighed but relaxed a slight bit. He knew Adder would still be fuming but the camera footage would have already been reviewed and he didn't have to state the conclusion the other cutters thought was obvious. The cost could just show up as auto withdrawals on Adder's account. Nothing personal. No disrespect of one of the scariest convicts on the moon. He switched off the feed as the cutters went to gossiping among themselves about what might be in the latest Earth side shipment still being offloaded behind the blast wall at the far end of the track. With containers on the ground the incident became little more than a bar joke to tease Adder with.

Pepper wanted to leave it at that. It happened. Men out there in the black saw the world through ice eyes and ice minds and sometimes coming out of the blind gave them ecstasy like the light was heaven. Maybe they were as near to God as they were likely to get. But Adder hadn't sounded ice happy and it was Pepper's job to keep the rail clean. He felt like he'd missed something. With the emergency averted or at least shelved he limped out of the grim room that housed his particular set of computers. A pillbox, he thought, for the millionth time, he worked in the equivalent of a concrete underground pillbox.

Earth called the Moon's first colony the City of Eternal Light. Locals called it the Peary Tube because it was a reformed lava tube between Peary Crater and Little Big Crater. It was a monster size tube more than forty meters wide, ten meters tall and running under the Moon's surface for six usable kilometers. Early miners cut light shafts through the 65 feet of Regolith crust as a constant free light source. In the 50 years since, the locals had determined the constant light created a form of sunlight affective disorder contributing to agitation, insomnia and suicide. It was like an eyeball always watching and the locals got to calling the shafts the 26 Eyes of God.

Pepper lived adjacent to Sleepy Eye, a shaft which had suffered a partial cave-in between its transparent aluminum panels several years before Pepper arrived. He got 'the shaft' because he was considered a new arrival with limited prospects. Five years underground with minimal likelihood he'd ever tramp about the surface made him a gimp pearydog. He was gimp for his post polio syndrome muscular weakness and a pearydog for living full time in an underground hole. He still liked the sunlight that flooded several hundred yards of the tube from what was left of the shaft.

It wasn't good grow light though. It was too hard and it still tricked his eyes with the way it created ink black shadows. Everything was stark in Moon sunlight, unforgiving and naked. He stumped from shade patch to shade patch as his eyes dilated with the extreme shifts in light. They sold sunglasses that moderated the light. He owned a pair but habitually left them on the sink in his bathroom. The shaft light strobed his eyeballs until his desperation to escape the visual torment produced his equivalent of a run in the light gravity making him an ungainly and awkward sight which added new pain and embarrassment to his thoughts. The moon had promised to free him from the near immobility of his disease. A promise it kept, but he was as much disabled here as he had been on Earth. Now he could walk but everyone else could nearly fly.

As if to accentuate the morose of his thinking three young people leapt, flew and bounded past him, laughing while words like freak escaped behind them. Pepper want to curse after them, make any one of them feel the shrivel of healthy limbs. Let them become for a minute the pariah people looked away from, the hurt of old friends no longer returning phone calls because polio was contagious in their thin memory, unaware that post polio couldn't be caught. Bitterness soured his mouth again.

His hand was twisting the key in his door lock when the emotion of his thoughts drained away leaving him with the same nagging feeling; he was missing something. He turned to look after the now distant forms of the young people; so far down the tube they had entered the shade, their bodies now graceful dancers in the half-light glow of the central tube's perpetual dawn. What was it about them? His gaze followed them until shadows consumed them into suggestions of movement. Town. The central part of the tube was more than a kilometer of housing and shops divided by the natural looking but very artificial stream that continuously recycled through the center.

Low-light gardens flourished on the banks of the stream under the radiation-doctored grow lights of the central shafts. Town smelled good. It produced high quality oxygen and abundant raw foods. He could find a café and pay for dinner. See people. Some might even talk to him, they might pretend an interest in news from the ice or they would ask him about the delivery schedule for the latest shipment from Earth and what would he see? Women he couldn't have, relationships he would only lust for as they politely turned away. Convicts had better prospects than the disabled, even here, even if his problem wasn't genetic and wouldn't pass to children. He turned back to his door to discover his hands were shaking.

"Heard you had some excitement today." Anna Seiko's voice preceded her from the same office pillbox where he worked. He always wondered how she knew when he left or when he arrived and why she bothered to talk to him at all. Still, he lowered his shaking hands and turned to face her. He'd heard she chose the Moon, followed her father as part of a convict family enhancement incentive. At forty she already had children and a former domestic partner she'd refused to marry. The cutters gossiped about her and sometimes he listened in as they exchanged schemes on how to gain her intimate acquaintance. She knew the way of things with the Moon. It never managed to attract enough women to get near 40%, much less half the population.

"Derailment." He swallowed, wishing he could step into the shade without stepping, without showing his disability. The stark sunlight of the shaft caught his doorway full on, drying him out like a dehydrator. And he figured it didn't help his features any either. Direct downward light made every man look Neanderthal.

"Got a power play or someone ice happy?" She glided up to just that bit too close where he could smell the sweetness of her, a new torment for a man who hadn't touched a woman in more than a decade.

"The ice is clean." He answered, and then realized he hadn't really answered her. "Adder didn't seem ice happy."

Anna shaded her eyes and looked up at him.

It surprised him to realize she was shorter than he was. Somehow her presence always felt bigger, as if she carried part of the world with her, part of the mass of an Earth lost to both of them now.

"I'm making you stand in the light." He felt his face flush. She would move on now. Courtesy complete she would glide in the fast Moon way down the sidewalk and into the life that flourished in town. He fumbled with his key in his fingers.

"I'll step inside for a beverage." She answered.

Pepper blinked hard for a moment, as if wetting his eyeballs would sharpen his hearing. A visitor? Better still a woman visitor?

He fumbled with the lock again, this time trying to recall if he'd dumped his laundry in the bin or left any food bits on the table. The door opened, answering his internal queries with a disappointing yes.

"Sorry. I didn't expect . . ." He lurched forward and did his best to wave her past him and into the expansiveness of his private quarters. The Moon didn't stint on space. He had a comfortable lounge, open concept kitchen, handicapped bathroom and comfortable bedroom with both the lounge and bedroom with doors out onto a fountain courtyard. Every residence maintained such courtyards both to help circulate water and as a replacement for view windows. It was some Moon engineer's answer to claustrophobia and for the most part it worked.

Anna strode past him to the kitchen, gathering a handful of dirty dishes off the eat-on counter. He tried to follow her, intending to stop her from seeing his mess but she didn't stop or move away when he joined her at the sink, to even more dishes. She found the plug and as his embarrassment increased she began to fill the sink with soapy water.

"No need for that." He tried to pull her away. He touched her upper arm. Then he was too close again. Her clean scent disrupted his thoughts. The firmness of her arm muscle under his fingers suggested more.

"If Adder wasn't ice happy and the ice was clean then what are you thinking?"

For a long moment he couldn't fathom the meaning of her words, they seemed to come from another planet and made not the least bit of sense.

"Huh?" he blurted.

"The derailment." Anna glanced over at him exactly as if she found nothing out of the ordinary in his behavior.

"Oh right." Pepper collected himself. Maybe she had a thing for dishes or maybe she got off on charity to the disabled. He wanted to hate her and mostly he wanted to stop sniffing at the air where she stood, trying to imprint her body odor into his memory. "Adder." His mind flitted back over the derailment details.

"I keep thinking I missed something." The words escaped him before he thought how it might sound.

"Like what?" She was neatly stacking his now clean dishes in the dry rack and wiping at the counter, circling him in a way both natural and comfortable.

"I have some lemonade." His mind finally caught up with her request for a beverage allowing him to open the under counter fridge for the glass carafe. When he turned back she'd placed two glasses on the counter and was moving on to wipe off the entire counter. It gave him a chance to pour, even with his shaky hands. He didn't spill any. She arrived back at his side before he could offer her a glass. Instead she took both and slid them across the counter to spots in front of his barstools, followed by the carafe.

"Like what?" She repeated.

He swallowed another huh and stumbled around the counter wondering why his leg muscles felt weaker than normal. Was he having some kind of relapse? Rescued from his thoughts by the barstool he sat down.

"Adder." He repeated, all the while watching her settle on his second stool exactly like they'd been old friends and this were a common occurrence. He looked away from the confidence of her. "Adder wasn't ice happy and he seemed damned sure he hadn't rammed the rail."

"What did you miss?" Her tone was fluid, inviting, like a confidant.

Pepper contracted inside. Her first words to him, what had she said? "Was it a power play?" He mentally kicked himself. Convict politics, always playing the angles with secretive alliances and blood feuds as the families jockeyed for position in any way they felt might profit them the most. The disabled and volunteers remained the minority in the moon population.

"Probably nothing. The shaft might be getting to me." He took a deeper drink from his glass. Maybe he could touch her arm again, pretend to stumble against her. It sounded cheap and a bit dirty, even in his mind.

"Most of Adder's generation are gone now. He's been out on the ice twenty-five years and unfriendly to boot. A lot of guys would like his contract." She left the thought open.

But Pepper knew that most men wouldn't be able to find the ice that Adder brought in. It wasn't like a man could lower a cutter anywhere in the crater and come up with pristine black cubes so clean it could be separated into top grade rocket fuel with minimal loss. And Adder would notice anyone trying to spy on his claims, wouldn't he?

"Contract is only as valuable as the man working it." Pepper risked eye contact with her again. So she might be playing an angle. Who was he to judge her motives for sharing a beverage with him in his home?

"My dad says the last three containers surface dropped all had bins of satellites and tech debris from near Earth orbit. He said some of that was old time spy stuff and a man might get some of it to work again, if he were computer savvy and say worked technical, like you or me."

Pepper tried to figure out if Anna was offering him a job or just stating one of the many rumors he too had been hearing. He took another drink of his lemonade. Moon duplicity was a high stakes game, one he'd fallen prey to when he signed on. He was shown footage of a primitive moon base depicted like a rugged wild west boomtown of the 1800s. The ads invited him to share the romance of being part of the solution to a population expansion into space. He could be a man on the Moon. He could make a difference. It was a fabrication the locals carefully manufactured when they marketed the Moon to future residents. Collectively they were in the business of milking as many resources from Earth as possible while never letting on that they'd long since crossed into sustainable and were expanding their goals toward the control of space traffic.

"I'd heard as much, at least about the bins. I haven't seen any bits and pieces though." He glared down at his empty glass.

"Well, if someone was, looking to jump a claim—you're the only eyes out there, Paul."

That she knew his real name shocked him, as did the realization that she might be giving him a warning.

"My cameras are limited to the cables' ranges." Even as he said it he knew it wasn't accurate. He generally only looked at the rails. That was his job.

"The cutters think you are 'the man.'" Anna finished off her glass and instead of rising to leave she refilled both of them.

Pepper flinched. 'The Man' was as close to the word enemy as it got out here. "I'm just trying to have a life."

"If you're not a con or hooked up with one, then you're 'the man.'" Anna repeated.

She didn't have to be sitting on his stool telling him anything. That was the thought he clung to, as his sense of personal security seemed to ooze out every pore of his body. No one had approached him to look at any space junk so he wasn't on the inside of a claim jump. Why would he be a target?

His mind filled with an image of Adder squeezing him by the throat and then shaking him till he was dead. Then the bastard would harvest his water and compost the rest of him to sell to the gardeners. He rubbed his hand over his throat.

"My dad says only 'the man' would live this far up in the oldest part of the tube and you've stayed here for five years listening in and peeking in on all kinds of electronic traffic. People figure you know things . . . secrets."

Pepper faced her more deliberately. That meant she was consorting with 'the man' too. Someone would have seen her enter his home, would be gossiping about their conversation, maybe even listening in. Her presence, wasn't that a type of intentional presentation?

"Who are you showing me off to today?" The words hurt, even as he spoke them.

Anna held his gaze. "Adder will think twice before stomping down here frothing with disrespect and retribution."

Pepper felt his gut tighten. She shouldn't smell good, not when she was talking like she was buying him off the shelf at a corner store. She couldn't want him, not on a personal level but it sure felt like she was marking her territory.

"You can't afford to be a convict's bitch though, Paul, and they won't give you much time now to throw the first punch."

She slid off his stool and leaned close to him. "Think about it."

He thought back on women he'd known before polio crippled him. They didn't like a man they could get with a sultry look. They wanted to think the man didn't want them. He slid off his own stool knowing she expected him to kiss her or touch her, the gimp being thrown a breadcrumb. How long had her family been setting him up? He leisurely brushed his body against hers, just enough to watch her assume the position of expected contact. Instead he lightly grasped her upper arm, steering her toward the door. He thought she gasped, felt the slight stumble of her feet. He didn't look down into her face, not wanting to crumble in front of her.

"I enjoyed sharing a beverage with you, Anna." He kept his tone light and a bit bored. He saw a flicker of confusion on her face before she was standing outside and he was shutting the door on her. He sagged back against the wall, his leg muscles tenderly close to collapse. Her scent surrounded him . . . moist, as if a part of her remained, touching him.

Insomnia tortured his evening and no matter how he adjusted his black-out curtains they always seemed to find some way to gap, allowing fingers of light into his bedroom. Even if Anna had ulterior motives her advice had been sound. Convicts lived by establishing and maintaining a reputation. If you avoided conflict they saw it as weakness. If you didn't belong somewhere then by default you belonged to authority. He should have seen it earlier, should have understood why other newcomers stayed in the old housing units for only a short time before finding elsewhere to go.

Why hadn't he tried to move? They were constantly building deeper into the tube so housing was plentiful. He'd told himself being close to work meant less walking, less presentation to people of how broken he was. He didn't want them staring at him and what if things got worse and he couldn't manage the distance? Sure, he could probably rig a scooter. Excuses. All his reasoning came down to thin excuses. Now his lack of engagement and interaction with the locals was turning on him.

His restless night became a tired, irritable morning. He left his house early, uncomfortably alert to every sound and movement along his short walk to work. Only four people worked the front end of the tube regularly and all of them carried an emergency beeper in case something failed. They were their own backup. Including Anna and himself, that left only Toby Feist and Manuel Gonzales. Both of them worked the water recyclers and clarifiers. Anna handled communications with Peary Station and ran interface with the loose network of tube politicians. He expected she would be considered a PR person Earth side, but on the Moon her job extended, like everyone's did, into doing what needed to get done. Pepper was entering the pill box when he saw what looked like the same group of young people racing past him on the other side of the stream, still jumping and yelling at each other and mocking him as they passed him by. By the time he slammed the thick metal door closed on the computer center he'd convinced himself that Anna's paranoia was ridiculous. He was still the same disabled guy who worked in one of the lowest jobs on the Moon. Nobody wanted a piece of that, of him.

However, he didn't have to be such an easy target for any stray woman who crossed his path either. He powered up his main computer and surfed to the tube's community website. There were half a dozen ads for housing available and he quickly signed up to tour two of them after work. After hitting the button he pushed his chair back and realized he was quivering, like it was some big deal. He ran both hands through his hair and regretted not bothering to wash and shave. His hair was too long and the absence of a shower made him feel gritty. Free water was the great luxury and necessity of life on the Moon. Residents were encouraged to bath or frolic or otherwise de-dust themselves as often as three times a day. Pepper knew it reduced mechanical problems as well as improving air quality but for him, it was all about getting rid of the grit. "Damn." He brushed at his arms, as if scattering fine dust onto his keyboard was an intelligent decision.

"You didn't even bother to check to see who is managing those houses." Anna's voice made him jump, until he realized she'd backdoored his computer's microphone and camera. That level of security penetration made him feel violated.

"You don't have the right to snoop in my computer." He scowled at the screen.

"Really?" She was only using audio on return so he couldn't see her and that didn't seem fair either. Plus, he wasn't sure if she had authority or not. Authority was very gray on the Moon.

"It's rude."

"Well it's stupid not to know who might be your new landlord, don't you think?"

He did think and again she was right and it annoyed him. "So maybe I need a little stupid to get things done. Pleasant as it is to have my morning violated by another employee, you will understand that I need to get back to work now." He disconnected the feed and changed his login and passwords. Maybe she could see that too.

He didn't want to work. He didn't want to sit in his gray pill box of a life arguing with a blank screen female and her detached voice. If the Zamboni or the cutters had a problem, they could beep him, right?

But first, he needed a shower. The downstairs bathroom had a wet room to die for and there were coveralls left for anyone caught without a change of clothes. Fight the dust. He would be an environmental warrior and then maybe find something reasonable to eat. Stumping awkwardly down the stairs he had time to regret what he'd said to Anna. Ten minutes into the best shower of his life he'd decided to make it up to her and bring her some fresh fruit. That set him to humming and he didn't immediately notice when a second set of showers announced the presence of another person. Then the second shower cut off as the persistence of a beep announced an emergency. Pepper's mood headed south until he realized the beeper wasn't his. By then his shower had cut off too and he could hear someone's com crackle to life, making him an accidental eavesdropper.

"That bastard isn't going to levy my account. Once they get a hook in they're like vampires eating a man's soul." ... pause ... "Yeah, well he'll see me all right cause I'm too old to fall for a jump on my claim."

Through the wisping steam Pepper couldn't avoid the certainty that the man in the next shower was Adder and the bastard he was talking about was Pepper.

With his legs in his coveralls and his shoes in his arms, Pepper was edging to the door when his beeper went off. He scrambled, trying to find the thing before Adder got interested. His beeper, now under a pile of clothes on the floor chose that moment to switch to open com, the distinctive crackle of a cutter communication with a man yelling, ". . . the damn main rail flipped my load, clean through Dirty Ice my ass . . ."

Pepper looked up into the red, tattoo-covered face of Adder, both men holding their communicators in hand.

"Got another one." Pepper wanted for a whole set of legs with muscles that could respond and leap and flee and somewhere invincible to flee to.

"You stood there an peeped my conversation, didn't you?" Adder stepped closer.

The man was old, his tattoos bleeding into wet-comic-strip blurs. His skin with that thin papery look and fine sags that hid shrinking muscles. UV bombardment outside hadn't done him any favors but the isolation cons were the ones who couldn't stay underground, in a hole as they called it. Life was in the super cold, in the tractor rigs they called home, cutting the ice for fun, profit and the freedom of living unobserved by anyone but the dark gods of deep craters.

"Didn't mean to." Pepper straightened his own body as much as he could. "Did you mean to peep mine?" Equity between men. He needed to keep Adder thinking he was a man, not a snitch.

Adder's eyes narrowed. "What are you doing down here when you're supposed to be watching the loads?"

"Man's gotta shower." Pepper stumped toward the stairs, shrugging one arm into the sleeve of his coverall. Adder could jump him, could club him from behind, could break him up into firewood but he wasn't going to roll over and beg for him.

Adder grunted.

Pepper made his slow way up the stairs, certain with each breath that he would die before his exhale, only to discover he was still alive. By the last step he discovered he had a companion in the hastily clad, still dripping Adder. Not touching him. Not even bumping him.

Pepper didn't try to prevent Adder from entering the computer room, even though he knew it violated some rules. It was better to bend those rules than kick-start whatever Adder intended to do to him. He put on his shoes and adjusted the coveralls to the best fit while waiting for his additional computers to power fully up. Then he forgot about Adder because Randy Fox had dumped a load right where Adder had and the robot tractor was still recharging its batteries and wouldn't be available for another twelve hours putting the rail down at least that long.

Pepper ran the tower footage at maximum detail. Even slowed down what he saw didn't make sense. The load was running the rail fine and then it toppled only there wasn't anything out there that could topple a load. No wind, no rain, no flying objects.

"Is that what mine looked like?" Adder interrupted his thoughts.

"What? No. Here . . ." Pepper punched up the tower footage on Adder's load. It didn't look too fast. The load entered the curve with appropriate compensation and angle and then it popped, throwing ice fragments back while the giant cubes fell right on top of the main rail.

"What was that?" Adder pointed at the popped spot.

"This is our best resolution." Pepper answered. "Maybe a band broke or the ice cracked in a weird way. I've seen some weird stuff when the loads round the corners."

"That's no band." Adder hovered behind Pepper's chair. "That looks like a projectile hit."

A projectile? Pepper switched back to current view with the toppled load of ice fragmented out like enormous glass blocks. He was supposed to shut the rail down for a manual inspection; that was his job but he kept staring at the pile of dimly lit ice. Back before the polio he'd enjoyed interactive detective fiction which was full of who done it and why scenarios, a hobby not supported by the moon's network. He was rusty. If all this happened in one of his games he'd be looking for what was missing.

What did he know? The rail went down twice in two days—no coincidence. Adder was standing behind him. When was the last time Adder left topside? Anna made a point of talking with him, warning him. Out there on the black ice cutters were stuck with loads they couldn't deliver. And on the other side of the blast wall robots were loading bins onto flatbeds that couldn't be delivered with no rail to ride on. He was supposed to shut it down. And through all of this there was a detail he'd missed.

He turned back toward his computer, pulling his camera view back to tower one and rotating its housing to maximum hard right. Adder's rig sat out on the thick ice. Ghost candles danced around it.

"What are those?" Adder growled, his finger stabbing at the flits of light.

"Those are the kids trying to steal your rig. They are highwaymen. Robbers. Like old time train robbers. All they need is a portable oxygen platform and your rig is perfect for that."

The candles. The skaters. They were the kids who escaped their boredom by donning vacuum bags with twenty minutes of breathable air, who strapped on skates and extended antennas topped with solar cells all the way up to where sunlight never died above the shadow crater line. Up in the light they harvested enough juice to run dim purplish lights ringing their helmets, lights that dipped and bobbed as they skated the dark ice. He hadn't been paying attention. They always raced the Zamboni, scooping enough shaved ice to buy a few things. He hadn't been paying attention.

"My rig? The bastards!"

Pepper flipped the view back to watching the Zamboni clear Dirty Ice Siding the day before. Behind the machine the shavings lined up in even rows, no kids there with hand-held scoops to steal little freebies. No kids because they'd already been on the ice too long to chase the Zamboni. Dirty Ice Siding was eight minutes from the front door so of course that is where they made their play.

"Got a back door on your rig?" Pepper asked.

The door to his pill box slammed open bringing both men around to see the flushed face of Anna Seiko who reached past both of them to commandeer Pepper's keyboard. "Of course he does." She said, "See how the little bastards like the smell of sulfur in the morning. Didn't you always say the moon was made of brimstone, Dad?"

Pepper inhaled a nice deep waft of her clean scent while his brain scrambled to conflate Adder and Dad.

His beeper went off, a young voice screaming, "Mayday, Mayday. Low oxygen."

He opened the com. "The air you are stealing is contaminated but sufficient for you to make it back inside the tube, if you hurry." On the split screen the candles spun around the bolted for the tube.

"Adder." Pepper looked up into the hard, hard eyes of Adder, "Maybe you would like to greet them?" he offered.

The old man smiled, patted Anna's shoulder and slammed the door behind him.

Pepper looked up into the careful gaze of Anna Seiko. "They're not the head of this you know. Give the robot loading those bins from the containers the go ahead. I'm supposed to close the rail for a three-day inspection based on a double derailment. That's time enough for three bins to disappear and I'll bet someone has turned an eye of God into a delivery chute. I always wondered how my shaft caved in. I bet someone used it for practice and it didn't quite work out."

A slow smile crossed Anna's face as her fingers flew across his keyboard, giving the go-ahead for transport.

"This is going to make someone quite unhappy," she murmured. "Bet those bins aren't clearly marked." She laughed. "That makes the contents community property."

"He won't kill them, will he?" Pepper liked the sound of her laughter but his thoughts couldn't quite leave what Adder might do to the young people.

"Dad? Probably not. Might scare them a little though. You sure the transport train will clear Dad's siding?"

Pepper shrugged. "It'll be close. Some of those ice shards are right on the edge of the tracks, but I'll bet on forward momentum to prevail." He leaned back in his chair thinking it wasn't so bad to be sitting in a pill box with a woman leaning over him.

"Want to watch?" he asked.

She turned to him fully. "You bet," she answered.

(In 2008, the average cost to execute a person on death row in California is estimated at $250,000,000—it would be financially appropriate for some state accountant to consider buying a prisoner's freedom for the cost of sending him to the Moon. This idea helped inform this story.
—F.R.R. Mallory. *Citation:* http://www.deathpenalty.org/article.php?id=42)

Misdirected
by Adam Israel

Chen rocked back and forth on his heels, glancing occasionally at the arrival schedule. The work order to meet the arriving flight was vague and unsigned, but he assumed it was from his boss, the Director of Communications for Luna City. Hahn hadn't been happy about losing a week's salary to Chen on a bluff at Friday night's poker game. Any other time Chen would welcome the distraction from work but he had plans for the night. He didn't want to spend his Sunday evening escorting someone's cousin or second uncle around the city but when a director said go, you went. No questions asked. It was hard getting hired over the thousands of other applicants vying for a position on the Moon. He had no intention of losing his job and moving back to Earth.

The only flight on the board was the Virgin Galactic spaceship *Zepher*. In the distance, a light twinkled on the horizon, just beyond Peary Crater, and dropped out of view. He envied those coming to Luna City for the first time. He still remembered the sense of wonder he felt during his arrival. Still starry-eyed and breathless from seeing the cosmos unfiltered in its raw glory, crossing the Sea of Tranquility and hovering over the site of the Apollo 11 landing before setting course for Clarke Spaceport. Just thinking about the experience put a lump in his throat.

Navigation lights flickered into view as the *Zepher* emerged from the crater and began its final approach. Guided by thrusters, the sleek ship glided towards the hanger. The outer hanger doors lumbered like monolithic hands opening to welcome road-weary travelers in for food and shelter, and closed back around them.

Chen stepped through the airlock doors to welcome the newest visitors to Earth's city in the stars. Setting foot on the Moon for the first time was like a warm embrace after a long walk on a cold winter morning. The first blast of pressurized air that hit your face carried with it the subtle scent of fresh grass clippings, deliberately added to make you feel like you were home. And for a few brief moments, he would recapture that lost sense of wonder by proxy.

The passengers were being assisted off of the ship by Jessi Torez, a familiar face on the Mohave-Luna City run. She smiled at Chen as he entered the hangar. He hoped that meant she had forgiven him for how their date on her last layover had ended.

Chen greeted the passengers as they took their first steps on Luna soil and directed them towards the airlock leading to the welcome center. Businessmen in sports jackets, young men and women, the occasional family, but not the non-descript elderly couple he was looking for. Until the last two passengers stepped through the doors of the *Zepher*. A short woman with grey hair in a bobbed cut, deep bags underneath eyes the color of jade. Her companion stood barely a head taller than she did, lean and with less hair than Chen remembered.

Chen stood dumbfound as the pair descended the stairs. His shoulders sagged in resignation as they reached the bottom of the stairs and wrapped their arms around him.

"Mom, Dad? What are you doing here?"

Chen's one-room quarters were what you would expect of a Tech Specialist with a degree in electronics, functional but stark. Gunmetal grey walls enclosed a bed in one corner and a desk with a computer terminal against another. He ignored the insistent blinking of the new message indicator and plopped onto the bed.

He had dropped his parents off at the first and only hotel open in Luna City so far before returning to his quarters. The building Hilton converted to be their flagship property on the Moon stood in the center of the primary dome and reached all the way to its peak. Now the twenty-story landmark and its already infamous Starlight Lounge stood as the focal point of tourist central.

The door chirped. He sighed and stood up, smoothing out the wrinkles in his clothes.

"Come in." The door, keyed to his voice, slid open.

"Hey Torez," he said, smiling. "I'm really glad to see you."

"Of course you are," she said, sauntering into his room. "You invited me here. I was a little surprised, though." She arched an eyebrow. "I figured you'd be busy entertaining your parents."

"I had no idea they were coming here."

She grinned. "I know. Your mother never stopped talking about their surprise visit to see their handsome little boy living on the Moon." She looked at him seriously. "Never stopped talking, the entire flight."

"That's my mom," he laughed.

She stepped close and pressed her body against his. One hand wrapped around his waist while the other stroked his smooth cheek. Warm breath tickled his ear. "Shall we pick up where we left off?"

Chen's cheeks flushed and his heart thumped against his chest as if it was trying to break loose. "Jessi . . ."

The door chirped again. He jumped backwards like he was five and caught stealing dumplings from his mother's kitchen.

"I, uh," he mumbled.

"You'd better get that," she said. Her eyebrow arched again, and this time he couldn't tell if she was amused or angry.

Chen's father rushed through the door as it slid open, sweating as if he had just run the New York City Marathon.

"Chen," he panted, "I need your help. Your mother has gone crazy."

"Dad," he said, "what the hell are you talking about?"

The senior Chen, a shorter, stockier version of his son, looked around the room and blinked. "Am I interrupting?"

"Not at all," Torez said, stepping past them. "I was just leaving."

Both men turned and as the door slid shut behind her.

"Who was that?" his father asked

"That—was my girlfriend."

"Oh," he said. "Oh." Realization flashed across his face.

"Yeah. So, what's Mom doing now?"

His father's shoulders slumped. "She wants me to apply for emigration, to move here and open up my practice."

"And you don't want to?"

"I'm not sure. Don't get me wrong," he said. "I'm sure it's lovely living here, but it's so different, you know?"

The terminal started ringing. "I should probably get that."

"I should be going, anyway. I told your mother I was going to pick up my tickets for the sports adventure tour. I hear they've just opened up the driving range at the Sea of Tranquility."

His father turned to leave. "If that's her, don't tell her I was here. We'll see you at dinner tonight."

Chen sat down and grunted.

"Chen," a genial voice said. The video feed was flickered with heavy static and the audio warbled like an angry songbird. "This is Jones, the Executive Director of Economic Development. We're having problems with our communications equipment."

Chen perked up. "So I see, sir."

"We've been having these problems sporadically over the past few weeks but they seem to be getting worse. We have a call in the morning that we've already had to reschedule six times. I know your parents just arrived, but this can't wait. We can't reschedule it again."

"You know about that?"

"Son," Jones said. "It's my business to know the who, what, and why around here. Right now there's something going on that I don't know and I'm not pleased by that. Understand?"

"Understood. I'll get right on it."

Jones' voice grew firm. "See that you do. Jobs are on the line here. You're working for me tonight. Do whatever you need to do to find out what's causing these problems and fix them by morning."

Chen's nose wrinkled as he passed through the airlock leading to the utilities dome. Water and waste services housed under one stellar roof, along with Communication. The engineers who designed this model of efficiency never had to walk through it during peak hours. It smelled like a cross between an oil refinery and a chicken coop. And the equipment room was on the other side of the dome.

The glorified closet was as immaculate as a clean room. Multiple loops of cable feeding from the external antennas spilled into the room and into a switchboard that connected them to the city's communications system.

He sat down at the terminal and dialed Hahn's office. Static flickered on the screen and Hahn's haughty voice filled the room. "What do you want?"

"Hahn," he said. "I'm in the utilities room, trying to track down a problem for the Executive Director."

Hahn grunted. "So I hear."

"Can you send a diagnostic signal from your terminal?"

"Hold on."

A minute later the screen switched to a multi-color display of vertical and horizontal bars and audio squelches that cycled for thirty seconds before returning to static.

"Well?" Hahn said.

"Everything checks out," Chen said. "There doesn't seem to be a problem between communications and the antenna array."

Hahn's laugh boomed. "Have fun crawling around inside the attic." The echo of laughter rang in his ears even after the line went dead.

Chen looked at the hatch in the wall that led to the utility elevator and sighed. Each dome was constructed with a wall that separated the inside from the out by way of a maintenance crawl space divided into twelve horizontal levels. The external wall of the dome shielded the inhabitants from solar radiation. The levels housed some of the equipment that kept the domes running smoothly: security cameras, lighting and communications. Far above his head was the mesh antenna array that he needed to test.

It only took a few minutes for the elevator to reach the top of the dome. Unlike the primary dome, there was no observatory at the peak of this one. He checked the schematics on his handheld computer and found the junction he needed.

He plugged his computer into the antenna controller and ran the diagnostics program. It scanned the spectrum of frequencies, from satellite television to the Internet. Every signal received was strong and clear. Every test ran successfully. Wherever the interference was coming from, it was definitely originating from inside the city.

Chen flopped into the chair in his quarters and sighed. His feet hurt, his body ached, his head was beginning to throb and there were seventeen missed calls on his terminal. One was from Jessi—no message—and the rest from his mother. He cycled through them; each one began with "Where are you?"

The clock read ten past midnight. He missed dinner with his parents by more than five hours and he forgot to call and cancel. He didn't relish the thought of the guilt trip he was going to receive from his mother, but the alternative was worse. He had no intention of being fired and having to move back home with his parents. The best he could do was meet them in the morning for breakfast.

He scrolled through the maintenance logs, looking for anything out of the ordinary. The only department reporting any problems with communications over the past few weeks was Economic Development. Over the last six months, Hahn had assigned dozens of work orders to himself that should have been given to a technician. Hahn may have been qualified to do the work once, but that wasn't his job anymore. He gave up the technician's lifestyle for the higher pay grade and spacious living quarters long ago. Every job done by Hahn involved either the building that housed the offices of the city government, including Economic Development and Communications, or its staff's personal quarters.

The duty log showed that Hahn signed out of the building two hours ago. A long day, but they'd all been working overtime since the switchover to the civilian government. Now that the city was accepting applications for settlement, every business on Earth wanted to claim their stake in the growing market and establish roots in the new frontier.

He tossed his sweat-stained work uniform into the laundry chute and glanced at the shower wistfully before putting on fresh clothes. An outside influence was causing the anomaly, but why was it only manifesting itself on calls relating to Economic Development and its staff? He didn't know the answer, but he suspected he would find some clues when he broke into Hahn's office.

The building housing the offices of the city government stood a few blocks away from the entertainment district at the city's center. The dome's lights were dimmed to late evening and the stars above were visible through the translucent top. All but the most dedicated or behind schedule employees had long gone home. Chen scanned his employee badge at security and entered the building. He technically had an office in the building, shared with the other technicians, but the last time he checked the space it was being used to store spare parts and tools.

The Communications office, recessed in the back corner of the second floor, was pitch black. Turning on the lights revealed barely controlled chaos—books and photocopies spread haphazardly across the conference table and empty stimulant wrappers lay discarded on the floor. He scanned a couple of the titles: *Riding the Wave: Economic Market Forces* and *Shifting Strategies: A Guide to Career Advancement.*

Hahn's office was sealed shut. Chen picked up a toolkit from his office and knelt on the floor next to the panel that housed the servomotor that controlled the Hahn's door. He rummaged until he found an electrostatic wrench and removed the access panel. He separated the bundle of wires and installed a splice into the one powering the door.

The Director's office was almost as cluttered as the rest of the office space. Chen sat down at Hahn's terminal and opened a maintenance window. His fingers tapped at the keyboard in rapid succession as he traced the commands that had been executed earlier in the day. He stopped when he reached the time period of his call to Hahn. Chen spent a significant amount of his working life maintaining the communications systems and he had never seen the commands that Hahn had run right before accepting the call.

A beep echoed in the hallway beyond the office. Someone was calling the elevator. Even though he was working under the orders of the Executive Director, the last thing he wanted to do is explain why he was snooping late at night. He typed frantically, dumping the data from Hahn's terminal to his own before closing the window and flicking off the lights.

Chen pulled the splice out of the access panel and power surged back into the door. It slid shut and sealed with a hiss. He killed the rest of the lights and ducked into the shadows next to a filing cabinet near the entrance to the office. A few seconds later the door opened and Hahn entered the room and paused. Chen caught his breath when he saw the open toolkit still lying on the floor next to the access panel. Hahn showed no sign of noticing it. He continued, footsteps clicking against the floor, into his office and disappeared. If he had turned around, he would have seen Chen huddled against the opposite wall.

Chen crawled into the hallway and, avoiding the elevator, took the staircase down to the street. Out under the quiet lunar night, he sighed with relief. His phone rang and he almost jumped out of his skin.

"Hello?"

"Hi, Chen, it's me." A familiar sultry voice.

"Jessi," he said. "Sorry I didn't call you back earlier."

"It's okay," she said. "I'm sure you were busy with more important things. Why don't we meet for a drink and talk about it?"

He hesitated.

"Well?"

"I'm sorry, Jessi, I really am. I'm in the middle of a minor work crisis. I'm heading back to my quarters to figure it out. Rain check?"

"That's fine," she said before hanging up, "I'll bring the drinks to you."

Chen sat down and looked at the data from Hahn's office. He instructed the computer to look for patterns related to the dates and times when communication issues were reported. He couldn't imagine what, if anything, would motivate Hahn to sabotage communications.

The door chimed.

"Come in," he called, standing up. Jessi Torez glided into the room wearing a slinky, curve-hugging red dress. In one smooth motion she wrapped her soft arms around his waist and greeted him with a kiss that left him breathless.

"Jessi," he stammered. "I, uh, hi."

Her smiling lips matched the color of her dress. "How about that drink you owe me?"

"I can't. I'm sorry. I would if I could, you know that."

Her lips pouted disappointedly. "You can do you anything you want to. The question is, wouldn't you rather have a few drinks, take me to Luna Point for a romantic dinner, and see how lucky your stars are tonight?"

Chen swallowed hard. "I really want to, but I can't."

"Well," she said coldly, "if you'd rather work than spend what's left of the evening with me, I think I'll leave you to it. I'll be flying out in the morning anyway."

She turned to go but he put his hand on her arm. The feel of her warm, goose-bumped flesh sent a shiver down his spine. "I'll make it up to you next time, I promise."

"Oh yeah?" she said, staring into his eyes. "How?"

He blurted out the first thing he could think of that might satisfy her.

"Dinner at Luna Point."

"Deal," she purred, stroking his cheek with a fingertip. She turned to the door and called over her shoulder before the door slid shut. "Next Friday. I'll schedule an extended layover."

Chen collapsed into the chair and wiped away the sweat from his forehead with his sleeve. Luna Point, at the top of the Hilton, was the hotspot of the city. The view of the city and stars was said to be awe-inspiring. It was no wonder reservations had to be made weeks in advance.

He sighed and turned back to the computer. It had finished searching the data and the results were displayed on the screen. Chen's eyes widened. He punched up the staff directory.

The phone rang a dozen times before a groggy voice answered. "Hello?"

"Sir," he said. "It's Chen. I'm sending something to you now. You're going to want to see this."

Chen sat in the office of the Executive Director, drumming his fingers against his leg nervously. The light shining through the window was beginning to brighten as the new day began. Outside, the shadows still draped across much of the valley.

"Thank you once again," Jones said, "for all of your work last night. My security staff were very interested in the data you uncovered."

Chen shifted nervously in his chair. "Did they say anything about how I uncovered it?"

Jones laughed. "No worries, son. I told them you were working under my direct orders."

"What's going to happen to Hahn?"

"That," Jones said, "is ultimately up to the court. The theft charges are solid. With the data you found, we can prove he was stealing confidential information and selling them to some less than principled contractors hoping to gain an edge in bidding against the competition. The truth is, Chen, we got lucky."

"How so?"

"As far as we can tell so far, Hahn's operation had been running for years, probably from the day he was promoted to Director. He'd recently accrued a substantial gambling debt."

"Uh, sir, I think I should tell you . . ."

"About the poker games?" Jones said. "A trifle. I may even take Hahn's place at the table, if there are no objections."

"None at all," he said, grinning.

"Hahn used his position in Communications to bury the records of his bets with his bookie in Vegas. He knew deleting the logs would set off the alarms with security so he just changed them so they appeared innocuous to the casual observer."

Chen nodded. "That makes sense, but why was he interfering with communications?"

"In Hahn's desperation, he accepted an offer from one of his contacts that would pay him enough money to settle his debts to Vegas. All he had to do was disrupt some negotiations that the contact stood to benefit from if they fell apart."

Chen's watch beeped. "I've got to run. I'm late for a meeting. Again."

Jones stood and extended his hand. "No problem. I'll see you tomorrow at the meeting, right Director Chen?"

"Yes," he stammered. "Oh, about that favor I asked for?"

"A reservation for two at eight on Friday night at Luna Point? Consider it done. Oh, and one more thing. Tell your father that we're on for golf tomorrow."

"You know my father?" he said, confused.

"Of course I do. He was my doctor, before I settled here. Who do you think arranged for his surprise visit?"

The lobby of the Hilton was everything you might expect. Trendy looking furniture arranged to give the sense of spaciousness. The water display in the center of the room cascaded under natural moon gravity, like a waterfall in slow motion. Chen slowed to admire the view as he passed on his way to the cafeteria.

"Hi Mom, Dad. Sorry I'm late."

His mother's fork paused in mid air as she scanned his face. "What happened to you? You look haggard."

Chen couldn't decide between laughing or sighing. "It's been a long day," he said, sitting down at the table.

His stomach rumbled loudly. He couldn't remember the last time he had eaten.

"Hi, Chen."

He looked up from the menu. "Hey Jessi. You're still here?"

"I'm heading to the spaceport now," she said. She was dressed in her navy blue uniform and pulling her luggage behind her. "Don't forget our date."

"Benjamin," his mother said, "you didn't tell us she was your girlfriend."

"Ben?" Jessi said, raising an eyebrow at him.

He groaned.

"I have to catch my flight, Mr. and Mrs. Chen, but it was nice seeing you again," she said before hurrying away. She paused at the door and stuck her tongue out at Ben.

"Mom, did you have to tell her you named me Ben Chen?"

His father chuckled around a mouthful of scrambled eggs.

"So, Mom," he said. "Have you considered moving to Luna City? I'm sure Dad's practice would be a huge success here."

His father grimaced before swallowing.

Final Arrangements
by J. M. Fisher

MOON STATION *CONCEPTION*—March 14, 2028—06:12—Coordinated Universal Time (UTC).

I pulled my hand back from the carotid artery of Commander Garret Henderson's neck, where my fingers had searched for a non-existent pulse. He was warm, but lifeless. I bent down low to his face and listened for a breath.

Nothing. No sound of life. Just like the vacuum of silence outside on the Moon.

"Houston . . . Henderson is gone," I said.

My wireless comm earpiece picked up the somber words and two seconds later my voice echoed in Mission Director Alex Oberg's headset at Mission Control.

My earpiece cracked with his response. "Say again, Colonel."

"He's dead . . ." My voice sounded odd and disconnected from the reality.

"Henderson is dead . . . did we copy that?" Oberg said.

I looked at Henderson, lying face-up in his bunk, and gently shook him again. For a moment I expected him to sit upright, bellow his baritone laugh, and announce, "Gotcha, Bird!"

But his empty blue eyes told the story he had embarked on a new voyage.

My earpiece cracked again with the distant voice: "Say again, Colonel."

After a long pause, I softly said, "He has no pulse . . . no respiration . . . ."

"We've activated the in-room camera," Oberg replied.

I heard a slight whirl and saw the red light glow of the wide-angle camera mounted in the upper right corner of the stateroom. It swiveled and zoomed to Henderson.

"He looks peaceful . . . maybe he passed in his sleep," I said.

"Do you see signs of trauma . . . signs of hemorrhaging . . . anything?"

I didn't answer. I stared at Henderson and felt the aloneness—I was the only person alive on the Moon.

Conception was humankind's first baby step to colonize another world. The proponents of a permanently manned station on the Moon had won the debate.

The station was under construction and manned by Commander Garret Henderson, 47, and me, Colonel Nelson Avery, 42. The Commander hailed from the mountains of western Montana, and I came from the blue collar streets of Los Angeles. We'd left home four months and twenty-four days ago—but Earth and humanity were a lifetime away and the unwanted had actually happened—the mountain man was the first to die away from Earth.

It was 4:15 a.m. and the controllers in Houston lit up the hotlines. With the utterance of my words, "Henderson is gone," every mission manager on-and-off duty experienced an adrenaline shooter—the kind that accompanies dire news. The tempo of operations jumped into high gear as contingency plans were reviewed and work-arounds developed. Shortly, Mission Control would issue directives to me as the brain-trust made decisions about the next step.

Difficulties would come at the Mission Management press conference. Hordes of reporters would shout outrageous questions and report live about the first death of a human being on the Moon and the fate of me. Senior Management would state they were working to understand what happened and that, in any event, no evasive alien life-forms threatened Earth. They would reassure the public that if something unknown on the Moon did cause the loss of life, the remote location of *Conception* insured there was no risk to the population. In a measured manner, the cerebral, gray-haired engineers would explain the loss in sterile terms and assure the worried public they were safe and that every effort would be made to rescue me.

But I was not energized and not worried. I felt a strange calmness in the quiet.

I looked around Henderson's stateroom, an efficient and orderly environment, kept neat with military discipline. It was a place I rarely ventured—just as he avoided entering mine without an invitation. Gone were the days of cramped living, three bunks to a stateroom. Long term studies proved that a measure of privacy and the opportunity to get away from annoying crew mate habits greatly improved morale when far away from home.

I looked again at his face. His lips were blue and his mouth was closed. A thin stubble of gray and white whiskers covered his cheeks and chin. His cold, lifeless blue eyes stared past me—the same empty look he used with great success when we played poker during crew training. And, I imagine, it was the same piercing expression he carried when flying attack jets for the U.S. Marine Corps.

I reached up and gently closed his eyes.

Commander Garret Henderson was a fourth-generation Marine. His hair clippers were permanently set to Number One and he trimmed his head every Monday morning before his shower. He never tired of reminding me I was an Air Force guy who wore my hair longer. After each self-administered buzz cut, he'd walk around the station rubbing his nearly-bald head, and say, "High and tight never goes out of style, Bird."

He was the perfect selection to command the first Moon Station. He was the nephew of an astronaut who flew on several Space Shuttle flights and also tested the Manned-Maneuvering Unit while he floated untethered in orbit. Henderson was groomed from birth to lead our type of space project—a research laboratory to extract raw materials from the Moon.

He made life-and-death decisions in the cockpit and carried that self-assured military bearing to *Conception*. He was a bit like the Moon landscape—a black-and-white guy. But, when circumstance allowed, he also saw the nuance of beauty in the minor shades of gray and brown that added color to the stark, desolate moonscape.

As I stared down at him, I faded back to memories of the Q and A video conference we gave a few days back with school children. One young girl asked, "Why do we go to the Moon?"

Henderson always loved the question and smiled at the opportunity to share his philosophy, "We learn by exploring—it's in our DNA. When we stop exploring we stop learning—that is why God gave us an imagination."

*   *   *

197

Oberg's voice interrupted my thoughts.

"Colonel Avery, we need you to move his body to the medical ward."

I knew the drill. I'd carry Henderson to the ward, place him on the exam table, and remove his clothes. Then, a remote-operated MRI would scan the body and a medical robot would collect blood and tissue samples. After the post-mortem, I would place Henderson inside a body bag and then inside a sealed morgue drawer, where the body would await transport back to Earth.

There would be great concern I was in mortal danger and that the station was at risk. The loss of a crew member would stimulate the political opposition to the program. There would be demands to moth ball *Conception* because it was an expensive, windowless condominium in an exotic locale and a waste of taxpayer dough. Henderson's death would inspire Congressional inquires, newspaper editorials, and public discussion about the viability of the project and possibly the end of government funding.

Protocol demanded that I be quarantined until the cause of death could be determined. Although my gut reaction told me he died of natural causes, because I resided on government property, I'd be spared no quarter until management was convinced the danger had passed.

Conception was constructed on the lower rim of Shackleton Crater, located at the South Pole of the Moon. The rim of the crater was bathed in near perpetual sunshine, and the floor was in perpetual darkness. It was selected for the station location because the floor of the crater was cold and contained significant water-ice deposits. The water-ice provided raw materials for life-support and propellant manufacture.

One of *Conception's* mission goals was to better understand the effects of long-term human exposure to the Moon environment. Solar radiation was the most significant hazard we faced and it might be related to Henderson's death.

The problem of exposure to solar radiation was solved by covering the station underneath three feet of Moon dust and lunar soil, known as lunar regolith. As a result of the design, the station had only one window in the Command Center—the only place we could peer outside at the desolate lunar landscape.

There were twenty-six wireless cameras installed around the outside the station. Each camera could be swiveled in any direction and zoomed to any area, including the one we kept pointed to the sky at Earth. This was our default picture on the flat screens scattered throughout the living modules.

Our charge was to greet the autonomous space transports that brought new modules and consumables, and oversee the robotic construction of the station. We were the human element, able to trouble shoot and override the bots—the go-to guys when red lights flashed on the machines.

Assembly of *Conception* was far easier than on Earth because of the low gravity. It was constructed of hex-shaped modules fourteen meters long, six meters wide, and four meters tall. Mission Control launched new modules to the station every twenty days. An unmanned space transport landed near the station and the cargo was unloaded by robotic tractors called traks. The traks could be operated by handheld remote control units or from inside the station. They could also be controlled by the construction technicians back in Houston.

The traks hauled, positioned, and attached new modules to the station. After a visual inspection by us, the module was connected to the station via power latches that were designed to adjust and fine tune the connection. If the connection passed with a green light pressure check, it was deemed habitable. After a successful attachment, the traks scraped regolith over the top to bury the module and provide a protective layer against the intense solar radiation.

The design allowed for modules with a larger interior area. But, it was like living inside a submarine, or being delayed inside a jet airliner for six months, with no flight attendants.

The station now consisted of ten connected modules. It had a Command Center, a wardroom and galley, the medical ward, a lounge which included a library and small theater, and a module which contained three private staterooms, each of which featured a small closet, writing desk, large flat screen display, and a bunk. There was also a module that contained a gym, bath and lavatory facility.

We spent most of our time in the Command Center, which was fitted with a four-by-three foot plexiglass window. From this window, we could look across the dark crater floor at the stark, sunlit mountains on the other side of the crater, nineteen kilometers in the distance.

There were four additional modules designated for station operations. They included the water recycling facility, a life-support system, and energy storage. An airlock nodule connected the pressurized modules to the station garage and provided outside access. A solar collector farm, which produced 2.1 megawatts of power from seven solar towers positioned on the sunlit areas of the crater rim, provided our electricity and charged back-up batteries. We had one more safety feature—a small, lead-lined closet we could retreat to in case of high solar flare activity.

Consumables, including oxygen, nitrogen, and water, were transported from Earth until the water-ice extraction system was operational. When that extraction system came on-line, the station would be deemed self-sufficient, which included the capability to grow fresh fruits and vegetables. Eventually, *Conception* would be expanded to support a crew of twenty-five.

"Colonel, we are ready to conduct the post mortem. Please take his body to the medical ward," Oberg announced.

I looked at Henderson and said, "Right this way, Commander."

I hefted his six-foot-two frame over my left shoulder. His bulk and weight were quite easy to manage as he only weighed about eighteen kilograms on the Moon. Ever since our arrival, Henderson had joked about his feats of strength as compared to that "mediocre strong dude, Incredible Hulk, back on Earth."

I carried him down the hallway and into the medical ward. I placed him face-up on the exam table and undressed the body. I removed his watch, wedding ring, and the gold cross pendant that hung around his neck, and placed them in my pocket.

I moved away from the table and stood near the wall. A robotic arm, equipped with a wand, and commanded by a distant operator in Houston, disengaged from a mount on the ceiling and slowly scanned the entire body. The arm passed back over the body and stopped at his left forearm. It hovered and the wand retracted. A rotating needle mechanism appeared and the arm moved very close to the skin. A small needle poked into the skin and drew blood. The needle withdrew and the robotic arm moved over the abdomen. The old needle was pulled back into the rotating mechanism and a new six-inch needle appeared. It was inserted into the abdomen at the stomach and another sample was taken.

The arm moved up toward the chest area and another needle appeared. The robotic arm positioned itself over the right lung and the large needle was inserted about ten centimeters deep. Another fluid sample was collected. The needle was pulled out and the arm moved to the left section of the upper chest. A needle appeared and it was inserted about eight centimeters into the heart. A sample was taken and the arm moved up and away from the exam table.

"We're ready for you to turn the body," Oberg said.

I stepped back to the table and whispered, "Okay Major Tom, time to roll over for the man."

I grabbed hold of his left arm and turned him face down. His lifeless right arm swung away from the table and dangled from the edge. I shifted his body and lifted the dangling arm and laid it on the table and then stepped away. The robotic arm returned and scanned the body from head to toe, bathing it in an eerie bluish light. The arm moved up and returned to it's holding mount in the ceiling.

"Colonel Avery, the exam is complete. It's time to put him in storage."

"Roger," I replied.

I pushed a button on the console next to me. A small door on the wall opened upwards and a long flat drawer extended itself next to the exam table. I pulled a body bag from a storage locker and laid it out on the flat drawer. I slowly pulled Henderson's body from the exam table and into the bag. When I had positioned him inside, I looked at his face one last time, and zipped the bag closed. I reached over and pressed a button on the console. The flat drawer retracted into the wall, the small door closed, and Henderson was gone.

"Alex," I said.

"Yes, Colonel?"

"I need some time—I'm turning off my comm line." I flipped a switch on the comm unit attached to my waist and disconnected from Earth. I returned to my stateroom and set my comm unit down on my small desk. I lay down on my bunk and stared off.

My thoughts jumped back to the last time we explored outside the station. It was our last "liberty trip" together, taken just a few days ago. We went to our favorite spot—a place Henderson named "Waikiki Beach"—to share the view of Earth.

He was in a philosophical mood and switched off his simultaneous transmission to Houston as we sat down on the rock outcropping. A small basketball-sized Earth hung low on the horizon, just above the bleak moonscape—a dreamy spectacle floating alone in the black sky. From our vantage point, the Earth was just a small, smooth ball, with none of the achievements or imperfections of humanity visible.

After a while, Henderson said, "It's just a blue and white swirl—the dark and light of human emotion . . . That's the problem, Bird . . . all the emotions people carry around."

We sat without speaking for some time, looking at home.

Maybe Henderson intuitively knew his time would soon arrive. Suddenly, he raised his right arm, pointed at Earth, and said, "Bird, either you grow and change, or you're a rock on the river bank as the water flows past . . . that's why we are here . . . we must migrate to new places to grow."

A red light flashed at my stateroom work console and brought me back to the reality of my situation. Mission Control wanted to talk. I walked to my station in the Command Center and activated the comm. I looked up at the panel display and saw Alex Oberg seated at his console. I flipped a switch and a red light indicated the camera was beaming my picture down to Houston.

"Yes, Alex."

He looked up at his camera and adjusted his eyeglasses by pushing on the nose bridge with his left index finger.

"Colonel, we have considered your immediate evacuation via *Rescue One*—but—we want to keep you quarantined at *Conception* until we understand what caused Commander Henderson's death. The quarantine may last several weeks."

I nodded and said, "I expected that, Alex."

"Colonel . . . you will be required to stay inside the station—it's too great a risk to venture outside alone . . . . And . . . one more thing . . . you must keep the comm open at all times."

So, they decided they needed to watch me 24/7. Fabulous—nothing like being trapped and displayed in a glass tube with no place to escape.

Oberg looked at his console. He continued, "We will bring Henderson home on Moon Flight 141, which will launch in sixteen days. In the meantime, Autonomous Transport *Clarke* arrives in 36 hours and 28 minutes."

"Have you informed Elizabeth?" I asked.

Alex looked down, pressed his mute button, and turned to his right. He spoke to James Duffy, the second-in-command at the CAPCOM station. A moment later he reactivated communications and said, "We've not reached Henderson's wife yet."

"Garret asked me to break the news to Elizabeth," I said.

"Roger that, Avery. . . . Until we have the preliminary medical report, we are keeping this need-to-know. We will arrange a video meet with you and Elizabeth ASAP."

"What about the our weekly public Q and A? It's scheduled for tomorrow," I asked.

"Press relations will make a formal announcement at 2:00 p.m. EST. The Q and A has been canceled." Oberg shifted in his chair and added, "The suits want to make you available for an interview tomorrow."

Two hours later, at 8:50 UTC, Mission Control buzzed me that Elizabeth, Henderson's demure wife, was ready for the video conference. I sat down at my stateroom console and activated the comm. A moment later she appeared seated at a table in her home near Houston. Behind her was a wall with several digital frames that displayed various pictures of her and Garret. The largest picture showed a young Garret and Elizabeth holding hands and standing on a sandy beach, with a white line of surf crashing on a coral reef in the background.

Elizabeth's neck-length blonde hair was cut in a bob and framed her roundish face. She smiled, but I noticed she clutched a white tissue in her left hand—her red fingernail polish accenting her long and slender fingers.

I switched on my camera and said, "Hello, Elizabeth."

"Hi Nelson . . . . How are you?" she replied.

"I'm fine . . . considering. This must be a difficult for you—"

"It really hasn't sunk in . . . I didn't know how hard it would be."

"I'm very sorry, Elizabeth. . . ."

"I knew Garret might die doing what he loved . . . . I knew that . . ." A moment later she composed herself and said, "Sometimes I teased him and called him my Major Tom . . . . I really miss him."

I looked away from my screen. I turned back and said, "Major Tom was a good man and good friend. I miss him, too."

Neither of us spoke, then I said, "Elizabeth . . . Garret loved you very much . . . . He told me he was going to take you back to Hawaii for your twenty-first anniversary."

She stared away at something off-camera and said, "Nelson—he wore a gold cross pendant—his Mother gave it to him when he went to boot camp."

"I have it, I'll return it to you."

"No . . . . He wanted it to stay on the Moon . . . . Nelson, please leave it there."

"I understand, Elizabeth,"

"Nelson, I must go . . . . Thank you." She reached forward and pressed a button on her console. Her image vanished and my screen went dark.

Ten minutes later the comm lite flashed and Alex appeared on my screen.

"Colonel, there was a meeting regarding Commander Henderson's personal effects. We must remind you the International Moon Development Treaty of 2024 prohibits astronauts from leaving personal mementos or items of religious significance on the Moon. You cannot leave Commander Henderson's cross. All of his personal possessions must be returned to Earth. We cannot risk politicizing the mission with a controversy about religious symbolism."

"I know the drill, Alex."

A few hours later, I went to the airlock and sat down on a wide metal bench in front of pressure suit 2B, the white one with a blue stripe on the arms and legs. A rack held the suit open and in a standing position. Dressing was similar to stepping into a pair of overalls, with a personal valet to hold them up and open.

I stepped into the suit and fastened my gloves with a twist. Then I pressed a button on the console which closed the hard back plate.

I felt the plate latch snugly. I reached to the shelf above my head and grabbed my helmet. I pulled it down over my head, placed in the ringed metal collar, and turned it a quarter turn to the right to firmly seat the latch. I pressed a button to pressurize my suit and activate the life-support system. I heard the faint of hum of the suit air circulation fan. A small heads-up display lit up inside my helmet and gave me a reading of the suit vitals and my GPS coordinates.

I pressed the switch to depressurize the airlock and watched the digital read-out turn from green to red as the air pressure inside fell. In thirty seconds the airlock would be emptied of the warm station air.

My headset cracked with the voice of Alex. "Colonel, I see you activated the airlock and appear to be preparing to exit to the surface—"

I flipped off my comm line.

I pressed the hatch release switch and overrode the control from Houston. The hatch opened to the raw expanse of a desolate, gritty, and ancient Moon. The harsh, intense sunlight lit up the far wall of Shackleton Crater and it's razor sharp edge offset the blackness of the night sky.

I walked to the left side of a parked Moon rover, slipped into the driver's seat, buckled the lap belt, and pressed the green start button. The electronics came alive with an auburn glow which illuminated the gauges. The power recharge cable automatically decoupled and I was ready to roll.

I pressed on the accelerator and eased the rover toward the open hatch. I slowly descended the aluminum grid ramp and onto the surface of the Moon. The nearly horizontal sunshine was bright, even with the automatic dimming of the liquid crystal glass visor of my helmet.

I turned the rover toward the worn path off to the right—the one that led upwards to an overlook about 300 meters above the station—the spot Henderson dubbed "Waikiki Beach." I maneuvered the rover over the bumpy, winding pathway at a walking pace, and steered around several large boulders along the way. After a drive of about ten minutes, I arrived at the overlook, parked the rover, and turned off the power. The auburn glow of the dials disappeared and I sat for a moment and absorbed the view.

Then, I unbuckled the lap belt, pivoted to the left, and placed my left boot, and then my right, on the surface of the Moon.

As I stood up, I heard Henderson's voice echo in my head, "Bird, every time I step on to the surface, I hear those immortal words, 'One small step . . .'"

I felt the soft crunch of dry regolith under my boots and watched as small gray grains floated up and quickly rained back to the surface. A gray powder covered my boots—a gritty dust created by the impacts of micro meteorites and solar radiation over the past 3.1 billion years.

I slowly and deliberately traversed a few meters to a rock outcropping Henderson had named after a bar in Hawaii—*The House Without a Key*. I leaned against a smooth section of a large boulder and sat down on the dusty lunar soil. The area was crisscrossed with many of our boot prints—some distinct and undisturbed, and others partially covered by steps taken later. I saw a few of Henderson's large boot prints which marked the places he'd stood, as the first person since the creation of the Moon.

I looked up into the jet black sky. The half-lit Earth was just a few degrees above the jagged outline of Shackleton Crater on the far horizon. It resembled the Moon rising over the Diamond Head landmark near Waikiki Beach.

In one easy sweep of my eyes, I saw all of the Indian Ocean, the Indian subcontinent, and Sri Lanka. I moved my gaze westward, to the Middle East, where conflict still raged. My eyes moved up and across the brown deserts and savannahs of East Africa, where humanity first learned to walk upright. I looked further to the right and saw the terminator, that eerie, in-between twilight which announced dawn across the cloud-covered, western portion of the African continent.

It only took a few seconds for my eyes to travel across the breadth of life that was Earth, and across the history of humankind. In an odd way, I had just traveled faster than the speed of light. My eyes came back to the wild grasslands of East Africa and I thought about how early man may have looked at the Moon in the night sky, just as I now looked at Earth.

Perhaps that early man, like me, felt the same raw emotion when loss paid a visit—that deep sadness we feel when someone is no longer.

I fumbled with the Velcro closure on the small pocket of my left arm and pulled out Henderson's gold cross necklace and held it with my right glove. The pendant and chain hung and swayed in the bright sunlight.

I looked up at the majestic Earth, which silently hovered in the dark sky, and thought, *There it is, Major Tom—that tropical beach—the place of blue lagoons and coconut trees . . . . You'll be home soon . . . back to Bali Hai and your Elizabeth.*

I sat in the cold vastness of the stark, sharp vista—barren of green, red, or blue. Barren of any life, except Henderson, the Earth, and me.

I fingered the gold necklace with my glove and then carefully placed it on the rock with the cross facing Earth. It glinted boldly in the harsh sunlight.

I sat looking at home, and then, after a long while, I heard Henderson's voice echo in my head, "Carry on, Marine."

This Time to Stay
by Matthew Pavletich

"Houston, I'm going to do the Station Eleven panoramic now," Jana Stanley announced as she clamped the hi-resolution digital camera to her spacesuit's chest bracket. As Jana started the image captures, she regarded a landscape that was accurately described as *magnificent desolation* long ago. The raw sunlight caught fine scratches and scuffs in her gold-coated sun visor. They threw glinting, sun-sparkles across her vision as she turned this way and that, looking out across the lunar evening terrain of the Marius Hills. But if she stood still and raised the sun visor, she could see without the filter the subtleties that could easily be overlooked by a busy Astronaut. And every so often she would see a bright golden flash in the corner of her eye, and would attribute it to an odd reflection from her own visor.

In spite of the powerful light that bathed the landscape, the lunar sky was the deepest black, though still seemingly three-dimensional. The sun was a huge, arrogant spotlight that dominated the sky. The land seemed as if someone had taken a snapshot of a heavy ocean swell, then covered it in a blanket of frozen lava and powdery dust. The grey and tan regolith seemed to glow in a vaguely fairytale manner. And there was the littering of millions of rocks, boulders and craters.

When Jana had finished her panoramic shots she moved toward the rover vehicle that was parked near the rim of a house-sized crater. She bounded along in loping, side-to-side steps. Normal heel-toe walking was nearly impossible in her stiff spacesuit and the gentle one-sixth lunar gravity. Another spacesuited figure emerged from behind a big boulder toting a rock sample bag. It was Sasha, and he was gently humming a tune to himself. His white spacesuit glowed intensely in the powerful sunlight. Except from the waist down that is, for his suit was stained with streaks of dark grey and black from the ferociously clinging moondust. Jana glanced wistfully at her own suit. It too was grimy as hell from the many hours of EVA on the old, dusty Moon.

But Lt. Colonel Jana Stanley wouldn't have it any other way. It was her second visit to the Moon. Four years ago she had spent five days at Hadley Rille, re-visiting the 1971 *Apollo 15* landing site. She had been *Altair 4* Lander Pilot, with her Commander, Charles "Cee-Cee" Clarke and two other crewmates. Cee-Cee had really taken to lunar geology and he had grown to love the Moon. Jana remembered how bitterly disappointed he had been when Houston had recalled them back to Earth early after only five days at Hadley. They were to have been the first crew to spend a whole fourteen Earth-day daylight period on the Moon. But Cee-Cee had experienced erratic heartbeats after the fourth day, scaring the hell out of Mission Control doctors. And so home they came. Cee-Cee Clarke never got over that disappointment the rest of his life. He died of a massive heart attack two years after *Altair 4*.

Jana had planned to retire from the Astronaut office after *Altair 4*, but she considered her Moon mission to be unfinished. So she campaigned hard for command of *Altair 9* and won the assignment. Not only had she been the first woman to set foot on the Moon during *Altair 4*, but she was now also the first to command a Lunar mission. Eleven days before when she had once again placed her booted foot in the lunar dust, Jana knew she had done the right thing. She loved it here on this tiny world.

Jana and her crew, including her immediate companion, Cosmonaut Alexander "Sasha" Vlasenko, were the seventh crew to return mankind to the Moon after an absence of more than fifty years. This was a length of time that Jana and her astronaut cohorts thought was a bit disgraceful. Though mankind always seemed to have plenty of money for wars, she reflected sourly. Their two other crewmates, Jake Thomas and Dr. Claude Dubache, were in the pressurized rover, exploring a valley and chain of craters two days' drive away. They were scheduled to return two days before the lift off back to Earth.

The international press back on Earth seemed to have already forgotten about them. But Sasha and Jana's expedition was still fraught with hazards and because of this, they still had respectable viewership watching their moonwalks over the Net. Lunar exploration was still a long way from routine.

"Hey, Sasha, have you finished your sampling yet?"

Sasha grunted a distracted affirmative, between humming bars of a Russian pop tune.

"Yes. Er . . . What station stop is this again? Oh yes, Eleven-E." He stopped at the rover and opened one of the sample bins on the back of the driver's seat. He pushed his gloved fingers into the bin to settle its contents and then he stuffed his latest bag into it.

"This container is now full," he grumbled. "They are too small. How many times did we tell them that, eh? *Bah!*"

Jana rolled her eyes and smiled. Her old friend and lunar lander pilot was pedantic about the little details, a fact she had been grateful for countless times during training. It seemed that they had collected enough regolith and rocks to fill up Clear Lake, back in Houston. But Sasha was very dutiful about collecting any rock or soil clod that appeared interesting. After all the geologic training they'd had, the two explorers had become very adept at spotting the thousands of subtleties to be found on the lunar surface.

A voice came through Jana's earphones, as loud and strong as Sasha's though she knew it was from much further away.

"Altair 9, this is Houston. You might want to pack up for the press on to Station Twelve. We believe you have enough sampling from this location, over."

Jana leaned back to look high into the sky over Marius. A three-quarter full Earth hung in the black sky, shining blue, white and green, and brighter than a dozen full moons. The Earth also looked four times bigger than a full moon and clearly three dimensional, even from 380,000 kilometers away. Once again, her home planet took Jana's breath away for a moment.

"Er . . . Roger, Kathy," Jana said to the Capcom back in Mission Control. It was Kathy Seddon, a fellow astronaut and a geologist to boot. "Sasha has already stowed this station's sample and I've finished the panorama. As you probably saw on TV, I've already stowed the Magnetometer."

"That's affirm, Jana. Just for your information, you and Sasha are one minute ahead of the timeline. Well done."

"Thank you," Jana grinned. To be ahead of the tight timeline was the 'brass ring,' worthy of praise. Jana bounced over to the rover and with a hop and a twist she folded her stiff, semi-rigid spacesuit into the drivers seat. An inflated pressure suit had a tendency to "starfish" in a vacuum environment. Nonetheless, she got into the lawn chair-like seat with little difficulty and attached the seatbelt. With a small grunt of exertion, Sasha climbed aboard next to her.

"All set," he confirmed. Jana gave a thumbs-up and pushed the combination steering handle and throttle forward. With a lurch, the rover rolled forward and Jana steered the vehicle onto the shallow slope formed by the nearby crater rim. Sasha glanced at the lunar GPS Nav-unit then pointed roughly East of the down-sun angle.

"After this slope is the dune field. The Nav-unit will point the way to Station Twelve."

"Got it," Jana affirmed. Within minutes the explorers were steering across the boulder-strewn dune field and heading due east. A sudden, bright golden gleam in Jana's peripheral vision distracted her. The rover bounced through a deep rut; sinking up to its wheel hubs in dust for a moment.

"Bozhe moi!" Sasha exclaimed.

"Sorry," Jana apologized. "I didn't see that. I got that flash in the corner of my eye again for a moment. I don't know what it was."

"Could it be a large chunk of anorthosite?" Boris wondered. "Or perhaps a bright piece of impact glass, glinting in the sun."

Jana was non-committal. "Well, I'm not certain. There's plenty of shock glass about that's for sure. Anyway, we don't have time to go looking for it. I'm not even sure where I saw it, now."

However as they drove across the hot, dusty surface, Jana could not forget that golden gleam of light. She felt that she should somehow recognize it.

At the end of a grueling eight-hour EVA, a tired Sasha and Jana arrived back at base. On a level plain southwest of the Marius Hills formation sat their bug-shaped *Altair 9* lunar surface lander. A half kilometer from the lander was their small outpost "cabin module." The cabin module sat atop a common four-legged Altair landing stage in place of an ascent stage and was shielded from the brutal sunlight by shiny gold Mylar film, radiators and a solar panel assembly. The front facing leg of the cabin module had a ladder that led to a small airlock. Jana parked the rover at the foot of the ladder then she and Sasha wearily climbed up the ladder and repressurized the airlock. They got out of their spacesuits then hooked up the backpacks to the recharge station. After cleaning the lower halves of the suits as best they could, they finally attached ventilation hoses to the suits to help dry out their accumulated perspiration.

After this it was time to move into the main cabin for the rest of their housekeeping chores, which included sponge baths for their sweaty bodies, the evening meal and a twenty-minute debriefing of the day's activities to

Mission Control. They also said a quick goodnight to Thomas and Dubache, their signal relayed by Mission Control. Sasha put shades up on the small window to block out the powerful sunlight then he turned down the cabin lights. Finally, he and Jana lay down in their bunks, mumbling "goodnights" to each other. In the comfort of one-sixth gravity the tired Astronauts quickly fell asleep.

It was a nice day, Jana thought, though a bit hot. As usual, the sun in the black sky was devastatingly bright and the chances of inclement weather were nil. She might go for a picnic in the hills. Should she wake Sasha? No, he'd been working very hard, better to let him rest. Jana smiled and looked down at her open-toed shoes. Her painted toenails poked out and she wiggled them. The sand beneath her shoes was a very dark grey, almost black in places, though speckles of glass glistened within the clods of regolith soil. Suddenly, she longed to put her bare feet in that sand. She kicked off a shoe and plunged her toes into the sand. It was *hot*! With a frown she withdrew her toes from the stinging sands and put the shoe back on. I can't get a proper feel for this stuff with just my big toe, she thought. She looked at her hands.

They were clad in thin white gloves. Jana took off the gloves and noticed that her fingernails were very long and well manicured. Strange, I thought I'd cut them really short just two days ago. She adjusted her side-slit skirt and knelt down to grab a handful of the sandy soil. With a finger she stirred the textures in it, marveled at the sparkles of very fine glasses within the powders in her palm. Jana squeezed the soil hard and winced in surprise. She let the dusty grains fall from her fingers. She looked at her hand and saw that small cuts had been opened in a couple of fingers. Bright spots of blood welled from the cuts. As Jana brought her hand up to see better, the drops of blood fell in slow motion to the ground.

The blood immediately soaked into the dust without a trace. Jana squeezed her stinging fingers, hoping she might bleed out any contaminants within the cuts. More blood vanished into the dusty ground. This was getting annoying.

"*That's okay, Jana,*" an amused voice behind her said. "*It's not your blood the land wants.*"

It was a male voice, quiet and slightly nasal sounding.

Jana turned quickly to see who—

. . . She awoke in the darkened Cabin Module, disoriented and still

211

half-asleep. Sasha stood with his back to her, looking at the closed window shade.

"What's the matter?" Jana asked blearily.

"Nothing," he whispered. *"Nothing. Go back to sleep, Jana."*

She didn't argue. Some moments later she came awake again and groggily listened to the lavatory flushing. Vaguely uneasy but too tired to care, Jana went back to sleep and didn't dream again that night.

It was the "morning" of Day 12 and Jana and Sasha were about to sit down for breakfast before getting ready to suit-up. Jana reached up to unclip the shade from the Habitat's one window. As it had done for the last twelve Earth days, the sunlight burst into the room. Sasha turned off the main lights and looked over to see Jana staring out of the window.

"What's wrong?" he asked. Jana didn't answer for a moment, but then she seemed to shake herself from her reverie.

"Oh, nothing really. It's stupid, but I thought I saw something move out there."

Sasha blinked at that. "Well, that *would* be strange, for Claude and Jake wont be back until tomorrow afternoon, about fifteen hundred hours. Did you see that flash again?"

Jana turned from the window and hugged herself. She looked uncomfortable but nodded. "Yeah, I sure did. And I'll tell you what it reminds me of."

Sasha waited several moments but when Jana didn't reply he waggled his fingers to prompt her.

"You'll think this is nuts, but I've finally figured out that it reminds me of the reflection off a helmet's golden Sun visor."

"No, I do not think that's nuts," Sasha shook his head slowly. "After all, this is an alien environment. Beyond the aluminum and Kevlar shell and water tanks of this module, there is hard vacuum with brutal extremes of temperature between sun and shade. One meter above the ground here may as well be deep space for all the protection the Moon's environment gives us from exotic radiation that might have been traveling for a billion years. Who's to say you're not especially susceptible to cosmic rays? The flashes could merely be high-energy particles zapping your optic nerves. The Apollo astronauts used to see cosmic ray flashes all the time."

Jana smiled at his analysis. She patted his arm.

"You old bear, you always manage to make me feel better. I guess we've been here so long now that this place is starting to get to me".

Sasha smiled, nodding in agreement.

"Sometimes," she continued, "in the middle of our sleep periods I have to resist the temptation to get up and take a peek out of the window. I guess last night was no exception for you, either."

Sasha's smile changed to a quizzical expression.

"What do you mean? I didn't look out of the window at all. I did go to the toilet, yes. But I never removed the window shade, for that would wake you up."

Jana stared at him, not trusting the creeping feeling of unease. Perhaps it *was* time to return to Earth.

That next morning Jana stood on the dusty, rolling plains again. This time she had a picnic basket and was determined to reach the hills for that picnic. Jana knew that time was running out, even though there was still so much of this wonderful land to see. The dark sands seemed to promise that there was a beach somewhere nearby though throughout this whole holiday, she'd been too busy to find it. Jana changed her grip on the basket and set off towards the hills. The going quickly got tougher as the thick dust kept clogging her open-toed shoes. She'd pause every so often to take the shoes off and tap the hot sandy dust out of them. The tiny fragments of shock-glass scratched at her feet and to Jana's annoyance would draw shallow weeps of blood from her abraded skin. She bit her lip and continued on, determined to reach the hills.

The sun was bright in the inky black sky and seemed to be getting hotter as she trudged up a shallow slope, up and over the rims of craters. Her breathing grew more labored and the blisteringly hot and bright sun was getting ever more intense. Jana wiped the sweat from her brow with the back of her gloved hand and as she struggled out of a particularly deep crater she came upon what appeared to be rover wheel tracks in the dusty regolith. Jana frowned, for she knew that there shouldn't be anyone else here.

She looked towards the hills and they appeared to be no closer, despite the kilometers she had walked. Distances were certainly deceptive on the Moon where there were no helpful, Earthly reference points such as trees and lampposts to judge distances, let alone any air. She regarded the tracks and decided to postpone the walk to the hills. After all, these strange rover tracks were a mystery and Jana was an explorer.

She began to follow the tracks. And for the next kilometer or so they meandered from place to place over the pitted and rugged surface. But when she rounded a particularly large boulder, Jana was surprised to see a lunar roving vehicle parked near the rim of a small crater. Two spacesuited figures were seated within the rover. Jana glanced down within the little crater. The regolith soil within was splashed with greenish, glassy fragments. Looks a lot like olivine, she thought absently. But Jana knew she was fooling herself; what she really wanted to do was talk to those astronauts, who were just sitting there. She walked slowly up to the rover, seeing that the astronauts' gold sun visors were down. Jana waved at them.

"Hey guys! Come on, you'll never get ahead of the timeline just goofing off."

She raised the sun visor of the astronaut in the left seat. The face behind the clear visor was a glassy-eyed and obviously dead Sasha Vlasenko.

Jana staggered back with a grunt of surprise and shock and promptly stood on a sharp rock. She looked down to see that a glassy spur of the rock had gashed her foot through the side of her shoe. Bright red blood spurted from the cut and Jana cursed and staggered from the sharp pain. Blistering hot dusty regolith touched her injured foot and began to greedily draw out her blood. Jana hopped on her good foot, trying to keep away from the vampiric regolith. But as fast as her injured foot spilled the blood the hot, dark-grey dust would swallow it up.

"I thought I told you, Jana; the Moon doesn't want your blood!"

She spun around to see a spacesuited figure with red-striped legs walking out of the little crater, arms outstretched. Jana had to put her cut foot down or risk falling over. It felt like her very life was draining through that foot and into the dusty ground, into the very heart of the Moon itself. A movement in the corner of her eye made her turn again, this time to see the second rover astronaut climb off the vehicle and approach her. The second astronaut raised the gold visor and Jana saw her *own* face a moment later, smiling happily back. She gestured for Jana to come to her.

"NO!"

Jana's injured foot sank into the ground and she felt the inexorable pull of the Moon taking her down. Which didn't make sense: the Moon only had one-sixth gee. As Jana rapidly sank up to her waist in the Selenite quicksand, the astronaut with the red-striped legs grasped her hand firmly.

"Don't fight, Jana, otherwise you'll never be able to walk here freely!" the slightly nasal, male voice warned her. *"Don't fight,"* he insisted. "The Moon doesn't want to fight you; it's a peaceful place. There can be no struggle here."

So it *was* like quicksand then. Jana became still and instantly stopped sinking. With her free hand, she raised his sun visor and knew the smile within . . .

. . . The grip on her hand was firm and the deep male voice was insistent.

"It's okay, Jana, do not struggle."

She opened her eyes then squeezed them shut again as the bright cabin lights hurt them. Sasha loomed over her, concern etched on his broad, stubbled face. Jana felt so hot and thirsty and was dimly unsurprised to find herself covered in sweat. She cleared her throat, feeling it rasp dryly.

"Can I have some water, please Sasha?"

"You were having a bad dream, my friend." He moved to the galley faucet and filled a plastic cup. Jana took it gratefully and quickly drank the ice-cold water.

"I'm sorry I woke you," she said.

Sasha frowned but said nothing.

Jana forced herself to eat a full breakfast, despite feeling unsettled from her broken night's sleep. After contacting Dubache and Thomas and hearing that they were completing the last kilometers of their return journey to the *Altair 9* campsite, Sasha and Jana began to suit up for their final major EVA of the mission. Within the hour they were standing in the airlock waiting for the depressurization cycle to finish. Jana's suit smelled of the faint whiff of her own accumulated body odor and the slightly metallic tang of pure oxygen. The big green light on the airlock control glowed once more and Sasha yanked on the hatch's manual locking lever. Although the airlock was well lit, the two astronauts lowered their gold-coated visors when the raw, flat sunlight burst through the opening hatch.

Jana felt her pulse quicken as always to the sight of the Moon. *Her* Moon.

"*Once more into the breach, good friends,*'" Sasha quoted before he all but bounded down the cabin module's short flight of stairs. Jana followed more sedately, noting and savoring every moment. She felt the soft crunch and compression of the regolith beneath her boots. Jana looked up at the dazzlingly bright Earth that hung high in the jet-black sky and knew that within five days, she and her colleagues would be standing on the brown soil of their home world again. And then the Moon would be back in its rightful place, sailing the blue days and star-studded nights, just as it always had.

It was Sasha's turn to drive the rover and he turned the spindly little car towards Station 14. In silence, Jana watched the magnificent, desolate scenery pass by as the rover bounced along. She noted that the sun was now getting really low on the horizon, the shadows were lengthening and the landscape was taking on a more tan coloring up-sun and a darker grey down-sun. Within twenty-six hours it would set and the brutally cold, fourteen-day long lunar night would begin.

"You're quiet, Jana. Is everything all right?"

Sasha's question startled her. Her throat was dry so she took a sip of water from the suit's neck ring dispenser tube before answering.

"Yeah, Sasha, I'm fine. Just admiring the view." And she got back to doing just that. Sasha turned the rover towards a shallow dune field pockmarked with the omnipresent craters.

The *craters!* God, craters seemed to be the dominant feature of the ancient and battered Moon. From ringed basins larger than some Earthly nations, to holes big enough to swallow sports stadiums, right down to pinprick sized "zap pits." The Moon was craters on top of craters, right down to the microscopic level. And the dusty regolith that covered everything was the result of eons of ceaseless micrometeorite rain. This steady, Zen-like erosion had ground the rocks to textures that varied in coarseness from cobbles and sandy grit, to fine-blend coffee, to that of fragile cigarette ash.

Sasha steered the rover around the biggest crater rim and they started up a medium-grade slope towards the hills. Jana nodded approvingly, for it was a nice day and she was glad they would finally get up there before this mission was over. Sasha started humming a jaunty sounding tune. Jana saw a bright golden flash dead ahead upslope. She gripped her seat harness tightly and felt her pulse quicken.

"You, know, we should have brought a picnic basket this trip," Sasha said, laughing just as they drove across a set of rover tracks not their own.

"Sasha, stop the car."

"What?"

"Stop the Rover, now!"

He did so and Jana couldn't unstrap and get off the rover quickly enough. She clumsily bounded across the slope, side-slipping one-step for every three she took on the crumbly regolith. Sasha repeatedly called her name; worry keenly heard in his voice. Within moments Mission Control was on the radio, too, demanding a status report. But Jana ignored them all. She just kept running and bouncing up and across the slope, pursuing the golden gleam that now flashed like an irregular beacon.

The rugged slope abruptly gave way and she fell in slow motion onto her butt and slid perhaps a dozen meters down friable clods of regolith and dusty cobbles. Jana came to a halt near the bottom of the slope. A few meters below were more level ground with a set of rover wheel tracks. She was panting hard and her suit's air conditioning labored to clear the suddenly fogging visor. Jana struggled to get up but her dirty suit legs seemed to slip into quicksand. She peered through a now very foggy visor. It was just a small crater nearly filled with perhaps a half-meter of the finest, powdery regolith. It was almost like struggling in light mud, albeit a very dry mud.

She could get out of this easily enough but she'd have to be careful. But for the moment she would just have a short rest. Jana was becoming so hot and thirsty that she took a drink from the helmet's neck ring dispenser, which promptly stopped working. *Great.* She realized belatedly that her radio had gone silent, too. The stuffiness in the helmet grew worse and the visor was nearly completely fogged. She forced herself to close her eyes for a few moments, relax and take a few deep breaths.

"Need a hand, partner?"

Jana's eyes snapped open. The slightly nasal, male voice was loud in her cloth-capped earphones and the figure before her was diffuse from the foggy faceplate. She craned her neck forward and used her cloth-covered forehead to wipe a patch of the visor faceplate. The spacesuit revealed before her was pristine white and the sun strike off its golden helmet visor was nearly blinding. The man offered Jana his hands and she gratefully accepted his help. A moment later she stood before him.

"Cee-Cee? What are you doing here? Have you been following me?"

Cee-Cee Clarke raised his gold visor and grinned. His large green eyes creased mischievously. "Well, you ought to know me, Jana. I'm not an easy man to ignore, though God knows you've done your best to these last couple weeks. Although I'm happy you've come back to the Moon, I'm surprised, too."

Jana shook her head. "Surprised? Why would you be surprised? You know how angry I was we never got to finish exploring this place."

"Well," Cee-Cee chuckled. "What do you think I've been doing these last few years! I'm not one for lying around, as you well know. Now I've got all the time in the world—I mean Moon—to explore this place. It's pretty neat. Beautiful by day and even more so by night. You should *see* this place at night when there's a full Earth. It's fantastic. And by the way, many of the theories about the Moon have got it wrong, you know."

Jana sighed, partly annoyed and partly relieved. How else could these last few days here end up?

"And what would a dead man know about geology?" she asked, bemused.

Cee-Cee's smile broadened even more. "There's still a lot I don't know, Jana and you know a dead man can't tell tales."

"Well, here's a question," Jana posited, for she doubted she'd get a second chance. "Why are you here, Cee-Cee, and what do you want?"

Cee-Cee Clarke looked slightly offended but he still smiled. "I wanted to see you, buddy, I've missed you." He looked more somber for a moment.

"Jana, did you know that the mountain tribes of Nepal believe the spirits of their ancestors reside on the Moon?"

Jana shook her head. "No, I didn't know that. Well, *do* they reside here? Is the Moon a spiritual conclave?"

"If you were Nepalese, you'd probably have that answer already," Cee-Cee shrugged. "But I'd say it was more of a prophecy than anything else. I'd say the Moon was lonely, Jana. Whether by design or accident, it transpires that anyone who ever lives on the Moon will leave a piece of him or herself here for all time. Perhaps the longer you stay here, the stronger that bond gets. Only time will tell."

Jana looked around the dusty little world, at the beauty that walked hand in hand with lifeless desolation. You had to love the place, she thought. And if a part of Jana Stanley would remain here forever, then that was fine with her.

Cee-Cee clasped her gloved hands. "Well, I've got to go, buddy. And so do you. There's a lot of people worried about you right now and it wouldn't be kosher to end up like me."

He embraced Jana as best as their clumsy suits would allow and bounced lightly away into the bright lunar evening. At the top of a little hill, Cee-Cee paused long enough to give Jana a wave before he became just a gold gleam on the close horizon and then, not even that.

Jana was so preoccupied that she didn't notice at first the rover arriving with a clearly agitated Sasha. Through her foggy visor she saw him clamber out of the rover and rush to her. She only heard his one word in three through her obviously damaged radio and managed to placate Sasha by giving him a thumbs-up. He checked her filthy spacesuit over and found no serious damage. Jana gripped his arm and allowed herself to be escorted to the rover.

They hooked their suit's airhoses together in a 'buddy system' and Sasha's air conditioning unit soon cleared her fogged-up faceplate. After that Sasha drove them back to base camp at full speed.

On Surface Mission Day 14, Jana and her three crewmates made their final EVA after closing out the cabin module. They bounced across the dusty ground that was now decorated with deep and inky black shadows and approached their waiting Altair spacecraft. Their *Orion* Exploration Vehicle 'mothership' was right now undertaking a plane-changing maneuver to prepare for their ascent and docking. In less than four hours the sun would set and the long night would begin, illuminating the surface with Earthlight. Jana wished so much that she could be here to see that. But she knew that the likelihood of her flying to the Moon again was slight. The Shackelton Lunar Outpost project was about to start, Mars landings were still years away and she'd had a good career. She didn't want to take away a young astronaut's chance to fly here by monopolizing a third lunar mission.

Jana climbed up the Altair's ladder and paused in the hatchway to look across the landscape one more time. Those lovely hills that she'd never quite made it to were now succumbing to creeping shadow. And as it turned out, the 'other rover' tracks she'd seen were in fact from Thomas and Dubache's first traverse. It seemed now that the crew of *Altair 9* had traversed much of the Marius Hills area. But Jana knew that Charles 'Cee-Cee' Clarke had been doing a lot more exploration.

Or so she hoped.

It annoyed her to think that the whole incident had been nothing more than the double failure of her carbon dioxide scrubber and liquid cooled undergarment control units, giving her an oxygen-starved, overheated mania. But Jana liked to think she knew better. The Moon had never nurtured life of its own and had ridden the skies of Earth for eons, looking down in envy on the flourishing children of Mother Earth. And when the Earth no longer had use for them, Luna would gratefully give refuge to their shades.

As the night crept forward to cover the still-hot dunes, it was chased away a moment by bright rocket light, then softened by the stars and glow of a full Mother Earth.

One Last Haul
by Mark J. Soppet

"Contact light," droned the pilot's voice through the intercom system. The rumble of the rocket engines slowly tapered off as the jolt of the landing rippled through the body of Elijah McCoy. The lean, sinewy man inside the pristine white pressure suit never objected to the sensation, but the timing always surprised him.

Elijah traditionally put his face to the porthole at this moment, surveying the craggy majesty of the lunar landscape. But he just couldn't bring himself to do it today. The awe had long since worn off.

McCoy sat in his seat, a thin layer of nylon webbing stretched over an aluminum frame, while pensively longing to disembark. It was only supposed to take the pilot thirty minutes to complete his post-flight checks before freeing the hatch and releasing the eight passengers. But Elijah McCoy was very tense on that particular day in May 2067.

Eventually the notice came from the pilot, and the aft hatch folded down. McCoy and his seven fellow passengers eased out of their seats and shuffled down the stairs built onto the aft door. There wasn't enough headroom for the passengers as they left the two banks of seats for the single aisle, and they strained their heads down while plodding to exit the lander.

McCoy paused on the bottom step to take in the moonscape. The boulders and rocky spires dotted the lunar surface near the flat crater where the lander touched down.

The landing craft itself was a spindly-looking affair with four frail legs arrayed in two rows. The passengers sat in a cylindrical crew module, slung horizontally between the banks of legs. Two rows of three thrusters each flanked the passenger compartment. The engineers from the Wanliss Corporation in El Segundo thought of this ingenious design, which allowed

221

the same lander to carry either a cargo module or a crew compartment.

Like a giant metallic caterpillar, a pressurized rover lumbered over the crater rim to meet the eight passengers and their pilot. It resembled a tube with six wheels, each of which was nearly six meters tall. The head of the caterpillar was a gold-tinted glass dome on the forward end, affording the rover driver an unparalleled view of the path he was driving. But the passengers could anticipate a cramped ride with a nonexistent view. Both sides of the dust-covered white vehicle were adorned with the orange and magenta logo of the LuMinEx Corporation, still visible through the lunar dust that covered every manmade object on the Moon.

The rover came upon a cluster of seven squat, cylindrical buildings at Fra Mauro Crater, all connected by inflatable tunnels. Like the rover and lander, they all belonged to LuMinEx. The caterpillar docked at the building on the west end of the complex. The weary travelers shuffled out through another airlock and doffed their pressure suits. They hung the suits in their assigned lockers, only to attend the safety briefings and sign the waivers that were a legally mandated prerequisite for their expedition.

When all of the legalese was complete, McCoy retired to his chamber in the northeast building. The room was little bigger than the bed, and no taller than McCoy could stretch his arms above his head. Its computer workstation folded into the wall. But Elijah McCoy was wired, in spite of the long day he'd just endured. There would be little sleep for him as a full fleet of shuttlecraft streaked through his mind.

McCoy was no stranger to the Moon. During his first expedition, the initial feelings of trepidation were mixed with sheer exhilaration. But the adrenaline rush quickly vaporized when McCoy got word that his best friend from Lunar Mining Academy, Glenn Fordham, was killed in a mine collapse.

Death is never a pretty sight, but death on the Moon requires an exceptionally strong stomach. After the mine collapse and the rapid boil-off of his bodily fluids into the vacuum of space, there wasn't much left of Glenn Fordham.

McCoy was permitted to attend the funeral, where a small box containing his friend's remains was dropped in a hole in the ground. The dead were never sent back to Earth; their remains cut into the volume of cargo that could be stuffed into a lander, and keeping the bodies under pressure was deemed an unnecessary cost. Flight between Earth and the Moon was still an expensive prospect. Flights that didn't help to generate revenue were dismissed as an unacceptable waste.

Glenn's death catalyzed Elijah McCoy's spiral of growing disillusionment with the lunar mining enterprise. On McCoy's second expedition, LuMinEx told the miners that they'd make a fortune mining helium-3 isotopes for sale to the People's Republic of China in their fusion reactor project. When the reactor ran into myriad technical difficulties, the entire haul turned out to be a bust, and it was the miners who were left without their cut at the end of the six-month expedition.

The romanticized vision of being a "star voyager" had eroded for Elijah. As a boy growing through adolescence in the 2050s, he was enthralled with news reports of the initial lunar sorties launched by the Wanliss Corporation. Wanliss's astronauts were overnight heroes when they landed on the Moon, and they enjoyed fame and fortune when they returned from their first voyage.

Eventually the Wanliss Corporation receded from lunar operations and settled on building lunar vehicles for three private mining firms. The most prominent of the three was Lunar Mining Expeditions, or "LuMinEx" for short.

The allure of LuMinEx had been too much for Elijah to ignore. It promised a relief from the coal-mining life he had been raised into in West Virginia. Elijah engorged himself on claims from the LuMinEx recruiters about the fortune and the great education the company would grant him. Elijah saw himself as the guy everybody would look up to when he was back home between six-month tours on the Moon.

There had been one problem with the LuMinEx lifestyle, though. Aimee, Elijah's wife, hadn't approved of him being gone from home for half the year at a time. Especially after their twins, Josh and Beth, had been born. Elijah had to give up his family to pursue his dream. He hoped Josh and Beth would understand when they were older. Aimee was like an anchor, holding him back from chasing his dream. And if she wouldn't let him go, she must not have really loved him anyway.

But LuMinEx really didn't love Elijah McCoy either. Their promises of a great education amounted to nine months of Lunar Mining Academy, hardly the engineering education he wanted for an eventual career after LuMinEx. Once he was on the Moon, he toiled in the same mining work that his father and grandfather performed in West Virginia. And even as advanced mining robots became commonplace in the mines on Earth, LuMinEx insisted on using humans to perform the jobs that were both rote and dangerous. The Chief Technology Officer at LuMinEx was taken by surprise at the rapid advances in robotics. The company struggled to keep pace with the technology, and the CEO couldn't justify the high startup costs of the robots. LuMinEx had already spent millions in training a glut of human miners.

Elijah had to stop dwelling on the painful past. It was making his stomach churn, and he was having a hard enough time adjusting to the lunar sleep cycle without having to taste the bitterness of the last few years. This mission would be his last stay on the gray, barren rock known as the Moon. He was determined to leave with his head held high.

Elijah made it to the mess hall on time and shuffled through the serving line, grabbing the same stale toast and same rubbery eggs he'd grown accustomed to. He sat at an empty table, followed by George Muntz. He had worked with Muntz on previous expeditions and knew him well. Muntz had greasy silver hair, slicked back and terminating in a short ponytail. The loose folds of skin under his jawbone betrayed that he was pushing sixty.

Two more men took their seats at McCoy's table. The man to his left was Bob Sanchez, a fellow miner from the Helium-3 debacle. Across the table, and to the left of Muntz, sat a boy who didn't look a day over twenty-one. Technically he was a man, but his smooth skin hadn't known the rigors of working the LuMinEx mines. His thin face and its pale skin contrasted with his jet-black hair atop his head, neatly parted down the left side.

Elijah tore off a mouthful of toast, put the rest down, and looked at his breakfast-mates. "So how was your lunar shuttle flight?" he asked them.

"Can't complain," said Sanchez. "No better, no worse than any other time I've been here."

"Well, I wasn't expecting the jolt when we touched down," said the boy with a bit of hesitation. McCoy reached across the table with his right hand. After holding it out for a second, the boy tepidly shook it.

"I'm Elijah McCoy. You can say I've been around the block a few times."

"Oh, I'm Jeremy Steffens, and this is my first time on the Moon."

"We should probably keep him away from you," said Bob Sanchez. "We don't want your attitude to rub off on him."

"Don't question my attitude," McCoy replied, somewhat defensively. "I'm just realistic about the situation, that's all."

"What situation?" inquired Steffens.

"Nothing in particular," McCoy said, brushing him off. With a raised eyebrow and a sly grin he added, "You'll have a good time here, kid. There's a lot of important work to do here."

"What kind of important work do you got lined up?" asked Muntz.

"I'm on a strip-mining operation near the Taurus Mountains. The next big thing in lunar mining is Orange Soil, and I'm going to be a part of it."

"That's what they've been saying," Muntz replied between bites of French Toast sticks. "If they can extract oxygen from Orange Soil, the whole mining operation will be less dependent on oxygen from Earth. Then the lunar mining business can really take off."

"I wish I could be around to see it," McCoy said insincerely. "But I think this Orange Soil expedition is going to be my last haul on the Moon."

"Why?" asked Sanchez.

"I've been letting my life pass me by, Bob. This business of doing six months on the Moon and six months on Earth is really wearing on me. I'm almost thirty years old, and there's so much of life I need to experience. Hang gliding. Rides in hot air balloons. Getting a real education. Working a steady nine-to-five job, and going out for lunch with the guys on a daily basis. And if I play my cards right, maybe I can patch things up at home and finally start being a real dad to my kids. I mean, is it fair to them that daddy is too busy playing astronaut? I'm not a dad. I'm not even a sorry excuse for a dad. I'm just a bum . . ."

"Jeremy," interrupted Bob, "why don't you go back through the line and get me some more sausage links?" He needed to get Elijah off this tangent of self-destruction, before he got the kid too jaded. "Elijah, you knew getting into this that the life of a lunar miner wasn't for everybody."

"Yeah, but when I got into this, I was young and selfish. I was naïve to the way the system worked. I didn't have any sense of what really mattered in life until we lost Glenn."

"You still don't have any idea of what you really want in life," Sanchez shot back.

"No, but I'm trying to figure that out. And there's no better time to start than now," McCoy sheepishly admitted.

Muntz was the next to interject his opinion. "Maybe you need to face facts. That boat sailed a long time ago. There's no going back to what you had, or what you could have had. You're a lunar miner now, and you need to put all of your effort into being the best lunar miner you can be."

McCoy slumped back in his chair with a look of resignation on his face. The boy returned with Bob's sausage, which the elder miner wolfed down. The miners left for their lockers, with McCoy assuring the boy that all was well on the Moon.

In their full pressure suits, Elijah McCoy and his team of four made their way through the airlock into the cabin of the hopper. Resembling a lander, a hopper was configured for the fastest point-to-point travel that the lunar transportation infrastructure had to offer. The men strapped themselves in as an automated voice recording counted down from ten, a voice with a dehumanized and mechanical quality to it. The voice reached one, then announced "ignition." The engines rumbled to life, and the passengers were greeted with the sensation of movement, followed by weightlessness as they reached the apex of their ballistic arc over the lunar surface. The sensations of falling were rebutted by the jolt and rumble of engines firing again to brake the hopper as it came to a landing at the prepared pad for the Taurus Mountains mining site.

The miners disembarked to be greeted by the behemoth machine they'd be operating. The bucket-wheel excavator was the preferred tool of the strip miner, on the Moon just as it was on Earth. The massive mechanical beast's metallic skeleton towered three hundred feet above the surface of the Moon, and stretched across the length of two football fields. Two trusses stretched like arms to the front of the vehicle and held the most important component: the massive wheel carrying the scoops that would wrest the Orange Soil from the Moon.

Building the excavators on Earth was a challenge; building them on the

Moon was a different kind of hurdle, but no higher or lower than the one on Earth. The reduced lunar gravity held certain benefits for the construction of such large machines. But the logistics train to get the equipment from Earth to the Moon was still too slow for most people's satisfaction.

From the cabin, the miners extracted themselves from their pressure suits to work in the shirtsleeve environment that the cabin afforded. Over the radio, they contacted Expedition Control at Fra Mauro.

"Control, this is Tiger 1," informed McCoy over the radio. "Crew members Kohl, Eiserman, Stone, Evans and McCoy present. All systems nominal. Ready to commence mining operations."

"We copy, Tiger 1," replied the twangy voice of Expedition Control. It could only be Dean Strait, an operator that McCoy was too familiar with. "I'm looking over my telemetry and all looks nominal. Cleared to commence mining operations."

The crew manned their stations and flipped the switches to awaken the metal leviathan. The cabin responded with a shudder and a regular reverberation as the bucket-wheel excavator lurched forward.

The operation seemed to go well for the first ninety minutes before McCoy noticed the temperatures rising in the number one fuel cell. The needle wasn't holding steady, wavering between borderline and safe levels. It looked like an instrumentation problem and McCoy wanted to press on. Besides, the LuMinEx management would eat him for lunch if he cost them productivity and money over a ratty instrument reading.

Thirty minutes later, the bad temperature gauge stabilized. Unfortunately, it stabilized on the high side of the range over which the measurement had been uncertain. McCoy informed the crew and took a look at the reading again. It was in the yellow range, but still not out-of-limits. The operation would carry on.

After fifteen minutes, the needle on the temperature gauge wavered briefly, and then went red. The bucket-wheel excavator reacted with a shudder and a thud, its motors falling silent. The beast was dead, broken down for the indeterminate future. Emergency lights went on in the cabin as the miners suited up for extravehicular activity.

"Kohl, grab the emergency checklist for a dead fuel cell," McCoy called out. Kohl used his emergency flashlight, a tiny stick concealed in his suit's pen pouch, to find the checklist in the storage compartment under a crew seat. "We're probably out of commission, but we don't want to rule out something simple as the source of our problem." The men reviewed all of the maintenance steps on the fuel cell checklist, but it was clear that the problem was beyond their capacity for field repairs. It would require a maintenance crew, and it would probably take weeks of schedule to push the bucket-wheel excavator back into service.

It was never a good thing when Dean Strait pulled you into his office. Anxiety and nervousness coursed through Elijah McCoy's veins as he made his way through the corridors of the Fra Mauro base to Expedition Control. "Take a seat," Strait commanded, his voice not betraying the anger that was certain to come. McCoy sat in one of the swivel chairs that Strait kept at his desk for just such an occasion.

"I guess you want to hear me say that I screwed up out there in the field today," McCoy stated.

"That's an understatement, if I ever heard one." Strait's voice mixed a tone of sarcasm with the anger.

"Well, you're not going to get that admission from me. I followed procedure, I used my judgment, we were within our limits, and the problem arose too fast to take corrective action."

"So not only are you irresponsible with multi-million-dollar LuMinEx equipment, but you've also got an insubordinate attitude that measures up to the repair bill you dropped at my feet today." Dean wrinkled his brow as the blood rushed to his face. "In all our years working together, all I've seen out of you is poor judgment."

"What did you expect me to do? I can't suspend mining operations for a piece of hardware that's still within operating limits." McCoy turned his right hand to expose the palm. "If the cell didn't break down, you'd have praised me for showing some ambition." He repeated the gesture with the left hand. "If I suspended operations and found that it was just an instrumentation problem, you'd have busted me for being excessively cautious. You just can't win around here unless the chips fall in your favor." McCoy threw his hands up in exasperation.

"It's not about judgment, McCoy! It's about sloppiness! If you had checked the secondary telemetry before starting the excavator, you'd have seen where the problem was!"

McCoy had a burning sensation of embarrassment deep within his core. Strait rose from his seat and turned his back to McCoy, staring out his window. The stars appeared as points of light that didn't twinkle. It was just one aspect of life on the Moon that McCoy had never completely adjusted to.

"Well, I don't know what to say, except that I messed this one up big-time, and I was wrong to be so defensive about it." Really, McCoy didn't know what was in the secondary telemetry. Strait could have been making up the entire story, for all he knew. But now seemed like a pretty good time for being conciliatory. Strait opened his mouth again, but the passion was now missing from his voice.

"I had high expectations for you when you first arrived from the Academy. But your heart was never in it. I should really put you in a desk job until the next Earth-Moon shuttle arrives, and then send you back where you belong. You're a dead-ender, and I can't have you screwing up the mission."

"Dead-ender?" McCoy asked, feigning ignorance. "What makes you say that?"

Strait turned around again to face McCoy and took his seat again. "I listen to the grapevine. I know what you think of LuMinEx, and how you want to get out. I need not remind you that you're committed here for one more expedition after your current one, as a result of your education at Lunar Mining Academy."

"Yeah, but if this Orange Soil is as valuable as they say it is, I can use my cut of the haul to buy my way out of the last year on my contract."

"Let me give you some friendly advice. If you're not going to give your full effort to this program, you need to leave now. It's better to repay your debts than to make yourself miserable while detracting from the mission." Strait took a deep breath and said, almost accusingly, "McCoy, are you a Selenite? Is that what your insubordination is all about?"

The Selenites had grown out of the environmental movement on earth. Every night they would look up in the night sky to see that the Man in the Moon had scars and pockmarks all over his face, like he'd been in a motorcycle accident. The Selenites wanted, at a minimum, to restrict mining on the near side. Some Selenites wanted to ban lunar mining altogether.

"Politics has nothing to do with my attitude," McCoy replied. "I just want to make a buck. The only politics that bother me are the rotten LuMinEx politics that take advantage of guys like me."

Strait paused for a second. "What drew you to this job in the first place? I mean, don't you appreciate the Moon for the sense of the unknown and the thrill of adventure you get here?"

"I don't feel any of that rush anymore," McCoy said, taking a gulp and choosing his next words very carefully. "I mean, I thought I'd feel that way, but LuMinEx made me a lot of false promises when they took me in. And after I got here, I don't feel like an adventurer or a celebrity or even a member of this 'LuMinEx Family' that all the corporate propaganda talks about. I just feel like a pawn. And every day I spend toiling for LuMinEx is a day I could have spent trying to better myself or trying to be a better dad for my kids." Now it was Strait's turn to be conciliatory.

"Well, I want you to keep in mind that the real world isn't any better than LuMinEx. The rocks will always be grayer on the other side of the fence. You might not have gotten what you wanted, but LuMinEx has given you valuable skills that will help you succeed wherever you go."

It was as rehearsed a response as McCoy had ever heard. McCoy fought the urge to make a sarcastic retort and asked to be dismissed. He sulked back to his chamber with his head tilted back, staring blankly beyond the ceiling.

The bar was quiet that night, a perfect time for McCoy to clear his head. The burly bartender poured the usual scotch on the rocks for McCoy. In the diminished gravity, the act of pouring was unbearably slow, while the act of downing a shot was too fast to truly savor it. As he sat at the bar, the river of regret began to race between the boulders of his memories.

Elijah still didn't know what to make of Strait. He wasn't a bad guy, but he didn't have any loyalty towards his people. The center of his universe was "The Mission." Anything that didn't contribute was extraneous. Elijah knew that Strait could always be worse, like the passive-aggressive Division Chief who sat in his office on Earth and appeared to be clueless about the lunar operation.

It was Aimee who warned him about LuMinEx. She told him that it wouldn't be glamorous; it would just be another job that would work him to the bone, like the mines in West Virginia. By the time he got to the Moon, there would be over 400 people working the mining colonies, plus a smattering of scientists. He'd just be another face, and certainly not a celebrity. Besides, she explained, he needed to grow up and be a man. He needed to be responsible and hold down a steady job that would allow him to spend time with his children.

Why did he ever doubt her? She'd known him since high school, and was in a better position than anybody to figure out what would make him happy. But Elijah repaid her by slapping her upside the head one night when they had that discussion. Was he drinking at the time when he slapped her? *He must have been,* he assured himself. *Definitely.*

Elijah wished he could roll back all the hurtful memories. He longed to make everything right again. But he knew deep down that there was no going back to the way things were. A girl like Aimee would probably have a new man in her life by now, one who would treat her like the queen she was. And one who would actually be there for the children, to celebrate the birthdays, and play catch in the yard, and make them feel like the greatest kids in the world.

He could only settle for making things better than they were now. He could cast off the chains of LuMinEx and try to discern his life's calling. He could tell Aimee that while she might never take him back, she was right all those years ago. He could at least get visitation of Josh and Beth, and let them know he was a responsible daddy who still loved them deeply.

Elijah left the bar and went to bed. Tomorrow he would try to fix things. There was one last haul to make.

The plan was to take the hopper back to Taurus and see if he could do anything to help the technicians fix the fuel cell. He couldn't guarantee that it would get him his spot back in the Orange Soil effort. But he could guarantee that if he did nothing, it would earn him a one-way trip back to Earth, to soak in his debts to LuMinEx.

The technicians welcomed McCoy's helping hand, as LuMinEx never kept enough technicians to deal with all the problems that somehow managed to erupt. It took two hours to disconnect the fuel cell. Another thirty minutes were required to transport it on a rover, outfitted as a pickup truck, to a pressurized service facility. The technicians had to swap out air tanks once, using the shirtsleeve environment of the rover-truck to perform the switch. They were amazed with all of the sweat they dumped out of the suits when they pressurized the service facility.

Elijah McCoy was in the middle of inspecting a hydrogen valve when a grainy but familiar voice came over the service facility's radio. "We have a cave-in at the Taurus Rutile Mine! Need all units to respond at once!" McCoy thought about the voice for a second before it registered in his brain. It was the boy from the dining hall, Jeremy Steffens.

The boy was too inexperienced for mining the Titanium-rich Rutile ores, McCoy thought to himself. LuMinEx had probably doomed another expendable miner to his death. But Elijah McCoy also had a say in the matter.

"Does anybody here have any mining experience?" McCoy barked the question to the technicians, and got only blank looks in reply. *It was no use bringing three guys into the field and getting them killed during the course of rescuing one*, McCoy realized. He would be the only person from the service bay making the trip into the Rutile Mine. But he couldn't go without a hard suit, the kind the miners wore during operations. And he needed a pick and shovel. As he scrambled for the necessary equipment, he spotted the suit and tools suspended neatly from a metal frame. It must have been repaired recently, but it appeared as a gift of divine providence to McCoy.

Disembarking from the rover-truck, McCoy surveyed the lunar horizon. The stars still didn't twinkle. They simply stared accusingly, regardless of how McCoy cocked his head. The void of space was still deep and endless. Peering down the mineshaft, McCoy noted that the inner space was equally as void.

Elijah took the agonizingly long elevator into the abyss of the mineshaft and rode the nearest cart through the mine towards the site of the cave-in. A duo of miners set to work in hard suits, furiously picking away at the wall of rock and scooping out the debris. McCoy stood by for a moment, stunned by the soundless scene of men pounding away at rock with a fellow miner's life in the balance.

"How long has he been in there?" McCoy asked over his microphone. He started to pick away at the rock wall.

"Over thirty minutes," revealed one rescuer. If the kid was good at regulating his breathing, he might be able to last two more hours, but still

232

not long enough for McCoy's liking.

McCoy thought back to breakfast the day before. The boy was too young to go down like this, in some freak accident. LuMinEx wouldn't take this young man from the world when he had so much more to offer. LuMinEx had taken his own pride, but they at least let him keep his life. He guessed he should be thankful for that, and put that life to good use for a change.

Swinging his mattock with all his strength, McCoy grunted and snorted and grimaced as he broke through layer after layer of rock. Bits of boulder flew in every direction. The other rescuers stepped aside, unable to see through the frenzied mist of rock fragments. "He's going at it like a rabid badger," one of them remarked. They stood by and scooped away as Elijah McCoy became a twirling mass of purposeful violence. His face burned red with the intensity of a thousand suns, while the sweat pooled in his boots as it overwhelmed the suit's cooling system.

With every swing of the mattock into the barrier of rubble, McCoy imagined himself lashing out at everybody who made LuMinEx into the remorseless juggernaut that he despised with every inch of his being. Every thrust of the shovel was a stab into his own heart, a heart that forgot what was worth cherishing so long ago.

An hour of non-stop digging produced a small hole into which the rays from McCoy's helmet-mounted light disappeared. Jackpot. The other men were quite far behind. He broke down enough of the wall to fit a hard suit through, then peeked around the barely-lit chamber.

There was no trace of the boy to be found.

McCoy realized the error of his hastiness upon second inspection. Jeremy was slumped against the darkened corner of the chamber, sitting motionless. Heavy perspiration condensed on the inner surface of his helmet. No—he couldn't lose him like this, not after coming this far. McCoy checked the oxygen pressure gauge on the back of his suit. There was still enough for him to get to the surface, but barely. Maybe there was still hope after all.

Elijah tapped on the front of Jeremy's helmet, only to be met with the closed eyes behind the glass. He grasped Jeremy by the shoulders and jerked him side-to-side. The boy's limp body shuddered. He jerked his head in McCoy's direction.

There was no time to waste. McCoy pushed Jeremy towards the opening in the rock wall, then put his hands under the boy's feet and pushed him through the escape. After a brief halt, Steffens disappeared through the hole. All that was left was to get himself out through that narrow passageway. McCoy put his left hand on the hole's rim, then his right foot followed partway up the rock wall. The wall felt shaky, and it was with great dread that he continued. Next came the right hand, then the left foot. His head and arms were through the hole. Freedom was just around the corner.

Then he felt the thunk against his back. It sounded like the suit was dented, perhaps severing the internal plumbing. The two rescuers, dragging Jeremy by his hands, looked back at Elijah McCoy as he was pinned helplessly in place. Elijah managed the strength to raise his arm and motion to the rescuers that they had to get the boy to safety immediately. They could come back for him later. It was his own sloppiness that created the second cave-in to begin with. He'd have to solve his own problem in the only way he knew.

Elijah clawed at the dirt in front of him. It seemed like he was just pawing away at the ground and making no progress. Eventually he felt his hulk lurch forward. His breathing became increasingly labored with each lurch forward. The stones that had pinned him down trickled backwards over his legs and behind him.

Then the stones stopped moving.

The failing radio in McCoy's suit crackled with an acknowledgement from Expedition Control that the medical team had arrived at the mineshaft. The doctor radioed once Jeremy had arrived.

A wave of euphoria swept over Elijah. The boy wouldn't be another casualty of LuMinEx.

Elijah McCoy was unresponsive when the rescuers returned to the accident site. The coroner would claim that he was already dead by the time they arrived.

After a brief stay in the infirmary, Jeremy Steffens returned to work. His new team loaded ores into the landers that would rendezvous with the Earth-Moon shuttle at the L1 Lagrange Point. The cargo would then transfer to LuMinEx's space station in Earth orbit and LuMinEx's landing strip in Nevada. The ore shipment was a bit skimpy this time around.

Once the ores were secure in their storage racks, an unusual cylinder arrived for loading. The top and bottom domes were securely sealed to their tube. The men exchanged surprised and solemn glances. Jeremy placed his hands on the extraordinary object and wistfully gazed at the brushed aluminum surface as if to ask, "Why?" The cylinder walls contained the vindictiveness behind the sacrificial act.

The time had finally arrived to return home.

Dean Strait leaned forward at his desk and punched his assistant's speed-dial button on the speakerphone. He would need to submit a statement to the accident investigation board that afternoon, but a different statement consumed his thoughts.

"Yeah Mary, this is Dean."

A high and raspy yet comforting voice emerged from the other end. "Yes, Mr. Strait."

"I need you to draft me a letter. Address it to Josh and Beth McCoy."

"And who would they be, Mr. Strait?"

"Did you know Elijah McCoy, by chance?"

"I met him in passing, Mr. Strait. Seemed like a pleasant gentleman. Very quiet. You could detect a trace of anger, but it seemed like he was filled with a sense of resignation above all else."

"Yes, that's him. I wanted to tell Josh and Beth what we thought of their dad."

He gave his whole heart to the mission. It was all that Strait could ask for.

Inherit the Moon
by Fran Van Cleave

Colonel Jake Rowan steered the Looney Bug over the rolling plain, the Earth a creamy crescent in the rear-view mirror. Ahead, sunlight spilled like a white phosphorus bomb over the vast Aitken Basin, an impact crater large enough to hold North America. Though not as beautiful as from orbit, the sight always made him forget to breathe. He should've relished this trip as a vacation from the joys of mining ice and hauling dehydrated pee.

But only a genuine lunatic could've relaxed with Mother Catherine Connelly as a passenger, let alone looked forward to arriving at Heavenly City.

"So what's this about?" Jake said, squinting as his Smart Visor swiveled toward the rotund figure in the passenger seat, clutching her vacuum-safe freezer case. "Two million in prize money wasn't enough—now you want sainthood? And maybe a book deal with appearances on Oprah."

The suit radio transmitted Catherine's snort with such fidelity Jake almost ducked. "You're a cynic. With all your medals, Colonel, why fear an epidemic? You've been vaccinated."

"My immunity to biowar agents wore off years ago. And if General Barrett doesn't kill me for disobeying orders, the Chinese won't have any such worries."

"Spoken like a man with a guilty conscience. Be grateful for a chance to redeem yourself. You see, Colonel, God sent me here for a reason."

Jake stared out at the kilometers of candy-colored rock ribboning the fantastically steep slopes of the basin, a finger-painting experiment for giants. The collision with the gigantic asteroid that formed it would've made plowing the Grand Canyon in an instant seem a mere twitch by comparison.

Such a panorama made his own plight, and life, seem insignificant. "As I recall, it was NASA, not God. And I'm telling you right now, if you try converting the Chinese while we're there, we'll never get out alive."

"Two decades and 380,000 kilometers haven't improved your disposition, Colonel."

Jake ignored her, the Bug jouncing on its shocks as he skirted a bumpy craterlet. The truth was, the NASA bureaucrats, the Chinese, and this psalm-singing harpy had all come here over the dead bodies of American astronauts. Jake and his moon-dusted brothers and sisters had sacrificed everything to be kings and queens of the solar system for a brief, shining moment. Next to what he'd lost, the little episode in Singapore meant nothing.

But there he'd had the bad fortune to cross paths with Catherine. One little misstep, and St. Joseph, the patron saint of astronauts, had sentenced him to astronaut hell.

From the rim of its home crater at the southwestern edge of Aitken, Farside's Heavenly City made *Freedom Base* look like a kid's fort in a sandbox. A forest of low-g drills and spindle-legged refineries sprawled thickly over the Chinese settlement, black tailings from the enormous asteroid mine strewn over the lighter basalt with total disregard for esthetics. Solar cells snaked around the long string of habitat bubbles and partway up the crater wall, glittering blindingly in the low rays of slanting sunlight. Three lunar landers perched on a paved runway; a telescope dish looked like a tiny steel flower.

A Made-in-China Tomorrowland.

"So much for capitalism, eh?" Catherine mused.

Jake found it ironic that NASA had flown such a leftist to Freedom Base as a publicity stunt. But the suits were idiots.

He felt the Bug rattle like a C-130 as it descended the bulldozed road, its low center of gravity and wire-mesh wheels making a bobbing, floating ride; unwilling to risk the Bug's delicate solar panels, he gave the wall a wide berth. His instruments showed more than a kilometer straight down to the crater floor. Compared to the rest of the basin, this was the smallest of bubbles.

"Can't you drive faster? Lives are at stake."

Jake threw her a disgusted look. "Yes, ours. I'm getting us down in one piece." He cornered a sharp turn, skidding as the road narrowed to hug the shadowy black cliff as sharply as if cut with a laser.

Maybe she saw a face-full of vacuum in her immediate future, because she quit complaining.

The closer they got to Heavenly City, the more deserted it seemed. Nobody came in or out; the equipment stood immobile like so many petrified insects from a bad SF movie. Yeah, could be an epidemic.

Or maybe they were building a new slave-labor production facility for genuine Surveyor souvenirs. That'd be a high-dollar item at Wal-Mart.

Catherine had said the doctor begged her to come in Commander Sun's name. Pleaded for diphtheria antitoxin because their own government, terrified of a real-life Andromeda Strain, had flatly refused to help. Nevertheless it did not surprise Jake when the suit radio erupted into a litany of complaint in Mandarin as he turned into the paved parking area. Two figures in China's red-and-silver spacesuits popped out of the airlock and headed straight for them.

Jake did a donut around the parking lot near the main entrance and shut off the Bug's engine. "All out for the worker's paradise."

Catherine stared at the ghostly dust-haloed *taikonauts* trotting their way. "You'll be a gentleman and escort me and the vaccine inside, won't you?"

"Fat chance. As you know, I'm not a gentleman. The angel-of-mercy gig is your business."

"If that's how you want to play it." She unsnapped her seat belt.

Jake slouched back in his seat. "I wonder how long the President will quarantine your plump posterior when he finds out about this."

"He'll understand." Slinging her case under one gauntleted arm, she climbed out.

"Who's going to change his mind—you?"

"Oh ye of little faith."

The two Chinese skidded to a halt in front of the Bug, like warrior ants behind the mirrored glare of their faceplates. Pointed at Jake, their pulse weapons said volumes.

Instantly Jake raised his hands. "Don't shoot! We're unarmed!"

"Americans!" one said in English. "You under arrest!"

"I'm from the EU," Catherine corrected in an upbeat tone. "Commander Sun and Dr. Zhou authorized me to bring you life-saving medicine."

Unfortunately, dropping the commander's name didn't have the desired effect. "You under arrest. Move or die!"

Furious, Jake unbelted and climbed out. "Thanks a lot, *Mother*." Bird flu, anyone?

"Sorry for the inconvenience, Colonel. Commander Sun will release us."

Jake declined to voice his skepticism to the listening Chinese.

The entrance ahead sported a metal sign in sun-faded Chinese characters above two airlocks, a single-person and another large enough for several spacesuited humans. A stack of what appeared to be white plastic coffins did nothing to lower Jake's rapid heart rate.

The guards crowded them into the bigger airlock, and presently Jake heard the cycling of pumps and the whoosh of air. When the pressure normalized, the door popped open; the two Chinese had already removed their helmets.

"Forward!" Jake felt the barrel of the pulse weapon press into his suit above his left kidney.

The interior hall began grandiosely, with red and gold Chinese flags, a colorful Great Wall mosaic, and what appeared to be an unfinished fountain, but within a few yards morphed into bare walls and rough gray mooncrete floor.

A door slid open behind a stern iron statue of Mao. Racks of hard-vacuum spacesuits hung on both sides of the room; helmets, boots, and gloves lay everywhere, in the scattered haste of a high school locker-room. All of the equipment showed the dents and dings of hard wear.

"Nice little place you got here," Jake said sarcastically, undogging his helmet. He hated desuiting in front of Catherine, but at least he wore a flight suit underneath, enough to preserve his dignity.

Whatever was going on, he'd deal with it. *The Andromeda Strain* was *fiction*, for Pete's sake. Bio-weapons weren't, but they'd be very expensive to make and maintain here. And what would be the point, when a lunar base could slam Earth cities simply by throwing rocks?

The guards directed them against the wall, where automated grapple-arms raised the hard upper torsos of their suits, allowing them to step free.

Before removing the bottom part of their suits and boots, Jake and Catherine had to stand on the hissing metal floor vents, bright as scars in the mooncrete. An ultrasonic pulse knocked off the dust, which was then sucked away into the vents. Over the gunpowder tang of moon dust, Jake detected the bitter tang of disinfectant. The Chinese were efficient, he had to hand them that.

The guards searched them, right down to their cooling underwear, then took Catherine's case and marched the two of them down a hall through three sets of vacuum doors. The fourth and final door had steel bars woven into it.

Jake's stomach tightened; he fought down a futile impulse to flee.

"You can't *jail* us!" Catherine said, outraged. "Commander Sun will not tolerate this! People are dying!"

"Indeed so!" a guard said as he slammed the door to the cell. "Commander Sun and Dr. Zhou are both dead!"

The lock clanged shut.

Lacking a window to see out of or a chair to sit on, Jake sat on the floor, as far from the filth as possible. He wasn't resigned to dying, but he had to admit things didn't look good. Being an Iraq war veteran didn't help his cause; China's Xinjiang province was virtually all Muslim.

Strange, how his first few years as a pilot had led here. All the jobs disappeared after 9/11 except flying freight, so he became a freight dog, hauling just-in-time cargoes in all over the world in poorly maintained aircraft.

He almost smiled, remembering the Boeing 747 loaded with condoms he'd flown to Rio for Carnival.

On approach, a freak wind shear had ripped off his No. 1 engine. Despite that, he made a perfect landing. Next day, he and his flight engineer celebrated in Miami over a pitcher of Watney's at Bryson's Irish Pub. Jake had felt so bulletproof, a few months later he joined the Air Force and went to Iraq.

And miraculously, after two years of that, he hadn't been killed.

If anything should've killed him, it would've been women. Dubai had had the finest—

"I'm sorry," Catherine said. "This is all my fault."

Jake took a deep breath and exhaled slowly. "True."

"When was the last time you went to confession?"

"How 'bout we focus on our problem here? Your two pals are dead, probably from this epidemic. Any ideas? Maybe you told the President of the U.N. where you were going, so he'll phone the new Chinese commander and tell him pretty-please to let us go?"

"I'm afraid I didn't think of that. But I've prayed for guidance."

"Yeah? God helps those who help themselves." Jake got up and examined the lock. It was a Yale, and rock-solid. He checked his pockets for something that might prove useful, but of course his pockets were devoid of both lock-picks and pulse weapons.

"Do you have family, Colonel?"

"Families don't rate an air allowance, not unless you're married to an astronaut-scientist-ice miner."

"So you have family on Earth?"

"I don't want to talk about it."

"Considering our circumstances, I thought you might like to talk about something pleasant."

"After joining NASA I got AIDS, also known as aviation-induced divorce syndrome. So, nothing to talk about."

"Children?"

"Catherine, did you ever hear the expression 'no means no'? Get off my back."

They sat in cold silence, Jake mentally rehearsing knockout punches and trying to recall the route back to the airlock. If their suits weren't locked up ... but they probably were. Okay, then steal a suit—there'd been enough in the desuit room. Just get outside, and if they'd taken the Bug, then he'd borrow one of their Lunar Modules. The Chinese had copied the design from the Russians, and simplified it—Jake had flown one in sim enough to know how easy it was to handle. Even an amateur could do it.

The outer doors banged open, admitting two buff young PLA-uniformed guards brandishing carbines, handcuffs, and a set of jangling keys.

"You come! Now!"

With no opportunity to escape, Jake and Catherine were handcuffed and taken to an ugly little room, barely large enough to enclose a steel desk flanked by two Chinese flags and six plastic chairs. It looked like a courtroom in a phone booth.

Jake was kicking himself for not at least *trying* to grab a gun when the door opened. Two stony-eyed Chinese males entered, escorting a poker-stiff old codger in a neatly pressed green uniform. All three wore white facemasks over their noses and mouths.

The old man's brand-new epaulets bore the silver star of a brigadier general, but he sounded like an angry drill sergeant as he unleashed a barrage of hoarse, high-pitched Mandarin.

"Who is he?" Jake muttered.

"I don't know," Catherine whispered back. "It's not Commander Sun."

The shiny new insignia said he'd been a lower-ranking officer until recently.

Jake had a bad feeling about this. Commander Sun was either dead or in prison, which meant the new boss would be anxious to prove his authority.

The escort on the right set Catherine's box of diphtheria antitoxin and vaccine on the desk. The other escort cleared his throat. "This is General Po Yun, commander of Heavenly City."

The Boston-accented English set Jake's teeth on edge. A Harvard or MIT alumnus. How nice for him.

"He says," the escort/translator continued, eyeballing Jake, "that if you tell him which of your people was the first to try to kill us with your Andromeda Strain, he will not throw you out the airlock without your suits. You will instead be shot."

"There is no Andromeda Strain," Jake said as calmly as he could manage. "That was a made-up story."

"And you, sir, are you a physician?"

Jake shook his head. "I'm only the driver."

"*I* am in charge here," Catherine declared firmly. "You will address your questions to me."

The translator sighed. The general clearly didn't like the thought of having to talk with a woman. Jake might've sympathized if not for General Po's permafrost expression that said he was picturing an airlock in Jake's immediate future.

"There is no Andromeda Strain!" Catherine declared heatedly. "I am

Mother Catherine Connelly, winner of the Nobel Peace Prize. This is life-saving medicine, brought in Jesus' name at the request of Dr. Zhou. She stated that an infected crewman from Earth brought the sickness here."

Jake was thankful she didn't mention the Freedom Base pharmacist who donated the medicine. It'd be awkward trying to explain why NASA stockpiled surplus drugs but couldn't keep astronauts in toothpaste.

"Dr. Zhou was a man," the translator snapped. His eyes flickered anxiously as he spoke to General Po in Mandarin.

"That makes no sense. She told me—"

The old man flushed blotchy red and snatched a vial from the medicine box. "Toxin!" he shouted, jabbing a finger at the vial. "Number ten!"

Sweat trickled down Jake's spine. Number ten meant "bad." The general didn't read enough English to understand antitoxin, and the translator was afraid to tell him.

Catherine shook her head. "It's 'antitoxin'! 'Anti' means it fights the poison produced by diphtheria. Antibiotics defeat bacteria, just as—"

General Po interrupted loudly, the translator cringed. "He does not believe—"

But Catherine didn't let him finish. She leapt into a rapid-fire speech in Mandarin, and in a matter of seconds, she and the general, his face now purple with rage, were both shouting at each other.

Was she insane? Jake wanted to crawl under the chair, but rule number one of the astronaut corps was *better dead than look like a coward.*

The old man pounded his fist on the desk and roared. Catherine tried to outdo his volume, then shut up. The translator exhaled as if he'd been holding his breath.

"General Po will permit the woman to inject herself."

A grinning guard pressed the muzzle of his gun on Jake's left temple. The other guard removed Catherine's handcuffs and slapped a vial of antitoxin, a needle, and a syringe from her kit on the desk.

Jake breathed shallowly, trying not to inhale the guard's garlic breath. Even burning to death on a launch pad beat being shot like a dog. Am I considered more dangerous with handcuffs than she is without, or is killing me part of the deal?

"Give me an alcohol wipe, please," Catherine said. "It's the little red and white packet—"

Po spat a reply, which needed no translator. *Do as I say or we shoot him now.*

Catherine's hands shook as she screwed the needle onto the syringe and popped the top from the vial. Inserting the needle through the rubber stopper, she withdrew a small quantity, which she injected into her left deltoid.

"See?" she said with a smile. "It's perfectly safe."

General Po flicked a hand at the translator, who delivered the assessment with a scowl. "You may have taken the antidote before you came here. Therefore you must inject someone else."

This sounded like progress to Jake. But the gun muzzle continued to press its cold metal mouth on his temple.

Catherine shrugged. "Why not a sick person this time? I don't want to waste any doses."

This time, the interplay between Po and the translator was as brief as a lightning bolt. The latter bowed and scurried from the room.

Jake threw an interrogatory look at Catherine. Her expression said she didn't have a clue what was happening. Neither of them dared speak.

Presently the translator returned with a young Chinese woman, who carried a blanket-wrapped bundle—a baby with dull eyes and ruddy cheeks, throat swollen like a bullfrog in mid-song. A sawing noise came from the baby's open mouth.

Shocked that the Chinese brought kids to the Moon, Jake felt his hopes crash and burn. Catherine had described the throat swelling as end-stage. Even with a full dose of antitoxin, the child would probably die before it took effect.

The translator's brown eyes focused on Catherine with laser-like intensity. "General Po wishes you to inject our son."

Catherine smiled brightly. "Be glad to. What's his name?"

"Peter." A tear trickled down the young woman's pretty face; she ducked her head when the translator snapped at her.

An old memory flashed in Jake's brain, of the night Addie got meningitis. She must've been about five or six. Jake had rushed her to the hospital—his ex-wife met him there—and didn't sleep for thirty-six hours, until the doctors pronounced Addie out of danger. Up till then, Jake had wanted to strangle her doctors on at least four different occasions. Like when they stuck her eight times for one IV, for example.

"Set him on the desk," Catherine ordered briskly. "I'll need a fresh syringe and an alcohol wipe . . . ."

Despite having a gun to his head, Jake wouldn't have swapped places with that translator. What did a fancy education get you, when you had to watch your dying kid turned into a guinea pig?

Too weak to protest the needle in his thigh, the child wheezed and flailed his skinny arms. Gray phlegm trickled from his nose; his mother blotted it with a tissue and picked him up, as gingerly as if he were made of glass.

The baby wheezed again, a harsh mechanical sound, then went limp in her arms.

The guard cocked the pistol; Jake's heart hammered. Were these the last few seconds of his life?

Her face pinched, the young woman looked up. "He's sleeping. Finally."

General Po snarled at the guard, who lowered the gun. A moment later, the handcuffs were removed.

Rubbing his numb wrists, Jake remembered to breathe again. Thank you, God. Or whoever.

The translator scowled. "Since our son has survived, General Po will allow this treatment for others at the clinic. But if anyone dies . . . ."

Catherine shook her head. "I can't promise no one will die from the disease. That's unrealistic."

She and Po argued it back and forth, but when the general finally released them to the clinic in the custody of the translator, the issue remained unresolved.

In the hallway with his family, minus General Po, the translator actually smiled. He took the child from his wife and introduced himself. "I'm Lee Ma, and this is my wife, Tina. We both went to school in America."

Jake's strongest impulse at the moment was to bolt for the airlock, but he managed to reciprocate the introduction.

Tina rubbed her eyes tiredly. "I studied to be a nurse, so I knew what would happen. He's got that horrible diphtheria membrane growing over the back of his throat."

Catherine smiled beatifically. "He'll be all right now, child. Don't worry."

"I'll show you the clinic," Lee said, shepherding them down the hall. "We have a lot of sick people here."

"I hope we can vaccinate everyone who isn't sick, too," Catherine said, falling into step beside him.

Jake found himself walking next to Tina. Unable to think of anything else to say, he said, "Was the boy sick before the epidemic?"

"Yes. He coughed all the time."

"Wouldn't be surprised if he's got looney lung," Jake said.

Lee turned, frowning. "Ah, you mean dust-inhalation syndrome. That is not serious, not like this."

"For some it is. NASA sent a friend of mine back to Earth—his lungs couldn't take it. With all the mining you guys are doing, you must know what I'm talking about. People track in so much dust, the vents and filters can't get it all. That dust trap out front is new, isn't it?"

Tina was nodding; Lee looked away. "Yes, but . . . ."

Jake decided there was no possible way Lee worked outside, let alone in a mine. He had to be a science weenie.

You'd think they'd all understand about moon dust being so primordial, but they didn't. Earth dust was soft and rounded from billions of years of rain and weathering, which had never happened here. Moon dust was still as sharp as the day the asteroids blasted it from the ground. A fortune awaited the man who built a better air filter.

Lee led them through another set of vacuum doors, behind which were apartments—small even for one-rooms, to judge by the spacing. A lunar Segway leaned against a wall, together with a pair of disassembled housecleaning robots. The odor of bleach made Jake's eyes water.

At least he didn't see any weapons lockers. No one knew what the Chinese would do when they landed eighteen months ago, a full year before NASA broke ground on *Freedom Base*. For all anyone knew, they could still decide to claim the Moon. Short of war, they couldn't be stopped.

And maybe not even then. America's vaunted Space Force consisted of two rocket ships, one of which was being refitted—Congressional budget permitting.

There might've been a privately run American base before the Chinese, if there hadn't been so much talk in Congress about how easily an American business would be corrupted by all their money. As much as Jake hated Never-A-Straight-Answer bureaucracy, he could see how a business without any oversight might be worse.

Lee gave the sleeping child back to his wife, and ushered Jake and Catherine into the cramped medical clinic, its single ornament a pixel window displaying a scene of an improbably perfect Earthly garden. It made an appalling contrast to the wretched-looking people lying in narrow beds, or more frequently, on dirty mattresses jammed together on the floor.

The air was moist as a swamp, redolent of Tiger Balm and the smell of unwashed bodies. A few looked dead already.

The next hour or so seemed to last forever. Tina and Su-Su, another exhausted young Chinese nurse, showed Jake how to give shots. He didn't care for it, but mastered the technique quickly, figuring they'd never get out of here if he didn't.

Presently Su-Su brought him green tea and a bowl of fragrant noodle soup, which he reluctantly turned down. He never drank anything right before going outside in a spacesuit.

Instead he popped a piece of gum, the astronaut's second-favorite remedy for dry mouth. Alcohol, unfortunately, was out of the question.

Notwithstanding Tina's evaluation of her son's condition, if this turned out not to be diphtheria, but something Jake wasn't immunized against, he couldn't go back. Even if good old Po didn't shove him out the airlock, he couldn't risk the lives of everyone at *Freedom Base*.

And it was only a matter of time before General Haskell realized he was AWOL. Then what? Explain to Haskell that he and the nun had been on a mission of mercy to the Chinese? After their own president refused to help them because he was scared of space bugs?

Yeah, that'd go over well. All things considered, Jake preferred the airlock. He'd be shipped back to Earth in about the length of time it took a quark to decay. If he were lucky, he might get a job flying helicopter tours of Cleveland.

"Last one," Catherine said, upending an empty vaccine vial.

Hallelujah. Jake looked up to see a man waving at him as he made his way toward him, a broad smile on his face. His mask was gone, but it had to be Lee.

"The child is better," Lee said happily, handing Jake a diamond the size of a golf ball. "This is for you, with my thanks."

Wondering how much this bauble was worth, Jake hefted it in his palm. With a sigh, he handed it back. "NASA would take it, just like it keeps everything else we find."

Lee's eyebrows knitted. "That isn't right. Now I can only repay you with friendship."

"That's okay," Jake said, unable to imagine a Moon in which that could happen. "Come to Freedom Base sometime and buy me a beer."

"Done. And whatever data you or your friends wish from my radio-telescope, you can have."

"Radio, huh? I bet you're an expert on communications."

"Something like that," Lee shrugged, looking oddly relieved as Catherine came up. "Uh, General Po wants to speak with both of you. Follow me."

Bracing himself, Jake followed Lee into the hall. Some of the first to be injected had managed to sit up, though they still looked like death warmed over. But the nurses carried out three bodies in the last hour, so . . . .

General Po stood outside, arms folded stiffly. "You take too long. What is problem?"

Catherine smiled. "Your wife's recovering, General. What a lovely Christian woman."

Lee turned pale. "She's not a Christian!"

"Really?" Catherine said sweetly. "She is now."

Sweat matted Lee's temples as he babbled in Mandarin. Even Jake could see he was lying.

"You leave now! You never here!" General Po shouted, storming off.

Jake went limp with relief. He'd been here way too long, but he could fake a shift at the ice mine to cover. The Bug's solar-cell recharge meant he didn't have to account for fuel. General Haskell would never know he'd left.

Back in the Bug, Jake ignored Catherine as he focused on his systems check. He wouldn't be within radio contact of the base until ninety-five kilometers from the relay station. He could say he'd broken an antenna and stopped to fix it. Thankfully, weather was a non-issue. Solar storms would be preceded by at least twenty-four hours warning, and they were in the quiet half of the sun cycle anyway.

Only thing that bothered him was remembering General Po's expression. *Here's the freaking American rushing in to save the day!*

We made him lose face, and he'll never, ever, forget that.

Jake glanced at Catherine, snug in her passenger seat. "Ever hear the saying, 'No good deed goes unpunished'?"

"Of course. It's wrong."

"I'm talking about the here and now." Shaking his head, Jake switched on the motor and gunned the Bug onto the steep rim road. He'd pour out half his precious booze stash as an offering to St. Joseph if it ensured him kicking back with a cold one in three hours.

Once they reached the rim, they were making great time retracing their tracks when one of the tires hit a hole. Which had happened often enough before, except this time the hole collapsed into another and larger hole. In a blink, they were sliding down inside a crater, wheels spinning and gravel flying with dreamy slow-motion grace.

Careening around elephant-sized boulders, Jake turned the wheels into the skid, but with so much kinetic energy, stopping was impossible. Near the bottom of the crater, the right front tire sideswiped a granite slab. The Bug flipped in a crumple of solar cells, like a butterfly doing a barrel roll, and groaned to a halt in the dust.

Jake breathed deeply and told his pounding heart to slow down. His suit seemed intact, but obviously the solar cells were wrecked, and probably the recharger. He probably still had battery power.

When he tried to restart the Bug, it was silent as an OMS burn. *Nothing.*

"What's wrong?"

Jake found a hole in one of the fuel cells—the water had run out. He couldn't fix it, and he only had three hours of air.

The Bug of course had an automated distress call. Unfortunately, they were still on Farside, with Earth hidden behind the horizon. Sixteen kilometers short of max range for Malapert Relay Station.

Jake fired a signal flare, then tried all three Chinese radio channels. No response.

Well, he hadn't really expected them back on the air yet. Without knowing the height of their beacon, he didn't know if he was in line-of-sight.

And frankly, Jake could see General Po allowing a rescue party when NASA threw a surfing safari at the Sea of Tranquility.

"There must be *something* we can do," Catherine said.

Jake unfolded the topographical map. "Well, let's see. The dust shows our outgoing track with perfect fidelity, but the rock is a blank slate, you should excuse the expression. Can't navigate by the stars with polarized face-plates, compasses don't work on the Moon, and with the horizon two kilometers away, we won't see the beacon until we're almost on top of it. Running in spacesuits is exhausting even for Olympic athletes. If and when we get close enough to Malapert for them to hear our distress call, it will still take time for them to retrieve us."

"Is this the Right Stuff, Colonel? Why can't you fix a little problem like this one?"

"What would you know about the Right Stuff? I'm the one who had a gun to my head, while you were insulting the general. You almost got us killed."

She chuckled. "A calculated risk."

Jake wanted to kill her. He loped around to the back of the Bug instead. Wasn't there any way to fix this cursed thing? "Is there any water left?"

"No, I drank it all. Why?"

Great.

Despite his own no-liquids policy, he felt unpleasant pressure in his bladder. Could fuel cells run on urine? He could dump it through his suit's U-vent; if the tube fit over the cell intake, some would remain liquid. All he needed was a plug.

The chewing gum. It'd cost him a little air, but he could expel it through the helmet vent.

The fix worked for a whole twelve kilometers before they broke down again.

Deep shadows pooled around the silica-rich volcanic rocks, all the darker for the low sun and fading light. Jake told himself to watch his step, but stumbled often.

Where'd that track go? It was right here, dammit . . . .

"Sorry I said you didn't have the Right Stuff," Catherine said.

"I doubt it. I think you enjoy making life miserable . . . you would've been only too happy to rat me out to General Haskell about that little episode in Singapore."

"'Little episode'? Is that how you refer to selling girls into slavery at 'Four Floors of Whores'?"

"At least it was truth in advertising." Jake cast back and forth, searching for the lost track in the polar twilight. A few stars shone overhead, but he couldn't see any constellations.

"You wretched Americans, blathering about freedom! You've no idea what it means."

He felt colder with every passing second. His suit heater must be freezing over. "Twenty years ago, I owed money to the kind of people you should never owe money to, okay? The girls, their families needed money, too. You want to hold me to a higher standard than their parents? Anyone who'd sell his own kids for thirty dollars . . . ."

They both saw it at the same time.

A blue cloud slowly levitated above the horizon. The Earth, swimming in the starry black.

Seeing those beautiful continents and sparkling white clouds made Jake's eyes blur. He stumbled and fell flat, remembering the time he'd been expected to lead the Houston Rotary Club in singing "America the Beautiful," and he'd frozen when the camera focused on him. Forgot the words.

But in space, you can't see any borders, that's why he'd gotten confused.

Blinking hard, he crawled forward and grabbed a shiny fist-sized nugget with icy gloved fingers. "Know what this rock is, Catherine? It's platinum. Almost pure, from the looks of it. And that outcropping there . . . it's platinum, too. If I could ship this acre back to Earth, I'd be a goddamn billionaire. But no, NASA runs this plantation."

Yeah, he knew about freedom. Because he didn't have it.

"How's that? Didn't China claim mining rights?"

"Since China didn't sign the Space Treaty, they could've claimed the Moon and let the courts fight it out. But they couldn't risk pissing off the rest of the planet, especially the U.S.—I guess we still pack enough clout for that. So they got a civilian to claim their mine, but that's all. NASA claims everything an employee invents or discovers. Otherwise, we'd all be running around looking for our own strikes like the Alaska Gold Rush, and we'd never get any work done."

"Oh, rubbish! Without working, you won't be breathing. I'd call that a motivator."

"For most people, yeah."

"Look, *I'll* claim it. I'm not employed by NASA, so I'll claim this strike. I'll give it to you, and your . . . son or daughter?"

"Daughter," Jake said faintly.

"Right, your daughter. And all the Earth's poor who wish to come here . . . ."

"Hey, wait a minute! Addie won't have anything if you split it a billion ways!"

"There aren't a billion people who will actually come here, Colonel. I meant for those who want to live here. It'd get them here, give them a stake."

"Why?" Jake asked suspiciously.

"Without you, my mission would've failed. You did as much as I . . . perhaps more."

"Then tell that to your suit recorder. Say it's your last will and testament."

Jake started laughing before she finished dictating. "You're the one who opens up the Moon. Next to you, Neil Armstrong and all the rest of us . . . we're nothing."

Catherine giggled. "Oh, no, I wouldn't say that."

"Yeah, right." Jake couldn't feel his arms or legs much, but his heart was pounding like crazy—a sure sign of carbon monoxide poisoning. "You wanna be the first lunar saint."

"Does it matter?"

"I guess not." Jake thought carbon monoxide poisoning wasn't so bad. You die seeing beautiful things, like retro rockets firing on a lunar lander. He lifted his head, but that only compounded the illusions.

A suited figure bending over him, a woman's voice on his suit radio.

Tina's voice.

"What . . . how did you . . . ?"

"You two saved my baby's life. Did you think I wouldn't monitor your transponder after you answered my call for help?"

Catherine staggered upright, following as Tina helped Jake into the lander. His smile hurt, but he didn't care.

Maybe it's doing the right thing that makes borders disappear.

In Their Own Words
by Brenta Blevins

Question: How did you approach the task of directing the Lunar History Project?

Answer: Well, that is *the* question with which I found myself charged, isn't it? How do you construct a narrative of a world? It wasn't my job to be thinking about history at all when I first arrived here. But I realized that what we were doing was making history. It wasn't in my job duty, but it was my obligation as one of the first lunar residents to preserve our stories. And not just a single story because there's not one simple fairy tale to living here. All these historians on Earth were writing about what was going on here, and not a one had ever set foot in the regolith. Once I came to that conclusion, I couldn't wait a day longer and set about trying to answer: Who are a history's main characters and who are merely the supporting characters that belong in footnotes?

Maria Diaz, M.D.

I've written a lot, but it's a little awkward for me to make this recording about *me*.

The problem with Luna is that it has no mythology of its own. As a doctor, that's my official diagnosis. Oh, I know what everyone thinks. Humans have been worshiping the Moon probably from the time they'd evolved eyes to look up into the night sky.

But there's nothing about this place that needs to be deified, no more than the Earth needs to be deified. Sure, sometimes people here worship that blue and white mirage hanging above the horizon once they're separated from it—in a way they never did when they were on the planet.

"Earth sickness." That's what we call it.

Of course, the Moon figures prominently in myth. The Man in the Moon. Werewolves. Full moons causing strange behavior. But the problem is: those are Earth myths.

So, I set about writing some distinctively lunar stories. What really surprises me is how popular my fiction is on Earth. I never set out to create stories about a world that appealed to Earth-based cultures; my ideal audience—albeit small—has always been lunar residents. I know, the "The Earth Always Rises: A Lunar Murder Mystery" is "genre" fiction—but it's not mystery. It's the lunar genre. I'm not sure why, but everybody seems to love a good suffocation story. I have to tell you that I've never run into the villainous characters on Luna (maybe on Earth) that inhabit my novel, "The Ghosts of Kennedy Station."

Earth readers seem fascinated by the little details that Luna residents take for granted. Like the way people walk here—how some walk in the lower gravity with a perky little skip and others bounce like kangaroos. They seem to take almost sadistic delight in how we get gray regolith coating everything; people on Earth still think of the Moon as being one undifferentiated lump as white as mozzarella cheese.

Luna is a different kind of existence; there's not one place on Earth that's as deadly. (The submariners who've come here might disagree.) Earth weather can turn ugly, but here, Luna is always deadly. You don't ever stop thinking about the lack of atmosphere, which means no air to breathe, no protection from solar storms, no food growing on the surface. Luna's environment is a character that's always present in my stories in a way that I never see Earthlings thinking about their planet.

I guess I should wrap up this recording. Go read my latest book, "Crisis at Armstrong." It's about a mysterious medical crisis that occurs during solar storms that prevent the trucks from bringing necessary care to the remote Eagle outpost. I'll admit I wrote that novel just after the reactor breakdown here at Aldrin. We spent agonizing days wondering if, from losing all the power that keeps our oxygen flowing, we'd lose everything. But even though we had mechanical dysfunction, I'm pleased that our people and our relationships were all functional. That brought us through that one. I hope that unique Luna spirit shows in my writing.

I'm looking forward to seeing what stories will come from other Luna residents, from Mars, the asteroid belt, the Jovian satellites . . . and beyond.

Question: Would you consider yourself a historian?
Answer: I like that the word "history" is based on a Greek word meaning "to inquire." I think all of us here on Luna are always inquiring. I can't help wondering how our past, albeit our near past, is shaping our future. If I've learned anything about being a historian, it's that history is messy; it doesn't create a clean, easy narrative. For good or ill, I'm glad the Lunar History Project has preserved that.

Mary Sturgill

Forget that whole "Man in the Moon." I'm the "Woman in the Moon." My great-grandfather and grandfather were coal miners in West Virginia, on Earth, so maybe I've got digging in my veins. I've moved from one project to another here, digging up the lunar regolith and getting to the matrix below. Playing in the dirt, my mother would say. Everyone knows about the He-3 extraction that goes on to fuel the Earth's new and miraculous fusion reactors, but there's more that we dig. We've mined "rare earth" metals, for example, to build hybrid batteries. I'm looking forward to finding, digging, processing, and prepping the next resource that will help us continuing living—on the Earth or on Luna.

Some people have protested because we're mining the Moon, but the way I look at it is as long as humans are alive, we're going to be affecting our environments. Honestly, I don't know how humans can survive without having some sort of impact on the places in which they live.

When my grandfather was alive, they shifted coal mining from something that happened belowground to aboveground work. Instead of tunneling into the mountain, my grandfather worked for a mining company that simply removed the mountain, as if it were an annoying impediment in the way of progress. The mountain went from being a solid green forest in the summer or a frosted purple majesty in the winter to being an open scar on the world.

When the dysprosium site first came up, I proposed we use remote tunnelers to dig into the matrix and harvest the metal, both minimizing risk to the underground miners and the impact to the surface of the Moon.

After I proved how we could use the tunnelers, the site managers agreed. I think the people on Luna and Earth value the unique appearance of the Moon.

Some group back on Earth gave me a special award for encouraging environmental awareness on Luna. I guess that's all right. But I didn't do that for an award. I did it for my grandfather, who couldn't save the mountain his family had once taken for granted as a beautiful presence in their lives. Maybe I made history in that demonstration; I'm glad it was a better history than the one my grandfather had to make.

Question: But you can't preserve everything as history, can you?
Answer: I wish I knew how to solve that problem, but it's true to an extent. If you preserve everything, are you preserving anything? I think that's why history focuses on firsts—the first time something is accomplished, the first time someone does something different; it provides a nice cutoff. There are many firsts here on the Moon—the first woman, the first permanent surface systems, the first death, the first successful medical intervention, the first road, and it just goes on and on. I understand the need to save the first footsteps on the Moon, but if we try to preserve the first road, the cost of doing so means creating new roads until the entire surface is covered in roadway and we're ultimately doing more damage in our preservation systems.

A risk of preserving only firsts is ignoring all the people who contributed to an achievement. It's a nice story to say that Thomas Edison was the first person to invent the light bulb, but it's not the truth, is it? The goal of the Project is history, not nice stories.

Charles Farrow

I'm a little embarrassed about being included in a history project. I mean, I never thought I'd make history—not unless you count being the kid who got the most detentions at St. Andrew's Middle School. I'm just a truck driver. I drive the supplies that come from Earth, the things we can't make here—because we don't have the people or because we don't have the resources to do so. Besides, it's fair trade, the exchange of goods and supplies between Earth and Luna.

They hired me because I'd done a lot of remote trucking on the Canadian ice roads and was used to being alone, used to being self-sufficient if I ran into a problem. A couple other guys who drove those road trains down in Australia work here, too. I call 'em the "Kangaroos," and they call me "Maple Leaf."

The rigs feel a little different here on the Moon: you know, if you're driving too fast and hit a pothole or a new micrometeorite crater, you leave the road. And don't come down for a while. You just don't do that on Earth. I imagine my old ma would get pretty motion sick here with my driving.

But some things are the same. I still listen to the weather reports; here, I'm keeping an ear open for sun storms. CMEs, Coronal Mass Ejections, sun barf. During my training, they told me the sun storm protons could kill me if I wasn't careful—or that I might have to go back to Earth for treatment. I'd hate to cost everyone that kind of money, and it'd feel like being sent home from school. But if I hear a storm's coming, I stay at the station. If I'm between stations, I have to stay inside my rig; it's protected with aluminum and polyethelene. As long as my rig stays functional and my oxygen holds out, I'm okay. Of course I worry about what might happen if my rig broke down and I were a long distance away from help. My environment suit isn't—can't be—thick enough to provide radiation protection, and it's not like I could carry enough oxygen to hike across the lunar surface to safety. When I was driving the ice roads, I worried about falling through and freezing to death in some remote Northwest Territories lake. As long as you're living, you're at risk of dying; doesn't matter where you are. Maybe some things are the same no matter your location?

I like driving on Luna for the same reason I liked driving on Earth; I love looking at the scenery. And sometimes I listen to the Doc's stories. Of course, lunar days are fine, and I get a lot to look at—mountains and valleys and plains. I nearly drove into a monster crater the first time I saw Mons Huygens; that mountain is huge! But the lunar nights are long. My time driving the winters in Canada gave me good preparation for it. Some people get a little depressed from the long dark or from being stuck in their stations all the time, but the Doc gives 'em medicine, prescribes them some time with the sun lamp, and then they count the Earth days back to the lunar day. Doc pulls 'em through every time. Maybe we need more Maple Leaves up here.

I do okay with the darkness, but sometimes I feel a little funny on the Far Side where you never get to see the Earth. Sometimes I'm driving along and I forget where I am, and I catch myself looking up in the sky for Earth and when I don't see it, I feel really lost. I realize what's going on before I catch a real case of Earth Sickness. Some people can't stop themselves and have to go back.

Like I said, I'm just a truck driver. I do my job getting water, food, supplies, and such shuttled from the main depots out to the remote bases. It's important work, but I'm only doing my job. But, let me tell you, I felt like I was a Nobel prize-winning scientist when I finally showed up at Wu base with their long overdue shipment of condoms. I've never heard so many cheers.

Huh. Should I have offered that comment for history's sake?

Question: You've no doubt heard the criticisms of the Lunar History Project: That critical events have been ignored, that your perspective has been skewed by not including the impact of Earth politics on the Moon, that your subjects have elided their own accounts to enhance their importance or to hide mistakes, that perhaps you focused on too many minor players.

Answer: I have to say it's fair to criticize the project. Every attempt at recording history will be flawed. When NASA first came to the Moon, they went to a great deal of effort to document and broadcast the first manned lunar landing, but think about the primary recordings of the first man, Neil Armstrong, on the Moon. "One small step for man. One giant leap for mankind." Of course, he claims he said, "One small step for *a* man." There's always controversy in history. I guess that's up to the public to decide. And then communist Russia didn't publicize their successes like the United States did. I mean, a British newspaper scooped their Luna 9 photos!

Karen Park

One of the first things I learned on Luna was that everybody pitches in and does whatever is needed. You have to. If you don't do it here, you die. I think that's one of the things that makes us different from people on Earth.

I never expected to come here, but after I first saw the job ad, I found myself looking up that very night into the sky (there was a waxing half moon) and I realized if I didn't come here, I'd spend the rest of my life thinking, "*What if?*" The Moon would be an accusation hanging in the night sky every time I saw it. My mother's not entirely happy I've got two degrees in microbiology and I ended up a mechanic. (Sorry, I can't help laughing.) "My daughter, the wrench monkey." I can hear her telling her friends that at her bridge club. Sure, I miss her, but we e-mail and she's gotten better about the time delays and not talking over me on my monthly phone call home.

We've got it all here on the Moon: commercial interests, research and development, pure science, and all the sorts of folks who have to help get it done: scientists, secretaries, administrators, nurses, IT specialists, cooks, electricians, civil engineers, builders, plumbers; you name it, we need it. We all have to juggle jobs; we've got a primary job and then avocational work.

Me, I lead tours. I think there's nothing better than showing around tourists, company bosses, and politicians—from Congress, from the House of Commons *and* the House of Lords, the Bundestag, and more. I don't mind. I know some people think the tourists can never appreciate Luna like we do, but I think they can get a taste of it when they see all the historic sites. I've ridden with them on rigs to all the major lunar sites—the Apollo landings, the Lunokhod Russian rovers, the Chandrayaan impactor, the first Altair landing, and so forth. Every time I go with them, I try to see the sites with their fresh eyes and I can't help but *ooh* and *aah* along with them. A lot of us on Luna don't want to admit any dependency, but the more advocates we have on Earth, the better off we'll be. I always show them as much current work going on as I can. It's important for Earth residents to see that they're now as dependent on us as we are on them. We're all in this together. I've heard accusations on both sides that the other side is "out of touch," but we have to keep talking to each other and keeping in touch. My mother reminds me of this every phone call.

The tourists spend a lot of time asking me how I get used to wearing an environment suit every time I go out, how I get used to the space weather forecasts, how I get used to worrying about the gardens, the water supply, and the power. I tell them, it's hard, but it's like President Kennedy said, we do these things "not because they are easy, but because they are hard."

I still read about life on Earth and I see a lot of people there talking about "mindfulness," about approaching everything, walking, eating, and so forth, with a mindful awareness to truly pay attention to everything they do. That's what living on Luna is. Mindful living. There's not one thing here that you can ever take for granted. Well, maybe you can take the gray dust for granted. But every basic need humans have? We have to work hard for it. There's no convenience store on every street corner. I'm not sure if our trucking roads even count as streets, so we sure don't have a Starbucks here.

It's hard and I juggle at least two jobs, but I'm going to keep renewing my contract as long as they let me.

Question: What do people on Luna think of the project?
Answer: I guess there are always a few narcissists in the crowd who worry about how they'll look both in the now and in posterity, but I think if you listen to the recordings of the Luna residents, a lot of them don't feel like they're history. Yet, we're all a part of history, whether we're on Luna or Earth.

Chad Desai

When I first came to Luna, the other Luna residents told me that I was coming here for the adventure. When I renewed my contract and stayed on Luna, they told me Luna dust gets in your blood. You won't fit back in on Earth—no matter how many supplements you take or how much time you spend in the full gravity workouts to keep your bones strong. You're officially a lunatic. A Luna-tic.

I've got one of those jobs that nobody ever wanted to see on Luna. I'm a security officer, a sheriff on the new frontier. I feel like I've got some things in common with those old sheriffs of the American West. One of the most important things I've learned is that when disputes arise, sometimes you just have to get people to talk and then listen. Listen to what people are saying. Sometimes people think something is willful wrongdoing, they offer accusations like "sabotage," but when you get both sides talking, sometimes they realize that the problem wasn't purposeful, but an accident. They work together to figure out how to resolve the problem. I won't deny that we've had some international conflict, but I think people here are coming around to thinking of themselves as Luna residents first, and later of their prior nationalities. There's something very unifying about the common problems of air, food, and water—particularly when we all work together to ensure those needs are met.

The first couple times we ran into problems with Luna residents, we sent them back to Earth. After a while, though, we stopped treating the Earth like old Australia and decided these were our problems and we were going to take care of them ourselves. Now, if someone needs treatment or rehabilitation that can only take place on the Earth, we'll send them there, but otherwise, we have the people here work out what should happen as rectification or treatment. It's been working for us and I hope it continues to work for us.

Of course, my job is about more than going after people for infractions. Unfortunately, I've gone on search and rescue. I have to say that tourism here scares me; sometimes people come to hike mountains here and they're not even prepared for hiking a mountain on Earth. While gravity may not be as strong here, working out in a suit isn't as easy as the type of walking you've done the previous thirty, forty, or fifty years of your life. Most of our tourists are good people, but sometimes people get a little crazy here. I guess they think, "What happens on Luna, stays on Luna." Wu station can sometimes get rowdy. When they get out of control, I talk to them, sometimes put them up some place where they won't hurt anyone or themselves, and then send them on back to Earth, minus charges for the damages they've inflicted (it's now always part of their carriage contracts).

I undertook a hobby here at Aldrin to create a Zen rock garden. No matter how much we love it here, we all miss something from Earth; I can't tell you how much I miss seeing a waterfall plunging off the side of a green cliff, its mists spraying my un-helmeted face. Visiting the water treatment plant doesn't offer the same feel. Anyway, I've used the local aggregate to create a garden for people to calm down, to think about something other than the stresses of their dorm roommates, their worries about the physical environment here, their families back on Earth, and so forth. Maybe it's a stretch, but I think that's part of the job of sheriff—eliminating stresses before they get as out of control as a drunk tourist.

Ugh. I've gotten emails from Earth complaining about me building my garden, about "robbing" and "disturbing" the surface of the Moon, but I've never gotten one from any lunar residents. I'm not sure why, but a lot of people on Earth feel like they have the right to tell us what to do on our home. But I'm recording this because, as I mentioned, I feel like it's important for people to communicate.

Maybe my neighbors are right. I never would have gardened on Earth; and if I had, I would have grown more than rocks. Maybe the Moon does change a person.

Question: Did you participate in the Project by including your own history?

Anya Volsky

I suppose there's some hubris in including my own recording in the Lunar History Project. But everyone's included in this project; we try to do things the "fair" way.

I paid my launch dues here as the first manager of Altair Base; there weren't too many of us then. I'd done some similar work at McMurdo in Antarctica. In short, my job was to worry about everything—oxygen, water, logistics of all varieties, workers, *everything.* Anything that could go wrong was for me to address. But one of my other duties was to celebrate our successes. I tried to arrange celebrations every chance I could because each day we stayed here alive and functioning was a success. Maybe because I'm an old-timer I felt the need to start the Lunar History Project. I wanted to document what did or did not go right.

I went home after I'd fulfilled the obligations of that contract. I was proud of the work I'd done and prouder yet of the work being done by all the other people on Luna, but I felt I needed to go home and see my family. My father had just died and my son was graduating from college and I thought I should go back to Earth and work for Luna there.

I started worrying about Luna the moment we launched from its surface and continued through my first wobbly days re-acclimating to full gravity. That first night on the Earth when I looked up into the night sky and couldn't see the Moon for all the clouds, I realized I had to come back.

More and more expeditions were scheduled to head to the Moon. I wondered how the Moon's new local concretes would be used for creating habitats. I wondered which station would be the first to build its own bowling alley and just how long an alley they'd have to create. I realized that I had to go back and see all this for myself. I also realized that other people deserved to see what I had seen. So, before the workers and the tourists started showing up in droves, I wrote a request to the United States government to preserve the historical sites associated with Apollo and Altair. I lobbied hard. That's how I ended up coming back and overseeing a glass viewing platform installed over Neil Armstrong's and Buzz Aldrin's perfectly preserved footprints—footprints retained for future generations of Earth and Luna to appreciate. I've turned those sites over to new park officials and now they're worrying about how to manage visits to the site, how much to protect and how much to interpret for the tourists. I've worked with other governments eager to maintain their own lunar histories. And, at some point, I realized that I wasn't just interested in retaining this Earth-Luna joint history, but that we needed to preserve Luna history. When I started thinking about what should make up this account, I remembered the equalitarian approach Luna residents have tried to adopt in terms of their jobs and hobbies here. I realized no one person should write Luna history; we all needed to share in the responsibility of our chronicles.

As an aside, the first time I came to the Moon, I was limited to a few pounds of personal effects that I could pack. The second time I came, I didn't bring anything with me. I knew my memories were on Earth, but my life was waiting for me on Luna.

Question: What's next for the Lunar History Project?

Answer: One of the jokes in history circles is, "So, not much new going on in your field, is there?" But history isn't dead. It's being made all the time. We're adding new stations, new work sites, and some day soon, I suspect we'll have our first babies born here, growing up, and becoming the first Lunar natives. Those are stories that aren't yet recorded.

I'm looking forward to seeing how lunar history will continue to write itself.

About the National Space Society

The National Space Society (NSS) is an independent, educational, grassroots, non-profit organization dedicated to the creation of a spacefaring civilization. Founded as the National Space Institute (1974) and L5 Society (1975), which merged to form NSS in 1987, NSS is widely acknowledged as the preeminent citizen's voice on space. NSS has over 12,000 members (and more supporters) and over 50 chapters in the United States and around the world. The society also publishes *Ad Astra* magazine, an award-winning periodical chronicling the most important developments in space.

For more information, please visit www.nss.org.

National Space Society

www.ingramcontent.com/pod-product-compliance
Lightning Source LLC
Chambersburg PA
CBHW032025240626
47154CB00003B/794